WRONG MEANS
RIGHT END

By the same author

Right Fit Wrong Shoe
Xcess Baggage

WRONG MEANS

RIGHT END

VARSHA DIXIT

RUPA

First published in 2012 by
Rupa Publications India Pvt. Ltd.
7/16, Ansari Road, Daryaganj
New Delhi 110002

Sales Centres:

Allahabad Bengaluru Chennai
Hyderabad Jaipur Kathmandu
Kolkata Mumbai

ISBN: 978-81-291-2046-5

10 9 8 7 6 5 4 3 2 1

Varsha Dixit asserts the moral right to
be identified as the author of this work.

Printed in India by
Thomson Press India Ltd
18/35, Delhi-Mathura Road
Faridabad 121007

*For the mother I'm the daughter to and
the daughter I'm the mother to!
Maa & Anvi!*

Contents

1

Find me a doctor

'Kabootar Ja Ja Ja! Kabootar Ja Ja Ja!'

'Shut up!' Sneha sleepily moaned. Jerking a lazy arm out of the flowery duvet, she grabbed her incessantly ringing cell phone before it awakened her three-year-old son, Advey, asleep next to her.

'WHAT?' She whispered fiercely, instead of the usual hello. Sneha kept her eyes closed, hoping to catch a few more winks afterwards.

'Hi Sneh! Did I wake you up?' Nandini cooed in her ears.

'Sunday morning! Calling me at...hold on,' Sneha lowered her cell phone and raised the end of the comforter to glance at the slightly scratched, white and green dial of the small rectangular clock on her side, 'at 7.45 in the bloody morning. What do you think, Sethani?' Sneha retorted, using the new moniker she had anointed Nandini with after her wedding to Aditya Sarin, the mega successful entrepreneur who, over the last few years, had become the globally recognized face of Indian business.

'Sorry!' Nandini chuckled. 'Just wanted to remind you about dinner tonig—'

'How many more of these torturous things do I have to go through before you realize you are not Shaadi.com?' Sneha hissed. In class ten, Sneha had once saved Nandini from the bullies and after that, she had vowed to protect Nandini for life; from everyone and everything. However, after Sneha's divorce and consequent move to Mumbai a year and half ago, the tables had turned. Nandini was now Sneha's self-appointed guardian angel except for one problem that Sneha voiced sullenly, 'You may have angelic looks, kulta, but on the inside you're all devil.'

'Kulta? Me? I'm not promiscuous,' Nandini chuckled softly.

'Never say never!' Sneha shot back.

'Very funny! Don't forget, 7.30ish tonight. Wear something sexy.' Nandini hung up.

Sighing, Sneha slid the cell phone back on the table. She turned to watch her toddler son who slept facing her. Sneha's hazel eyes softened as she watched him snore softly, his chubby lips slightly apart. His little chest, under a worn blue and grey dinosaur sleeping suit lifted every time he breathed in and out, his soft dark hair falling onto his forehead. His small, puckered hand fisted tightly around his stuffed toy giraffe that with wear and tear now looked more brown than yellow.

'You are beautiful,' Sneha whispered softly, cupping the curve of his plump cheek. Even in his sleep, the boy felt his mother's touch and turned his face into her hand. Planting a soft kiss on his cheek, Sneha gently slunk out of her bed. Sethani had killed her sleep.

Yawning and stretching, Sneha came out of the bedroom. She saw less-her-maid-more-Advey's-nanny Amla, sitting on the floor in the living room perusing the English newspaper. Amla was the eldest daughter of a driver who had worked with the Sarins for over thirty years. Amla too, like Sneha and Nandini, had a connection to Kanpur; her family resided there with Aditya's mom.

'Baba sleep?' Amla asked. The young south Indian maid only spoke either fluent Tamil or halting English. When Sneha had walked out of her marital house in Kanpur, it had been with wounded pride, shredded confidence, four suitcases and two bodies—Advey and Amla.

'Yes, Baba asleep,' Sneha replied.

'Coffee now?' Amla asked, gathering and folding the newspaper.

'Yes, please. Thanks!' Sneha walked to the end of the living room of her apartment in Lower Parel that had the tiniest of balconies, just wide enough for her to stand without bumping her ass to the wall. Oh, the joy of living in the city where houses were worth more than the families and their assets combined. The glorious city of Mumbai! If the East India Company had a crystal ball that actually worked, they would have chucked the Kohinoor diamond and taken the city.

It still surprised Sneha that in Mumbai, a city so congested and so crowded, she experienced such soul-filling joy of being free like never before. Free from a shell of a marriage, free to be true to her son, to her dreams and the prerogative to lead a life that might have her question the hours in a day but never her sanity or self-respect.

Sneha pushed her dark brown curls, currently crowding her face, behind the ears. 'Coffee, madam!' Amla stood at the door, extending a cup to her.

'Thanks.' Sneha took the cup. 'No dinner tonight. We are going to Nandini's house.'

Amla snorted and walked back inside.

'Eggjactly!' Sneha and Amla held similar opinions about Nandini's recent matchmaking efforts. Sneha's fast-track divorce from Ankit was as old or as new as Nandini's marriage. Ironically, the day Nandini had moved into a new house post-marriage, Sneha had walked out of hers.

'Mama!' Sneha turned at the gurgle.

'Good morning, sunshine,' Sneha crooned, picking up her son with one arm, loving the feel of his chubby soft body next to her. Advey was trying to get past her into the balcony, the only space in the house he was barred from. 'No, not in the balcony. No kiddo.' Clasping her son tightly, Sneha came inside. Thus began Advey's first tantrum of the day.

The rest of the day passed in completion of chores and activities centred around Advey. The only downer about being the sole bread-earner of the house was that family time was mostly limited to weekends.

At 7.30 sharp that evening Sneha, Advey and Amla were at Nandini's palatial flat in Colaba. None other than the suave and gorgeous man of the house, Aditya Sarin himself, opened the door.

'Hi! Come in,' Aditya flashed a broad smile. Advey squirmed in Sneha's arms ready to launch himself at Aditya.

'Where's Advey? Did you forget him in the car?' Aditya acted as if he did not see the vigorously moving child.

'Here! Adi here!' Advey excitedly bounced up and down in his mother's arms and stretched out his small arms, grabbing the collar of Aditya's denim blue shirt.

'Oh, there you are little fella!' Aditya took Advey with careful ease. Sneha watched the gorgeous hunk handle her son like he was his own. Aditya's chiselled face broke into a wide crease that pushed his cheekbones higher, revealing a smile that could warm any woman, any age inside out. Sneha too was no exception; however, her friendship with Nandini was strong enough for her to feel only asexual, sisterly affection for Adi.

Aditya and Nandini had gone through a tumultuous four-year relationship before finally tying the knot over a year and a half ago. Even a cynical person like Sneha could not remain unaffected by their chemistry, thus she had happily played a pivotal role in bringing the lovers together.

Smiling, Sneha headed into the larger than large living room divided into two levels, complete with a bar and an aquarium for a wall. She sank into a large, dark brown recliner. 'Where's Sethani?' she asked.

'Getting ready,' Aditya took a seat across from her. He put Advey down next to him on the beige sofa.

'He might leave some stains on the sofa. He was eating apples in the car.' Sneha gestured for Amla to pick Advey up.

'Don't worry. That's what kids are supposed to do.' Aditya motioned for Amla to stop and said to her, 'Why don't you go and get something to eat from the kitchen?'

'Yes Aditya sir,' Amla gave a rare, shy smile to Aditya that revealed a gap between her front teeth and her crush on him.

'Truly a ladies' man!' Sneha mocked, taking in Aditya's fresh-from-the-shower look, complete with tousled wet locks brushing his forehead.

'Please!' Aditya replied, his tone defensive. 'What will you drink?' He rose smoothly to his feet.

'Adi, who's the bakra today?' Sneha came to the point.

'You!' Aditya smirked and quickly scooped Advey off the sofa, herding him to the gigantic aquarium.

Guilty man walking, thought Sneha. 'Can't you make her stop? Please.'

'Make her stop? You've known her much longer than I have,' Adi pointedly reminded Sneha over his shoulder.

'You owe me!' Sneha threatened.

'For?' Aditya faced her, his tone teasing.

'Hellllooo! I was the one who did the famous reveal, let the cat out of the bag! Remember?'

Aditya shook his head, still confused.

'Oh my God, did I not tell you about your mom and Nandini? The big secret!'

'Oh that!' Aditya's tone was casual.

Sneha scowled at him. 'Yes, *that*. The big *that* that made all *this* happen.' Sneha gestured at the wedding picture of Nandini and Aditya in the glided golden frame adorning the wall in front of her.

'Made all of what happen?' Nandini voice interrupted.

Sneha waved a dismissive hand in Nandini's direction. 'OM Jizzles!' Sneha exclaimed, seeing the flawless, short-sleeved, grey gown Nandini was wearing. It fastened at her waist with a silver belt and fell smoothly to the floor, clinging to her every curve as she moved.

Aditya came next to the few steps between the foyer and the living room. He extended his hand but Nandini did not take it. 'I can manage a few steps without your help, Adi.' Aditya dropped his hand, smiling genially. Sneha rebuked her senses for reading more into the irritation that briefly coloured Nandini's voice.

'Isn't this a bit too much? I thought we were setting Sneha up,' Aditya said, watching his young wife closely as she bent to pick Advey from the floor.

Sneha glared at them both. 'I knew it.'

Nandini, giving Advey a smackeroo, paused. 'Gee, thanks, Adi!'

'What? You think she doesn't know?' Aditya sneered.

'Behave, children! All three of you,' Sneha remarked.'OM Jizzles? Still watching *High School Musical?*' Nandini teased from Aditya's side.

'And what about Kabootar Ja Ja Ja?' Sneha voiced, her expression dark.

Nandini giggled, 'Sorry! My bad!' She was unapologetically and solely responsible for getting Advey hooked on to the damn pigeon song.

Just then, the doorbell chimed. Nandini went to the door. Sneha took shelter behind Advey, bracing herself to grin and not growl at the new suitor Sethani was about to throw her way.

And then she heard the voices. Sneha grimaced. On second thoughts, she would rather face ten ridiculous suitors than this woman.

'Sneha, you are here!' With a greeting sweet on the outside and patronizing on the inside, Mona Punt, Nandini's recent self-proclaimed best friend, came strutting through the door. HITCH! (Thanks to Advey's habit of picking up only cuss words from entire sentences, Sneha and Nandini's colourful lingo had downgraded to age-appropriate but confusing material).

'Hi Mona! Good to see you,' Sneha mumbled between pressed lips. With a quick disinterested glance, Sneha noticed Mona's short, satin, magenta sheath dress with horizontal pintucks to flatter her slightly full figure. Mona's hair was a short, stylish bob with perfectly maintained light brown highlights. Mona was blessed with a pair of beautiful dark eyes, a slightly hooked nose and thin lips which were usually pursed, making them appear to be mere painted lines in her face.

'Hi Advey!' Mona animatedly called out. Advey ignored her. 'He's adorable. Isn't he, Sam?' Mona turned to her husband who gave Sneha a quick curt nod.

'Hi Aditya! How's it going?' Sam Punt, a portly figure in a business suit at least a size smaller, came down the steps and boisterously shook hands with Aditya. 'Heard about the new deal you signed. You will be needing consultants. My firm can help you with that.' Mona's husband only had work on his mind. That could explain why, even after seven years of marriage, they had no kids. *Sorry!* Sneha rebuked her mind for its pettiness.

'Sure! Let me look into it,' Aditya replied, lightly extricating his hand from Sam's grip.

'I'm going to check the hors d'oeuvres!' Nandini smiled and went towards the corridor that led to the kitchen. Mona followed and so did a reluctant Sneha even as she gestured at Advey to behave.

Just then, the doorbell chimed again. Nandini stopped, glancing at the door. Sneha caught her sudden gulp. Nandini walked past Sneha to get the door. She was close enough to Sneha for the latter to glower and mutter, 'Who the hell have you invited, kulta?'

'Someone we all know,' Nandini chirped. Sneha followed her into the foyer as she opened the front door. Just as Sneha halted behind Nandini, a man stepped in.

'Bloody hell. She did not!' Sneha snarled to herself, her brows touched her forehead, shock writ large over her face.

'Sneha, Dr Saigal! Dr Saigal, Sneha!' Nandini trilled, flashing a wide smile while refusing to meet Sneha's shocked eyes.

Dr Saigal took a few steps inside and Sneha, regaining her composure, obligingly put her hand forward, 'Dr Saigal...Advey's ...paediatrician?' Sneha's surprise had her speak disjointedly.

'Sneh, remember last week when we had gone together for Advey's appointment with the doctor? While you and Advey were with the nurse, Dr Saigal and I got talking. That's when I realized that we all have so much in common. That got me thinking—we should all spend some time together. So here he is.' With a bright smile and a sweeping gesture of her hands, Nandini moved, partially hiding behind the doctor who stood at around 5 feet 10 inches.

'You are very kind and you have a beautiful home,' the doctor said, clearing his throat and turning around to get Nandini in his line of vision.

With a smile that was more of a grimace and eyes that shone bravely and pleading simultaneously, Nandini was busy trying to gauge Sneha's response, wondering if it was safe to leave her hiding place.

'I'll be in the kitchen,' Sneha sharply turned around and walked away. The kitchen was at the back of the house and far—far away from the living room, giving Sneha room enough from the few people she wanted to strangle.

Just outside the kitchen door, Sneha stopped and took a few calming breaths. 'Sneh!' she heard Nandini call out tentatively from behind.

Sneha turned to face Nandini. On seeing the guilt on Nandini's face, Sneha's anger quickly dissipated. After all, kulta and her warped convictions and schemes only had Sneha's good in mind. 'What are you doing, crazy woman?' Sneha asked gently.

Nandini let loose a relieved sigh. 'You're not mad?'

'I'm beyond mad. I'm stumped. You have to stop this insane matchmaking. Please Nandini. Advey's paediatrician? Seriously?'

'I just want you to be happy!' Nandini started with her usual defence.

Frustrated, Sneha raised her hands to the heavens. 'For the last time, woman, I'm HAPPY. Seriously ecstatic.'

'Because of Dr Saigal's being here?' Nandini asked, her expression somewhat unsure.

'Nooo!' Sneha indulged in a few *anulom-viloms* she had learned during a free yoga session at work. 'Because of Advey, because of you, my work and yeah, even my divorce. There I said it. I'm a happily divorced single mom.'

'But how can you really be...' Nandini trailed off, her expression saying it all.

'You would be miserable without Aditya, you *were* miserable without Aditya. I remember that time. But Ankit and I were never you and Adi, Sethani. My marriage was a pain in the ass not only for me but even for my ex. I've told you everything.' *Almost everything!* Sneha kept that musing to herself.

'Ya, after you separated,' Nandini accused.

Sneha gave her a direct look. 'You know me, Nandini, I deal with my own crap. Ankit and I got married for the wrong reasons. If Advey had not happened, we might have lasted only two months rather than two years, give or take. We did try to make it work though.'

'*You* tried to make it work. He just freaking started on with his ex-girlfriend,' Nandini said, her face tightening.

'Forget all that. It's in the past. I don't blame him. I have moved on—but coming back to you, Shaadi.com, please no more of these matchmaking schemes and blind dates. I have suffered so many of these clowns. I'm scared of coming to your house now.'

'C'mon Sneh. Dr Saigal is a good match. He's good with kids.' Nandini cajoled.

'Duh...that's his job!' Sneha added sarcastically.

Nandini continued her tirade. 'He's recently widowed and has a four-year-old daughter. Can you imagine being married to your child's paediatrician? Advey is growing. You know kids tend to fall lot sicker in their growing years, building up immunity and all,' Nandini paused, satisfied she had made her case.

Seeming to deliberate, Sneha scratched her right temple, 'Given that very good logic, you know who'd be perfect for me?' she asked matter-of-factly.

Nandini walked into the trap. 'Tell me who? I'll have him over tomorrow.'

'My doodhwala!'

2

Sethani, are you okay?

Sneha continued, 'After all, Advey will consume more milk as he grows up, right? I could save some serious dough with that alliance.' Nandini, pursing her lips huffed, giving Sneha the evil eye.

Sneha wasn't done yet. 'Maybe I should try and see if same-sex relationships are for me. Because Amla is irreplaceable. It'll be perfect! Advey will have two moms and a mad massi,' Sneha lightly touched her chin in wonderment. 'It's a foolproof plan! How did I not think of this before?' Sneha's pose and face briefly shone with sheer bliss and then she sobered. 'Idiot!' she lobbed at Nandini's irked face.

'Very funny!' Nandini stalked past Sneha into the kitchen.

Sneha followed her, determined. 'Hold on missy! Seriously, you'd better find me another paediatrician first.'

Nandini stopped mid-step. 'Why?'

'Because after tonight, I'm not going back to Dr Saigal.'

Grimacing, Nandini said out loud, 'Now instead of a date I have to find you a doctor.'

'Good luck!' Sneha, putting on her best smile, turned around and headed for the living room. On her way, she passed Mona going in the opposite direction.

'Nandini?' Mona asked.

'Kitchen!' Sneha found Sam talking to Adi, Adi replying in monosyllables and Dr Saigal perched awkwardly on the sofa. As Sneha was on a damage-control mission, she headed for the doctor. In the kitchen, Mona found Nandini standing next to the counter that the staff were laying the appetizers on. Nandini appeared lost in her private thoughts.

Mona waved a hand in front of Nandini's face. The diamond ring on her third finger and the chunky diamond bracelet on her wrist caught the light and glimmered brightly. 'So what did Sneha say? Is she going to be a sport tonight?'

Nandini focused her eyes on Mona. 'I don't know, maybe inviting her paediatrician wasn't the smartest thing to do,' she confessed.

'Excuse me,' Mona twitched her mauve-painted lips, 'I wish my other friends would be half as caring as you. You are only thinking of her good and of her son's.'

Nandini shook her head. 'I'm not so sure. Sneha keeps reiterating that she is happy. Maybe I shouldn't butt in.'

Mona uttered a priggish snort. 'C'mon. No woman likes to be on her own. It's lonely and crippling for her self-confidence. I'm a psychologist, I know what I'm saying. Sneha's in denial. You have to help her.'

Nandini's face held a wry grin, 'Help Sneha? She's the damsel who kicks butt.'

Pursing her lips, Mona pressed on, 'I know she's strong, or at least she's good at pretending.' Nandini opened her mouth but Mona continued. 'Moreover, being around you and Aditya and all your couple friends probably makes it worse for her. If I were you, I would not invite her to my parties.'

'Excuse me!' Nandini's face and tone were affronted.

'Let me rephrase that. Not invite her to all your parties. I'm positive Sneha feels lonely being around us couples. She just won't admit it.'

'Sneh's fine,' Nandini replied firmly. This time her lips clamped closely.

Mona let loose a kittenish laugh, 'I just—'

'Let's go back to the living room—everyone must be wondering where we are,' Nandini softly suggested. And she was right. Sneha had that exact thought as she was about to exhaust the topics she could converse on with Dr Saigal or Pradeep, as he preferred to be called.

Aditya appeared at Sneha's side with a drink. 'For you!' He held a funnel-shaped glass. Sneha caught the cherry and grated coconut swimming in the blue liquid.

'Strong?' she whispered, keeping her smile bright and fixed.

Leaning close to her in lieu of handing her the glass, Aditya whispered back, his face bland, 'Two of these shall knock you out.'

'Perfect!' Sneha took a big gulp of the drink.

Aditya fixed a glass of red wine for Pradeep as the latter insisted on sharing the cardiovascular benefits of drinking red wine.

'Maybe they should make it mandatory while working out,' Sneha voiced sweetly.

'That is one gym I wouldn't mind frequenting,' Aditya smirked.

'Which gym?' Nandini and Mona joined them.

'The one Sneha is planning to open that would have the patrons drinking red wine as they worked out,' Aditya replied.

'Sign me up for that one too!' Mona replied.

Nandini and Mona headed towards the other sofa. Sneha moved her feet to make way for them.

'Oh gosh, her skirt is ripped,' Mona whispered fiercely near Nandini's ear.

Nandini took note of the hole in the hemline of Sneha's simple khaki skirt. 'She mustn't have noticed it,' Nandini defended her quietly.

'Get her a new wardrobe. She's always dressed up for work or in jeans.' Mona made sure to keep her voice free of any judgments. 'Shopping should pep her up. Works for every female I know. Trust me, I'm a psychologist,' Mona threw in as they sat down.

Unaware of how interesting her skirt had suddenly become, Sneha tucking her feet under her knees, struck a demure pose while carrying on a forced conversation with Pradeep. Aditya duly provided the drinks and Nandini the food.

After dinner, Sneha followed the others back to the living room. Pradeep followed her. He even joined her on the love seat she opted for. 'I'm glad that Nandini got us together,' Pradeep spoke, shifting his glasses further up the bridge of his nose as he fell back into the comfortable leather.

'Hmm.' Sneha smiled, trying not to focus on the large blackheads glistening around his nostrils. She let her eyes skim over his receding hairline, creased forehead, dark eyes behind a pair of rectangular glasses, broad nose and wide mouth that was prone to gentle smiles. Pradeep's personality was pleasant, avuncular.

'Advey is such a nice kid,' Pradeep remarked.

'Thank you.' Sneha hid her face in her drink—this time it was a glass of water.

'So Advey's father…?' Pradeep probed further.

Sneha lips stilled near the rim of the crystal tumbler she held. 'What about him?' she hedged.

Pradeep's expression was kind. He seemed to undertand Sneha's reluctance to talk about that subject. 'You know what I mean.'

Lowering her glass and taking a deep breath, Sneha looked at him squarely in the eyes. 'I'm divorced. Advey's father works in Hyderabad. I'm his ex-wife and his ex-girlfriend is his present spouse.' Sneha was thankful that the others were engrossed in their own conversations or at least pretending to be. This was the only part she hated about her divorced status; revealing how quickly the ex had moved on.

Pradeep exhaled. 'I'm sorry!'

'Don't be. I'm not,' Sneha replied sombrely.

'Well, I lost my wife to cancer last year,' Pradeep confided.

'I'm sorry! Were you close?' Sneha almost bit off her tongue at the doctor's surprised look. Just because she did not understand closeness between a man and a woman did not mean that it did not exist, her kulta was a live and kicking example after all. 'I'm sorry. Please don't answer that,' Sneha apologized. She stood up. 'Excuse me. I need to check on Advey.'

She found Advey rollicking on the carpet next to the train set Adi had set up especially for him in one of the five guest rooms. Amla was keeping a close watch as *Ben 10* played loudly on the gigantic flat screen on the wall.

'Mama!' Advey got up and rushed to her on his short legs. Grabbing him off the floor, Sneha hid her face in his soft hair and inhaled his baby smell. Heaven!

'You're okay?' Nandini called out from behind.

Sneha turned with Advey still in her arms. 'Mathi!' Advey lunged for Nandini just as she lunged for him.

Sneha looked at Amla. 'Why don't you go and have your dinner? I'll watch Advey.'

'Okay, madam!' Amla rolled her eyes as she went out, letting them know that she knew when she was being politely kicked out.

'So give me a number, kulta,' Sneha remarked, sinking down on the bed. The bloody thing almost ate her whole. She quickly moved to a carved and upholstered mahogany chair.

'Number? What?' Nandini let Advey tug her to the train set.

'How many more of these blind dates do I have to go through?'

Sheepishly, Nandini met her eyes.

Sneha continued, her face unknowingly glum, 'You know what is really hard for me is not that I'm divorced, but having to tell complete strangers why I failed at something every woman is expected to adapt to like a second skin.'

In a second Nandini was across the room, sinking to the floor in front of Sneha, her expression guilty. 'Crap! I'll back off, I promise, if you agree to something.'

Sneha grimaced, 'Oh God, what now?'

'Let's go shopping! How about tomorrow?' Nandini implored.

Sneha could not help an inadvertent smile. 'I have to work.' Sneha slid down, joining Nandini and Advey on the floor.

'And I don't?' Nandini suddenly bristled.

'Not for a living!' Sneha pointed out in all honesty.

'So your work is more important than mine?'

Sneha made amends. 'No, Sethani. I didn't mean it like that. Seriously.'

No, you did, just like Aditya, Nandini thought as her hands straightened a section of the toy railway tracks.

'Sethani, are you okay?' Sneha asked, closely watching Nandini's face.

'I'm fine,' Nandini brushed her off.

The two friends were not as alone as they thought themselves to be. They missed the person hiding behind the partially open door. Mona had a smug smile as she went back to the living room. Her mind games were working...they had to. After all, she was a psychologist.

3

You guys know each other?

Next day, late in the afternoon at work, as Sneha was busy tweaking a photoshopped image on her computer, her desk phone rang. She knew the extension. It was the reception desk of her advertising agency.

'Sneha Gupta!'

'Ms Gupta, ummm…' the receptionist had trouble finishing the sentence. Sneha gave an impatient sigh. The receptionist spoke hurriedly, 'Sethani is waiting for you here,' and hung up.

Sneha gazed at her wristwatch. 'Shoot, it's 4 o'clock already.' She hurriedly saved the open file, logged off her PC and grabbed her bag. She got to the lobby, dishing out hurried goodbyes to her team and colleagues. As Sneha entered the lobby, she stopped short, her mouth open. Sethani was planning another weekend massacre.

'Nandini!' Sneha called out with more force than usual.

'Hi Sneh!' Nandini smile was a healthy mixture of guilt and some more guilt. 'I was just talking to your colleague, Jigar!' She pointed at the bespectacled young man with curly dark hair in a pastel pink shirt.

'Were you talking to him or exchanging numbers with him?' Sneha's smile was ghoulish as she joined them.

'Hi Sneha! Did not know Mrs Sarin and you were childhood friends,' Jigar's smile spilled out of his face.

'Ya, till death-do-us-apart kind!' Sneha felt some satisfaction as she heard Nandini's nervous titter. 'See you later! Gotta go.' She spied Nandini uttering a quick goodbye and whispering something to Jigar that she obviously wasn't meant to hear.

As they got into the elevator and the steel doors closed on them, Sneha's first words to Nandini were, 'No frigging way. Not him.'

'But he's so nice, Sneh,' Nandini tried her best pouting expression.

'That Jeegar is freakin' vying for the new promotion. He's my competition.'

Nandini's smile was dazzling. 'Well then, dinner's a perfect way to bury the hatchet. You know, blur the line between enemies.'

Sneha's smile was threatening. 'I shall blur both you and him.'

Nandini snorted, 'Fine! Looking forward to shopping?' she changed the topic.

'Sure.' Sneha rummaged through her bag and pulled out her cell phone. 'You did promise to grab a drink and a bite.'

Now Nandini threatened, 'Yes, but after shopping. With the emphasis on *after*.'

'Ya, ya whatever, kulta.' Sneha was busy typing a message.

'I already spoke to Amla. Advey is fine. He's had his evening snack and she was about to take him to the park.'

Sneha's smile was genuine. She put her cell phone back in her bag. 'Thanks, Sethani! So where are we going?'

'You'll see!' Nandini answered as the elevators came to a halt.

Half an hour later just as the rush hour traffic, like an overflowing dam was about to burst upon Mumbai's roads, Nandini and Sneha, from Sneha's office in Mahalaxmi reached Phoenix Mall.

'What a wedding present!' Sneha remarked as she caught the reflection of Nandini's maroon Aston Martin Vanquish in the adjoining thick glass wall.

'I liked my older one just fine!' Nandini said while looking for change in one of the numerous slots in the console between them. 'Adi kicked up such a fuss when I thought of getting my old car here.'

Sneha's laugh was rude. 'I can just imagine that car parked between the fleet of obscenely expensive cars the Sarins have.'

Nandini rounded on her, her expression resentful. 'Ya, but I'm not a Sarin. Should I simply discard everything I hold precious just because I married rich?'

'Don't be such a mirchi-ka-pakoda, kulta. I'll willingly trade my car for this one if you wish. I'll even paint it a garish red,' Sneha remarked calmly.

Nandini made a face. 'Forget it. Why the hell is the checking taking so long?'

'Ask and you shall be answered.' Sneha brought the window on her side down to have a short tête-à-tête with one of the uniformed guards nearby. 'Some big-ass jewellery exhibition! It'll be crowded. You still wanna go?'

'Heck, yeah!' Nandini worked the stick shift and moved the car forward. 'To shopping!' Nandini exclaimed and promptly clipped the side of the car against the security post. 'Oops!'

'And that makes it dent number seven. Stop punishing the poor car just because it's not your other khatara.' Sneha saw the slight dent from the sideview mirror. 'Will Adi be mad?'

'Nah! He'll just ask if I'm okay and again try to press the need to keep a driver,' Nandini grumbled, pulling into an empty parking spot.

An hour and a half later, the two friends flopped into the cane seats of a chic bar on the topmost floor of the mall.

'Two measly bags, that's it! You're impossible, Sneha. Any other woman would have bought a store in this much time.'

'Chill ya! You know I'm not much of a shopper. I appreciate the effort, but I know the real reason we are here,' Sneha remarked, grinning as she went over the laminated red and black menu card.

'You're such a twenty-nine-going-on-fifty.' Nandini frowned confused, 'What reason?'

'Nearly thirty-going-on-sixty,' Sneha's smile was goading. 'You just wanted to hang out with moi!'

'Ya, that too. But I did want you to buy a new wardrobe.' Nandini should have been more careful with her words. 'Mona suggested a makeover—'

Losing her happy face, Sneha smacked the menu card on the table loudly. 'Mona! She suggested a what!'

Nandini backtracked, 'Of course I wanted to chillax with you.'

'Un-freakin' believable,' Sneha sat back in her chair, her lips twisted to one side of her face. 'Who is that Mona to critique my clothes? And you listened to her?' Her tone was accusing.

'Oh man! What a crowd. Look there!' Nandini tried her best to distract a glowering Sneha. She knew she had just put her entire array of footwear in her mouth.

'What!' Sneha peeved, tossed a careless look over her shoulder. They were seated right across from the pub door. Just then, Sneha's eyes fell on the group of people entering the pub. Her breath jarred in her throat and Sneha felt time simply freeze around her. Her body went slack; had she not been holding the armrests of the chair she would have surely slid to the floor in a tidy heap. The man in the middle of the crowd seized all of her attention and breath—the one with slightly wavy and thick raven hair that sat upon a sculpted face with arched dark eyebrows over piercing green eyes that she knew by memory were dark green at the rim and a mixture of paler green, yellow and brown in the centre, shielded by long lashes. She had not forgotten those eyes. The nose in a straight line started in a gentle slope under his eyes and ended firmly over a generous mouth with a slightly plump lower lip. The chubby boy she remembered had chipped away into a tall and lean specimen of raw masculinity. His strides were long, graceful and confident, commanding others to fall in a step behind.

No way, José! Sneha thought, watching the man, her mouth agape. His recent pictures did no justice to his actual persona or physical aura.

'Sneh! Sneha!' Nandini's voice broke into her catatonic state.

Sneha turned to face Nandini, her eyes round as saucers, 'Super canary shit! I don't believe it.'

'What happened, Sneh?'

'Just don't look that way, okay?' Sneha ordered vehemently.

'Jalti jawani calm down!' Teasingly, Nandini reached out to poke Sneha's hand. She struck her glass of water instead. The glass tipped over the side of the table spilling all the water on the table before it shattered on the floor.

'Hit, kulta!' Sneha winced. 'Loody bell! You just had to, didn't you?'

'You are acting like you have a fire in your pants. You want this water?' Nandini bantered, giggling.

A waiter appeared at their table. 'Mrs Sarin, we will take you to another table.' He briskly began cleaning the mess. Another smiling server stood at their side, ready to whisk them away.

'I'm really sorry!' Nandini straightened to her full height. Sneha too stood up, making sure the menu card covered her face. 'I'll pay for it,' Nandini insisted.

'No problem, Mrs Sarin!' Even the manager joined the brouhaha. 'Please come, I have a table ready for you.'

'Is there anyone who doesn't know you?' Sneha mocked quietly, swiftly falling in step behind a still-apologetic Nandini.

Sneha caught a glimpse of their new table and the others in its vicinity. Keeping the menu in front of her face, Sneha grabbed Nandini's elbow and pulled her back. 'Hammit! No, kulta. Not there, please, anywhere but there.' The menu card dribbled the last few drops of water on Sneha's wrist. Reflexively she brought the menu card down and it caught Nandini's wrist.

'Oww!' Nandini's soft yelp was loud enough to be heard by the people around them.

Panicking, Sneha closed her eyes. And when she opened them a second later, her eyes of their own accord slipped to the next table where a party of three businessmen in similar dark suits sat. However, one of them was staring at Sneha, as if some old forgotten memory was waking up in his head. In a nano second, realization dawned in the familiar light green irises, and in response, Sneha's face turned a bright shade of red. She broke the eye contact.

Sneha watched from the corner of her eyes as the man, who she knew to be three years older than her, come out from behind his table. Turning her face away, Sneha cursed under her breath, 'Hit!'

The man did the unexpected, he greeted Nandini. 'Nandini? Right?' Surprised, Sneha turned to gaze at him and then quickly averted her face as his rapier glance collided with hers. Sneha averted her eyes, thinking and praying that he had not recognized her. After all, she had changed a lot since their last meeting.

Nandini stared at the newcomer for a few seconds and then her words came out in a rush, 'Nikhil. Nikhil Chandel. Gayatri's friend?'

Sneha kept her curiosity to herself. *How did they know each other? And how did Gayatri feature in this equation?*

'How are you?' Nandini tried to eclipse the sudden stab of guilt on her face and conscience but failed.

Sneha, in spite of her own unease, felt a twinge of anger. She did not have to see Nandini's face to imagine what she was feeling. Her kulta was guilty of nothing.

'Very well, thank you. Congratulations on your wedding!' Nikhil Chandel's voice was deep and suave, hitting all the right notes of aloofness. Sneha scowled yet she did not look at him. *Jerk!* She formed an opinion of him right then, right there.

'Thanks… How is…' Nandini trailed off awkwardly. The colour in her face rose.

'How is? Who?' Nikhil asked with banal curiosity but there was nothing banal about the glint in his eyes as he kept them fixed on Nandini's face.

Sneha, at Nandini's side, stiffened. Nikhil must have noticed the tiny movement. He finally swivelled his eyes to Sneha.

Nandini obligingly made the introductions, 'This is my goo—'

Nikhil cut her off. 'Hello Sneha. It has been a while. Remember me?'

Pulling in a deep breath even as her hands fisted at her sides and her chin came out at him, Sneha gave Nikhil her full attention. She schooled her expression to match the indifference she saw on his arrogant face, 'Hi Nikhil! It has been a while.'

'You guys know each other?' Nandini asked, surprised.

'Hardly!'

'Maybe!'

Sneha and Nikhil answered simultaneously.

4

Worried face, anxious eyes!

Observing Nandini's comical expression, Sneha sheepishly rectified, 'It was ages ago. He's a friend of my cousin in Amsterdam.' Nikhil did not add to her statement. He watched them, his eyes cold, face impassive, not giving any of his thoughts away. Sneha kept her eyes fixed on Nandini.

'Your table, Mrs Sarin!' the server interrupted.

'Well, it was nice meeting you,' Nandini made a move towards the table. Sneha had already grabbed a chair for herself. Nikhil did not move, prompting Nandini to murmur, 'Would you care to join us?' Sneha bit her lip in annoyance and then noticed Nikhil watching not Nandini but her, his eyes hooded.

'How can he join us? He already has company,' Sneha reminded her, defiantly thumbing her chin again at him.

Sliding his hand into his black trouser pockets that sat well on his muscular and lean build, Nikhil smoothly disagreed, 'I would like to. Thank you for asking.' The flash-in-the-pan smile that started and ended at his mouth was solely for Nandini while he ignored Sneha. That only added to the building irritation in Sneha, even though she knew she wasn't her smartest when irked.

'We were almost done.' Nikhil glanced at the two men on his table. They promptly immersed their faces in their cell phones. At seeing the alacrity with which the men reacted, Sneha deduced that they worked *for* him rather than *with* him.

Nikhil moved forward to take the chair from the waiter and pulled it out for Nandini. Before he could extend the same courtesy to Sneha, she hurriedly pulled out her own chair and sat down with a thump. The table shuddered slightly.

'Sneha!' Nandini reproached, grabbing her glass before it fell again.

'Sorry!' Far from polite, Sneha shot back, busying herself with the menu again. By the time they were out of here, Sneha had a feeling she would remember this menu by heart. *All his loody fault,* Sneha cribbed to herself.

Nikhil took a seat between both of them. For few minutes, there was complete silence at the table. Sneha kept her mouth closed and eyes exclusively on the menu, purposely ignoring Nandini's frantic gaze. *Sorry, kulta, in this you're on your own; if I step in you might have to rue more than a broken glass,* Sneha thought.

Nikhil for his part appeared content to sit quietly and stare indifferently, although his eyes kept straying back to Sneha's lowered head.

Clearing her throat, Nandini broke the ice, 'So what brings you to Mumbai?'

'Work!' Nikhil turned his head to give her the briefest of smiles. 'My firm has organized the jewellery exhibition.'

Saala sunhaar (goldsmith)! Sneha thought acerbically, refusing to contribute to the conversation. Sneha was surprised by the intensity of angst she felt for the cold man sitting across from her. A rational part of her could not help but wonder, was it dislike for him or dislike of the embarrassing memories he awakened?

'Whatever!' Sneha blurted scowling fiercely at the table linen but both Nikhil and Nandini heard and misunderstood her.

Nandini hurried to smoothen the awkward moment. 'Your firm?'

Nikhil's nod was brisk. With an effort he moved his eyes off Sneha who avoided his gaze as if he had the pink eye.

Abruptly, Nandini lost the nervous look in her eyes and a slow saintly smile climbed all the way from her lips to her eyes. 'As in you own the firm or do you work there?' Nandini asked brazenly. Sneha widened her downcast eyes. She could strangle Sethani.

Nikhil's smile was downright frosty, 'A bit of both.'

'Ohh okay!' Nandini replied, smug. The waiter appeared on her side. 'Mangotini for me,' Nandini said.

'Make that two please,' Sneha said, keeping her eyes pinned to the menu.

Nikhil had a sudden urge to grab that blasted menu from her hands and fling it across the room. Years of rigidly practised self-control came into play and Nikhil instantly thrust all emotion away from his face and mind.

The waiter glanced at Nikhil. 'Glenlivet with club soda,' Nikhil emphasized in a deeper voice, his words sounding more clipped than usual.

As the server moved away, Nandini trampled over all etiquettes of PC. 'So Nikhil, did you re-marry?' Sneha nearly choked on her breath. She shot Nandini a warning look. It fell off Nandini like water off a duck's back.

Nikhil watched Nandini. His answer was a sneer accompanied by a single word, 'Never.'

Nandini wasn't finished. 'Seeing anyone? Anything serious?'

A sudden shake enveloped the table. Nandini and Nikhil grabbed whatever they could. Thankfully nothing spilled or shattered.

'Why did you just kick me?' Nikhil asked, levelling his indifferent glance at Sneha. However, the mere glance altered to a reluctant gaze as his eyes ran over Sneha's features. Her forehead was clear and currently housed a few lines of tension which he knew with some satisfaction were there because of him. Her deep-set hazel eyes fringed by thick dark lashes with a natural upward tilt at their ends gave her face a perpetual saucy expression. The nose, thin and petite, was the kind that suited a nose ring or a stud. Her lips free of any colour were a light pink, well defined with rounded tips, the kind that could alter from a grimace to a grin in seconds. Hastily, Nikhil swung his face away, surprised at himself for noticing such details. He had seen and known far more alluring women with better manners and opinions.

Sneha grudgingly admitted, 'That wasn't meant for you.' The next word was even harder to utter, 'Sorry!'

Nikhil answered her with a silence that further maddened Sneha. He moved his hand from the table to let the server place a single malt scotch in front of him. 'So how often do you play footsie with each other?' He kept his sombre face turned to Nandini, his tone disparaging. There was no emotion visible on his face. He could have been talking about anything from the weather to a bomb.

'Ha! Ha!' Sneha muttered darkly, tucking her feet under the chair. Had she left her wits behind in one of the trillion shops they had visited? What was wrong with her? How could she let Nikhil speak to Nandini and her like that? Angrily, Sneha looked up and opened her mouth the very second Nikhil shifted his face and met her eyes. Her hazel eyes widened at the caustic expression that briefly lightened the inner circles of his irises. Confused, Sneha shut her mouth without uttering a single word and reached out to take a desperate sip of the mangotini.

'Which cousin of yours is Nikhil friends with?' asked Nandini.

Sneha obstinately clamped her lips and picked up her glass.

Giving Nandini his signature cool smile that did not spill out of his lips or cause creases around his eyes, Nikhil stayed mum.

Sneha finally voiced softly, 'Kim di. My first cousin on Mom's side. You've met her a few times,' she reminded Nandini.

Nandini nodded. 'Oh, Kim di. Of course, I remember. She came down for your—' Nandini bit the word off. Just then, Nandini's cell phone buzzed. She glanced at it. 'It's Adi. Again and of course,' her smile was quick. 'Excuse me.' Nandini got up and walked away, leaving Sneha and Nikhil alone. Sneha nearly put out her hand to stop Nandini, a sudden bout of awkwardness surging in her. Fresh colour climbed from her neck to her face as she felt Nikhil's eyes scrutinizing her.

After a few seconds of silence, Nikhil finally ventured a question, 'Adi?'

Sneha deigned to shoot him a quick pointed look, 'Aditya. Her husband? You knew that!' Sneha glanced at Nandini who was busy talking on her cell phone. She shifted uneasily in her chair. *C'mon kulta, come back!* Sneha tried sending Nandini a few cuss words telepathically.

'How well you know me,' Nikhil's tone was lazy and mocking.

Taking a deep breath, Sneha resignedly faced him, 'We were just kids back then. I can't believe you are still mad about it.' She watched his face closely for a reaction. She didn't see any.

'I'm not.' Nikhil took a sip of his drink and put it back on the table with an air of finality. He smoothly got to his feet and looked down at her. Sneha unconsciously tipped her face back at him, realizing in that instant that even if she were standing he'd be towering above her. Nikhil eyes ran over Sneha's upturned face framed by dark brown, soft curls that fell below her shoulders. A sudden expression in Nikhil's eyes had Sneha feel some nervous flutters in her stomach. Perplexed by her reaction to him, she hurriedly looked away.

'Gayatri is back from Europe. And she's not over Aditya.'

With those ominous words, Nikhil turned and walked away. *And they call queens dramatic*, Sneha thought, even as she tried to fully absorb the meaning of those threatening words. Nikhil passed Nandini who was still on the phone and waved her a casual bye. He stopped to hand over a few notes to the server at their table.

In seconds, the two men from the adjacent table followed him out. Nikhil might have freed her and the room of his magnetic physical presence, yet those green eyes and his parting words haunted Sneha's anxious mind.

5

Waiting for someone?

In a few minutes, Nandini came back to the table. Sneha had regained her composure by then.

'So what was all that about? You and Nikhil?' Nandini asked, sitting down in her chair.

'BORING!' Sneha waved her hand dismissively. The less she said or thought about that insufferable man, the better. However, Sneha was still surprised by the intense revulsion, anxiety and everything else she had experienced around Nikhil. *Has to be the shock of seeing him, it won't happen again,* Sneha decided with a firm shake of her head.

'BS!' Nandini disagreed loudly.

'What?' Sneha asked distracted.

'You both were positively rubbing sparks off each other. Tell me, woman! NOW!' Nandini whined, shaking her stylish dark hair vigorously.

'He did mention Gayatri was in town.' Sneha knew how to distract her friend.

Sneha's words had the desired effect. Nandini sat back, chewing the side of a finger. 'Nikhil is extremely tight with Gayatri and her family. They go back decades. If he's saying it and it's about Gayatri then it's true.' Nandini grimaced, 'Tit.'

Sneha rolled her eyes. 'The whole idea of mispronouncing cuss words is to bring them down a level, not make them worse.'

'What?'

'I don't say dammit, I say hammit. For bloody I'll say loody or poody. For shit I'll say hit or bit, not tit. Yuckkk!'

'Sorry!' Nandini grumbled even as she flipped Sneha the bird.

Sneha sighed, 'Get that tattooed on your head if you must! You and Adi did no wrong. Aditya was always in love with you and even a blind person in the room with you and Adi can sense that. Okay?' Sneha demanded an answer.

'I know, but he did break off the engagement with Gayatri because of me!' Nandini replied dully.

Sneha snorted, 'If I remember correctly, Adi broke off the unofficial engagement even before the official announcement of their wedding date. He did the right thing.'

Nandini exhaled, 'Oh, well.' She shook her head as if to clear it and continued, 'Adi called. I have to go home. We have to go out with someone from work.'

'Cool!' Sneha grabbed her bags and got up.

'So you didn't tell me how you and Nikhil met,' said Nandini matching Sneha's strides.

'BORING!' Sneha reiterated as they exited the pub. The two headed for the elevators. Sneha firmly kept her face angled off the exhibition going on across from them. Thus she missed Nikhil standing at the entrance, his enigmatic glance steadily watching Sneha.

As Nandini pulled up in front of Sneha's apartment complex, her nagging was still very much on. 'Why the fudge aren't you telling me?'

Sneha raised a shaking fist in front of her, 'Oh God, kulta, for the last time, he and I met ages ago and very, very briefly. Will you please quit now? Can I go? Advey will be waiting!'

Grumpily, Nandini pressed the auto unlock button. 'Fine. Wait and see who I invite this weekend,' she muttered under her breath.

'What did you say?' Sneha asked, grabbing her bags from the back seat.

'Nothing.' Nandini's smile was a ghostly spectre.

Narrowing her eyes momentarily and menacingly at her BFF, Sneha alighted and a quick goodbye later headed for the building elevators. The rest of the evening was lost in cuddling, bathing and feeding her son, followed by an hour or so of pending office work before she hit the sack.

Next day, after work, Sneha headed straight for an exhibition. A very expensive and crowded exhibition.

She went up to the topmost floor and walked straight to the entrance of the large hall. Sneha swung open the tinted glass doors only to be instantly engulfed by humanity. The kind that wore excessive perfume, spoke softly and carried small clutch bags that housed multiple credit cards. The person she sought stood close to the doors conversing with a young couple.

Nikhil noticed Sneha just as she saw him. A slightly raised eyebrow was all Sneha received as a greeting and then he went back to the conversation.

Uncertainly, Sneha moved to the side as she allowed others coming in behind her to pass.

A woman approached her. 'Could you open case number 14? My sister would like to take a look.'

Sneha straightened. 'I'm sorry. I don't work here,' she replied.

'Oh sorry!' came the reply. 'It's just that your clothes…' the woman trailed off and hurriedly walked away. Sneha ruefully glanced at her clothes. A crisp white shirt tucked into slim-fitting black pants may make her look taller and take some voluptuousness away from her curves, yet it was the most common dress code for staff in the service industry.

A bemused Sneha was about look for a place to sit when Nikhil approached her. 'Looking for someone?'

Sneha immediately altered her expression to severe, 'Yes. You!' Unconsciously, Sneha's hands balled into fists at her side. Why did she feel as if she had a fight on her hands? 'Is there somewhere we can talk for a few minutes in private?' she asked evenly.

'I've already accepted your indirect apology yesterday,' Nikhil reminded her coolly. He knew he was purposely goading the woman in front of him but he could not help himself. Nikhil was no longer the eager to please, always polite kind of bloke. The sooner Sneha realized that the better. He knew better now, life itself had taught him that harsh lesson. Only give an inch if you can take a mile!

Sneha felt like gnashing her teeth but she would not give the exasperating man in front of her that satisfaction. 'Very generous of you,' she quipped sarcastically. 'It's about something else.'

Nikhil seemed to debate for a few seconds; all the while he stared at Sneha, his look piercing as if he were trying to pick on her thoughts. Sneha met his stare and stood her ground. Her obstinate expression clearly proclaimed that she wanted to talk and she wouldn't be taking no for an answer.

'Let's step out.' Nikhil did not wait to see if Sneha followed him. With quick, familiar, long strides he headed out of the already open glass doors. Sneha assumed that they would be heading to the pub across from the exhibition hall. On this floor that was the only other place with chairs. She was wrong. Nikhil marched straight up to the elevators and waited for her there.

'Here?' Sneha murmured, surprised.

'You said it won't take long so I'm guessing you have somewhere to go,' Nikhil shot back. The icy tone of his voice told Sneha another story; he was eager to get rid of her.

Sneha tried not to feel insulted but failed completely. Her hazel eyes positively shot sparks at him. 'What did you mean yesterday when you said "Gayatri hasn't gotten over Aditya?"'

'I meant exactly what you heard,' Nikhil's reply was smooth even as he could not help but notice how in anger Sneha's hazel eyes took on a reddish blackish tint around the rims. *Hmmm... different*, he thought. Sneha had her hands pulled back, her stance defiant. The action only strained her blouse tighter across her chest, drawing attention to her downright attractive curves.

'Was it a warning?' Sneha demanded, crossing her hands over her chest, oblivious to the fact that it hid a part of her that Nikhil had suddenly discovered to be very fetching.

Pity! Nikhil pushed that thought away from his mind. 'Are you going to challenge her to a duel?' Nikhil kept his expression bored as his eyes skimmed over Sneha's head back to the entrance hall.

Sneha saw what he wanted her to see—his eagerness to get back to work. 'Of course not. I just want to make sure that Gayatri knows her boundaries. Aditya and Nandini are married.'

'And marriages are forever?' Nikhil shot back. Abruptly his eyes intensely, and very briefly, clashed with hers. Sneha noticed the sparkling yellow flecks in his green eyes.

'Yes, some are,' Sneha retorted. 'And as Gayatri's friend you should give her correct advice.'

'Is that all?' Nikhil was terse.

Sneha was taken aback by his curtness. 'Ya… that's all.' Not too many people on this planet left her tongue-tied. The Nikhil she remembered wasn't one of them. *What happened to him*, Sneha wondered, staring at his chiselled face that held no softness.

Sneha thought she saw a flicker of amusement sparkle in his dead-as-a-fish stare but it was so brief that she was sure she had imagined it.

'I'm not the only who's changed!' Nikhil countered, his look astute.

Sneha inwardly cringed. *Crap!* Had she said that out loud? 'Whatever. That's all! Bye.' Beating a hasty retreat Sneha punched the button to call the elevator. Nikhil did not stop her.

Even though they did not exchange another word, Nikhil quietly stood at her side until the elevator came and took Sneha away from him. 'Horrible man!' Sneha blurted to an empty elevator.

As Nikhil walked back to the exhibition he could not help but recall the Sneha he had met ages ago. Even then, she had been a pesky slip of a girl with an equally pesky affliction of meddling in other people's lives. She had worn her hair differently then. Short curls that framed her face and ended above her shoulders, unlike the tight bun today. Then her body had been that of a girl's, lean, with a child-like gait of perpetually trying to move faster than her legs could carry her. However, now her body was that of a woman with generous curves and inherent grace as she walked. He recalled the way her blouse had pulled taut over her torso. Frowning, Nikhil stopped short of the glass doors. How had her body of then and now stayed in his memory? He liked his relationships to be uncluttered and functional. And his gut told him that Sneha would not know uncluttered or functional even if they were her first and last name. She seemed like the kind to bring knives to a gun fight and it would make no difference to her if the cause was hers or not. That very instant Nikhil made a solemn resolution to stay as far as possible from the cumbersome woman. She got under his skin in a manner he did not appreciate. Nikhil walked back inside the exhibition hall.

However one thing that Nikhil did not know about Sneha was that she wasn't easily thwarted. At the exhibition Sneha had discreetly picked up a business card of Nikhil's firm, DC Inc., which provided his office address in Worli.

'I will find out where Gayatri is and meet that tart face-to-face, once and for all and without any of that insufferable jerk's help,' Sneha muttered, heading out of the elevator. The exhibition was on until tomorrow so she knew Nikhil would be here and not in his office.

The next day around noon, feigning an appointment in Worli, Sneha left her office. A woman on a mission, all she was lacking was a cape and a plan. After a short drive, Sneha pulled into the parking lot of the multistorey building with a completely tinted glass exterior. As she walked into the lobby, Sneha made sure to read the names of a few other offices in the building. Seven of the uppermost floors in the building belonged to DC Inc.

Casually, Sneha slid into the elevator behind a group of professionally attired people. After pressing the button for the topmost floor, she hovered in the back.

Sneha was nervous. By the time the elevator reached the top floor, she was alone in it.

'Ohhh!' Sneha recoiled just as she stepped out.

6

A. Patel and Associates

Did the building house a prison? Why were there so many security personnel? she wondered. Near the elevator alone, she counted four.

'You are here to meet...?' asked the guard closest to Sneha, brandishing a forbidding-looking gun.

Sneha gulped, 'Uhh umm, Nikhil Chandel.'

'You have an appointment, ma'am?' he asked next.

'Umm yes, kind of. I mean yes I do,' Sneha replied with more confidence that she felt.

'The code number please,' he requested, as another guard with a paper and pen joined him, ready to jot it down.

'What code?' Bewildered, Sneha fumbled.

'Whenever meetings are scheduled with Mr Chandel or any other directors, a code, ma'am, is sent via email.'

'Well I wasn't sent any code. No problem. I'll just come back some other time.' Sneha knew this to be a wise time to turn back. Another guard stepped between her and the elevator.

'Just a minute. We need to check you.'

'Excuse me! Check me? What rubbish!' Sneha nervously pulled her bag and folders in front of her body. *Where the heck had she come?* Sneha thought, panicked.

'Please come this way!' the guard replied sternly.

'No friggin' way!' Sneha made a move to jab the button to call the elevator. A strong vice-like grip on her elbow stopped her. She was about to scream her lungs out or do something equally rash when a woman popped her head out from a room at the end of the corridor.

'What's going on?' The elderly woman dressed in a well-draped cotton sari asked, stepping out of the door.

'Help me. Please!' Sneha wailed. The woman, with her salt-and-pepper hair tied neatly in a bun at her nape, beckoned the guards with some authority, 'Bring her to my office please.' She disappeared back into her room.

'You heard her. I want to go to her office.' Sneha brought out her repressed indignation. The guard hustled her into the room. Sneha caught a glimpse of a clean, expansive room in muted shades of cream with a small fountain and expensive-looking art on the walls.

The woman sat behind a clear glass desk that appeared as spotless and well-kept as her appearance. 'Your name, Miss?'

'Who's asking?' Sneha fidgeted between the guards, buying time. 'Who's that?'

Sneha looked around. It was Nikhil's voice, sounding somewhat muffled. 'Where is he?' Sneha whispered to the woman in the sari. As an answer, she swivelled her computer screen towards Sneha. Sneha and Nikhil came face-to-face with each other yet again. Nikhil's expression was incredulous and Sneha's smile flustered. 'Hi!' Sneha raised her hand awkwardly in greeting.

'What are you doing there?' Nikhil barked. His jaw clenched tightly and his nostrils became pinched at the ends. His expression turned dark and ominous as his green eyes glowed hostile. The guards left the room.

Sneha's chin rose defiantly and, purposely ignoring Nikhil's angry eyes burning a hole in her, she addressed the woman behind the monitor, 'I was actually looking for A. Patel and Associates and came here by mistake. A. Patel and Associates have an office here, right?'

Nikhil spoke with obvious impatience, 'Who at A. Patel and Associates were you going to meet?'

Sneha was a good chess player with a bad poker face. 'I'm here to make a presentation to the managing director. A… Adarsh Patel.' She waved the folder in her hands in front of her. 'I'm trying to get their business.'

Nikhil was not impressed. 'Mrs Ali!'

The woman swivelled the monitor to her. 'Yes sir.'

'Please have Sneha take a seat in my office. I'm on my way. I'll be there in a few minutes.'

Sneha leaned forward, speaking urgently to Mrs Ali, 'Please tell him I have to be somewhere else.' Sneha heard an impatient cluck from the monitor.

'Seriously. I should be on my way.' Sneha pointed at the door.

'Mrs Ali, call Hiren,' Nikhil emphasized on the name, 'the MD of A. Patel and Associates and tell him Sneha is going to be delayed.' Nikhil did not get the satisfaction of seeing the expression on the bad poker player's face.

'Sure!' Mrs Ali put a headpiece in her ear.

Sneha hastily put her hands out, surrendering. 'Fine. I'll wait. I'll send Mr Hiten Patel an email from my phone right now.' She held up her BlackBerry and gave Mrs Ali her most winsome smile. Mrs Ali rotated the monitor back to Sneha.

Feigning coolness that belied the anxiety eating at her insides, Sneha met Nikhil's rapier-like gaze. 'Hiren and not Hiten,' Nikhil said. He saw Sneha inadvertently sink her teeth into her lower lip, a mindlessly endearing gesture that revealed her nervousness even though she bravely glared back at him. 'I'll see you in a bit.' Nikhil purposely made his words and tone rather imperious and chilly. She would see no softness in him.

'Fine!' Sneha voiced, her face composed except for the thin line of sweat above her upper lip and a rather red chewed-out lower lip. Nikhil's eyes slipped to her mouth, again. Biting off a cuss word that was directed more at his treacherous mind than the bothersome busybody in his office, he cut the connection and the screen went blank.

Haramchor! No, haramkhor magnified! Sneha fumed. It wasn't her fault that the first name of A. Patel and Associate's MD was Hiren and not something with an A.

Mrs Ali got to her feet. 'This way Ms?'

'Gupta. Sneha Gupta.'

Mrs Ali and Sneha walked into the foyer. The security guards were back at their post outside the elevator. She caught one or two smirks as she passed them. Sneha ignored them for she had a bigger problem coming her way in a few minutes.

Sneha and Mrs Ali stopped at the last door that stood apart from the others for it was the only one monogrammed with two small gold leaves entwined at the stems.

Opening the door, Mrs Ali ushered her in. 'Mr Chandel's office. Please have a seat. Can I get you something? Cappuccino or tea?'

Sneha was tempted by the cappuccino but she declined. Mrs Ali left her alone in the large room that housed sleek, contemporary furniture. The walls all around were lit up with lights lined discreetly at the bottom of the walls. A sleek rectangular glass table sat in the middle of the room and a wire mesh black chair sat empty behind it. On the upper half of the wall behind the table was some kind of a mural painted in muted colours with an uneven surface. On the lower half of it was a quiet waterfall making soft lapping noises as the water flowed. The floor under Sneha's feet was dark and echoed her footsteps more than she would have liked to hear. Nikhil's office was overwhelmingly modern and stark. *Just like him!* Sneha fumed.

Apart from the dominant desk and chair she was staring at, there was another seating arrangement in the room. Just to the side of where Sneha stood lay two, rather large, black leather chairs, a black leather sofa and an oddly-shaped glass table that had a silver coloured stump for its base. Sneha gingerly put her stuff on the table and sank into one of the black leather chairs.

A soft humming sound distracted Sneha from her scattered thoughts. It came from the desk. Curiously, she walked over to the other side of the glass table. The 27-inch Apple flat screen lay blank except for the minuscule blinking green light at the bottom right corner. A tempted Sneha chewed her bottom lip and smoothed some imaginary creases in her clothes. Her right hand shot out for a mouse. Except there was nothing on the table. Her hands searched the glass surface for a keyboard, or something to bring the monitor to life. It was then that she noticed the faint pale blue light on the surface next to her, a shining faint imprint of a hand. Tentatively looking up to make sure she was still alone in the room, Sneha placed her hand on the imprint.

'Whoa!' The screen sprung to life. Her luck had just changed. Nikhil's dayplanner was open on the screen. Using the imprint, which was a mouse of sorts, Sneha quickly turned the pages. 'Jackpot!' she exclaimed, her face lit up as she caught the entry for the day after. Sneha scanned a few more dates and then quickly shut the planner.

She moved back to the leather chair, her mood much more buoyant than what it was minutes ago. Sneha did not have to wait for long. Soon, Nikhil walked in, his steps sure and glance seething as he sank into the chair behind his desk. With trepidation that Sneha would not show, she watched the animal-like grace of his taut muscular body further enhanced by his smooth grey and black pin-striped trousers and a white shirt that sat well on his broad shoulders. His hair looked tousled as if had run his fingers through it multiple times. Sneha felt some satisfaction hoping she was the reason for those running fingers. Nikhil glared at her before she could hide her smug smile.

'You wanted my attention? You have it. Why are you here? Don't give me the A. Patel nonsense,' Nikhil snapped. He did not raise his voice but every word he spoke sounded threatening.

Sneha hid her irritation but not all of it, 'Well, hello to you too.' Her words earned her the narrowing of those glimmering green eyes. Unfazed, she continued, 'Like I mentioned earlier, I am here by mistake. A. Patel and—'

'Show me the presentation,' Nikhil cut Sneha off mid-sentence.

'Excuse me? What presentation?' Sneha asked just as she realized what Nikhil was alluding to. Before Nikhil could say more, she waved her hands dismissively. 'Oh, that presentation. The one for A. Patel and Shah Associates?' Nikhil nodded, his eyes glinting. 'Sorry can't do. It's confidential.'

'What can your advertising company do for a tax accountant?' Nikhil fired next.

'Ughh, well you know—'

'What is the name of your contact there? The MD is no Hiren Patel. The company is run by Anand Patel. A. Patel and Associates,' Nikhil's informed her caustically.

'I knew it,' Sneha reflexively snapped her fingers. 'The name had to begin with an A.' Sneha's self-righteous smile was brief and died a slow, torturous death under his scrutiny.

'I'll repeat my question. Why are you here? Bear in mind I have only so much patience.' Sneha's face stayed defiant but Nikhil saw the slight flush on her cheeks and how her pink lips parted to take a quick gulp of air. She was nervous. *Good!* he thought. *She should be!*

'What will you do if I don't?' Sneha spoke quietly and braced herself as though she was anticipating him to lunge across the room at her.

Lunging might be a tad too much, but Nikhil definitely wanted to give Sneha a thorough shake till all her hare-brained schemes fell out of her head. Silently counting till ten, Nikhil ran a hand through his thick dark hair. A few of those dark locks fell on his forehead.

Sneha dragged her eyes away from his face. A cold man with colder manners, she dubbed him. Even still water held more ripples in comparison to Nikhil's impassive face. 'I want to meet Gayatri,' Sneha finally came clean.

Not saying a word, Nikhil leaned back in his chair and watched Sneha with hooded eyes revealing nothing of his thoughts. Sneha stared at him uncertainly; she was the first to look away.

'Are you a friend of Gayatri's?' Nikhil asked, emphasizing his words.

A rude snort from Sneha answered that question better than words.

'Thought so. Are you married to Aditya?'

'C'mon! Really?' Sneha slung her bag on her shoulder. Talking to him was futile. She had to get out of the room. Nikhil's presence was stifling and overwhelming, especially when he stared at her with those hooded lids. That look was once again giving her flutters in her belly.

'Then whatever happens between Gayatri and anyone else is not your business,' Nikhil retorted just as Mrs Ali brought in a tray with two cups filled with steaming liquid. The coffee teased Sneha's nostrils.

'You can take one cup away. Sneha was just leaving,' Nikhil ordered the older woman, his smile as usual starting and ending at his lips.

Even Mrs Ali seemed a little taken back at her boss's manners. Nikhil noticed the hurt on Sneha's face. He refused to feel sorry for her, yet he continued to stare at Sneha, wanting to see all the emotions that chased across her face and eyes. Mrs Ali made a quick exit with the extra cup. Sneha waited just long enough for the secretary to exit the room.

'Your reasons for protecting Gayatri and my reasons for protecting Nandini are the same,' Sneha said, getting to her feet.

'I truly doubt that but do enlighten me.' Nikhil tore off the edge of a packet of sweetener as he poured it into his cup. He wondered if he should after all, offer her a cup of coffee. It was the civil thing to do and he was a civil, rational man. Except he had a feeling that after his earlier rudeness, the hot coffee might just end up being thrown in his face.

Oblivious to Nikhil's thoughts, Sneha reasoned, 'Nandini is my best friend just like Gayatri—'

'Gayatri is family,' Nikhil cut her off 'Anything else?' Even as his hand lifted the tiny spoon to stir his coffee, his unblinking eyes did not leave Sneha's face for a second.

Sneha valiantly fought the urge to upturn the hot coffee on his head. So maybe Nikhil was a closet psychic. Giving him a last, quelling look with her nose in the air, Sneha turned and wordlessly walked out. She wanted to stomp on the wooden floor and leave marks on it.

Sneha was oblivious to the elderly bespectacled man, who after a few floors entered the elevator she was going down in.

'Rotten behaviour and buffoons with weapons! You just watch Chandel, you just watch. Ha!' She threatened no one in particular as the elevator continued its descent.

The bespectacled man standing next to her gave her a wary look.

'What?' Sneha countered belligerently.

'Nothing!' Mr Anand Patel of A. Patel and Associates meekly countered, moving a little away from her.

A few minutes after Sneha left, Nikhil buzzed Mrs Ali on the intercom.

'I need the CCTV footage of the time she was alone in my office,' Nikhil asked off-handedly, reading his emails.

'Yes sir.' As an afterthought she added, 'She seems harmless.'

Nikhil was quiet for a moment in which he was sure Mrs Ali was squirming. 'The footage.' He hung up.

Mrs Ali hurried to the security room. Her boss was a man of very few words who tolerated even fewer mistakes. The turnover ratio of their company was high, not because of the employees but the employer.

In less than ten minutes, she knocked on Nikhil's door.

'Come in.'

Mrs Ali opened the door. 'The CCTV footage.' She carried a thin opaque CD case in her hand. Nikhil nodded. She placed the CD on his desk.

'Thank you.' Nikhil gave her his usual smile, the one that was forbidden to touch eyes.

'Thank you.' Mrs Ali left his room.

Nikhil inserted the CD and watched the video. At the point when Sneha shouted, 'Jackpot!', he frowned. Nikhil re-opened his planner which he knew he left open on his computer by habit and went back and forth over the appointments of the next few days.

'Hell, no!' Frustrated, Nikhil rubbed his temples. He knew what had Sneha so excited. Sneha Gupta—the woman he did not want to meet again as her antics and actions, and not to forget her blouses, caused a cannonball-sized chink in his armour—he knew, would be soon paying him a visit.

7

You knew I was coming!

The next day Sneha was lost in what she held most precious—Advey, work and of course, phone calls exchanged between Nandini and her. The day after was another story. As she got ready for work, Sneha pulled out a sleek black and white dress suit from her wardrobe. She knew she had a fight on her hands and she wanted to look her best. The more confident she felt, the stronger her arguments would be. Sneha laughed at her own reflection in the mirror; strong was all she knew.

Sneha reached office early and took no lunch break. She had deadlines to meet that translated into a recurring paycheck. However, close to 3.00 p.m. Sneha logged out of her machine and slyly gathered her things off the table. It was time for a far-ass drive to meet equally asinine people. And then Sneha remembered how Nikhil had stared at her with hooded lids; she hated the telltale warmth that crept up her nape.

An hour and a half later, Sneha slowed down in front of 525 Hunter's Lane, Powai, nearly on the outskirts of the outskirts. Switching off the AC, Sneha stepped out of her car. She walked up to the large iron gate that must have been at least 12 feet in height. Loud, whining mechanical sounds filled the air and Sneha could smell more than usual dust here. *What is this place?* she wondered as she rapped on the door. As no one answered, Sneha was forced to press hard on the car's horn. Immediately, the gates opened and a guard with a burgeoning potbelly and khaki uniform complete with a beret stepped out.

'Yes madam?'

'Gayatri Dutta?' Sneha spoke haughtily, sliding her sunglasses to rest on the top of her head.

The guard's expression appeared puzzled.

Sneha made an impatient sound. 'Nikhil! Nikhil Chandel?' she fired next.

The guard bobbed his head. 'Yes, yes. Wait please. Your good name?'

Sneha decided to do something mischievous and said with a straight face, 'Me. Gayatri Dutta. I just told you.' Taking her eyes off his confused expression, Sneha glanced at her watch, 'I don't want to keep Mr Chandel waiting.'

'Yes madam.' The guard opened the gates. *He might not know Gayatri but he definitely knew the ice prick.* Sneha smiled at her bawdy wit.

Sneha drove in. She recognized the two security guards loitering inside. She had encountered them at Nikhil's offce. Sneha parked at the only free spot near a big, black German car with a white and blue circular logo.

In the rearview mirror, Sneha saw Nikhil's security guards approach her car. They were still at some distance. She pushed her door open and promptly banged against the German car next to her. 'Flock!' Sneha hastily trotted down to the adjoining white warehouse-like structure. She went past the glass doors and stopped dumbstruck. The loud sounds were deafening now. Sneha had found its source. 'Go-karting? What the…?'

The reception comprised and a gleaming dark L-shaped wooden desk with an open register and a computer standing empty and forlorn. Across from her, Sneha saw four panels of thick glass doors. They led to an open courtyard cordoned off by a fence of rusting iron bars. Beyond it were several track lanes that had rubber tyres stacked on either side. Sneha pushed open the glass doors and the first thing to hit her was copious amounts of dust. It stung her eyes and nostrils. Choking and hacking, Sneha stepped back inside. As she stood wondering what to do next, several karts rushing at tremendous speed passed the tracks in front of her. All the occupants were dressed in flame-retarded clothes and helmets emblazoned with large red and white numbers. Sneha counted four karts.

A man wearing dusty overalls, the lower part of his face covered with a white cloth mask, pulled the door open from the other side and joined her. 'Madam, this place is only for members. Who are you here to meet?' He asked, lowering the mask from his face.

'Nikhil Chandel!' Sneha replied peering at the shiny name tag pinned to his chest. Sher Singh. Such names just plant themselves in your memory whether you like it or not.

'This place is only for members, madam,' Sher Singh repeated emphatically. His thick and bushy moustache seemed to go on forever. *The things people do to add character to their personality,* Sneha thought. The deafening whirring sounds came to an abrupt halt. Sher Singh turned around, 'Wait here. Please wait here.' He jogged back through the door to the tracks.

Soon the thick glass doors opened, letting in a slow stream of four men of various shapes and ages. Sneha met their curious passing stares with a curious one of her own.

Nikhil was the last to come out. In his snug, flat-fronted, dark navy blue trousers that showed off an athletic lower body and a pale blue silk shirt, he looked quite dapper. *Pity one can't say the same for his disposition,* Sneha scorned. It seemed like Nikhil had not seen her for he was busy wiping his face with a wet tissue. Clearing her throat, Sneha stepped up to him. 'Hi!' she called out tentatively.

Nikhil gave her a brief glance. Chucking the used tissue into a bin near the door, he simply said to her. 'GD at 4.45 p.m., means Go-Karting Date at 4.45 p.m., not Gayatri Dutta.' Stumped, Sneha watched him saunter out of the reception. Sneha felt like breaking something. His explanation sounded expected and rehearsed. *Flock! He knew I was coming.* Sneha hurried after Nikhil, anger churning inside her.

As Sneha went down the few stairs, she found Nikhil chatting to a portly man of around fifty and another one close to Nikhil's age. Sneha came to an abrupt halt near them. Her anger turned to confusion. She hated making a scene in general, especially publicly. Sneha was forced to wait, unsure of how to approach Nikhil. The older man glanced at her.

'Nikhil, you should not keep pretty girls waiting,' he winked at Sneha. Genuinely puzzled Sneha looked behind her. Who was the oldie referring to? She had seen no other woman here. When Sneha turned around to face them, she caught Nikhil watching her with his familiar hooded eyes. Sneha's face tinged warm even as she cast at Nikhil a look so foul that she could nearly smell its pungent odour.

'I can wait!' Sneha said, her voice tight.

'What did you do to deserve that look? Good luck, bud!' The younger man slapped an easy hand on Nikhil's shoulder and moved to an expensive car, low and bright red. Nikhil moved back to stand near Sneha, giving room to the reversing cars.

As the cars headed for the gates, Nikhil wore his dark aviator shades and began to head for the black German car.

'I will find a way to meet her,' Sneha called out just as one of his security guards opened the driver's side door for him.

Nikhil just stopped short of getting in his car. His shoulders moved briefly and then he turned around and steadfastly walked back to where Sneha stood, watching him, her eyes narrowed.

Nikhil slowly took his shades off, 'Stop following me and trespassing. Next time I'll call the cops.' His tone was even and the only sign of barely controlled irritation was in his flashing green eyes.

The more nervous Sneha became, the bolder she acted. Some may term it a death wish. 'You don't scare me. In fact, you are an insufferable lout of the first order and I care two hoots for your high-handed—'

'Sher Singh!' Nikhil's sudden shout startled Sneha who visibly jerked. Immediate footsteps behind them announced Sher Singh's presence. 'Call the police and tell them we have a trespasser. I'll sign the complaint,' Nikhil's tight jaw proclaimed his seriousness.

'Are you mad?' Sneha was taken aback. Her hazel eyes were incredulous as her shoulders rolled back. Nikhil knew, without glancing down, that her blouse must have tightened across her chest. Giving a silent inward groan and with Herculean effort, Nikhil kept his eyes on Sneha's fuming face even as his own lost some of its ire. Sneha was still busy telling him off. Maybe he could steal a downward glance, Nikhil speculated. On second thoughts, forgets the idea; he would not put physical assault past this spitfire. 'You know if I didn't have a reason to go home, I would play this whole thing out. Your wife was right in dumping you and I thank God that Kim di never fell for you. You are despicable,' Sneha walked past him, mad enough to explode.

The part about his ex-wife caused Nikhil to see red and lose whatever little patience he had with Sneha. As she huffed past him, Nikhil's hand shot out and grabbed her forearm in a vice-like grip. He pulled her back and with a startled cry, Sneha fell against him. Her chin bumped into Nikhil's chest as she attempted to regain her balance. Nikhil did not lift a finger to help her. His grip bit into her soft skin.

'You little—!' Nikhil bit off the angry word as his green eyes blazed in his face, his eyebrows bunched above them. Nikhil's grip brought Sneha much closer than he had anticipated. Even through his anger, he felt the softness of her body against him, smelt the sweet hint of vanilla and some flower in her perfume and could not ignore the various shades of brown, golden and hazel mingling in her startled eyes. Disgusted at his unexpected reaction to this sudden closeness Nikhil flung her hand away. 'Get out!' he said quietly.

Sneha immediately tottered away from him. Her breath was uneven and colour rose high on her face. Unconsciously, she rubbed her chafing skin. Nikhil felt a twinge of guilt for unknowingly hurting her. He did not enjoy this one bit and a part of him wanted to apologize. However, he knew that if he wanted to see the last of Sneha, he would have to break a few rules of his usual cordiality. How could any woman affect him so? And just because Sneha did she would have to go, Nikhil decided.

'Tutta!' Uttering that word loudly and to his face and enjoying the confusion she saw there, Sneha turned around and marched up to her car. Nikhil's security guard awkwardly jumped out of her way as she bore down on him. Sneha yanked open her car door and with immense satisfaction, heard it connect loudly with the adjoining dark car. The guard made a choking sound. From her peripheral vision, she saw Nikhil remain where he was.

'Sir, do I call the police?' Sher Singh asked uncertainly, holding out his phone to Nikhil. Nikhil's answer was lost as Sneha sat in her car and shut the door. She reversed fast and headed for the gates. She did not glance even once in the rearview mirror. This chapter was over in her life, even though the marks would remain on her skin for a few more days.

8

What is your game here?

For the next couple of days, aspirin became Sneha's new best friend. Headaches are common symptoms of shouldering emotional burdens. Sneha wanted to confide in Nandini. However, she did not want Sethani worried unnecessarily. She never wanted to be the messenger who'd need to fear a bullet. Sneha rubbed her right throbbing temple.

On Friday evening, just as Sneha reached home, her phone buzzed. 'Hi kulta,' she smiled, stepping into the elevator.

'Hi! Are you free for dinner tomorrow night?' Nandini asked. Sneha heard the excitement in Sethani's voice.

'Okay now who's my blind date?' Sneha asked, immediately wary.

'No babes. It is someone we all know. Will you come?'

Sneha leaned against the wall. She let the others behind her get in the elevator and carry on without her.

'Fine, I'll come. Hey listen, I have to talk to you about something important,' Sneha said quietly.

'Sure,' Nandini answered nonchalantly. 'Listen, wear that beige dress we bought at the mall, okay?'

'Excuse me—' Sneha realized she was talking to a dial tone. Nandini had hung up. 'I'm so not wearing any beige dress. Jeans and a top it is,' she proclaimed as she pressed the elevator button for going up.

Next day, close to 7.30 in the evening, after Alma and Advey stepped out, Sneha locked her apartment door. Advey tugged at Sneha's dress.

'No, Baba, no. Mama dress go bad.' Amla tried to pull his hands away.

'It's okay, it's just a dress.' Sneha grabbed Advey's hand and led him into the elevator. She ignored the faint hand imprints her son had left on the hemline of the beige dress with a scooped neckline, sheer short sleeves and a light smattering of golden dust all over.

In less than forty minutes, Sneha and her brood were standing outside Nandini and Aditya's opulent digs. Sneha held up Advey's hand so he could ring the doorbell.

Instantly, Aditya thrust his body out, grabbed a startled Advey and shut the door right back. Advey's surprised gurgle turned into chuckles. Sneha grinned on hearing the sounds from the other side. Aditya and Sneha repeated the move for Advey's squealing pleasure. Sneha heard Amla murmur 'good man'. She heartily agreed. Nandini had struck gold in her choice of a husband.

Soon Sneha stepped in and Amla followed. Looking at her, Aditya gave a low whistle, 'Stunning, Sneha. If only if I wasn't married!'

Sneha gave a mock grimace, 'I know, and that too to my best friend. Shucks!'

'Who is not stopping either of you,' Nandini joined them. Today her dress was a simple sheath of olive green. Big diamond hoops swung merrily in her ears.

Aditya planted a lingering kiss on her cheek, 'Hey you! Where were you today?'

Embarrassed, Nandini put some distance between her and her husband. 'Adi! I had gone for a meeting.' At Aditya's insistence, post-marriage, Nandini had joined his vast business. Currently, she was moonlighting with various departments to figure out which one she wanted to permanently take over. 'I left a message with your secretary.'

'Why didn't you just call me? I tried your cell quite a few times.'

Nandini gave an exasperated shake of her dark hair. 'Oho! It was like only three hours.'

As Aditya opened his mouth to protest, Sneha interrupted, 'Children. The bedroom is also for other things besides making babies.'

Aditya lost his indignant look 'Millennium Behenji doesn't think so.' His look was sly. He had just used a nickname for Nandini, a nickname from the past, from his first meeting with her. The one he knew Nandini thoroughly hated. 'I am so sleep-deprived thanks to your best friend.'

Nandini gave him an irritated look. 'Yeah, right.'

'Put a small mandir in your bedroom?' Sneha said to Aditya.

'Huh!' Aditya asked. Both his and Nandini's expressions were puzzled.

'Arrey mandir hoga then you can say, chod do, mujhe bhagwan ke liye chod do,' Sneha grinned.

'That was such a bad one.' Aditya shook his head.

'Our gardener's name is Bhagwan,' Nandini added. She and Sneha exchanged a look and burst out laughing.

'Horrible women.' Aditya left the still-laughing women and walked over to the wet bar. Nandini bent down and gathered Advey, who stood fascinated by the fish in the aquarium. Soon the two friends began making Advey pose all over the room. Sneha was more than glad to take pictures. As she was taking a picture of Advey held jointly by Aditya and Nandini, she felt a lump in her throat. Nandini and Aditya had welcomed her and Advey warmly into their life. New beginnings, especially for a single mom in a strange city of this size could be frightening but not when you had such good friends. Sneha's resolution to watch Nandini and Aditya's back grew stronger.

'Choo, choo!' Advey cried out. Amla who was hovering nearby came to his immediate assistance.

'Baba hurried,' she announced loftily.

'Whatever that means,' Sneha muttered under her breath, capping the camera. Amla gave her the stink eye.

'Yes, of course. He wants to go to the room and see the train set,' Sneha was quick to agree. Working women can take on the mafia but never their maids.

'Let me get something to munch on,' Nandini said.

'Please, I'm starving.' Sneha stuffed her camera in her bag. She turned to Aditya and asked, 'So who's the bakra tonight?'

Aditya smirked. 'Isn't that you every Friday or Saturday night?'

'Ha! Ha!' Sneha gave him a mock glare. 'No, but seriously, who's coming?'

Aditya shrugged his shoulders. 'I'm just here to make the drinks.'

'Then please just keep them coming. The stronger the better.'

'Says the one-drink-wonder,' Aditya teased. 'Anyhow I have a video con in an hour. So I have an early pass.'

'Lucky you! Do you need somebody to hold the laptop?' Sneha griped.

Just then, the doorbell rang. A uniformed household staff member opened the door. Nandini trotted behind her. 'Got it.' Smiling hastily, she sent the maid away. 'Helloo…oh!' Nandini's greeting ended with a strangled sound.

Sneha moved to the side for Nandini obstructed her view of the door and she saw the guests. Sneha experienced sudden sharp anger coursing through her veins. 'I will kill him,' she murmured. Forcing herself to move quickly, Sneha joined Nandini, her smile grim.

Sneha turned to Nandini, keeping the surprise obvious in her voice. 'You invited them?' Sneha purposely made her words sound like an insult. She gave Nandini a quick wink, forcing her dazed friend to come out of her stupor.

'Well actually, Nandini invited me and I saw no reason not to bring Gayatri along. For she is more familiar with you all than I am,' Nikhil drawled. His stance was casual but the look on his face and glittering green eyes was smug. And all of it was directed at Sneha.

Bring it on, jerk! Sneha thumbed her chin at Nikhil, her hazel eyes kindling with contempt.

'We should go back,' Gayatri murmured quietly from the side. She appeared nervous. From behind her, Sneha heard Aditya's soft intake of breath.

Nandini smile was shaky. 'No, please. Forgive my manners. Do come in,' she moved to the side, giving room to her guests to enter.

Sneha glared at Nikhil and Gayatri as they went past her. Her eyes became hard as she saw Nikhil clasp Gayatri's elbow and shepherd her in.

Sneha gestured at Aditya with her eyes. He instantly loped over to them. Putting an arm around Nandini's waist, he drew her close. Sneha saw Gayatri observe the gesture and the other girl's lips tightened. Sneha slow smile at Nikhil was taunting.

Nikhil looked away. 'You have a beautiful house,' he said, extending a gift bag towards Nandini.

'Thank you. You didn't have to,' Nandini replied with a strained smile. She took the bag.

'Let me!' Sneha took the bag. 'Why don't you seat your guests?' Sneha said to Nandini and Aditya, laying emphasis on the word 'guests'.

'This way,' Aditya led Gayatri and Nikhil to the steps that opened to the seating area. Sneha noticed the slight quiver in Nandini's hands.

Sitting down, Gayatri tucked her red off-shoulder dress under her knees. She glanced at the interior of the room. 'Lucky you. This is beautiful,' she chirped to Nandini. Sneha heard the edge behind the innocent words. She hastily came down the steps and took a seat at some distance from Nandini and Aditya.

'Thank you,' Nandini replied.

'I love doing up the interiors too,' Gayatri added with a smile.

'She's quite good at it,' Nikhil remarked conversationally.

'I'm not. We hired an interior decorator,' Nandini answered honestly, her expression sheepish.

'You'd be good if you wanted to. However, you have a real job,' Sneha added hastily from the side. That remark earned her another one of those veiled glances from Nikhil. Abruptly, he leaned forward and then pulled out the rug from under Sneha's feet.

'Well Sneha, you should be happy to finally meet Gayatri. Considering the times you've come to me wanting to meet her.'

Sneha became the cynosure of everyone's eyes. Nandini's face was incredulous and Aditya's mildly displeased.

'Really! How sweet, Sneha,' Gayatri crooned, giving her a surprised smile.

Sneha gave Nandini and Aditya, especially Nandini, a helpless look, 'I can explain—'

'Sneha came up to my office earlier this week. Even when I was go-karting with some associates, Sneha showed up. She was so eager to meet Guy.' Nikhil sat back watching Sneha with a cruel smile.

'Oh, how nice of you,' Gayatri murmured.

Sneha went into damage control mode. 'No! Okay, hold on—'

'We did get to a bad start last time,' Gayatri threw another one of those innocent smiles at Nandini and Aditya. Of course, 'last time' as Gayatri had just called it was around two years ago when Aditya and Gayatri were engaged and Nandini was the other woman. 'Maybe this time we all can hang out some time. It should be fun,' Gayatri finished timidly, a perfect picture of grace and openness.

Sneha snorted, wanting to punch some cushions on seeing Gayatri's sickly smile and Nandini's attempts at avoiding her eyes.

'What will you drink?' Nandini politely asked Gayatri. 'Adi can make it for you.' Nandini got to her feet. Aditya also rose.

'Sex on the beach. Do you know how to make it?' Gayatri asked, keeping her eyes lowered.

'Sure. Let me call for some peach schnapps.' Adi pressed the intercom button on the wall that connected him to the kitchen. 'And for you?' He asked Nikhil.

'Single malt. On the rocks. Thanks.' Nikhil's smile as usual was brief. Not just brief, but freaking barbaric, decided Sneha, eyeing Nikhil with repugnance. Aditya walked away to the bar, Nandini headed to the kitchen and Gayatri waited for no less than five seconds to follow Aditya. Sneha felt torn. Who to go after? Nandini or Aditya? Sneha's troubled eyes clashed with the hooded lids of a still-seated Nikhil.

Let's deal with you first. Sneha walked over to Nikhil. Her body stiff, her hands feverishly smoothing the sides of her dress. 'You are a jerk of the first order!' she hissed down at him. For a few seconds, Nikhil stared at her, his eyes not reflecting any of his thoughts and then he languidly got to his feet. Sneha had not realized how close she was to him. He utterly towered above her. Keeping her stare still hostile, Sneha slid a step back—just a teeny tiny step to lessen the smell of his cologne permeating her nostrils or the silk of his pale green shirt from touching her upturned chin.

'Open season for trading insults? Sorry, I don't abuse women,' Nikhil's words were clipped. He saw anger darken her hazel eyes and add colour to Sneha's heart-shaped face.

'No, you just throw them under a bloody bus,' Sneha challenged haughtily. A nerve twitched on one side of Nikhil's tightly clamped cheek. Sneha was right, he had acted badly. However, Nikhil himself did not understand how this little spitfire with her wild accusations, challenging eyes, taunting smile and defiant chin could provoke him to such an extent. It had to be that short dress the colour of skin that clung lovingly to all her curves and made Sneha appear breathtakingly dangerous—like a sultry siren who could control a man with a mere look. And since Nikhil liked being the one in control, his self-detestation tonight was even more intense. It had all begun with the first look at Sneha in that beige dress.

'You had no business bringing her here,' Sneha flung a scornful glance at Gayatri who still stood close to Aditya as he measured the ingredients for her drink, 'or showing up at Nandini's house.'

Nikhil's look was one of suffering. 'Let Nandini tell me that.'

'Look around. Is she here? She's probably in the kitchen cursing the moment she bumped into you at that pub.'

Glancing at his shoes as if he were weighing his words, Nikhil took his time in answering her, 'Nandini herself called me and invited me for dinner. She was quite insistent that I come.'

Sneha glared at him, 'Oh, don't flatter yourself, she called you here for me.' In her fury Sneha did not realize what she was revealing. 'You were my blind date.' She could have bitten her tongue off.

Nikhil's surprised look said it all but he was far from done. Sneha was shocked to see all his pearly teeth at the same time as his cheeks hitched a little higher and he laughed a genuine, soft chuckle that was loud enough for Aditya and Gayatri to glance in their direction.

Gayatri pivoted toward them and spoke amusedly, 'Well, that's a rare sound. That man rarely laughs.' Nikhil stiffened and sobered. Sneha continued to stare at him, still trying to absorb the shock of how good-looking and amicable he became when he laughed. 'You two must know each other quite well,' voiced Gayatri loudly with a beatific smile. Hastily, Nikhil moved away from Sneha and joined the others at the bar.

Sneha met Aditya's eyes. Why did she feel like a kid who had been caught eating her own snot? Just then Nandini joined them, and from her stiff expression Sneha sensed that she had overheard Gayatri's last words.

Nandini came and stood next to her. Her hushed words to Sneha confirmed it. 'Wish you had told me you were so tight with them.'

'I'm not, Nandini,' Sneha implored.

'Yet you went to Nikhil's office or whatever go-karting place. And you didn't even tell me?' Nandini kept her voice low. To the others, who could not hear them, they would appear to be having a casual conversation.

Sneha shook her head. 'I did but—'

'You wanted to meet Gayatri?' Nandini asked quietly.

'I did but not—'

Nandini pointedly turned her face away. Sneha stood stumped. How could Nandini doubt her? After that, Sneha's mood took a nosedive. She excused herself and went to the room where Advey was playing under Amla's watch.

Sneha gave them a limp smile as she settled on the floor next to her son, her legs folded under her.

'Madam, dress,' Amla pointed out, her voice loud.

'Screw the dress, Amla. Just screw it,' Sneha snapped.

'Screw! Screw!' Advey gave a wide smile as he waved a blue plastic toy engine in front of her face.

In spite of her low mood, Sneha could not help a wry smile, 'Out of the million words I must have said to you today, this is the only word you pick up from Mommy.' She gently pulled Advey's cheeks and tickled him under his fleshy chin. Advey gave a hoot of laughter and squirmed. Sneha bent over and held him awkwardly but tightly to her shoulders. Her eyes, full of love, fell on a pair of black leather shoes at the door. They trailed up as she straightened, still holding Advey. Her eyes still held some of the love she felt for her son as she met a certain pair of hooded eyes.

Nikhil hid his surprise well on seeing Sneha with a child. Her dark chestnut-coloured curls spilled over the dark curls of the child. Her slim hands held the boy with such tenderness and her eyes showed such absolute love that they found a soft spot in his hard demeanour. The vulnerable look in Sneha's eyes made Nikhil feel every inch of the ogre that he knew he was.

'Your son?' Nikhil asked, giving Sneha just enough time to recover her composure.

'Yes,' Sneha answered, her lips pursed.

'Advey. Baba three,' Amla added proudly, holding up three fingers of her right hand. Sneha glared at her.

Advey turned to look at the stranger at the door. 'Hello, man!' he gurgled; his chubby cheeks blew some air along with the word.

Nikhil smile was deep enough to reveal a dimple on his left cheek. 'Nikhil.' He waved his hand at Advey.

Sneha chewed her lower lip, unsure of how to proceed. 'Nik!' Advey very appropriately shortened his name to the syllables he remembered.

'Where's his father?' Nikhil asked Sneha with a directness not expected of him.

Sneha mulishly kept quiet and chose to distract Advey with his toys.

'Madam divorced,' Amla replied sighing.

'Amla!' Sneha rebuked sharply.

Amla gave her a mutinous look.

Sneha knew it was a wise time to change the topic. 'Why don't you go and get Advey's dinner?'

Amla got to her feet. As she walked past Nikhil, she again sighed loudly. Nikhil pressed his lips together and averted his eyes so Sneha would not see the flash of humour in them. Sneha wanted Amla to choke on that sigh.

'She seems to be quite a character,' Nikhil remarked, watching Advey chase the whistling engine on his chubby feet.

'One of many I know,' Sneha retorted, without taking her eyes off Advey. After a few seconds when she heard no reply, she sneaked a glance at the door. She and Advey were alone in the room. Nikhil had left as soundlessly as he had come.

Having fed Advey, Sneha had to force herself to go back to the living room. She immediately picked up on the tension in the room.

For the rest of the night, the conversation was forced. Gayatri talked endlessly about herself. Aditya had cancelled his video con and he sat next to Nandini, nodding his head at appropriate intervals and keeping everyone's glasses full to the brim, especially his. And Nikhil, the blasted man would not take his cold clinical gaze off her. Sneha felt as though she was sitting in a petri-dish rather than a sofa worth $10,000.

At dinner, Nandini ate enough for all five and Sneha used her food as an excuse to keep her eyes lowered. Even though Sneha and Nandini were seated alongside one another, they did not exchange a single word and it was not because of a lack of trying on Sneha's part.

'So how's married life?' Gayatri chirped as the uniformed staff placed the food on their plates.

The flash of guilt on Nandini's face made Sneha see red. She put her fork down with a thump.

'By the looks of it, I would say it's going great,' Nikhil remarked serenely. Sneha swallowed her caustic words as she saw Nandini give Nikhil a small smile.

Aditya clasped Nandini's hand on the table gave it a gentle squeeze. Nandini and Aditya exchanged a look fraught with feelings. Sneha's smile was warm as she watched them. She swung her eyes to Gayatri whose mask briefly slipped and Sneha caught the flash of anger.

I was right, this hitch is up to no good, Sneha decided. Her eyes met Nikhil's who sat next to Gayatri. Still holding Sneha's frigid stare, Nikhil raised his glass, 'A toast to the happy couple!' Sneha gazed at him suspiciously as she took a sip from her glass. She kept her eyes on him. *What is your game here?* she wondered.

Not one you can guess! Nikhil thought, staring right back at Sneha over the rim of his glass. His eyes gleamed. Everyone on the table might be steeped in various shades of misery but Nikhil abruptly realized that after a long time he was actually enjoying his evening and only one person could take credit for that. The one who was moving her knife over her food as if it was his heart under the blade.

9

Couples only!

After dinner, Gayatri and Nikhil seemed ready to call it a night.

'It was great meeting you all,' Gayatri sent a sultry smile in Aditya's direction and took a step as if to embrace him. Nandini duly turned her face away. Sneha intervened.

'It was such a pleasure.' Sneha quickly stepped in between and hugged Gayatri.

Nikhil, standing behind Gayatri, gave Sneha a pointed look. *Grow up!*

You first! Sneha glared back at him. Sneha felt Gayatri go stiff and perversely, she tightened her embrace.

Gayatri extricated herself, murmuring self-consciously to Sneha, 'It was good seeing you too.' Aditya had moved closer to Nandini.

Gayatri simply addressed them together, 'Well then, goodnight. Thank you for having us.'

'Our pleasure,' Aditya responded amicably and his wife flashed a polite smile. Nikhil excused himself.

Just then, Nandini walked away from Aditya. Bending down, she picked up the gift bag that sat to the side of the sofa. Sneha refused to budge an inch away from Aditya and Gayatri. Nandini opened the bag and took out something. 'It's beautiful,' she murmured, her back to the others.

Sneha was curious to see what Nikhil had brought. Probably a jewel-crusted dagger with a poisoned tip.

'What is it?' Gayatri asked. Nandini, pirouetting, held out the gift so the others could see.

Sneha was partially right. It was definitely jewel-crusted but it was not a dagger, but a Ganpati with his right hand raised in blessing.

'Keep it on the table in the foyer,' Aditya said as he moved to marvel at the craftsmanship and the play of small, multicoloured jewels encrusted all over the idol.

'That's what I was thinking,' Nandini replied. Nikhil joined them.

'It's beautiful. Thank you.' Nandini unexpectedly gave Nikhil a quick hug. Nikhil appeared taken aback.

'Glad you like it. Shall we?' he addressed Gayatri.

Gayatri moved to his side. Sneha stayed where she was. Nandini and Aditya walked the guests to the door. As they stood at the door saying final goodbyes, Nikhil's eyes sought Sneha's. He raised his hand in a quick farewell. As everyone else had their backs to her, Sneha could show her true emotions. She twisted her lips to one side and made a face at him. Nikhil turned away before Sneha could catch his dry grin.

'Tutta!' Sneha griped, leaving the room. She found Amla putting Advey's toys in the diaper bag. A sleepy Advey sat snug on the bed, lightly holding a pop-up book.

'Nik said bye,' Amla mentioned.

'To?'

'Baba and I,' Amla said.

Sneha was surprised. 'He did?' She picked up Advey who trustingly placed his small face in the crook of her neck. Hugging Advey close, Sneha rubbed his back. 'And next time, Amla, please don't just give out personal stuff about me to anyone and everyone.' Ignoring Amla's baleful look—the maid had obviously issues with any kind of authority—Sneha, holding Advey, went back to the living room. She found Nandini gazing blankly at the dark wood piano in one corner of the room.

'Where's Adi?' Sneha asked.

'He's in the study. Following up on that video con he missed. Is he asleep?' Nandini pointed at Advey.

'Almost! You look tired,' Sneha said to her. 'Listen, about tonight...'

'I'm tired, Sneha. I'm going to bed. If you don't mind, can you show yourself out?' Nandini asked, walking past Sneha.

'Ya, sure. Goodnight.' Sneha mumbled to Nandini's back, trying not to feel hurt. Given her level of sensitivity for others, tonight's dinner must have been hell for Nandini. *Poor thing*.

'Night, night, Nik,' Advey murmured into Sneha's shoulder. Sneha's anger awakened as she walked out of the elevator.

The next week was a blur for Sneha. It was the deadline for her first new account for which she was solely in charge, the campaign for an upcoming children's TV channel she and her team had prepared. If they got the account it would easily earn them a few crores for a few years.

It was around 2.30 p.m. another Friday afternoon when Sneha grabbed her cell phone to call Nandini for the umpteenth time this week. All her conversations this week with Nandini had been either in monosyllables or in messages left on her voicemail. Sneha got more conversation out of her son who was still learning how to speak. Sethani had completely misunderstood the reason behind Sneha's shenanigans involving Nikhil and Gayatri. Sneha was hoping that in time, Nandini and she would just move on and laugh over this like so many other things. And until that happened, Sneha would just keep reaching out to her kulta.

'Finally! Hello kulta.'

The laughter on the other end wasn't her best friend. 'This ain't Nandini.'

'Uggh, okay!' Sneha was low on patience. 'Who's this?'

'It's me, Sneha,' the voice giggled.

'No. I'm Sneha,' Sneha murmured haltingly. Her brows met between her eyes.

'It's me, MONA!'

Sneha quietly banged her head on her desk a few times and then she said, 'Of course. Hi Mona. Is Nandini there?'

'She is but she is kind of busy,' Mona replied. Sneha could hear a smile in her voice.

'She's in the restroom?'

'No, she's trying on clothes.' Mona lowered her voice conspiringly, 'We are at a very exclusive designer's place. He doesn't allow phones in his changing room. Worries people might take pictures and copy his one-of-a-kind designs.'

'Okay. Can you have Nandini call me when she gets free?' Sneha requested.

'Sure! Aren't you going to ask me the designer's name?' Mona asked, surprised.

'I'm sure he's beyond my pay grade so why bother? Enjoy, ladies.' Sneha hung up. She glanced at the picture on her desk of Nandini holding Advey a few days after he was born. 'You have time to go shopping with that hitch to some snotty designer's store but no time to return my calls or messages. I was only trying to help, Sethani,' Sneha sadly confessed to the picture.

Sneha rubbed her nape. 'Maybe I shouldn't help. I'll back off kulta but just talk to your crazy friend.' She felt depressed. *I'm made of stronger stuff*, Sneha reminded herself. She pulled a folder out of the file cabinet next to her and using it as reference, she began phrasing bullet points on a PowerPoint slide for the client.

That evening around 8.30 p.m., the phone in the CEO's office rang. The CEO, Mr Baig, wasn't alone. He had Sneha and her immediate boss, Mrs Aiyyar, there for company. The conversation was short but Mr Baig's smile was wide. 'We got the account, Gupta. You beat the others. Well done.' His handshake was vigorous enough for Sneha feel it from her hand to her shoulder.

'Thank you. Congratulations to you too, sir. It was a team effort,' Sneha remarked, overwhelmed with the sense of achievement.

'We should celebrate! How about at the bar across the street?' The CEO gave Sneha another smile.

'Sorry, sir, some other time perhaps. Please!' Sneha turned

him down very courteously. The man signed her paycheck for goodness' sake.

'Oh, c'mon, one drink,' Mr Baig, a portly man of over forty with spiky salt and pepper hair, cajoled.

'Oh, she'll probably celebrate with her fiancé,' Mrs Aiyyar interjected.

'Bingo!' Sneha gave the two present in the room another one of her polite smiles that involved heavy-duty crinkling of her eyes and some stretching of the lips.

'You're engaged, Gupta?' Mr Baig asked, surprised.

'Yes, sir.' Sneha dutifully displayed the ring finger of her left hand. On that finger sat a small, sad-looking round solitaire set in yellow gold.

'When is the wedding? Your son must be excited,' Mr Baig said.

'Advey is! We haven't set a date yet though.' Sneha gave the reply she had been giving since the day she had announced her engagement—as in a month after she had started working here and that was now nearly a year ago.

'We have to meet your fiancé, Sneha. She has not introduced us to him yet,' Mrs Aiyyar complained.

'Sorry, he travels a lot.' Sneha dished the trite response.

Mrs Aiyyar snorted as Mr Baig said, 'Well then, ladies, goodnight and have a nice weekend. I know I will have a nice one.' A few more rounds of polite conversation and then Sneha and Mrs Aiyyar walked back to their cubicles.

'So how long have you known him?' The ever-inquisitive Mrs Aiyyar asked, her brows wrinkled with concentration.

'Since he became our CEO,' Sneha replied, puzzled.

'Not Mr Baig, your fiancé?' Aiyyar asked.

'A while.' Sneha wanted to end this conversation as soon as possible.

Mrs Aiyyar opened her mouth but Sneha interrupted. 'Got to use the ladies' room. I'll see you on Monday. Congratulations once again.' Sneha made a hurried exit.

In the restroom, Sneha made quick call to Amla. 'Amla. How's Advey?'

'Sleepy. Tina play Baba,' Amla replied in her usual drone-like voice.

What you just said sounded so wrong, Sneha thought. Tina was the four-year-old daughter of her neighbours who fawned over Advey as if he were a live doll.

'Okay fine. I have to go somewhere—'

'Eppo?' Amla switched to her native tongue, Tamil.

'Huh?'

'Now?'

'Yes, Amla now. Eppo!' Sneha replied. Sometimes Amla got confused about who she was watching over. 'You have your dinner and put Advey to bed. I might get late.'

'Okay!'

'Bye.' Sneha got into the elevator. On her way to her planned rendezvous, Sneha stopped at a corner store and picked up several flavours of ice cream cones. She entered a familiar apartment complex where the guards knew her.

Sneha was happy as she took the elevator to the penthouse floor. Nodding to the security guards flanking the door, Sneha couldn't help but grin as she pressed the door bell. Sethani had a weakness for hazelnut and chocolate ice cream, especially if it came in a cone.

She caught the guard on her right giving her office attire comprising grey-striped pants teamed with a black shirt with three-quarter sleeves and ruffled front a closer look. She could hear some muted sounds of conversations coming from inside. Sneha cocked her head to a side. The TV must be on.

Someone from the staff opened the door with a polite smile. Sneha instantly caught sight of a few heads in the living area and heard sounds of ongoing conversation. 'Is there a party in there?' Sneha asked the man holding the door for her.

'Yes madam.' He moved to the side, forcing her to step in.

As Sneha took a hesitant step inside, her cursory glance took in the elegant gowns and cocktail dresses in the living room. She did not see Aditya and Nandini but one face in the crowd startled her. Nikhil Chandel, looking sharp in a dark suit, an ebony silk shirt casually open at the neck, was staring right back at her. His hair was smoothed back over his face and the dark colour of his clothes made his green eyes sharper and his features appear even more sculpted. Nikhil acknowledged her with a slight nod of his head. Sneha shifted her face and awkwardly glanced away. She caught Gayatri, dressed in muted shades of lavender, standing next to him engaged in conversation with a few others.

'Sneha!' On hearing her name, Sneha turned to the side and spotted Mona coming towards her. Sneha groaned silently. Mona stopped right next to her, looking chic in a slinky, short dress in various shades of whatever. Sneha did not care much for Mona or her clothes. 'I didn't know you were invited.'

'I wasn't. I just happened to stop by,' Sneha replied quietly.

'Oh I'm sorry you had to find out this way.' Mona looked discomfited. 'Nandini had said it was a couples-only party so I guess she didn't...' Mona trailed off. She abruptly put a hand on her collarbone, 'I didn't mean how it sounded. I'm sorry...' She trailed off again. 'Let me get Nandini.' Mona pointed at the terrace garden to the left of the foyer.

Sneha was quick to stop her. 'Oh, please don't bother. I'll come back another day.'

'Are you sure?' Mona asked.

'Of course. After all this is a couples-only party, right? I'll stop by some other time.' Sneha's smile might have been contrived but the dull ache she felt in her heart was very real.

'Oh Sneha,' Mona grimaced. 'I'm not sure if Nandini told you that she and Aditya are spending next weekend at our farmhouse in Lonavala. Just a FYI,' Mona spoke haltingly, her smile apologetic.

'Thanks.' Turning around with enough force to cause a

minuscule tornado around her ankles, Sneha heaved the front door open and walked out.

Near the elevator, Sneha chucked the plastic bag with the ice creams in a trash bin. Sneha knew why the light on top of the elevator appeared blurred to her. She blinked a few times and took in a few deep breaths. 'You are made of stronger stuff. You are,' she chanted softly, tilting her head slightly to the back, refusing to let her tears trickle down.

Nikhil's eyes stayed fixed on the door Sneha had just shut behind her. He found the upside-down smile on Sneha's face as she had left and Mona's sunny-side-up smile at Sneha's departure interesting. *Interesting but not my business*, Nikhil decided. Though he wondered if he should go after Sneha, for he was really tempted to. He wanted to give Sneha one of his veiled looks that always brought heat to her face or purposely say something provoking just to see how the feisty spitfire tried to put him in his place. Nikhil realized thinking of Sneha had brought a rare smile to his face. Irritated with his wandering mind, Nikhil stayed where he was, forcing himself to listen to the conversation Gayatri was having with a Brazilian model who from time to time gave Nikhil a slow smile to let him know she might be interested in his… ahem…jewels.

By the time Sneha reached her apartment complex, she was able to walk, talk and appear normal. Advey was fast asleep on his side of bed, with several pillows propped up to prevent him from falling off. Refusing any dinner, Sneha changed her clothes and brushed her teeth as quietly as she could. Switching off the lights, she got into bed. She put her hand out to stroke Advey's forehead. A few shuffling sounds later, he shifted his small body next to hers so his head butted her shoulders. As Sneha soaked in her son's feel against her, she let the few tears pestering her lids roll out.

The next morning, refusing to remember or acknowledge last night, Sneha got out of bed and went on with her day as usual. She had not heard from Nandini.

Close to evening as Sneha, Amla and Advey were returning home after watching a children's animation movie, Sneha dialled a number on her cell phone. A child picked up on the other end. 'Hi Tina, this is Advey's mom. How are you?'

Sneha nodded, listening to Tina's response. 'Tina, can I speak to your mom?' A pause later, her mom came on. 'Hi, Maala! I'm good, thanks. Listen, if you guys are not doing anything, why don't you all come over. I'll order pizzas. Great! See you then.' Sneha snapped her phone shut. She glanced at Advey, 'Tina's coming.'

Advey's wide smile full of drool was answer enough.

'No Aditya and Nandini madam?' Amla asked.

'No.' Sneha's tone didn't invite any further conversation which was fine by Amla. Sneha was sure that she and her Amla got along beautifully because they both had a penchant for few words.

Next day, Sunday, had Sneha caught in hectic planning. She had decided to throw an impromptu get-together at her place. There was still no news of Nandini. Maybe it was time to make some new friends and be less clingy around older ones, Sneha decided. It was the right action for the wrong reasons! The guest list was made up of two couples with their kids and four singles. Close to eleven that night, as Sneha bid adieu to the last of her guests, she surveyed her living room. It was quite a sight, full of used glasses and plates with smelly, semi-dried leftovers.

Grimacing, Sneha picked up as many things as she could manage with her two hands and went to the kitchen. The sink was loaded with dirty dishes, pots and pans with remnants of food and grease. 'Ah, the joy of having a party,' she muttered, turning on the faucet to rinse the plates. Amla joined her.

'Advey's asleep?'

'Baba sleeping, very tired.'

'Nandini and Aditya?' Amla enquired.

'They're busy.' Sneha banged a spoon rather loudly. Next, she rinsed the dishes equally loudly. Amla took the not-so-subtle hint.

Amla and she worked silently until the kitchen had regained

some semblance of order. That night, even though Sneha managed to grab a few hours of sleep, she felt quite lethargic while getting ready for work the next day. As she stepped into her office, one of her team members quickly came up behind her.

'There's a business meeting for all account managers at 10.00 a.m. today.'

'Who called it?' Sneha asked grumpily.

'Mr Baig!' He left her alone to chew on the thought.

Sneha managed to get a few smaller issues off her to-do list and then headed for the conference room. She was running ten minutes late. On entering the room, she saw the rest of her colleagues already seated around the oval conference table. Sneha slid into a seat next to Mrs Aiyyar.

'What's the agenda?' she whispered to Mrs Aiyyar.

'New business. But you don't have to bother about this. Your hands are full with the new account,' her manager whispered back.

'True.' Sneha sat back. She let the others talk as her mind wandered. It chose to meander down a path paved with resentment and fresh hurt. Irked, Sneha forced herself to listen to the ongoing conversation.

She noticed the letters DC Inc. being thrown around quite a bit across the table. For some reason those letters seemed familiar. 'What's DC?' Sneha asked Mrs Aiyyar.

'An international jewellery firm that has just entered the Indian market.'

'Ughh!' Sneha felt her stomach heave. 'They can't be that big to justify our attention,' Sneha panicked, taking deep breaths while talking.

'Wrong, they are bigger,' Mrs Aiyyar was quick to refute.

'But like you said, I'm too busy for some new yuppie.' Sneha sat back once again. However, this time she heard the ongoing discussion until they went on to another name, another potential client.

Later that afternoon, Sneha had two visitors to her room: Mr Baig and the new client manager, Tanya, who had legs that went up to her face.

Sneha, who was busy crunching numbers on some deliverables of the campaign she was heading tried not to look disgruntled. She gave them a brief smile. 'What's up?'

The CEO and Tanya took the two chairs across from Sneha.

'After today's meeting, Tanya made a few calls to DC Inc. She spoke to the top guy's secretary,' Mr Baig looked at Tanya to continue.

'Mrs Ali,' Tanya quickly took over. 'I sent her a quick hello email with the company bio and then in a few minutes I received a one-liner email.' Tanya paused for effect.

'Go on!' Sneha felt some fresh heaving in her abdomen area.

'It just asked if Sneha Gupta was playing a lead role in the presentation. It came from Nikhil Chandel himself. You know him?' Tanya inquired.

10

Slice of life!

'Barely. Met him at an exhibition. I was there with a friend,' Sneha lied, trying hard to disentangle her professional life from her personal one. 'Why don't you forward the email to me? I'll follow up on it and then you can take over. Sounds good?' She included the CEO and Tanya in that question.

'Perfect!' Mr Baig got to his feet. 'Right?' he asked Tanya.

'Sure.' She, too, got to her feet, tugging her tight leather skirt down. Once they were gone, Sneha muttered churlishly, 'Who wears leather skirts to work?'

In minutes, Tanya forwarded her the email. Sneha opened and read it. It truly was a terse one-liner. 'Hmmphh, man of few words and fewer manners.' Sneha copied Nikhil's email address. She clicked 'compose a new email' from her private email account and executed a 'ctrl+v'. Sneha's email was equally short and terse. It read:

I have no wish to lead or be the back seat driver on this presentation. —Sneha

Satisfied with her response, she sent the email. Clicking 'enter', Sneha muttered, 'To sunhaar (goldsmith) with ewww from luhar (ironsmith).' The sunhaar chose not to reply.

After a long day at work, Sneha got into the car to head home. She joined the mêlée of traffic on the roads that nowadays appeared to be made of more potholes than tar.

Sneha questioned the strange melancholy that enveloped her. Taking deep breaths, she focused on driving. People with names that began with the letter 'N' were causing her much turmoil. In future, Sneha would shun any contact with Nikhil. And it appeared that Nandini had adopted a similar policy with her. Nothing good could come out of this situation, she was sure.

Next day, Sneha had to use some make-up to hide the residue of a sleepless night. On her way to work, Sneha called Nandini. She answered after two rings.

'Hi.'

'Are you okay?' Sneha asked, concerned.

'Of course. How was the weekend?'

'Good, and yours?'

'Nice, very nice,' Nandini was quick to reply.

For the first time, probably since their universe had collided with each other's in class 10, the two BFF's experienced an awkward silence.

'So what's happening?' Nandini chirped.

'Uhh you know, work and all,' Sneha replied.

'How's my doll?' Nandini asked sombrely.

'He was asking about you and Adi the other day.' Sneha expected Nandini to say something but all she got was silence.

'Listen, I have to hang up, I'm getting another call.'

'Ya, of course. Bye.'

Sneha hung up questioning her sixth sense that screamed that Nandini had wanted to say something more to her. Sneha pushed the thought away. 'You've become a clingy hitch,' she chided herself.

The whole of the following week for Sneha was a frenzy of activity at least at work. However, just like Sneha always made time for Advey, her mind always made time to think of Nandini and unexpectedly, even the loathsome sunhaar. 'Hammit!' With feeling, Sneha crumpled the paper she was doodling on. She had mindlessly drawn a caricature of Nandini; however, the eyes were all Nikhil.

Just then, Mrs Aiyyar popped her head in Sneha's cabin. 'Listen a few of us are going for drinks after work at Oasis, the new pub at Linking Road. Are you in or are you out?'

'I'm in,' Sneha replied. 'What time?'

'Close to six in the evening.'

'Cool. Let me know when you are ready to leave,' Sneha called out as Mrs Aiyyar disappeared.

Sneha rubbed her forehead. Growing a back-up circle of friends was proving quite tedious. Close to five-fifty, Sneha, Mrs Aiyyar and a few of their colleagues walked into the pub—it seemed to be in the middle of a power cut. The girl next to her reassuringly informed them that the darkness was just for effect and asked them to follow her.

'If we could see we would.' Mrs Aiyyar, grabbing Sneha's hand, took a few tentative steps. Even the servers who knew the run of this place ambled about slowly.

The group grabbed the first chairs they could find around two circular tables. Sneha chose to order a long island ice tea and chose wraps as an appetizer. Being a one-drink wonder, it was very important that she eat more and drink less.

Sneha listened to the conversation, contributed in parts and quickly realized that this was just a fishing expedition. Everyone wanted to know what the other was working on or trade some gossip. After a few sips of her drink, Sneha got to her feet. Her bladder demanded attention.

'I'll be right back.' Sneha made her way slowly to the bright red glowing sign proclaiming 'Restroom'. There was a queue outside it but Sneha couldn't wait that long. She saw a wide staircase that led upstairs to a lounge area. There was a sign to the right of the stairs that read, 'Members only'.

From where she stood, Sneha spotted a 'Restroom' sign up there. Sneha hurried up the stairs. She had barely climbed a few steps when a person accosted her.

'Ma'am, are you a member?' The man obviously worked here.

'No!' Sneha replied testily.

'This area is only for members. Sorry. You will have to go down.'

'I really have to use the restroom.' The man opened his mouth to protest but Sneha cut him off, 'Either you get me to the front of the line for the women's restroom downstairs or you let me go upstairs or,' Sneha took her time finishing the last sentence, 'I use the men's restroom. Your choice.'

The man did not waste time deciding. He stepped aside and let her carry on. 'Please be quick.' A few minutes later as Sneha exited the restroom, she caught a familiar silhouette sitting on a love seat near the bar.

'Adi?' As Sneha stepped forward to meet him, she paused when she saw who sat next to him. 'Gayatri. What the flock? Where's kulta?' Sneha whispered to herself, worried. She felt relieved when another woman joined the two.

'There she is.' As the woman turned, Sneha saw her profile. Dang! Mona darling was here, not Nandini. 'Okay, what the heck is going on?'

Resolutely, Sneha moved towards them. 'Hi Adi.' She was amused to see the look of relief that flashed on his face. Getting up, Adi hugged her.

'Thank you,' he whispered in her ear and then moved away. 'Good to see you, Sneha. How have you been?' Adi asked, his pitch normal.

'Good, ya!' Sneha answered even though she noticed Gayatri's annoyed expression. Aditya urged Sneha to take the spot he had just vacated. He grabbed the ottoman next to it. Sneha lowered herself next to Gayatri who pointedly moved away, pulling her white mini dress a little lower.

'So where have you been, Sneha?' Aditya asked. Before she could answer, he fired his next question. 'What are you going to have?'

'I have been very busy at work. And I'll have anything that is sweet and alcoholic,' Sneha smiled. Aditya was genuinely glad to see her and she to see him. Nowadays she could not imagine

Nandi without Adi. He was a great man, the kind *only* her kulta deserved.

'Adi, where's Nandi?' she asked him. Aditya quietly took a swig of his drink.

Mona answered. 'She's at a spa. She is getting ready for the weekend.'

'You've invited Sneha and Advey, right?' Aditya asked Mona. Mona seemed surprised by his question.

Sneha took pity on her. 'Nope, Adi, I can't make it. I have a few deadlines. I'll be working this weekend.'

'And how's the prince?' Aditya asked.

'He's good!'

Aditya ordered Sneha's drink. So far, Gayatri had not said a single word to her. Sneha felt obliged to lob a smile in her direction but she didn't get a response.

Sneha shrugged her shoulders indifferently. *Die hitch*. She addressed Aditya, 'Listen, I'm here with office colleagues. They are downstairs. I can't stay long.'

'C'mon, let's go and meet your office people.' Aditya made a move to get up.

Sneha put a hand on his knee, stopping him. 'No, they don't know I know you. Let's keep it like that.'

Aditya's smile was rakish, 'C'mon, I'll give you a bear hug in front of them.'

'Ha ha!' Sneha replied. She noticed that Aditya was hardly talking to the other two.

'Okay, fine. I'll stare everyone down. C'mon, let's go!' Aditya got to his feet, pulling Sneha up with him.

'Adi, please,' Sneha protested, half-heartedly letting him hustle her towards the stairs.

As they went down the stairs, Sneha had to ask, 'What are you doing with those two bimbettes?'

Aditya gave her a disgruntled look. 'I was ambushed! And it seems Nandini planned the whole thing. She wants me to spend some time with her new best friend.' Adi caught Sneha's expression. 'I didn't mean…' he trailed off.

'It's quite all right. I won't shatter, don't worry. Nandini is not to be blamed. She told me you had asked her to mingle a little more in your circle.'

'Sure I did. But not at the expense of you and her. I just wanted Nandini to get to know my friends too. That's all. And more importantly, Mona and her husband were never a part of my circle,' Aditya clarified as they went down.

'You too don't like them?'

'Can't stand them. Especially the opinionated snob of a husband who is forever asking for work rather than earning it.'

'Once this weekend is over, we'll go out or something. Just the four of us,' Sneha suggested.

'Five,' Aditya corrected. 'Who were you forgetting, Amla or Nandini?'

Sneha couldn't help laughing. 'Oh, you are bad.'

'Sneha you have to stay with me the whole time I'm here, please. I'm begging you!'

'Okay dude-in-distress, I'll hold your hand,' Sneha teased him.

'Very funny. My turn.' Aditya gave her a sly smile just as they reached the table where her colleagues were seated. Short of running across the room holding Sneha in his arms, Adi just did and behaved as he usually behaved with her—tight!

Sneha gritted her teeth as she saw Mrs Aiyyar's expression. She could literally see the wheels turning in her head.

As Sneha and Aditya walked back up the stairs, Sneha grumbled, 'You've got me into a load of crap now. The CEO is going badger me to get work from you.'

Aditya gave her a quizzical look. 'Any time! Nandini will give an arm and a limb to work with you.' He sounded glum.

Sneha did not beat around the bush. 'Are you and Nandi doing okay?'

Aditya gave her a crooked smile. 'The first few years are the hardest, right?'

Sneha stopped in mid-step and gave Aditya a closer look. She was at a loss for words.

Aditya gave her a familiar breathtaking smile, 'I'm kidding. Relax.'

'I nearly had a heart attack!' Sneha's smile was one of utter relief.

Mona and Gayatri stopped talking as they approached. Looking at Sneha, Mona patted the ottoman next to her. Ignoring her, Sneha purposely took the seat next to Gayatri.

'Oh, I wanted to ask you even the last time we met at Nandini and Aditya's place. What brings you back to India?' Sneha addressed Gayatri.

'Old habits. Also, Amsterdam, where my family has chosen to settle was beginning to bore me,' Gayatri replied, pushing her styled dark hair off her shoulders, revealing a well-rounded, toned shoulder and forearm.

Gosh, I really should exercise, thought Sneha. Everybody was sporting buffed bodies and the only thing Sneha had mastered was holding her breath while getting into her pants.

'Old habits?' Sneha quizzed.

Gayatri waved an airy hand, 'You know I love this country. The people.' If only Gayatri had not glanced at Aditya at that moment, Sneha might have bought it.

Sneha chose to take a few sips of her drink. The food she decided to miss, thanks to Gayatri's darn shoulders. Aditya gulped his drink. He got to his feet. 'I should be heading home.'

'One drink, Aditya, that's all. What's the rush? I don't see the ball and chain on your feet,' Gayatri drawled tauntingly.

Sneha itched to reply but she wanted to hear Adi's response. Any other man would have probably seen the comment as a window of opportunity to generally grumble about his marriage. However, Adi was no other man. 'If only my adorable wife would use the darn ball and chain that I bought her on me, I would be ecstatic.'

Ouch! Sneha's smile to Gayatri was smug. Adi bent down and gave Sneha a casual hug, 'We'll be seeing you and Advey soon. Right?'

'Right,' Sneha got up. 'I too should be going. Bye.' She included Gayatri and Mona in that farewell.

Just then, Aditya received a call on his phone. He moved away so he could hear better.

'Is gatecrashing your part-time job?' Mona asked, not bothering to hide her malice.

'Was this a couples' party too?' Sneha shot back. She walked away, satisfied that her barb had hit home. The weekend passed with Sneha warding off numerous questions from Advey regarding Nandini and Adi and a few were even about Nik. Monday came and found Sneha warding off questions from her CEO about the same group of people. Slice of life!

11

I miss Kanpur!

Around Wednesday, heavy rains besieged Mumbai. Sneha loved the rain from her balcony and hated it on the roads. The drive to her work, which usually took around twenty minutes, became a nightmarish trip of over an hour and half. 'C'mon, we deserve better,' Sneha muttered as she saw the news on the TV in the office cafeteria. A section of the road on her route home had collapsed. If she didn't have Advey to go home to, Sneha would have happily camped overnight in the office like some of her colleagues were doing.

Around 3.30 in the afternoon, just as the rain was hammering the windows of her tiny office, Sneha got an unexpected email.

```
From: n.chandel@dnc.com
To: snehag@flagshipad.com
Did you not go to Lonavala this past
weekend?
```

'Very polite,' Sneha muttered as she typed an equally terse reply.

```
From: snehag@flagshipad.com
To: n.chandel@dnc.com
??????
From: n.chandel@dnc.com
To: snehag@flagshipad.com
Mona's weekend party at her farmhouse?
From: snehag@flagshipad.com
To: n.chandel@dnc.com
```

```
    Nandini's  new  best  friend  had  not  invited
me.  Why?
```

After five minutes or so, she got the reply. Sneha hated to admit it but she had waited all that while for it.

```
From:  n.chandel@dnc.com
To:  snehag@flagshipad.com
Thanks.
```

'That's it?' she muttered reading his reply. 'Oooh, horrid man!' Sneha's inbox gave her an automatic option of saving the new email address in her contact. Sneha chose to cancel it in sheer vengeance. Minimizing that window, she went back to completing an expense report. Half an hour later, Sneha was still muttering the foulest of curses for a certain green-eyed businessman and when she realized her that her mind was still stuck on HIM, she immediately turned to chastise herself with the foulest of curses. *Hmmmphh blasted blackguard...* Sneha abruptly left her room to find an actual distraction.

Next day, close to four thirty in the evening just as Sneha was coiling her phone's charger to put it in her bag, she heard a tap on her door. She looked up to find the receptionist. 'Hi, Sandra.'

Sandra held an 8X10 brown envelope in her hands. The bottom corner was damp from the rain still coming down hard on the city. 'A courier just dropped this for you.'

'Thanks.' Sneha extended her hand and took her envelope. 'Who's it from?'

Sandra shrugged her shoulders. 'There's no return address. I asked the courier but he had no idea.'

Sneha studied the large bold scrawl in the front of the envelope but she did not recognize the handwriting. She slid a finger between the fold to tear it open.

'Maybe something from your fiancé,' Sandra suggested, an impish smile on her face.

'Sure!' Sneha said.

Sandra left just as Sneha opened the flap of the envelope. Peering inside, she saw a single sheaf of paper. She pulled it out. It was a print out of a photograph.

Curiously, Sneha put the envelope down and looked at the picture. From the familiar blue beading around it, she immediately recognized that it was copied from a popular social networking site. She looked closely at the photograph.

'Definitely a school picture,' Sneha murmured, gazing at the girls in the maroon and green uniforms, standing in a semi-circle, looking at the photographer. What was mystifying to Sneha was the number of foreigners in the picture.

'This doesn't look like a school in India.' Putting down the picture, Sneha gazed at the rain pelting the glass on her window. Confused, she again checked the name and address on the envelope. It was definitely addressed to her.

'What am I supposed to see in this?' Sneha again picked up the picture and this time she gave her attention to the faces of the students. In less than thirty seconds she put it down with a gasp.

'I don't believe this.' She picked up the picture and walked to the window where the natural light was better. She studied it. 'Hammit!'

Sneha rushed out of her office and made a quick call to Amla as she waited for the elevators.

'Amla, I'm going to be late. This could take time. Put Advey to bed if I do not come back by nine. And don't go anywhere, it's raining hard outside. And make sure you lock the doors and windows.'

Sneha made sure Amla said yes to all her requests. Just as she was about to hang up, she added, 'Also, keep your phone charged. Keep that and a torch near you. Thanks.'

Sneha's nightmare on the road began and lasted for over two hours. She drove into the parking lot of a familiar building, and took the elevators to the penthouse level. 'Nandini's in?' Sneha asked the guards. She got a loud, 'Yes ma'am.'

'Where's she?' Sneha shot at the staff member who opened the door for her.

'Madam is resting in her bedroom.'

'Where's Adi?' Sneha fired next.

'Sir is not here.'

'Thanks.' Sneha trotted to Sethani's boudoir. Stopping outside the door, she sharply rapped on it.

After a second or two, she heard Nandini call out, 'I don't need anything.'

Sneha pushed the door open. 'Wrong, kulta, you de—' Sneha came to an abrupt halt, as did her mouth. Nandini wasn't quick enough to avert her face smeared with black streaks of mascara and kohl washed by tears.

Nandini, sitting on the ornate canopied bed, turned her face away. Sneha fled to her side. Her first instinct was to grab Nandini and get an answer out of her. However, the awkwardness of the past few weeks caused her to stop next to Nandini and put a reassuring hand on her best friend's shoulder.

'What happened, Sethani?'

Abruptly, Nandini pressed her face into Sneha's abdomen and hugged her tightly around the waist, all the while crying softly. Sneha lowered herself and put her arms around the other girl, holding her close. 'What happened babes? You're scaring me.'

'It's over, Sneha. It's over. It's over.' Nandini sobbed against Sneha.

Sneha felt her stomach churn. 'What's over, Nandini?'

Nandini's voice shook as she replied, 'Aditya is sleeping with Gayatri.'

'Bullshit!' Sneha exclaimed.

'I have proof.' Fresh tears flowed down Nandini's face. She handed Sneha her phone.

Sneha saw the picture on the phone and the blood drained from her face. 'It is Adi...with...Gayatri.' Sneha's head spun. All colour drained from her face and her hands holding the phone began to quiver. Aditya's betrayal took Sneha back to a very dark place that she had strongly repressed. Memories of her own devastation came back, when Sneha had discovered Ankit with another woman. Sneha wasn't even in love with Ankit, yet she had felt slashed. Nandini's sniffles grew louder.

'How did you find out?' Sneha's voice was thick as she rubbed Nandini's arm sympathetically.

With her head resting in her hands, Nandini replied, 'Mona sent it to me. She caught them.'

Sneha instantly recoiled. 'Hold on! Mona sent you that picture? You didn't see it yourself?'

'How is that an issue?' Nandini replied bitterly.

Sneha stuck to her guns. 'I don't know. I don't trust Mona, neither should y—'

'I know you don't like her but...and seriously, right now I don't give a shit about that,' Nandini snapped at Sneha, wiping her face with the back of her hand.

'You will in a minute. Hold on.' Sneha picked up her bag that had dropped on the floor as she had bent down to hug Nandini.

Nandini grabbed her phone and stared at the picture of Aditya holding Gayatri tightly in his arms. Aditya's lips were on Gayatri's, their eyes closed in the ecstasy of the moment. Fresh howls tore out of Nandini's mouth. Sneha grabbed the phone away from her and put another picture in Nandini's hand. 'Look at this!'

'What is this, Sneha?' Nandini asked feebly.

Grabbing a pen from her bag, Sneha took the picture back from Nandini and drew a circle around two faces. 'Now look at it.'

Nandini took the picture and for a few seconds gazed quietly at it with red-rimmed eyes. 'It's Mona with...'

'With Gayatri. And that too in school uniforms. Those two go back a long way, Nandi. Did you know that?' Sneha said urgently, keeping her eyes on her friend.

Nandini looked confused. 'No! But how is that important?'

'There is something off. Look at this picture again.' Sneha held up Nandini's phone.

Biting her trembling lips, Nandini stared at her cell phone. 'You can't make this up, Sneh. It is Adi and Gayatri kis—' Nandini broke off with a sob.

'Agreed. But look at the picture. Whoever took it, took it standing very close to them.' Sneha put the phone a mere foot away from Nandini's face. 'Mona is so close to them and they didn't see her. There is no one else in the picture, no people, no background. So it's somewhere where these three were alone.'

Nandini gave her a blank look. 'What are you getting at?'

'Last week I bumped into Aditya. Gayatri and Mona were there. He said it was your idea?' Sneha asked.

'I know about that. I was the one who told Mona where Adi would be and she arranged for Gayatri to be there,' Nandini replied wearily.

'Are you demented? Why would you do that? Why would you want Gayatri to meet Aditya without you?' Sneha demanded.

Nandini raised her hands, exasperated. 'You know how guilty I feel because of what happened between Adi and her. And I was the reason for all that. I just thought that I should give Gayatri a chance to get some closure with Adi. Air her feelings, part on a happy note. And it wasn't like they were alone. Mona was there.'

'Who we know now to be Gayatri's chaddi buddy? This closure thing, whose idea was it?'

'Umm, what do you mean?' Nandini appeared to have a sudden fetish for picking on the silky duvet with twitchy fingers.

'Nandini, you *were* feeling idiotically guilty about the whole Adi and Gayatri fiasco and the last time we had discussed this you were convinced that you and Adi were meant to be together, plain and simple. No one's to blame. So what changed?'

'You threatened to sew my lips if I ever brought it up again,' Nandini reminded her quietly.

'Don't digress.' Sneha used the same tone she used on Advey

sometimes and Amla used on her often. 'Kulta, whose idea was it that Gayatri get some alone time with Adi?'

'Mona's.' Wincing, Nandini closed her eyes and then looked straight at Sneha. Sneha saw a glimmer of hope in her eyes.

'Okay, kulta. I'm going to get to the bottom of this. I think you need not doubt Adi just yet.' Sneha got to her feet.

'We had a big fight this weekend. Adi and I,' Nandini added sombrely.

'At Mona's farmhouse?' Sneha asked. Nandini nodded.

'What was it about?'

'Adi is a control freak and he was smothering me. And I told him that. He was very mad at me.' Nandini commenced the explanation with vehemence and ended it with a sniff.

'Most men are control freaks.' Nandini glared at her. Sneha raised her hands appealingly, 'I'm not saying it is right. I'm just saying that is the flip side of possessiveness and Adi is a possessive man. But I also know that he would not cheat on you.'

'I don't know.' Nandini's voice was sullen.

'Okay, we'll debate that later. Let me find them first. Did you try calling Adi?' Sneha began to walk away.

'His cell is switched off.' Nandini needed to get something off her chest so after a loaded pause she continued, 'We fought about you, too.'

Sneha turned around, surprised. 'What? Why?'

'A…Adi accused me of not being a good friend to you,' Nandini looked up at her. Sneha opened her mouth to say something but Nandini beat her to it. 'In that he was right. I have been acting horribly with you.' Nandini bit her lips to stem her tears but it did not work. 'I even had a party at my place two weeks ago and didn't invite you.'

'I know,' Sneha replied. 'I showed up anyhow, realized that I was gate-crashing and left. Mona and I talked for a few minutes.'

Nandini gasped. 'She never told me.'

'I think driving a wedge between us was a part of her plan.'

'What plan?' Nandini's asked, her eyes perplexed. 'She told me that you needed to be less around couples.'

'For I'm a divorced woman. And all divorced woman are evil witches who steal husbands and can't be happy for their happily married best friends.' Sneha hated that her voice cracked as she said the last words.

'I'm so sorry, Sneha. I am so stupid. I don't deserve you. And I think I've lost Adi too,' Nandini cried, anguished.

Coming back to Nandini, Sneha said, 'Kulta, listen to me. Please look at me.'

Nandini raised a tear-stained face that was now wholly black. Sneha bit back an inadvertent laugh, 'I, too, should have tried to sort out things between us but during those few weeks our egos got the better of us. My fault was that I wasn't using my brains and your fault that you were using someone else's. And about Adi, we will figure it out together. Right now, you remind me of the black-faced langurs that frequent our terraces in Kanpur. And I don't like langurs. So go wash your face. I'll be back soon.'

Sneha was at the door when she heard Nandini say softly, 'I miss Kanpur.'

As Sneha closed the door behind her, she voiced quietly, 'Me too, kulta. Me too!'

12

How did it get this far?

On her way out, Sneha took out her BlackBerry to send a short email.

```
From: snehag@flagshipad.com
To: n.chandel@dnc.com
I need to talk to you. IT'S URGENT!!
```

She did not have to wait for more than a minute.

```
From: n.chandel@dnc.com
To: snehag@flagshipad.com
I'm in the office till 8.00.
From: snehag@flagshipad.com
To: n.chandel@dnc.com
I'm coming over. Thanks!
```

Sneha drove like a maniac. In such heavy rains, even thirty kilometres an hour is for the fast and the furious. As Sneha ran from the parking to the building, the rain soaked her hair and shoulders. She got into the elevator and tried to get rid of whatever water she could off her clothes. It wasn't much.

As she got off on the floor of Nikhil's office, the guards did not stop her this time. She walked into Mrs Ali's office who immediately smiled as she pressed a button in the console in front of her. 'Mr Chandel's waiting for you.' Two knocks later, Sneha entered Nikhil's office.

On seeing her, Nikhil stood up. Today his shirt matched the colour of his eyes and his trousers were black. His hair, carelessly pushed away from his forehead, made him look no less impeccable or imposing. Immediately, Sneha became conscious of the fact that she was checking him out. She blurted out, unexpectedly breathless, 'It is very serious otherwise I would not have bothered you.'

For a few seconds Nikhil and Sneha unconsciously drank each other in, unable to take their eyes off the other and then Sneha's sudden sneeze brought them both out of the strange moment.

'Bless you! Have a seat,' Nikhil gestured at black leather seats at the other side of the office. With a few quick steps, he was at her side.

As Sneha was about to sit, Nikhil observed, 'You are soaked.'

Self-consciously, Sneha hestitated while sitting down, her bum extended awkwardly in mid-air and then embarrassed, she stood straight. Nikhil arched an eyebrow at her. 'I might get your sofa wet,' she bit out stiffly.

'That's fine. Sit. Coffee?'

'Please. Thank you.' Sneha sat on the edge of the sofa. She waited for Nikhil to finish talking to Mrs Ali and then he took the leather recliner across from where she sat.

'Shall I turn down the cooling?' he asked politely.

'Huh?' Sneha was taken aback.

'You are shivering,' Nikhil continued to take in her dishevelled look. Damp curls, wet eyelashes, and glowing eyes, lips that opened slightly and then shut uncertainly, a chin that probably itched to put him in his place and... Nikhil didn't dare to go lower than her face. He did not understand the slow pleasure building in him at this unexpected meeting. Impatient, he had done nothing but wait once he had known Sneha was on her way.

'Sure, thanks,' Sneha replied.

Nikhil, still focused on her appearance, gave her a blank look.

'You offered to turn down the cooling,' Sneha reminded him. Gathering her feet under her, she crossed her arms across her chest as Nikhil got up and touched a dial on the adjoining wall. Sneha wished Nikhil would not stare at her. Right now she could very well do without a fluttering belly. No such luck! Sitting down, Nikhil again turned those two green devils loose on her. Unaware of the other's thoughts, they were both recalling their last meeting. Not a nice memory!

Nikhil's sudden ardour cooled off and he sat back in the recliner—a familiar coldness seeped in his gaze and face. Sneha, too, straightened and the feisty chin came up as her expression turned belligerent and her shoulders stiffened and slumped back.

Damn her! Nikhil inwardly cursed her signature shoulders-back-blouse-taut move again. He forced himself to stay immune and not let his gaze dip.

Thus, Sneha and Nikhil both stayed quiet, openly sizing up the other adversary. 'Ohh!' Belatedly Sneha sprung into action. Taking her phone out of her bag, she opened a picture she had forwarded to herself from Nandini's phone. Rudely, she thrust the phone into Nikhil's face.

Giving Sneha a pointed look, Nikhil coolly leaned forward and took the phone from Sneha, making sure not to touch her fingers. He studied the picture. Nikhil didn't yell or curse but Sneha could feel his surging anger. A scowl broke out on his face, his expression became tense, his lips pursed and his shoulders tightened and bunched under his shirt.

'How did it get this far?' Nikhil asked, carefully placing the phone on the table between them. He wanted to smash it against the wall. Gayatri had really outdone herself and Nikhil did not think that as a compliment.

Sneha felt a responding anger in her. 'Good question. You tell me. You are the one who brought the tramp here.'

Nikhil sat back, reminding Sneha of an animal who sits back just before it springs. Sneha kept her attack coming. 'Oh yeah, I forgot...' Sneha mimicked a thinking pose. 'Gayatri is *your* family. So please tell me, why is *your* family stuffing her face in the face of another woman's husband?'

Nikhil leaned forward sharply. Sneha reflexively broke eye

contact with him and had to force herself to look back at him.

'We could go back and forth on this. However, I think that would not really help Nandini. So let's keep it quick and short. How did you get this picture? And how old is it?'

Sneha glared straight into his hard eyes, 'It is recent. Probably today afternoon or early evening. And Mona sent this to Nandini.'

'Mona sent it? She was there?' Nikhil asked. Sneha wanted to say eggjactly but given the present company she did not.

Just then, there was a knock on the door. Mrs Ali came in pushing a trolley. Sneha went to help.

'Please sit, Ms Gupta,' Mrs Ali requested and Sneha sank back in her chair. *Everybody has a demi-god complex in this place,* Sneha scorned. The older woman placed the cups in front of them and a plate of delicate-looking sandwiches and another with fragrant cookies.

'Thanks,' Nikhil said just as Mrs Ali pushed the trolley to the door. 'Can we get a few bath-sized towels?'

Sneha and Mrs Ali looked at him, surprised. Nikhil nodded his head pointedly at Sneha. 'For Ms Gupta.'

'I'm fine. Seriously.' Sneha addressed them both.

'Yes, Mr Chandel,' Mrs Ali nodding headed out.

'So what do you need from me?' Nikhil asked quietly as he raised the cup to his lips.

'Isn't it obvious?' Sneha's upper lip curled disdainfully. 'I want to know where Gayatri is. And thank you for sending me the picture of Gayatri and Mona.' Leaning forward, Sneha took a sip of the coffee. It was hot and scalded her tongue. Sneha put the cup down quickly and some of it splashed on the saucer and table. 'Hammit.'

'Hammit?' Nikhil's question was loaded with sarcasm.

As Sneha grumpily picked up a napkin to wipe the table, she explained, 'Because of Advey's inherent knack of remembering cuss words, I change a letter here or there. Therefore if he repeats it, it is just a meaningless silly word.'

'So "Hammit" is for "Damn it"!'

'Hes, I mean yes.' Sneha, feeling awkward, glanced away.

Nikhil did not let his unexpected grin colour his voice, 'How do you know I sent the picture?'

Sneha rolled her eyes. 'In our emails yesterday, I implied that Mona was Nandini's new best friend. So why would Nandini, given Gayatri's history with her husband befriend someone so close to Gayatri? She wouldn't. And if she did, it was only because she did not know of Gayatri and Mona's closeness.' Sneha paused. Nikhil continued to watch her over the rim of his cup, waiting for her to continue.

Sneha hurried into the explanation, 'Mona is inherently a Mumbaiker. Gayatri is not. So where could they have met? And what school Gayatri went to or who her friends were, only someone close to Gayatri would know. It's quite simple.'

Nikhil's face softened as he took another sip from his cup. 'And you want me to find Gayatri now?'

'Yes! Because if you did not want to stop this, why would you send me the picture?' Sneha felt she had to add, 'You should have gone for that weekend party in Lonavala. You must have been invited?'

'I was but I was very busy that weekend.' Nikhil did not elaborate on what he was busy with. 'Nandini did not have you invited there?'

Sneha flared at the accusatory tone in his voice. 'Nandini is capable of only seeing the good in people. That's what makes her so likeable.'

'And gullible,' Nikhil responded.

'And what does all this make Gayatri? A tart?' Sneha snapped. She took a big sip of her coffee in anger and set the cup down with a thump.

Nikhil eyes flared as he got to his feet with a jerk. 'You look ridiculous with the foam on your nose.' He remarked, walking to his desk.

Giving his back a vexed look, Sneha rubbed her nose clean. Just then, a soft knock later, Mrs Ali walked in with a few towels. She handed them to Sneha, who thanked her. Mrs Ali left them alone.

Sneha, not wanting to bring too much attention to herself, self-consciously and quietly wiped her bare arms and neck with the towel. Nikhil dialled a number on his cell phone. He spoke a few numbers into the phone and then waited. Sneha glanced at him. His computer and whatever he was doing had all his attention. Nikhil must have felt Sneha's eyes on him for he spoke without looking up, 'I'm having someone trace Gayatri's exact location through her cell phone.'

'You can do that? I thought only cops could do it,' Sneha said, surprised.

Nikhil glanced at her briefly. 'Some of us have micro-chips in our cells, so they can be traced.'

'Why?' Sneha put the towel down.

'Our business is worth a lot of money. And also open to dangerous thefts, forgeries and other threats. Our top personnel need to be protected because we have information, information about multimillion dollar transactions all over the world. I had put it in for Gayatri while she is in India since she's my responsibility.' Nikhil went back to his computer and Sneha realized that this was the longest she had heard Nikhil speak. He probably felt the same for he became quiet and went back to his computer screen. He was not really a person to make small talk while he waited for his head of security to get back to him about Gayatri's whereabouts.

Quietly, Sneha drew her feet out of her black pumps and rubbed her ankles with the opposite foot. She stretched her calf and crunched her toes; it felt good.

With a sneaky glance, Sneha made sure that Nikhil wasn't looking at her. She thought he wasn't but Sneha was wrong. Nikhil was looking at her, but on his computer screen.

Just then in the 2X3 window open on his computer that had live feed coming in from the sitting area in his room, he noticed

Sneha's tiny movements. Curious, he expanded the screen and watched Sneha as she used the towel to pat herself dry over her clothes. Sneha pressed the towel to her shoulders trying to absorb some of the dampness from her clothes. Sneha felt her nape. It, too, was wet, so was her hair above it.

Nikhil couldn't look away from the grace with which Sneha stretched her legs, the way she furtively moved her hands over her shoulders and her nape. Nikhil froze when she brought the towel in front of her, pressed it under her collarbones and moved it lower. Her chest rose and fell with her soft breathing. Nikhil could not help wonder if she would be as immune if his hands were the ones drying her. He would be more thorough, he would unbutton those pearl buttons to make sure her soft skin inside wasn't damp. Nikhil felt his breathing grow uneven as he imagined Sneha laying herself open to his greedy, all-seeking touch.

Just then, Nikhil saw Sneha peek at him. He schooled his face to be neutral as he watched her watch him on the screen.

Satisfied that he wasn't looking, Nikhil's saw Sneha sink her fingers in her hair as she searched for the clips. She slowly and quietly pulled out her hair clips one by one, Nikhil's eyes following the movement of her fingers reaching inside her hair, pushing in and then slipping out. Nikhil's mouth went dry as he watched Sneha shake her hair loose, her movements economical. It swirled below her shoulders, small curls at the ends. A strand flicked across her cheek and Nikhil watched Sneha brush it away carelessly. He knew if he had done that he would have done it gently and pressed his lips to the surface of her cheek and then trailed his hungry lips to her full mouth, tasting her skin, as he became a slave to her taste. And with that pretty pink mouth, too, he would be absolutely thorough and spend a long time knowing every crease, every fold of her crevice, every little dip in those lips would be his to explore...

Nikhil's sudden hiss startled Sneha. 'Everything okay?' Sneha asked her hazel eyes wide.

With long strides, Nikhil went past her to the door. He seemed angry. 'When you are decent, I'll meet you outside.'

'Decent? What?' Sneha looked down at herself, terrified that her blouse had come open. It had not. Even her trousers were zipped and buttoned in appropriate places. 'What did he mean by decent?' Sneha murmured to the empty room. She was clothed from her collarbone to her ankle. 'How is this indecent?' Sneha threw the towel on the seat next to her but then on second thoughts she folded the towels and put them on the floor to the side. Quickly stuffing a sandwich and then a cookie in her mouth (it had been a long day), Sneha grabbed her bag and waited impatiently as her mouth took its own time chewing.

In minutes, Sneha was out of Nikhil's office. She found him leaning over his secretary's shoulders, looking into her computer.

'Did you find her?' Sneha asked briskly. Her mouth was tight. If it wasn't for Sethani she would not step anywhere within light years of this curt man.

'They are at a five star hotel at Nariman Point. Not far. Let's go.'

'Let's go.' Just as Sneha took steps to go towards the elevator, Nikhil took a quick step from around the desk to go to his office. He collided with Sneha who fell back with a startled cry. Nikhil caught her arms just in time and pulled her back up. Alarmed, Mrs Ali stood up.

'What are you doing? Nikhil asked, irked.

Sneha pulled her arms free of his hold. His fingers were warm against her skin and she did not like the tingling sensation. 'You said "let's go". So I was going.' Disgruntled, she pointed at the elevators with one hand and with the other hand, pushed back the hair on the side of her face.

Nikhil followed her hand. He liked the act of holding Sneha. She was petite, all woman, reminding his body that he was a man, a man with very little self-control around her. Mrs Ali's pointed cough made him self-conscious. Nikhil dropped his hands as if burned and simultaneously, he gave Sneha a small push away from him.

'I was going to my office,' he told Sneha off. His voice remained cold and flat even though his eyes literally burned in his face.

'Why? Is there a secret route from your room to Nariman Point?' Sneha snapped, frowning at him. She, of course, had misunderstood why Nikhil had pushed her away from him. Why shouldn't she? She was grappling with bewildering emotions that had nothing to do with either Nandini or Aditya.

'I was going to get my jacket. So if you will do the honours of not crashing into me, we can be on our way.' Nikhil taking long strides disappeared into his office.

'Thank you for the towels and the coffee,' Sneha said to Mrs Ali and angrily walked to the elevator. 'Horrid, horrid, horrid man!' The guards standing near the elevator wondered which of them she was talking about. They put some distance between themselves and Sneha.

Nikhil joined her shortly. They got into the elevator and it was a silent ride to the lobby. As they got out of the elevator, Sneha moved to the right and Nikhil to the left causing them to bump into one another again. This time Sneha steadied herself against the adjoining wall.

'Where are you going?' Nikhil could not camouflage his exasperation this time.

'To my car. I'll follow you?' Sneha let go of the wall.

'It's easier if we go together. And my driver can get your car.'

'Why? Are you a better driver than I am?' Sneha snapped.

Stuffing his hands in his pockets, Nikhil looked out at the rain still hammering the ground. Sneha got a feeling he was counting to ten.

'I don't care who drives better but yes, my car is more comfortable,' Nikhil glanced at Sneha and then went back to looking outside.

'Fine.' Irritated beyond measure, Sneha took her car keys out.

'Thank you.' Nikhil gestured at his car, which stood near them in a covered parking spot.

As Nikhil moved forward, he realized Sneha was not with him. He turned around. She was still standing near the elevator. She stood there watching him. As a question, Nikhil raised his eyebrow.

'My car is quite comfortable for me. I know where that hotel is. I'll get there by myself.' Sneha coolly walked away, leaving Nikhil staring after her in exasperation.

13

Room service

Sneha didn't see Nikhil curl his fists and raise an irritated face to the skies. She jogged to her car parked out in the open. The rain beat hard on her back and open hair. It was getting dark. Sneha hurriedly got in and flung her bag at the back seat. As she pulled on her seat belt, she heard a loud knock on the window opposite to her. She saw a form outside. It was Nikhil.

'Open the door, Sneha,' she heard him shout loudly. Surprised, Sneha unlocked the door on her side.

Nikhil got in and shut the door behind him. It didn't close fully. Sneha politely pointed out, 'You'll have to close it har—'

'Ya, ya I know.' Nikhil slammed the door harder the second time round.

Flicking some water off him that landed on Sneha's face, he turned to her. Sneha glanced at Nikhil. Most of his hair was wet, there was moisture dripping all over one side of his face, and there were wet patches on the front of his jacket. When Sneha brought her eyes back up, Nikhil was staring back at her. His face was an impassive immobile mask but his eyes spoke volumes—highly irritated volumes.

'Shall we?' Nikhil spoke tersely, turning to look outside. Sneha could not help a sudden quick smile. 'Your driver is following us?'

'Yes.' Nikhil reached down and felt around the side of his chair. 'How do you push the seat back?'

Sneha sprung into action. He did not know of the lever under the car seat. Nikhil, too, remembered at the same time. They both reached down and Sneha's nose bumped into his shoulder.

'Ouch!' Sneha's eyes smarted and her nose stung with the contact even as it absorbed the pleasant smell of his spicy cologne mingled with rain water.

'Sorry!' Still bent, Nikhil turned his face, inadvertently bringing it mere inches away from hers. He felt Sneha's breath on his lips. Nikhil could not help but stare directly into her eyes as his own clouded over. He saw Sneha's hazel eyes dilate and darken to the shade of molten caramel. Sucking in an unsteady breath, Sneha straightened in such a hurry that Nikhil was sure she had pulled a muscle in her back.

Finding the lever under his chair, Nikhil pushed his chair back, all the way back. Sneha's unsteady breath both pleased and frightened Nikhil. She was not as impervious to him as she would like him to believe.

Sneha put the key in the ignition and started the car. She reversed with speed and saw Nikhil reach out and grab the door handle. 'Slow down, Schumacher.'

Surprised, Sneha glanced at Nikhil. Had he just cracked a joke? Avoiding her eyes, Nikhil pulled his jacket out from behind him. Sneha brought the car out on the main street. The traffic was heavy and slow, and Sneha put the wipers to test. As they meandered onto the Mumbai roads, the rain beating heavily down on the car, they felt as though they were inside a cuccoon. Sneha remembered Nikhil's rather long eyelashes which, when wet, made his eyes seem deeper and more luminous; the kind of eyes that were impossible to look away from. Sneha's hand reached out to turn on the music to distract her nerves that hummed like a pulled guitar string.

'I would request you to let me handle Gayatri,' Nikhil broke the silence. It did not sound like a request. Sneha removed her hand from the music system.

'You should have stopped her earlier.' Sneha inched the car forward.

'She is an adult.'

'High time she behaves like one too.' She caught Nikhil's look. 'Friends or family should give the right advice.'

Nikhil turned to partially face her, 'And what about Aditya dumping her? Gayatri doesn't have the right to be hurt?' He did not raise his voice but Sneha sensed his censure.

'Of course she does. Relationships break. You get over them and move on—not try and break up someone's marriage.'

'So as long as Nandini and Aditya have their happy endings, it doesn't matter who they hurt,' was Nikhil's cold retort.

Sneha snorted. 'I don't expect you to understand the sanctity of marriage.' Sneha bit her lip. Dang! She was as red as the traffic light they waited at.

Sneha glanced at him. Nikhil's pointed know-it-all stare made Sneha come to a rude realization regarding herself. She looked away discomfited. If he was the pot, she, sadly, was the kettle.

Nikhil bit off the caustic rejoinder hanging on the tip of his tongue. Sneha's vulnerable expression reminded him that if he could be not be chivalrous he could most definitely be quiet.

After a few minutes of silence, Sneha spoke haltingly, 'My marriage was such an unhappy blur that sometimes I forget it even happened.'

Surprised by how much Sneha had just revealed and hidden in the same sentence, Nikhil glanced at her. He felt compelled to lift her spirits. 'I'm guessing in your case the break up was amicable.'

'It was. We both couldn't wait to see the last of each other.' Sneha's wry laugh sounded steeped in anger.

'Good.'

Sneha glanced at Nikhil. The unexpected empathy Sneha saw in his gaze put her at some ease. She put her eyes back on the road. After a few seconds passed, Sneha said. 'I'm waiting?'

'For?'

'For you to elaborate a little more on your own...?' Sneha trailed off.

'I won't.' Nikhil was back to being terse.

'Fine!' Irritated, Sneha dropped the subject.

After ten minutes or so, Nikhil said. 'At this speed by the time we reach the hotel, Gayatri and Adi probably would have had kids. In plural.'

Sneha bit back her unexpected laugh. Instead, she said, 'Do you have a strong bladder?'

Nikhil raised a brow at her.

'I'll take that as a yes.'

Sneha slowly but surely increased the speed of the car. Nikhil caught the handle above him. 'How strong is my bladder expected to be?' he asked conversationally.

Sneha gave him a quick look. Nikhil stared at her, especially at her eyes that positively sparkled. 'Very!'

Sneha revved up and unleashed her true speed junkie self. She speeded up, weaving the car amongst others while receiving a few honks and taking some corners sharply. From the outside it might look as if Sneha was driving rashly but Nikhil could see that she did not lose command over the car, even for a second. Sneha changed the gears in perfect tandem with her speed, direction and space.

Nikhil made a quick call. Sneha heard him give his driver directions to their destination. Nikhil was sure that they had lost the other car quite some time back. The rain had dwindled. Soon Sneha was pulling in the valet parking of the five star hotel.

'I think some car race somewhere is missing a driver,' Nikhil said blandly, opening the door on his side.

Sneha could not fathom if that was an insult or a compliment so she simply ignored Nikhil. Giving her keys to the valet, Sneha marched inside the gleaming, spotless hotel lobby. Her stomach was knotted, nerves making her nauseous. What if they were too late? What if Adi had really slipped? In her rush to get to Adi, Sneha did not care whether Nikhil followed or not.

Sneha passed the lobby and reached the elevators. Just as

she was about to press the call button, she stopped. 'Hammit, HE knows where they are in this hotel.' Sneha swung her head to spot Nikhil but she couldn't see him anywhere. She glanced around and retraced her steps back to the front doors. There was no sign of him. 'Hammit.' She turned around and walked back towards the elevators. A sudden frisson of awareness had Sneha glance to her right. At some distance, leaning against the earth-coloured marble reception stood Nikhil, quietly watching her. He wasn't alone: two of his security details stood next to him. And all three had their eyes fixed on her.

'Doody cools!' Sneha muttered making her way to them. 'You couldn't call out?' she accused Nikhil as she came close to him.

'And interrupt your brisk evening walk?' Nikhil gave her the briefest of smiles loaded with sarcasm. Observing him one would think it was illegal to smile or have a sense of humour. 'They are in the penthouse. Just play along.' He said the last part quietly.

'What?' Sneha asked just as a woman in a green silk sari with printed white flowers joined them. She was the hotel's concierge.

'Mr Chandel, just as you requested, we have arranged a cake, a bottle of wine and flowers for our guest.'

'We are celebrating this?' Sneha's expression was one of utter shock.

Nikhil narrowed his eyes at Sneha. 'Of course we are. It is Gayatri's birthday. We are here to surprise her.'

Sneha caught on. 'I mean, of course we are.' She nodded at woman in the green sari. 'Why else would we ask you to arrange for all that?' Sneha added a fake laugh for effect. It sounded like a horse blowing wind. Nikhil briefly closed his eyes.

'Let me take you to the penthouse,' the hotel concierge said.

'Sure.' Nikhil stepped into the elevator with her. The ride was short but Sneha felt every second of it in her stomach. She dreaded what she would was about to find. *Please Adi, please don't do anything stupid.* Sneha shut her eyes tight and when she opened them, she found Nikhil staring at her. Just staring at her, not saying a word, just watching her with a strange stillness as if watching her was all he could do. As an embarrassed Sneha was about to look away Nikhil smiled at her, not the happy kind of smile but a gentle smile, a smile to say that she wasn't alone in this. Before Sneha could react, the elevator came to a stop. As everyone stepped out, they saw a waiter pushing a cart holding a cake with a lit candle, flowers and wine.

'That was quick. Thank you,' Nikhil said to the concierge.

They all walked to the only door on the floor. It was wide and dark brown, with the words, 'Presidential Suite' written in gold letters on it.

The woman in the green sari knocked sharply. 'Room service!'

A few minutes later, the door opened. It was Mona. Her face lost all colour on seeing Nikhil and then Sneha standing there.

'Shock, more likely,' spat Sneha as she and Nikhil went past Mona who stood mutely at the door.

Nikhil turned around and addressed the concierge and the waiter who stood at the threshold, confused. 'That'll be all. Send me a bill for the room and all this.' He shut the door on their surprised faces.

'Where are they, Mona?' Sneha demanded as Mona stood rooted near the door. Her eyes strayed behind them.

Immediately, Nikhil and Sneha walked into the living room beyond the foyer. Sneha caught glimpses of the pastel green, gold and pink interiors. They found Gayatri sitting on the love seat. Her face was tear-stained and her hair a mess. A box of Kleenex sat on her knees. She was wearing the same clothes as she was in the picture sent to Nandini.

On seeing her state, Sneha gasped. All the post-copulation scenes in Hindi movies bombarded her head. Gayatri noticed them and Sneha's horrified expression.

'Oh don't worry, nothing happened,' she tossed bitterly.

Making a growling sound in her throat Sneha went to her.

'Nothing happened? You little bi—' Nikhil passed Sneha and reached Gayatri first.

'Where's Aditya?' he asked.

'In the bedroom,' Gayatri replied uncaringly.

Sneha for the first time in her life wanted to punch someone. Her eyes met Nikhil's. Her chest was heaving, but she ate her angry curses and marched towards the direction of the bedroom.

'Adi!' She ran to the bed on which she saw Aditya sprawled on his stomach. She shook him. 'Adi! Adi. It's Sneha.'

Aditya mumbled something softly. Sneha couldn't make out what it was. She ran to the other side of the bed and put her ears close to his lips. Sneha smelled the alcohol on his breath. She made out what he was mumbling.

'Nandini, ughh Nand…'

'Oh, sweetie, I'll get you to her right away. Can you walk?' Sneha crooned, cupping his face in her hands.

'They gave him some sleeping pills.' Nikhil joined her.

'Some? Look at him, Nikhil. He's incoherent. Call a doctor, please.' Sneha sat on her knees on the bed.

'Let me take a look. You'll have to move, Sneha,' Nikhil said. Still on her knees, Sneha crawled to the side, still holding Adi's hand.

Nikhil timed his pulse. 'It's steady.' Next he felt Adi's forehead. 'His body temperature is normal.'

Just then, Adi made some gurgling sounds in this throat. 'He is going to throw up.' Nikhil quickly grabbed a vase from the side table and upturned it, letting the water and flowers fall on the floor. In seconds, he passed it to Sneha who shoved it under Adi's mouth as he barfed.

Lifting Adi's head, Sneha made it easier for him to retch. Nikhil got up and went into the bathroom. He came back with some towels. Aditya had by then fallen back on the bed, barely conscious. Nikhil took the vase and handed her a towel. 'Wipe his face.' Sneha took the wet towel and carefully wiped Adi's face and neck.

'I can't take him home like this,' Sneha spoke.

'We'll manage somehow.'

'What if someone sees us? A lot of people know him in this city, the kind who frequent such hotels,' Sneha said worriedly.

Nikhil went into the bathroom and came back without the vase. He picked up the other vase from the side table and emptied it, this time in the trash can. 'Poor flowers,' Sneha couldn't help murmur. Nikhil gave her a sardonic look. Sneha fumbled, 'I'm just saying...'

'We'll take Aditya out of the back entrance. The hotel should have one.' Nikhil picked up the hotel phone. Sneha wiped Aditya's face again with the wet towel. This time he opened his eyes with some semblance of recognition in them. 'Sneha?' he slurred.

Sneha smiled, relieved. 'It's me, Adi. Don't worry, we'll get you home.'

After a few seconds, his eyelashes fluttered again. 'We? Nandini?' he called out hoarsely.

'Sshh. Nandini's at home. She's worried sick. Do you think you can manage to stay up for some time?'

Aditya's eyes closed again. Sneha shook him. 'Adi, please wake up!'

Aditya opened his eyes weakly. 'Who else is...' He had to strain to speak, his voice hoarse and slurred.

Sneha bit her lip. How would Adi react to seeing Nikhil here? Nikhil took the decision out of her hands. He walked around to the side of bed so he stood in front of Adi.

'Asshole!' Adi said weakly, but clearly, to him.

'He got me here, Adi. He is helping us.' Sneha bit her lip surprised with the alacrity she had defended Nikhil. So was Nikhil. Aditya's head flopped back on the mattress.

'Call Nandini. Tell her to call a doctor.' From his pocket, Nikhil took out a bottle and tossed it on the bed towards her.

'This is what they gave him. Mona told me they gave him four tablets.'

'Four! Was she trying to sleep with Adi or kill him?' Sneha grabbed the bottle.

'Sleep…yes…slee…' Aditya muttered, digging his face into the pillow.

Sneha shook his shoulder, 'No, Adi, sit. SIT, don't sleep. SIT, ADI.'

'Oww, don't shout, Sneha,' Adi spoke more clearly. This time he opened his eyes and nearly lifted his head and torso up.

Sneha gave him a thumbs-up sign. 'Awesome.' Sneha glanced around. Nikhil understood and handed her his phone. 'Use this!'

Sneha quickly dialled Sethani's number. Nandini answered it in one ring.

'Nandi. We've got Adi,' she smiled into the phone.

'We've? Who's we?' Nandini asked her voice was anxious. Sneha rolled her eyes. Both husband and wife were equally interested in trivia.

'Umm, never mind. Listen, you have to call the doctor. Adi has some sleeping pills in his system plus some alcohol.' Sneha heard Nandini's sob on the other end.

'Nandi, don't cry. Babes, he'll be fine. He just threw up, he is somewhat coherent. Say something to him,' Sneha put the phone near Aditya's ear.

Aditya registered his wife's voice in his ear. He instantly responded, 'Nandini, baby…ughh…am fine. Sneha's getting…' He trailed off.

Sneha took the phone back. 'Nandi, we are bringing him home.'

'Who's we, Sn—'

'Listen, just call the doctor, okay Sethani?'

Sneha hung up. Her mouth twisted into a rueful smile as she fondly stroked Adi's forehead. 'You are going to be just fine,' she whispered to him.

Watching Sneha's tender expression, Nikhil felt an unexpected melancholy. 'I'll check if there's a wheelchair to take him down.' He swiftly walked out.

Sneha used Nikhil's cell phone to make another call. 'Amla, yes it's me. Is baba sleeping?' Amla answered in the affirmative. 'Good. Have your dinner. I don't know how long I will be here. Maybe the whole night,' Sneha tried to sound composed. Since the day Advey was born, she had never stayed a single night away from him.

Just as she about to hang up, she had to know. 'Advey didn't cry did he?'

Amla answered in the negative. 'Thank you, Amla. I'll see you later. Go to bed, I have my keys.' As Sneha hung up, she realized Nikhil was back in the room. He wasn't alone, his security guards were with him. Sneha jumped off the bed.

Aditya, still slipping in and out of consciousness, was smoothly lifted off the bed and settled gently into the wheelchair. Sneha was a little surprised to see Nikhil actively doing the lifting and making sure Aditya was comfortable in the chair.

Nikhil put a baseball cap on Aditya's head and pulled it down as low as possible. Next, he got a throw from the living room and he arranged it over Aditya's legs. Then he handed Sneha the empty vase, 'For the car. We are taking my car. I'll have your car dropped at Aditya's house.' Nikhil's face tightened, expecting a familiar my-car-your-car conversation.

14

Control your friend

'Sure!' Sneha quietly took the vase. 'The keys are with the valet.' Her voice was low-pitched.

Sneha's meekness made Nikhil feel as if he was cheated out of an argument. 'It has been taken care of, don't worry. My car is at the back entrance. You go down there and wait. The rest of us will get Aditya down.'

Sneha again nodded tiredly.

'Sit in the back, we'll put Adi in the back with you.' Nikhil watched as Sneha again nodded limply. As he watched Sneha head out quietly he felt like strangling Gayatri for the mess she had created.

Sneha entered the living room and realized it was empty. Gayatri and Mona were gone. She walked out and rode the service elevator with a member of the hotel staff. Outside in the unexpectedly chilly night, Sneha got in the back seat of Nikhil's already running car.

In a few minutes, Nikhil brought Adi, who was barely recognizable in disguise, down with him. Nikhil pushed the driver's seat to the front and he helped Sneha sit as best as possible with Aditya's head resting in her lap.

'You're comfortable?'

'Totally!' Sneha could not help the sarcastic quip.

Nikhil tilted his head slightly to a side as if to say, *I was just asking.*

Sneha, narrowing her eyes, gave Nikhil a closer look as if

to reply, *Bad question!* And then shook her head. *Big time!*

Fine! Shrugging his shoulders, Nikhil went over to the other side to help the others lift Aditya and fold his legs better inside. The drive to Aditya's house was uneventful except for a second barfing episode and Aditya's lovelorn incessant chanting of Nandini's name interspersed with 'asshole' solely for Nikhil's hearing pleasure.

Sneha bit her lips, feeling bad for Nikhil, which she had no business feeling but she did. Sneha met Nikhil's eye in the rearview mirror. *Sorry!*

Nikhil arched an eyebrow. *Sorry for me?*

Sneha pulled her lips to the side of her face. *Whatever!*

At the entrance of the building, Nikhil brought the window down on Sneha's side and she waved at the security guard.

'Let them in.' Nandini in her jeans, a thin blouse and flip-flops came running toward them. The gates opened and Nikhil drove the car in and parked where Sneha directed him.

'Adi! Adi!' Nandini called out from Sneha's open window. Her face was creased with concern, her eyes filled with tears. 'Adi! Adi!' she called, sticking her head in the partially open window.

Sneha tapped Nikhil's shoulder, 'Open the window completely.'

'Owwwww!' Nandini let out a strangled cry.

'Stop Nikhil. STOP! You're raising the glass,' Sneha yelled out.

'Nandini...na...' Adi added to the confusion.

'Ya, ya, she's here,' Sneha reassured the fumbling Adi. 'Open the door, Nikhil.'

'You said the window.' Nikhil turned back, confused.

'Fine, now I'm saying the door.' Sneha moved sideways to avoid Nandini's flapping hand that came dangerously close to her face. Sneha's knees shifted and Aditya's head fell forward and collided with the back of the driver's seat.

'Oww,' Adi feebly protested.

'Adi, Adi, are you okay?' Nandini hollered.

Sneha and Nikhil exchanged pained expressions.

'Nandini, where…are…you?' Aditya slurred, moving his head restlessly.

'Open the door!' Sneha yelled, exasperated.

'Don't yell at me,' Nikhil yelled back.

'OPEN THE DOOR NIKHIL!' Nandini called out.

'Opppenn the dooorrr assho—' Sneha shifted her knee so Aditya's head jerked and he was unable to complete his slurred sentence.

Finally, the door unlocked and Sneha got out as quickly as she could, still supporting Adi's head with her hands. Nandini quickly slid in her place.

'Do hanson ka joda,' Sneha murmured under her breath, not realizing that Nikhil was standing next to her.

'And who's that bald eagle?' Nikhil asked quietly, looking at the man with shining pate and rumpled clothes getting into the back seat from the other side.

Sneha choked on her startled laugh. 'Their physician, Dr De.'

'I smell vomit. Did Aditya throw up?' Dr De asked, trying to fit his rotund frame in the limited space.

Sneha moved to Nandini's side answering, 'Yes. Twice. Quite a bit.'

'Good. That means whatever was in his system is most probably out. Let's take him upstairs,' the doctor instructed.

With some crafty manoeuvring during which Nandini stepped on everyone's feet quite a few times, Aditya was put in the wheelchair.

Just as Nikhil was trying to push Aditya a little further into the seat, Nandini, trying to help, trod hard on Nikhil's hand.

Sneha grimaced as she saw Nikhil bite his lip, his expression pained. Nikhil glanced at Sneha. *Control your friend.*

Sneha hastily grabbed Nandini's arm and pulled her back. 'They'll manage.'

'No they can't do it. They need my help,' Nandini protested, moving forward. Her mouth opened once again to bleat out, 'Adi, Adi.'

'Nandini, behave,' Sneha gripped her friend's arm tighter. 'You stepped on Nikhil's hand. He wants you to stand back.'

'No he doesn't. He didn't say that.' Nandini seemed confused.

For a fraction of a second Sneha mirrored that same expression. 'Oh, never mind. Just stay here for a minute. They're almost done.'

Once Aditya was firmly ensconced in the wheelchair, everyone except Nikhil's security personnel took the elevator.

In the elevator, Dr De began his basic examination of Aditya. When the elevator halted, Nikhil pushed Aditya's wheelchair out. The others followed close behind. Aditya's staff anxiously waited at the door while two of the strongest men took the wheelchair handles from Nikhil.

'In the bedroom, Balaramji,' Nandini directed.

At that moment, Dr De turned around and addressed Nandini seriously, 'This would be a good time to call Mr Sarin's immediate family.'

Sneha gasped. Nandini pounced on the doctor's arm, her voice shrill, 'Adi is that sick?'

Wincing, Dr De disengaged himself. 'Just to find out if your husband is allergic to any medicine. You are newly married right? So you might not know.' And then he strode into the apartment.

Nandini's nostrils flared and her eyes narrowed at the doctor's cavalier manner. Sneha rubbed her friend's back, 'Control, kulta, control. We'll kill him once he fixes Adi.' Nikhil cleared his throat and the sound brought Nandini out of the red haze swimming in front of her eyes.

Nandini and Sneha followed the doctor into the corridor that led to the bedroom.

'Sneha,' Nikhil called out.

Sneha stopped and gazed at him. *What?*

'I'll wait here.' Nikhil's bothered green gaze said something else to her. *Is it okay if I stay here a while?*

'Please do, thanks.' Nikhil moved to the living room. Sneha and Nandini turned around, heading for the bedroom.

Dr De, with the help of the staff, already had Adi reclining on the bed.

Nandini moved to put some pillows under Aditya's head. She sat next to him, clasping her hand tightly in hers. She stroked Adi's forehead and he restlessly moved under her touch.

'What are you planning to do Doc?' Sneha asked as she saw the doctor setting up an IV. A nurse was assisting him.

'We'll pump his stomach. Might not be much left in there anyhow. I'll then check for any electrolyte imbalance.'

'What are the side effects?' Nandini asked still stroking Adi's head.

'Minimal. I am going to be here the whole night. Don't worry. Aditya will be fine,' he reassured her.

'Should we take him to the hospital?' Sneha mulled aloud.

'This is a low-risk procedure. Mr Sarin's vitals are great, his pulse and blood pressure are stable. Moreover, the sleeping pills he took were of the mild kind.'

'I could kill those hitches,' Sneha muttered as she saw the tears flow down Nandini's face.

'I'm about to begin. Why don't you both wait outside?' the doctor requested.

'I'm going nowhere,' Nandini said firmly. 'Sneh, why don't you go? I'll be okay,' she said giving her best friend a tear-stained smile.

'I'll be outside,' Sneha said, opening the door. 'I'll check in a few. Call me! Okay, kulta?' she reiterated at the door.

The doctor and nurse acted as if they had not heard the last word. Nandini gave Sneha a small smile, 'I will.'

Sneha walked to the living room. She found Nikhil sitting on the sofa, working off a digital tablet. On hearing her come in, he immediately stood up.

Sighing, Sneha sank into the sofa opposite him. 'The doctor is going to pump Adi's stomach. He is hoping most of it is out already. The sleeping pills, thankfully, were not the strongest.' Sneha rubbed her left shoulder. It felt excruciatingly tight.

'Should we take him to the hospital?' Nikhil spoke, noting how tired she looked. Fragile! That word he thought best suited Sneha even when she was being feisty and fierce.

Sneha shook her head. 'The doctor is saying that it is a minimal-risk procedure. The doc's been with the Sarins for a while.' She tucked her feet under her and shifted back to a more comfortable position.

'I have a few emails to reply to,' Nikhil spoke, watching Sneha's every movement with a fascination he did not understand.

'Are you leaving?' Sneha asked, her hazel eyes shooting wide open. 'I mean if you have to go. I mean...we all are here,' she finished lamely, smoothing a crease in her trousers.

'I'm not going anywhere,' Nikhil replied in an even tone, not revealing how much Sneha's brief dismay at his leaving pleased him.

Sneha raised her eyes to him and primly folded her hands in her lap. *Thank you!*

Welcome. Nikhil smiled slightly and went back to reading his emails on the tablet. Sneha watched him. With the eye of an artist, she studied the contrasts in contours and colours. Nikhil's thick raven hair held scant grey at his temples. The hair in front of his head had a tendency to fall onto his wide forehead that showed no frown lines, unlike hers. His eyes she knew by memory. In the sun, they shone lighter and became darker when he had his knickers in a twist. Sneha grinned at the thought. His nose was an easy prop for him to look down upon whoever disagreed with him. *I probably have the monopoly on that look,* Sneha thought ruefully.

As if he knew Sneha was at the end of her visual study, Nikhil glanced up. He looked at her discerningly and Sneha felt like a deer frozen in the glare of oncoming lights. She couldn't look away and she forced her mouth to say something, anything.

'What went down in that room tonight? Why was Gayatri crying when we came in?'

'Gayatri texted me some time ago, asking about Aditya. Some time tomorrow, she wants to come in person and apologize to

Nandini and Aditya. She'll try and explain everything,' Nikhil spoke evenly.

'Oh!' Sneha's single word response was terse.

Nikhil picked up on what she left unsaid.

'Excuse me!' Sneha stood up huffily.

Nikhil too stood up. 'Sit!'

Sneha glared at him. He added, 'Please.'

They remained standing for a few seconds staring at each other. Finally, Sneha sat down, her feet on the floor. Nikhil took a seat. 'It's not like I'm not telling you. It's just that I'm not good at explaining why I do things so it is even harder for me to explain someone else's point of view. And I don't like conjecture.'

Sneha said nothing to Nikhil but leaned forward over her knees, scowling at the floor and kept her chin lowered mulishly. Nikhil continued, 'I can tell you the events as they were told to me. I can tell you the what but don't ask me the why.'

Sneha still did not look up at him, her scowl stayed fixed on the floor. Looking at Sneha's bent head, Nikhil shook his own. He began, 'Mona purposely befriended Nandini. It seems she was able to drive a wedge between you and Nandini and brainwash your friend.' Nikhil's tone was flat, emotionless. He could be reading the instructions off a manual.

'Hitch!' Sneha raised her face.

Nikhil continued, 'Aditya and Nandini had quite a loud argument at Mona's farmhuse and of course, Gayatri was there. Today was Mona and Gayatri's final act. Mona ambushed Aditya after a scheduled press meet at that hotel. She gave him a spiked drink and once he was nearly incoherent, Gayatri joined them. Mona was to click pictures of Aditya and Gayatri in compromising positions. However, their plan backfired when Aditya passed out and became unresponsive thus scaring the daylights out of them.'

'Ohh, poor things,' Sneha mocked. 'So no pictures were taken?'

'One or two, similar to those sent to Nandini earlier. I checked both their phones and deleted all the images from their phones and emails.'

'Thank you,' Sneha said seriously. She was glad Nikhil, unlike her, had thought beyond getting Aditya out of there. 'So if the pictures had been taken, what would they do next?'

'Mona would send them to Nandini and then—'

'And then Nandini and Aditya would break up and Gayatri would offer her shoulder to her heartbroken ex-fiancé.'

Nikhil gave Sneha a humourless smile. 'Knowing Gayatri, she would simply walk away from the whole mess.'

Sneha was stumped, 'Then why go to all this trouble? Break a marriage?'

'Gayatri's ego is nearly big enough to be another person. And Aditya cut her deep when he dumped her for a small town simpleton.'

'Hey!' Sneha protested hotly.

'Just telling you as Gayatri sees it.'

'And you knew all this and did not stop it? Being an accessory to a crime is punishable by law,' Sneha could not help but accuse him.

Nikhil looked at her over his nose (Told you Sneha got an unhealthy dose of those from him!), 'I did not know about the plans those two were hatching. When Gayatri flew in with me to India all she said was that she wanted to talk to Aditya once and for all and close this chapter of her life. She needed to move on and I saw no wrong in that.'

Sneha felt some relief. 'Oh!'

'I wouldn't be a part of such nonsense. What? Were you thinking that I was?' Nikhil looked genuinely surprised.

15

Me or Nikhil?

'Complete the story please.' Sneha did not want him distracted.

'It is not a story,' Nikhil gave her his customary lofty look over his nose. Sneha gave him a sudden impish smile. Now Nikhil was actually distracted. He forced himself to look away from her cheeky smile even though his eyes wanted to linger...badly. 'Anyhow I got a sense of some deviousness on Gayatri's part when I observed her with Aditya at the party. The one Nandini had at her place.'

'The couples-only party,' Sneha added dryly.

'Couples only?' Nikhil's frown was one of confusion. 'No, it was Mona's party, one that she moved to Nandini's place at the last minute. Apparently, the plumbing at her place had gone for a toss.'

'Hit!' Sneha sat back stumped. Shrinks do mess with your head. 'Hit?'

Sneha waved a dismissive hand in the air. 'Do continue.'

Nikhil watched her steadily. *The magic word?*

Sneha gritted her teeth. 'Please.'

'Anyhow as I told you, because of work, I could not accompany Gayatri on that weekend to Lonavala, I assumed that you would be there. But when I heard of Aditya and Nandini's argument from someone other than Gayatri, that was when I shot you that email to confirm if you were there or not.'

'So you had no idea about today.'

'None. I was as much fooled by the two as were you all. However, I think Mona is more to be blamed than Gayatri.'

'Oh c'mon, don't give me that MS,' Sneha rolled her eyes.

'MS? Master of Science or Manuscript?'

'Bullshit!' Sneha clarified.

'That's BS.'

'Of course I know,' Sneha started getting all heated up before she saw the fleeting grin on Nikhil's face. 'Very funny.'

'Thanks.' Nikhil duly noted her expression. 'As I was saying, Mona is very good at manipulating people. Throughout their friendship, whatever stunts they both got caught for, Gayatri was always the one who took the blame or credit because of her silly ego but eventually she would always tell me how Mona had planned the whole thing.'

'Please,' Sneha disagreed.

'You don't have to believe me,' Nikhil added evenly.

Sneha sat back.

'What are you thinking?' Nikhil asked, his eyes straying back to his digital tablet.

'Nothing!' Sneha lied and put her head on the sofa. How had things spiralled so out of control and so soon? Nandini might be gullible but Adi was smart. He saw through these things, through people. And if he said something, Nandini would listen. Unless Adi was distracted. And the only thing that could distract him away from Nandini was Nandini herself. So had Adi and Nandini been fighting for a while? Not communicating? Sneha felt that if she closed her eyes she could concentrate better. Thus, she did just that.

After five minutes or so when Nikhil glanced up from the tablet, he saw Sneha had fallen asleep. She was curled up in a tight foetal position on the sofa. He saw her rub her arms in sleep. Acting on instinct, he got up soundlessly and draped his jacket over her gently, not wanting to disturb her. Sitting back down in his place, he went back to replying to his emails. He fought his urges.

Wanting to distract himself, Nikhil opened the latest stock market numbers. The urge only got stronger. He drummed his fingers on his knee, forcing himself to read the article as slowly as he could. The moment he went to the next word, he immediately forgot the one before. He could not concentrate. Nikhil kept his eyes glued on the screen in front of him. And then Sneha made a soft sound in her sleep, Nikhil looked up and then he did not look down. His urges won.

In her sleep, Sneha's expression wasn't guarded, angry, or pensive but simply peaceful and content. She nuzzled her face into his jacket and inexplicably, Nikhil was aroused by that tiny movement. What would he not give to replace the jacket with his chest and arms? He ran his eyes over Sneha's pointed chin, the chin she always raised at him just like a flag of a country proclaiming its unequivocal sovereignty.

The first time he had met Sneha was when she was twenty-one or maybe younger and that time, too, she had been 'all mouth and chin'. A rare, indulgent smile played on Nikhil's face. He ran his eyes over Sneha's mouth, her lower lip that had a natural pout. Even though her lips were not too wide, they were full and pink. Nikhil's eyes became a deeper green as they stayed on her lips. His own lips unconsciously parted. Hastily he shifted in his seat, only to see that her cheeks were slightly flushed in her sleep. Her thick lashes rested on the only things he did not like on her face—dark circles. Circles that spoke of long hours. Her hair was open and the soft curls at the end framed her face and brushed against its side. Nikhil could not stop himself from glancing enviously at his jacket that rose and fell evenly over her breasts. What would it be like to lie down next to her, her body soft and pliant against him? Stroke her face, taste her soft full mouth, explore her body like it was something that belonged to him. Damn! Nikhil's hand tightened in a fist over his knee and his eyes shone with hunger and yearning. Suddenly the room was starting to feel over warm. Taking a deep breath and loosening the collar of his shirt, Nikhil glanced away and his eyes clashed with Nandini's. She stood quietly at the edge of the living room.

Nikhil instantly got to his feet, wondering how much she had seen. Now not only did the room feel warm but it also seemed inordinately small. 'How's Aditya?' His voice sounded strangled to him.

Nandini came in. She seemed worn out. She sank onto an ottoman. 'He's better now. The pills were mild and he had anyway puked most of it out. They did not have much to pump. He woke up briefly, spoke a bit and then went back to sleep. I even fed him some clear soup.'

Nikhil sat down. 'I'm glad to hear that. Is the doctor going to stay?'

'He is,' Nandini yawned.

'You too should get some sleep,' Nikhil suggested, picking up his tablet.

'I will. Thank you for all your help,' Nandini said, looking up at him.

Nikhil stopped to look down into Nandini's earnest face and only saw genuine gratitude. He felt small. 'It's the least I could do. I'm somewhat responsible for all this,' Nikhil said quietly. And then went on to give her a succinct explanation of what had unfolded tonight.

At the end of his explanation, Nandini stayed mum for a few minutes. She finally blurted, 'I'm such an idiot.'

'You're trusting,' Nikhil replied.

Nandini gave him a small smile. Nikhil responded with a crooked one of his own. *He's got a great smile,* she thought.

'I'm just glad Sneha came to me when she did.'

'So you and Sneha know each other right? From before?'

Nandini saw how quickly he went from a concerned listener to a polite stranger. 'I should be going.'

'Sure,' Nandini stood up. Nikhil remembered his jacket. He glanced at Sneha. His jacket was still on her.

'I'll wake her up.' Nandini moved towards Sneha.

Nikhil stopped her. 'That's fine, let her sleep.'

'I was anyways going to wake her up. Sneh never stays away

from Advey in the night. She would want to go back now that Aditya is better.'

'But she might be too groggy to drive,' Nikhil reminded her.

'I'll have the driver drop her.'

Nikhil thought for a moment. 'I'll drop her.' His tone was firm. It was not a suggestion.

Nandini agreed. 'That's even better.'

'Can you tell me where the restroom is?'

Nandini pressed a bell on the intercom and a staff member instantly appeared. 'Bansiji will take you.'

Nikhil went with the staff member.

Nandini looked at a sleeping Sneha. 'Why was he staring at you like that? Hmm!' Nandini murmured. *Could a dark cloud hide a shiny glint*, she wondered.

'Sneh...Sneha.' She gently shook Sneha's shoulder.

Sneha opened her eyes and sat up with a jerk, eyes wide and very alert for someone who's been sleeping.

'Whoa!' Nandini jumped. 'You still wake up like that, freako?'

Sneha gave her wry look as she pulled the jacket off her. 'Whose is this?'

'Nikhil's I'm guessing.'

Sneha hastily put it down as if it burned her. 'How's Adi?'

'Recovering just fine. He's sleeping it off.'

'Did the doctor have to pump quite a bit?' Sneha wearily got to her feet.

'Thank God, no. He had thrown up most of it.' Nandini wrinkled her nose. 'Am I smelling puke off you?'

Sneha pointed to her knee, 'Your swami's peace offering.'

'Piece by piece offering,' Nandini smiled impudently.

'Eyuuck.' Whatever else Sneha was about to say was lost as Nandini enveloped her in a tight embrace.

'Forgive me, Sneh. I screwed up big time.'

Sneha winced. 'Okay chipku chameli.' She pulled herself out of the embrace. 'What the flock are you apologizing for kulta?

It's not your fault. If I had talked to you instead of the 'giving-you-space' bit, maybe tonight would not have happened. After all that you've done for me...I'm sorry Nandi,' Sneha held on to her best friend's hand.

Nandini rubbed her eyes with her forearms. Sneha ruffled her hair. 'I haven't done anything for you that you wouldn't have for me,' Nandini smiled even though her voice was thick.

With a final squeeze, Sneha let go off her hands. 'I definitely would not have made you a poster child for blind dates with one suthiya after another till there were way more than three,' Sneha said briefly, baring her teeth at Nandini.

'Oh no worries, I don't think I will need to do that now.' Nandini's smile was eerie.

'Excuse me?'

'Why don't you stay over tonight?' Nandini changed the topic as she caught Nikhil on his way back to the living room.

'No ya, if Adi is getting better and if you'll be okay on your own then I'll head back. I don't like to leave Advey alone. I'll be back tomorrow.'

'Great. But I'm dropping you,' Nandini said. Sneha opened her mouth to disagree but Nandini would not let her speak, 'No, don't be silly. I'm not letting you go with the driver at this time of the night.'

'Setha—'

'No! And that's final.' Nandini crossed her arms over her chest.

'Are you mad? You need to be here with Adi and you must be exhausted!' Sneha finally got a chance to talk.

Nikhil came and stopped next to them. That very second, Nandini loftily announced, 'Fine, then Nikhil shall drop you off.' Nandini ignored Sneha's protesting face and Nikhil's perplexed one. *What had just happened here?* he wondered.

'Sethani, listen to me—'

Nandini crossed her arms over her chest, her expression unyielding.

Sneha tried to sound reasonable, 'Nandini, listen—'

'Me or Nikhil?'

'Nandini!'

'Me or Nikhil?' This time Nandini even faked a yawn.

'Fine, Nikhil!' Sneha snapped, irked.

'Good choice.' Nandini innocent words earned her a glare from Sneha and a bemused expression from Nikhil.

Nikhil picked up his jacket and shrugged into it. Sneha looked away from him getting into his jacket. His shoulders slid up and pulled taut, drawing attention to his tall and lithe build. And Sneha was ashamed to admit that he had her attention.

'Why don't you take a day off tomorrow?' Nandini said to Sneha.

'I just might,' said Sneha, letting loose a yawn while she grabbed her bag.

'Does Advey miss me?' Nandini had to ask Sneha, a wistful look on her face.

'He does. A lot!' Sneha felt awkward because of Nikhil's presence.

'I want you both here tomorrow,' Nandini glanced at Sneha and Nikhil. They exchanged glances. Nandini hurriedly clarified, 'No! No! When I said you both, I did not mean you and Nikhil or Nikhil and you. I meant you and Advey.' And then she gave Nikhil a coy look, 'But you are most welcome here any time.'

'Last time I was at your place, Aditya shared a new business venture he wants to further discuss with me. Our meeting was scheduled for tomorrow,' Nikhil glanced at his watch, 'Or later today. Please ask him to text me if it is still on.'

Even though Sneha's and Nandini's curiosity was piqued, neither of them probed. 'Will do. Thank you once again for all your help,' Nandini walked them to the door. Nikhil stood aside and let Sneha pass.

Sneha and Nikhil rode the elevator down in complete silence. As they were about to get into Nikhil's car, Sneha stopped. 'You know, I can drive back. I'm fine.'

'What's the address?' Nikhil asked, ignoring her suggestion.

Sneha was too fatigued to argue. She got in and so did Nikhil. Nikhil's security personnel got in the back seat. Resigned, Sneha rattled off her address and directions. Sneha's last words were accompanied by a yawn.

'I know that area. Sleep if you wish,' Nikhil said, pressing the ignition of the car, which purred under his touch.

With her eyes partially shut, Sneha watched the dashboard with interest. She heard the power of the car in the way it smoothly cruised on the streets. Nikhil saw her glancing down at the gears. He decided he would make it a point to offer her a test drive some day.

Nikhil put some instrumental music on and the idea of asking Sneha out for a cup of coffee, on the shelf.

16

Just the way I like it!

Sneha remained mum for the rest of the drive. Her thoughts jumped from Nandini to Nikhil, and then to Aditya, back to Nikhil, then to Gayatri and then again to Nikhil and finally to her bra strap, because it was biting into her shoulder. She tried rotating her shoulders around. When Nikhil glanced at her, mainly because she was tired and sleep-deprived, she blurted, 'Sorry, it's my bra strap'. After her thoughtless confession, Sneha felt everyone in the car had fallen deathly silent, even the dude playing the complicated instrumental piece.

Closing her eyes in disbelief and utter embarrassment, Sneha sank lower in her chair.

'I can imagine. It has been a long day,' Nikhil remarked so casually that they could have been discussing the news. Sneha nodded vehemently, not trusting herself with words. Nikhil gave a crooked smile to the road in front of him.

After some time Nikhil reached the last of her given directions. 'Now where?' Nikhil asked.

Sleepily, Sneha rubbed her face and then her hair. Looking tired, she rubbed her eyes, smearing her kajal. 'You can take the next right,' she said to Nikhil.

'Hmmm!' Glancing at her, Nikhil fought to keep his face straight. 'You have something around your eye.'

'Oh, okay!' Sneha promptly took her finger and rubbed the wrong eye before Nikhil could stop her.

'Better?' she asked Nikhil.

Nikhil did not trust himself enough to speak so he just made a strangled sound, which sounded more like a grunt.

'Are you okay?' Sneha asked him. Nikhil nodded vigorously. 'Take the next left and the building on the right, Sukhshanti Complex, is where I live. Right there.'

Nikhil brought the car to a halt next to the cemented entrance to the apartment building lit up by garish tubelights. 'Thank you.' Sneha pulled at the door handle to open it.

'I'll walk you up.' Nikhil opened the door on his side.

'No you don't have to!' Sneha realized she was talking to an empty driver's seat. She heard the back doors opening. *Oh my God, three men walking me up to my apartment,* Sneha cringed. She did have curious neighbours.

'No,' Nikhil stopped his security. 'I'll be back in a minute.'

Out of politeness, Sneha turned around to nod a quick goodbye to them. She felt empowered after that goodbye because, going by the way the guards jerked as she turned around, Sneha realized she was bad ass enough to scare guys with guns.

Sneha, followed by Nikhil, trudged up the stairs. Nikhil waited until Sneha went inside her apartment. Sneha turned around to say a 'goodbye' or 'thank you' and realized Nikhil was already on his way down. 'Rude man!' she muttered, without any ire. Tonight Nikhil had helped her quite a bit.

Sneha walked into her apartment and switched on the living room light. A sleepy Amla came out of her room, her eyes groggy.

'It's me, Amla.'

As Amla came closer, the maid gave a startled shriek. 'MADAM!'

'Whoa!' Sneha nearly covered Amla's mouth with her hand. 'Shshhhhh!'

'Mannikkanum,' Amla whispered.

'Huh? What num?' Sneha asked perplexed.

Amla whispered, 'Rrraaped?'

Sneha's eyebrows reached her hairline. 'Who?'

Amla's face was confused. 'Yooouu!' she spoke haltingly.

'Me?' Sneha was dumbstruck. 'When?' Then she came to her senses. 'God forbid NO! What are you saying?'

Amla made swirling motions with her fingers around Sneha's face.

'What's wrong with you?' Grumbling, Sneha walked over to the ornamental wall mirror hanging opposite the dinner table. She drew in a startled breath at her own reflection. 'Oh my God!' She stared at her raccoon eyes thanks to the smeared kohl, her hair was a bird's nest at the side of her face, and there was white, flaky dried spit trailing from her mouth to the chin. Hammit! Nikhil had seen her like this. The guards were scared of this and not her and yes, Nikhil had seen her like this. Hit! Hit! Hit!

'Tired, Amla, not raped,' Sneha muttered to Amla as she went into her room. 'Goodnight. Oh and tomorrow, we are going over to Nandini's. For the whole day.' Amla's smile was wide. 'But please do not wake me up before nine,' Sneha requested, going into her room. She quietly went to the bathroom and scrubbed her face clean, changed into her nightclothes and then got into bed. Moving softly, she gently hugged her reason for existence, Advey. He sighed contentedly in his sleep and burrowed his face in her shoulder. 'Love you, baby.' She planted a gentle kiss on his chubby cheek. Slightly disturbed, he moved his face away.

Smiling weakly, Sneha rolled back to her side. Her legs were aching. An unbidden image of Nikhil getting into his jacket came to her mind. His shoulders had stretched tight as he had slid his arms into the sleeves. Sneha recalled the rest of him like he was standing next to her bed. Just the thought of Nikhil standing next to her bed made Sneha's face go red in the dark. The next image her overworked mind provided was that of Nikhil shrugging his jacket off his muscled shoulders rather than getting into it and all the while his hooded eyes stayed fixed on her prone form. Sneha's body felt hot in all the wrong places. Mortified, she stuffed her face in the pillow. She whispered to the dark room, 'God, some help please!' She was desperate to lose these unsettling thoughts and the tingling sensations coursing through her right now.

Next morning, Sneha's plan to sleep until late was disturbed by Advey waking up at around 7.30 a.m. and insisting on using her body as a road for multiple cars. Sneha smiled as she lay with her eyes closed, listening to her son make car engine sounds. She recalled the driver of a dark, German car. 'Hit!' Sneha sat up and all of Advey's neatly lined cars fell off the human bridge. Amla came inside the room.

'Baba! Good morning. No, Mama sleep.'

'It's okay, Amla. I'm up. I'll take care of Advey. Can I get some coffee, please?'

'Yes, madam. What time we leave?'

'I'll call Nandini in some time and ask.'

'Mathi! Adi!' Advey squealed, briefly forgetting his automobiles.

'Yes baby, Massi and Adi!' Sneha cuddled him in her arms. The rest of the morning passed in breakfast and baths. Sneha made a quick call to Nandini. Aditya answered it.

'How are you feeling?' Sneha asked.

'What's wrong with me?' Adi queried from the other end. Sneha heard the smile in his voice.

'Should I bring my puke-stained trousers to jog your memory?'

'I owe you!' Aditya said, humbled.

'No you don't. But seriously, are you feeling better?'

'I would be a hundred per cent fine if the doctor and his minions would stop following me,' Aditya griped. Sneha snorted. 'Why aren't you here already?'

'We are just leaving. Where's Sethani?'

'She's still asleep. You'd think she's one who ingested the pills.'

Sneha chuckled and hung up. In less than an hour Sneha, Advey and Amla rode up the elevators to Nandini's place. Aditya himself opened the door and Advey nearly jumped out of Sneha's arms into his.

'Hi buddy! It is good to see you too,' Aditya held him tightly and then threw him up in air and caught him neatly as he came down. Aditya did that a few times and Advey's loud chuckles and gurgles kept the adults entertained.

'Hand him over mister!' Nandini's voice had Advey, who had just landed on Mother Earth, hurtle to grab her legs. 'Mathi!'

'Oh, I missed you kiddo.' Nandini picked up Advey, hugged him close and then went on to twirl him around holding his chubby, soft arms. Advey's chuckles got louder. Sneha sighed. One only missed the boringness of normal life when anomalies replaced it.

Aditya enveloped Sneha in a bear hug, 'You are the man, Sneha Gupta.'

'Ya! Ya!' Sneha muttered smothered in his T-shirt. 'I can't breathe.' Aditya let her go and ruffled her hair affectionately. Sneha swatted his hand away, giving him a fond smile, 'You can thank me with food.' She moved toward Nandini.

'What's up kulta?' Sneha and Nandini bumped their fists.

'Such wannabe biker chicks,' Aditya teased and tackled Advey from behind, raising him in the air. 'I know you are going for the fishes.' He ran with a squealing Advey all the way to the aquarium.

'Careful!' Sneha called out. 'So how are Adi and you really doing?' she asked Nandini as they headed for the living room couch.

'Adi's better as you can see! We haven't had a chance to really talk about it yet. Just feeling very blah!' Nandini replied.

'It'll be okay, Sethani.' Sneha's smile was sympathetic. 'Talk it out. Don't internalize.'

'Like you do!' Nandini taunted.

'I do not!' Sneha acted offended.

Aditya joined them. Sitting down comfortably, he hooked his hands behind his head and came straight to the point, 'Nandini and I have been arguing quite a bit lately.'

Sneha glanced at Nandini who seemed surprised with Aditya's sudden admission. 'Maybe I shouldn't butt-in,' Sneha added diplomatically.

Aditya sauntered up and sat next to Nandini, taking her hands in his. 'I know you haven't said a word to anyone about this. But

I think we need to talk in front of someone we both trust.'

Nandini rubbed her forehead and slowly withdrew her hands from Aditya's. Then she jumped off the sofa and paced back and forth in front of them. Her restlessness was obvious.

'Talk, sweetheart, unload. I won't take offence,' Aditya sat back with a peaceful look on his face. Last night had brought a lot of things to the fore, things that he had no wish to ignore any more.

Sneha waited patiently. Nandini addressed Aditya first. 'I love you to death Adi, but you really are smothering me.' Aditya leaned forward and opened his mouth but Sneha put a hand on his knee.

'Hear her out,' she said gently.

'Sorry. And I love you too.' Adi's smile was encouraging.

'We live together, we eat together, we sleep together but we don't have to work together. I don't like working for you or with you because I want to do something on my own,' said Nandini, her words spilling out in a rush.

'Why?' Aditya asked, befuddled.

Nandini took a pause to find the words befitting her thoughts. 'I want to spend my life with you but not lose my identity. I have my own ambitions. I was never the kitty party wife. I can't stay on the shelf, I probably need to run the store, so as to speak. After our marriage, it's like I've stopped being a person of my own. I live in your house, I drive your cars, I use credit cards given by you; you even sign my paychecks! Its like there is no Nandini Sharma and Aditya Sarin in this marriage, it's Aditya Sarin and Aditya Sarin. I can't be happy like this. I'm NOT happy like this. I feel that if this goes on, I will begin to…begin to…resent you…big time!' Nandini became quiet, her expression sad, eyes damp.

Sneha noticed the stunned expression on Aditya's face. Then he gazed down at his hands linked between his knees. He appeared hurt.

'Nandini, do you love Aditya?' Sneha interjected.

'You know I do!' Nandini answered.

Sneha turned to Aditya. Even before she could ask, Aditya replied, 'I love her. Completely.'

'Okay then!' Sneha turned to look at Nandini, 'You know Adi. He will never hurt you knowingly. So, for five minutes, think about his motive behind wanting you both to do everything together.'

Then Sneha turned to Aditya, 'And you have five minutes to think about why she is feeling this way.'

Sneha watched her friends struggling quietly for a few minutes and then Nandini raised her hand. 'I think I know why!'

Sneha nodded.

'Because Adi's super-protective. He wants to do everything for me. He doesn't ever want me to go through anything on my own. And also because he's possessive.'

Sneha turned to Adi, 'Is she right or wrong?'

Adi, keeping his eyes on Nandini, grunted. It was not a denial.

'And why is Nandini feeling the way she is. Any idea, Adi?'

'Sheesh! I really have to do this?' Aditya gave them an awkward glance. 'After last night, I don't think I'm a hundred per cent okay yet.'

'See, I knew it. Adi would never talk it out,' Nandini huffily sat on the chair furthest from them.

With a resigned expression, Adi got up and took the chair next to Nandini. He did not touch her but he gazed at Nandini with all that he felt for her, 'Because I took Nandini for granted. Because I somewhere overlooked the fact that the love of my life is another person with her own ideas about how she wants live her life. I promise, sweetheart, the intention was never to clip your wings. All I wanted was to always keep you close. When you're around...that's my...my...utopia. You are simply my every thing.' Adi cocked his head to a side and gave Nandini a heart-melting smile.

'Adi!' Nandini flew straight into his arms already open to take her in. 'I'm sorry. I never wanted hurt you, which is why I kept all this to myself.'

Aditya held her close to his chest. 'It's okay, Nandi. I did overdo the death-do-us-part a bit. And sorry about last night. I was ambushed. Nothing happened,' he clarified, shifting Nandini a little more comfortably on his lap. 'And can we please have this kind of girly talk only once in every ten years and for never more than a few minutes?' Aditya added, with a pained expression. Nandini poked him in the ribs.

'I'm proud of you children,' Sneha said, smiling generously. Suddenly Advey clambered onto the sofa and within seconds, he was climbing onto Nandini's lap as she sat on Aditya's.

'Oh, so cute!' Nandini gushed, holding Advey.

'Stop shifting in my lap. That is cute but not in a PG-13 way,' Aditya groaned even as he held on to Advey from the side.

Sneha covered her mouth to stifle her laugh, 'Get a room, perverts. And spare my child. I don't want to pay for his college and lifelong therapy.' Sneha pulled a protesting Advey out of Nandini's arms. 'Seriously, I can spare you both for some time. I have a new book in my bag.'

'Okay,' Aditya got up taking Nandini along with him.

Nandini caught a corner of the sofa. 'No Adi, no way. We have guests.'

Aditya pulled Nandini's hand away from the sofa. 'Don't you dare call Sneha a guest. Come along Millennium Behenji.'

As expected, Nandini turned on him and pounded his arm, 'Oh no, you didn't. We'll be right back. Mathi is coming back Advey.' She grabbed Aditya's arm and led him away. Aditya turned around and winked at Sneha.

'Tell the staff to look after Advey and Sneha,' Aditya told Nandini as they entered their bedroom, thankfully free of any doctor or his paraphernalia. It still held a medicinal smell though.

Nandini punched the number on the intercom. As she finished mouthing off instructions, Aditya's muscled arm caught her at the waist, trying to pull her down on the bed. 'What's got you so hot, wifey?' his fingers slowly made their way up from her waist.

'Wifey? What about Millennium Behenji?' Nandini asked, trying to pull Adi's fingers away even as his touch made her skin tingle.

'She's turned out way smarter than I assumed.' Aditya nuzzled his nose in Nandini's nape. His tongue hotly traced the skin under her ear.

'What makes you say that?' Nandini shivered, arching in his arms, fighting the urge to turn around and wrap her arms around his neck. Abruptly Aditya moved away and Nandini fell back on the bed. He immediately pinned her down with his body.

'She married me, that's why.' Aditya gave Nandini a wolfish smile as his head swooped down, his lips clamped tightly over Nandini's chagrined mouth. Nandini did not back away but teased Adi, tracing his lips with the tip of her tongue. Aditya groaned into her mouth and he ground his body against hers, his hands stroking her breasts.

Nandini hastily pulled at the buttons of his T-shirt. In one fluid motion, Aditya got up and took off his T-shirt and Nandini's blouse. Nandini wrapped her legs around Aditya to move better under him. Kissing and tasting every silken inch of her, Aditya eased her out of her jeans. His movements were jerky, his breathing uneven and colour rode high on his cheekbones as he watched Nandini move restlessly to get closer to him. Just the thought turned him rock hard. He took in her creamy shoulders, bare under the thin straps, dark black hair that framed her petite face.

'God, I love you woman,' Aditya said, pressing his face into her cleavage. His hands moulded and kneaded her sensitive breasts. His words were muffled against her skin over which his open mouth moved with rapid heat. 'Make-up sex isn't overrated,' he groaned against her flushed skin.

Nandini moaned and thrust her hands in Aditya's thick black hair, holding him close as his hot tongue lapped her skin. 'Prove it!' Her voice was thick and her fingers dug into his hair. Nandini threw her head back and arched under him as an invitation. Aditya fell on her, hungry, gentle, urgent but thorough. 'Mmmm just the way I like it,' were Nandini's last coherent words.

17

Blow your horn!

While Nandini and Aditya were in a world of their own, Sneha was reclining on the couch where her friends had left her with a new, engrossing Nishant Kaushik book in her hand. Just then, the doorbell chimed. Sneha straightened herself and motioned at Amla to quieten Advey who was playing near her with his toys.

The staff member ushered in a tall, lean man. Sneha had never seen him before. He wore a simple checked cotton shirt crumpled at its ends and hanging loose over faded and overly washed jeans. On his feet, he wore black sneakers and in his hand, he carried a white plastic bag with big bold red letters written over it. The man took a seat opposite to Sneha without even glancing at her.

Sneha covertly studied his thin face, straight and narrow nose, arched eyebrows, dark hair that fell just below the collar of his shirt in a rakish style. He had high cheekbones and a long nose on which sat a pair of golden-framed round glasses. The man, with his unkempt look in their present surroundings, looked like a round peg in a square hole. Sneha watched him study Advey, who was focused on stuffing things under a plastic ramp so he could make his truck jump higher and crash more loudly.

Suddenly the man went to his knees near Advey. His shoulders almost collided with Sneha's feet. With a start she shifted away.

'If you want more speed then you have to increase the angle of the ramp to make it steeper. Here, you can try putting smaller but thicker objects.' The man proceeded to deftly sort Advey's toys scattered around him and chose the ones that fit his purpose.

Advey, with two fingers in his mouth, watched the man with rapt attention rather than focusing on what he was doing.

'There, done.' The man gave Advey a brief glance. 'This increased distance at that angle from the ground will not only give you more speed but make more noise when the trucks crash. Sound is essentially a pressure disturbance that travels via the means of particle to particle disturbance. The greater the disturbance and lesser the distance, the greater will be the sound you hear.' By now, Sneha saw, Advey nearly had his entire hand stuck in his mouth and there was spittle coming out on one side and his eyes were big in his small face. She bit back her smile.

Holding up a truck in his hand, the man continued unhindered, 'Also, the speed at which you hear a sound wave depends on the quality of medium it is passing through, like the quality of air temperature—'

'He's just a little over three. I don't think he can understand all that,' Sneha interrupted. The stranger glanced at her and then at Advey. Awkwardness shone on his face. Wordlessly, he went back to his earlier perch, the plastic bag in tow. Advey, after giving him a beatific smile, went back to his game. This time, thanks to the extended ramp placed at a higher angle his trucks made more noise as they hit the floor. Advey clapped his hands and looked at the stranger, 'Crashhh!'

The stranger's smile lit up his thin, intelligent face. 'I'm from Kanpur too,' Sneha said, pointing at the 'Tewari Sweets Kanpur' bag he held in his hand.

'Is it only people from Kanpur who buy sweets from Tewari Sweets? I could be visiting the town. And if I was not from Kanpur would you not talk to me?' The stranger asked his questions in a tone free of rancour, with honest curiosity on his face.

For a second, Sneha felt her jaw drop. She quickly closed her lips in a thin line, 'Well not—'

'Sorry to keep you waiting, Viraj,' Aditya's voice interrupted them. Nandini followed him. Sneha noticed they had changed their clothes. Sneha pointedly cleared her throat as she glanced at her watch. 'Forty-five minutes, not bad!' Nandini blushed and glared at her. Aditya passed her with a broad smile. He guided the stranger, whose name Sneha had just learned was Viraj, into his study located at one end of the apartment.

'Who the heck was that?' Sneha whispered to Nandini.

'Why, what happened?' Nandini asked, stopping next to her.

'He was trying to teach quantum physics to my three-year-old,' Sneha replied, her face sarcastic.

Nandini's gave a startled laugh. 'Really?' She made a face. 'I haven't been officially introduced to Viraj yet.'

'He works for Adi?' Sneha asked.

'He used to work for Adi's dad. He is the brilliant scientist whose idea would have been Papa's next big thing,' Nandini replied with a sigh.

'So essentially he is the guy who drove your late father-in-law to near bankruptcy.'

Nandini opened her mouth to protest and then she said as an afterthought, 'Yup that's him!' And before the conversation could go any further, Nandini nosedived off the sofa onto Advey and for a few minutes they tackled each other on the floor. Soon Sneha, Nandini and Amla had Advey enthralled in a game of hide and seek, where Advey, essentially trailed by an adult, located the others. Hiding wasn't really his thing.

As Sneha was trailing Advey, who was trying to find Nandini, the doorbell chimed. Nandini jumped out from behind the couch. 'Can you get it?' she asked Sneha.

'Sure.' Balancing Advey on her hip, Sneha swung the door open.

'Oh, hi!' Sneha said to the newcomer, feeling dazed.

Advey jumped out of her flimsy grip exclaiming, 'Nik!'

Nikhil caught him easily. 'Hi kiddo!' He lifted him in his arms and tossed him in the air. Sneha, alarmed, put out a hand.

Nikhil caught him deftly. 'Don't worry I won't let him fall,' he reassured her, smiling. 'More! More!' Advey bounced up and down in his arms.

Nikhil glanced at Sneha. *Shall I?*

Sure. Sneha nodded. *Just be careful!*

'*Of course!* Hi, Nandini!' Nikhil replied, as he obliged Advey first.

As soon as they entered the apartment, Advey squirmed to be set down. Nikhil put him down carefully and observed him as he slid down the stairs on his bum.

'That must leave burn marks!' Nikhil said to Sneha, his expression amused.

'Diapers do more than advertised,' Sneha replied, not completely at ease around Nikhil.

'Is it good for him to be in diapers the whole day?'

Sneha frowned, 'That's old school. Anyway, he's not in diapers the whole day. Only when we go out somewhere. The new diapers are—' Sneha turned her words into a cough as she became conscious of Nandini watching Nikhil and her with avid interest. Nikhil, too, seemed to remember his host.

He immediately turned to Nandini, 'So how's Aditya?'

'He's much better now!'

Nikhil glanced at Sneha who frowned slightly at him. *Ask her!*

He instantly turned to Nandini. 'Sorry! How are you holding up?'

Nandini replied with a broad grin, 'Much better, thank you!'

'I am here for the meeting with Aditya,' Nikhil said, coming to the point.

'Sure you are.' Those saucy words earned Nandini her first over-the-nose haughty look from Nikhil. She quickly added, 'Let me take you to the study. What can I send for you?'

'Coffee would be good. Black, please,' replied Nikhil, trailing her.

'Nik! Truck.' Advey's call made him stop.

Nikhil stopped and turned around, his expression wry. 'Sorry kiddo, but I have to go in there!' Nikhil said to Advey, pointing at the corridor Nandini was leading him into. Advey pouted and looked downcast. 'Excuse me!' Nikhil said to Nandini. In a few steps, he was next to Advey. He picked him up easily and along with his red and blue truck. 'Just like your mom. Prone to pouting.'

'Excuse me!' Sneha replied, frowning.

'See? Look at her right now, she's doing just that,' Nikhil teased with gleaming eyes and a surprisingly natural smile as he stopped right in front of Sneha.

'Only if you could carry her along so easily and simply take her with you,' Nandini added with an expression befitting a monk.

Sneha scowled at her. Nikhil ignored Nandini but his smile definitely disappeared. 'Is it okay if he is with me in there for a bit?' he asked Sneha.

'He won't let you guys work.'

'Don't worry about it. I downloaded a kids' game on my phone. I think Advey will like it.'

'Which one?' Sneha asked suspiciously.

'Fruit Ninja. Don't worry, it's age appropriate,' Nikhil assured her, taking along Advey who happily went with him.

Sneha's couldn't help the tremulous smile she gave Nikhil's back as Advey looked at him with such adulation. She promptly altered the smile to an evil eye as she caught Nandini looking at her. 'What, kulta?'

'Nothing,' Nandini shrugged her shoulders, 'nothing at all.' She rubbed her stomach, 'I'm hungry!'

'I can imagine. You just worked out or were you worked on?' Sneha winked at her.

'A little bit of both cheapo,' Nandini poked her tongue out at her friend. Sneha followed Nandini into the kitchen where her two chefs worked. 'Today you can make all of ours and your favourites,' she said to the chefs.

'So you guys actually don't have a feast at every meal?' asked Sneha, alluding to the Sarin tradition of having quite a few dishes at every meal, regardless of the number of people at the table.

'Found it a little wasteful. I just get the chefs here to cook to their heart's content once every week and we take that food to the nearby orphanage.'

'Very nice, Sethani.' They walked over to a guest bedroom. Sneha was in the mood to laze.

'Please!' Nandini waved a hand in front of her, 'What is commendable is what you do. Putting aside ten paisa for every rupee you spend. At the end of the year it must be accumulating to a decent amount.'

'There are always needy people, people less fortunate than us.' Sneha lay on her stomach. 'Listen, Sethani, I'm going to take a short nap.'

'Are you mad? We got together after such a long time. And you are going to sleep?' Nandini protested.

'I was up late last night, in case you forgot. Plus your nephew had me up really early today morning,' Sneha complained, stretching.

'Okay fine, old maid. Sleep as long as you want. Once Advey is done with the men, he and I are going to have a blast,' Nandini said to Sneha who was already tucking herself under the duvet.

'Be good!' Sneha said, her eyes closing the moment her head touched the pillow. After much time, Sneha felt something soft against her hand. It was Nandini holding a sleeping Advey. 'He fell asleep while we were playing after lunch.'

'What time is it?' Sneha asked, still groggy.

'Close to 3 o'clock. You must be hungry.' Nandini lifted the duvet away from Sneha and slid Advey gently under it.

'You have eaten, right?' Sneha asked, placing cushions on Advey's side.

'Nope, we snacked a bit. But I made Amla have her lunch.'

'Then can you send her in? I'll freshen up and come.' Sneha got up and then as a thought struck her she asked, 'Has the freako gone?'

Nandini nodded. 'It's just us.'

'Cool!' Sneha stretched. 'What did you and Advey do?'

'We had so much fun. We did some finger painting, read stories and watched Pokémon together. And yeah, we ate big bowls of ice cream, after his lunch of course.'

'Advey must be thrilled. He really missed you and Adi,' Sneha smiled sleepily.

Just as Nandini covered Advey with the duvet, she remarked, 'Advey has taken quite a fancy to Nikhil.'

'That man is good with kids I guess.' Sneha ignored how her insides did an irrational flip at his name. Obviously, her brains were still snoozing. 'I'm going to wash the sleep out of my sockets.'

While washing her face, Sneha saw her reflection and she remembered her raccoon eyes and the bird's nest hair from last night. Then she remembered who saw her like that. Sneha immediately splashed some water on her face.

'Do you need something?' Sneha asked Amla after coming out of the restroom. Amla already had the TV on low volume. She did the famous Indian nod that could mean a yes or a no. Sneha took that as a no; her help was very vocal about the tiniest indignation she might suffer.

'I'll be outside if you need me.' Sneha could have been talking to deaf ears. Nothing came between Amla and her soaps, except Advey. Atleast, so Sneha hoped. As she walked toward the dining room with its gold and beige wallpaper and tiered chandelier, she heard some muted conversation. Sneha stumbled when she saw Nikhil sitting across from Nandini and Aditya. She had assumed Nikhil too had left. A fourth place had been set for her right next to him.

Nikhil gave her an impassive look. *Shocked?*

Sneha waved her hand vaguely in the air. 'Noo. Pfft!' She made a funny sound with her tongue. Nikhil hid his sudden smile by dabbing his mouth with a freshly starched napkin.

Aditya looked at them confused, wondering what she was talking about. And then he glanced at his lovely wife. Her eerie, all-too-wide smile, which sometimes frankly scared the socks off him, was back. *Urggh*, Adi inwardly groaned. He just prayed he did not have even a cameo to play in whatever shenanigan Nandini was plotting.

Nikhil got to his feet and pulled out the chair next to him. Sneha sat down. 'Thanks! Hope Advey didn't bother you much.'

'No, he was fine,' Nikhil replied.

'Great!' Sneha replied. 'Enough, Ku—Nandini,' Sneha put her hand over the curry and chicken pieces Nandini was heaping in her bowl.

'You're good with children,' Aditya said to Nikhil as he handed his bowl to Nandini, who ladled a generous serving of a yoghurt mint dip. Nandini gave Aditya an extremely pleased smile as if he had just fished out a giant pearl from the bottom of the ocean for her.

'Advey is a very well-behaved child!' Nikhil replied, picking up his plate as Sneha placed a tandoori roti on his. He was amused to see three proud faces around the table.

Nandini turned to Aditya and said, 'You eat only khichdi. Your system might not be able to take the spicy stuff.'

'Nah! I'm fine,' Aditya said but under Nandini's stare, he hastily amended, 'I'll have that khichdi too.'

Sneha kept her head lowered and concentrated on her food, directing any conversation towards Nandini or Aditya. Nikhil followed the same pattern. The two did not even glance at each other.

Spoilsports, thought Nandini, eyeing the key players of her new pet project. Slyly, she pulled the fork closer to her plate and then purposely dropped it off the table. It fell down with a clang. Reflexively Aditya bending from his waist went under the table to pick it up. Nandini snagged the fork under the heel of her shoe and then, giving a quick smile to its other two occupants, she too disappeared under the table.

Nandini grabbed Adi's hand and pulled him closer. The table jerked at their end and Aditya's face was centimetres away from hers. Giving Nandini a know-it-all grin, Aditya puckering his lips, planted soft kisses on hers.

'Urghh, stop it! No!' Nandini whispered, shaking her head fiercely at her husband. From her peripheral vision, she saw Sneha move her feet restlessly. She had little time.

'No?' Aditya asked confused.

'NO! Not that,' Nandini shook her thick hair. Aditya could not stop marvelling at the way it brushed her cheeks. Nandini lightly tapped his nose with the fork but the smile she gave him was sweet. She planted a quick peck on the tip of his nose.

Before Adi could return the favour, Nandini hastily whispered, 'I'll blow your horn for two minutes if you drop food on Sneha's clothes. Something wet that will leave a stain.'

'Why? I'm okay with the blow my horn part though,' Aditya winked at her.

Nandini rolled her eyes. 'I'm sure you are.'

'But why am I supposed to drop food on her?' Aditya asked, his fingers now trailing a hot path under Nandini's collarbone.

'Focus!' Nandini swatted his hand away. 'The stains have to be big and like, all over her dress.'

At the table, Nikhil glanced at Sneha who was observing the fluttering and shuddering tablecloth across from them. She rolled her eyes. 'Loony bins are you planning to come up for air some time soon?' she asked sweetly and loudly.

'Just a second!' came Nandini's muffled voice.

Grinning broadly, Sneha reached over the bowls to slide some more silverware upon Nandini and Aditya, who still hadn't resurfaced.

Abruptly Nikhil reached out and cupped the underside of her forearm. Sneha felt his warm fingers against her skin. She swallowed at the rush of sensation. Glancing at him over her shoulder, her eyes locked with his as he watched her unwaveringly. Sneha could only stare, her mouth completely dry. Even Nikhil, who seemed to be in no hurry to remove his hand, appeared content to return her stare. Mindlessly, his fingers began taking a life of their own and rubbed the delicate skin at the underside of Sneha's forearm.

Coming to her senses, Sneha snatched her arm away. The look she gave Nikhil was bewildered. *What were you doing?*

Lowering his arm slowly and unable to glance away from her widened eyes, Nikhil spoke haltingly, 'Your elbow was about to dip into the curry.'

Sneha felt like dipping her face in next when she realized that she had her eyes fixed on Nikhil's lips, watching them move and form shapes as he spoke. Irked, Sneha hit the foot of the table nearest to her with some feeling. The entire table shuddered. Nikhil grabbed his plate and the bowl of curry that threatened to splash. 'Calm down!' he said to Sneha. That maddened her more. She was all set to kick the table again when Nandini, very much like a jack-in-the-box popped up. Aditya came up only a second later.

'What?' Glancing at Sneha, Nandini gave a breathless giggle. Adi's smile was pained.

Sitting back, Sneha crossed her arms and glared at both Nandini and Aditya, 'Where's the fork?'

'Which fork?' Nandini blurted and then realized her faux pas.

Aditya came to her rescue. 'It's dirty. She has another one.' He hastily passed Nandini his fork.

Nandini grabbed it with a flourish and a bright smile, 'Thank you Adi, my dear husband.'

'You are welcome, dear wife.' With a slightly lost expression, Aditya went back to his food.

'Would you care for some rice?' Nandini pressed Nikhil.

'Sure!' Nikhil replied.

'Let me get some more!' Nandini stood up and sailed out of the room before anyone could say another word. Just outside the kitchen, she made a quick call on her cell phone.

Adi's phone rang. He looked down and was surprised to see 'Hottie' flash on the screen. That was the nickname under which he had saved Nandini's cell number. 'Excuse me,' he said to Sneha and Nikhil. With a bewildered look, he put the phone to his ear.

Before he could utter a syllable, Nandini on the other end fired, 'Don't tell them it's me. Talk like it's a call from your office.'

'Ok…ay!' Aditya's hesitant reply had Sneha give him a sharp look and Nikhil gaze at him with mild curiosity. Aditya sat up straighter and began playing the part his madcap wife wanted him to play. 'Yes Ranga Rao, carry on!' he said, his manner brisk.

Aditya heard titters on the other end. He pursed his lips, irritated. 'Ranga Rao? What kind of a name is that? You know what it rhymes with?'

'Is that what you are calling to tell me? Well then we can talk about this on Monday at work, Ranga Rao!' Aditya kept his manner short.

Nandini immediately sobered. 'Sorry, sorry. Listen, please make some excuse and meet me outside.'

'Outside? Where are you?'

'Ssh! Outside the kitchen.' Nandini hung up.

Aditya continued the call on his end, 'Fine, I'll resend you the email but next time save a copy.' Hanging up, he turned to Sneha and Nikhil.

Nikhil cut him off before he could speak, 'Please go ahead and take care of that.'

Sneha too gave a hesitant nod. Aditya left the room. Sneha and Nikhil consciously chose to give the food in front of them their entire attention. Sneha decided that today was the day she would do everything the dentist advised. Today she would chew every bite thirty-two times. Nikhil on his part unconsciously rubbed the fingers of his left hand against his thumb trying to forget the feel of Sneha's silken skin. He was amazed at how aware he had become of the woman sitting next to him in just a few weeks. He found himself noticing even the smallest of her movements, a flick of her brow, a laugh line next to her eyes, a fluttering strand against her cheek.

Nikhil noticed Sneha smooth a crease on the tablecloth even

though her eyes were on the plate. She was anxious. But why? Was it because she was alone with him? And why were they alone? Where the hell were the hosts?

18

Earth to Mars!

The hosts were conspiring at the entrance to the kitchen, or at least one of them was. 'Nandini, what are you up to?' Aditya demanded of his wife.

'Why aren't you dropping food on Sneha?' Nandini immediately replied. 'I won't blow your horn,' she threatened.

Aditya shushed her, 'Keep your voice low, woman. The staff understand English.'

Nandini's face was perplexed. 'So? Praising your husband isn't really blasphemy. It is a very true blue bhartiya naari type thing to do.' Nandini made mock cow eyes at Aditya.

'Praise your husband? What are you talking about?' Aditya asked confounded.

'Praise your husband. Blow my husband's horn. Adi, keep up!' Nandini clarified impatiently.

'Praise me?' Realization and disappointment shone on Aditya's face. 'That is what you meant by blow my horn?'

Nandini nodded, confused. 'Ya! Of course. What did you think?' she asked innocently. Aditya arched a single eyebrow.

Nandini caught on. 'Oh my God!' She made a gagging noise. 'Two minutes? Oh my God. I think I'll throw up.' She made choking sounds.

Aditya coloured. 'Oh stop it Nandini.' He cleared his throat self-consciously. 'It's not that bad!' he countered defiantly.

Nandini instantly arched an eyebrow like he did at her several times, 'And you would know because...' she trailed off saucily.

Shaking his head and giving her a lopsided grin, Adi firmly grasped Nandini's arm and led her away. 'Because I'm smarter than you. Now do tell me about this grand plan that you are cooking up. '

In the dining room, Nikhil finally broke the silence that stretched between Sneha and him. 'Are they usually such attentive hosts?'

Sneha, just about to spoon a bite in her mouth, replied, 'This is normal. They can't see beyond each other.'

Nikhil's smile was wry. 'It must be strange to be like that.'

'Like what?'

'When someone becomes more important to you than yourself.'

Sneha, putting down her spoon, thought about it. 'It's just become a habit to see them like this, I guess. I mean, as a mom it is not strange for me.'

'Mother and a child, I can understand. But to care for another person like that?' Nikhil shrugged his shoulders.

'When you got married it must have been something like this. She would have been very important to you; you would always want to be around her,' Sneha voiced. She too had never known such feelings for a male other than her son.

Nikhil sat back and gave his usual brief smile. 'Are you fishing?'

'You are right. It's not really my business.' Embarrassed, Sneha went back to her food.

Nikhil opened his mouth to say something but he noticed Sneha's unyielding profile. She really did not want to know; sometimes he wasn't even sure if Sneha wanted to talk to him or be around him. It shouldn't have mattered but that thought bothered him. Nikhil to swallowed water from his glass.

'Rice!' Nandini came into the room holding a ceramic dish in her hands. 'Where's Adi?'

'I thought he was with you,' Sneha said. Nandini gave her a blank look. 'He got a call from work. He had to resend some email,' Sneha explained.

'Oh okay! Just hope he doesn't take long.' Nandini scooped

some rice off the dish and onto Nikhil's plate. 'So what were you two talking about?

'Nothing!' Nandini heard the same word in two voices.

'Ohh!' Nandini went over to her chair and sat down. She took a bite of her food and waited.

'Hope I did not keep everyone waiting.' Aditya came in, a large glass bowl in his hand.

'Ice cream in the middle of lunch?' Nandini asked him, playing out her self-scripted role.

'I was craving something sweet,' Aditya said, wondering if he looked as foolish as he felt. As he was about to go past Sneha what Nandini expected him to do happened unexpectedly. Some of the chocolate fudge fell on his fingers and trying to balance the bowl better in his hand, Aditya actually dropped the bowl right on top of Sneha's head.

'Shoot!' Aditya yelped.

'Adi!' Sneha shrieked. As she touched her head, her hand came back cold, smeared with vanilla ice cream, chocolate and nuts. Nikhil grabbed the nearest napkin and tried to get the mess off her hair. It landed smack dab on Sneha's lap and spattered her clothes and the tablecloth.

'Ewww!' Sneha's thighs danced.

'Sorry!' Nikhil and Aditya grabbed more napkins. Nandini caught Aditya's eye and glared at him and then the napkin. Aditya withdrew his hand.

Nikhil continued to wipe away the ice cream. Just as his hand collided with Sneha's crotch, Sneha gripped his hand, trying to yank it away from her. 'Thank you!' she muttered with all the composure she could muster, which wasn't much. She felt the ice cream dribble from her hair to her cheeks and chin.

Glaring at Nandini, Sneha stood up. Gritting her teeth she said, 'If I find out you have something to do with this…' Behind her, Aditya gulped.

'What are you talking about? Adi dropped it, I didn't,' Nandini retorted. Aditya gulped some more.

'Nandini!' Adi called out tentatively.

'You need to change. Do you have spare clothes?' Nandini asked as she saw Nikhil hand over some more napkins to Sneha, who took them murmuring a quiet 'thanks'.

'No! I did not get the memo that someone would be dropping ice cream on me today.'

Aditya quickly come over to Nandini's side. 'You can take something from Nandini's closet,' he suggested.

'Of course!' Nandini added. 'I'll find something in your size, Sneh,' Nandini glanced at Sneha who stood wiping the smears off her face as Nikhil pointed them out to her. 'You're a little bigger than me around the bust but...' Even though Nandini heard Sneha's growl and Aditya's startled cough, she felt some satisfaction when Nikhil's eyes reflexively dropped to Sneha's chest and then he immediately glanced away.

Cringing, Sneha shut her eyes briefly, and prayed this nightmarish experience would simply fade away. However, her nightmare called 'Nandini's rasoi' was just staging its first act, first scene. Nikhil could feel Sneha's discomfiture and he did not like it. He glanced at Nandini. His stare wasn't kind.

Nandini burst into action and immediately led Sneha away.

Nikhil and Aditya sat down. Nikhil pushed his food away, his appetite gone. 'Are meals always so eventful at your place?' he quipped.

'No, not really!' Aditya remarked, puzzled by the sheer drop of temperature in Nikhil's voice and expression. Nikhil had seemed to be in a congenial mood until now. Aditya hastily began discussing Viraj's concept, which was what he had invited Nikhil here for.

Just then in Nandini and Aditya's bedroom, Nandini was ushering a still-upset Sneha into her bathroom.

'I'm serious, if I find out that you put Aditya up to this, I will castrate you,' Sneha muttered, pulling the T-shirt over her head.

'Castrate me? What will you castrate?' Nandini asked, amused as she perched on her bed.

As Sneha carefully rolled her T-shirt so nothing would fall off it to the floor, she gave Nandini's question some thought. After a minute, she shrugged her shoulders. 'I don't know! Maybe a nipple.'

'Ewwww!' Nandini made a retching noise. 'Why is everybody around me talking such filth today?'

'Don't know about others but my mood surely has something to do with the ice cream sticking to my scalp.' Sneha went into the bathroom. 'Give me something sensible to wear,' she called out to Nandini from behind the shut door.

Pausing in front of the full-length mirror as she took off her jeans, Sneha viewed her body with the eye of an unbiased critic. To all those who think every woman has a Victoria's Secret store in her closet, it's a myth and only true for maybe Victoria's Secret models. Most women only colour co-ordinate their outerwear.

Sneha's eyes snagged on the mess that was her face and hair. *Yesterday, the raccoon eyes and today, he sees me like this.* 'Kulta, I'm going home after this,' Sneha called out just as she went inside the glass cubicle to take a quick shower

'No Sneha, you can't,' Nandini called out from the other side of the door.

'And why is that?' Sneha asked, taking out a fluffy, white bath towel from the stack of towels piled neatly atop a marble counter. 'Kulta?' Sneha called out when Nandini did not answer.

Sneha heard a tap on the door. 'I have to tell you something.' The urgency in Nandini's voice made Sneha wrap the towel around her. She opened the door. Nandini appeared nervous. She looked around her to make sure there was no one else in the room. *There better be no one else,* Sneha thought, panicking and holding the towel closer to her.

'Gayatri's coming over!'

Sneha remained quiet.

'Nikhil conveyed Gayatri's message. She wants to meet me and Aditya together.'

'And you agreed? After all that she put you guys through?' Sneha asked. She put a gentle hand on Nandini's arm.

'Adi doesn't know.' Nandini's expression was pleading.

Sneha said dryly, 'He will probably hit the roof.'

Nandini nodded. 'You'll stay, right?'

'Of course I will. But if that Mona comes, I'll kick her sorry ass all the way back to her house.'

Nandini's face was surprised. 'You are more pissed with Mona than Gayatri?'

'Because she's the mind behind this madness,' Sneha retorted, realizing just then that she had bought what Nikhil had sold. 'As in Gayatri stayed true to her character but Mona exploited you and messed with me too. Now before I freeze my tush, can I take a shower?' Sneha stepped inside the bathroom and as she was about to shut the door, Nandini put a hand to stop her.

'You still haven't told me how you and Nikhil know each other.'

Sneha made a face. 'Do you lack drama in your life?'

'So it was dramatic!' Nandini enjoyed Sneha's startled expression 'Like thunderbolt dramatic or crashing wave kind of dramatic?'

'Kick in your ass kind of dramatic.' Sneha shut the door on Nandini's grin.

'I'll leave clothes for you on the bed.'

After a quick shower Sneha, wrapping herself in the towel, tentatively opened the bathroom door. 'Anyone there?' she called out. Satisfied she was alone in the room and the door was closed, she stepped out. She quickly picked up the clothes Nandini had left for her on the bed.

'Oh God!' Sneha picked up the soft fabric and stuffed her face into it. 'I will kill you Nandini,' she murmured in the dress that slid like satin between her fingers.

In the living room, Nandini was working on her MacBook Air as Aditya and Nikhil sat at some distance, immersed in their discussion. Impatiently, Nandini kept glancing over her shoulder at the corridor outside the bedrooms. At some distance, she saw a swish of indigo blue. Instantly Nandini slunk deeper in the sofa and made sure to keep Nikhil's face in her vision just above the edge of the laptop.

Nikhil, completely obvious to Nandini's scrutiny, was crunching numbers on the initial investment required for Viraj's concept. He saw something move just beyond his line of sight. He glanced up and then halted mid-sentence. He stood up, forcing Aditya to turn around and look in that direction.

Sneha, feeling awkward to her bones, joined them. Her fingers twitched along the side of her dress. She glared at Nandini. 'It looks good on you!' Nandini remarked casually, making space on the couch next to her.

'This is all you could find?' Sneha muttered, sliding down next to her. She purposely avoided looking at the men in the room, particularly a pair of green eyes. If she had, Sneha would have seen him riveted by her damp curls, a face fresh from her shower, her petite creamy shoulders visible in the off-shoulder soft blue dress that hugged and caressed every curve of her body. Nikhil sat entranced by a drop of water than trailed from Sneha's hair onto her bare forearm.

Aditya cleared his throat, snapping him out of his stupor. Sneha took a peek from under her lashes. She saw Nikhil punch numbers on his cell. A big fat scowl sat between his brows. She saw him study the floor and then his eyes wandered to her feet. They slowly skated over her legs. Sneha reflexively flexed her toes. Nikhil's eyes slithered from her ankles to her calves and knees, all left bare by the dress. Sneha could feel his eyes on her skin like a touch. Unbearably warm and tingly all over, Sneha dropped an arm over her leg. Nikhil immediately glanced at her. Their eyes met and Sneha gasped. Oh! He wanted her. Nikhil's eyes burned with desire so strong that Sneha felt an answering leap in her belly. Her fingers curled at her side and her lips parted. Sneha could not look away but Nikhil somehow managed to.

Sneha sat shocked and strangely bereft. Confused she looked around the room and her eyes bumped into Nandini's. 'Are you okay? Are you cold, Sneh?'

Nikhil heard the words and he was sorely tempted to rip off his shirt, bundle Sneha in it and carry her into the nearest bedroom. He was going insane; Nikhil briefly shut his eyes and stood up. He needed some air. 'Is there somewhere I can make a call in private? A balcony or something?' he asked Aditya.

Aditya stood up. 'Sure, there is a terrace garden and pool area outside my study. I'll show you.' He led Nikhil away.

As the men left, Sneha slumped back into the cushions and the sensation similar to a whirlpool ebbed in her stomach. She felt Nandini touch her forearm. 'Earth to Mars! Earth to Mars,' Nandini called out.

Sneha swung her head left and right and she found the weapon of her choice—a cushion. Grabbing it, she turned on Nandini and slammed it several times on Nandini's arm and legs. 'Hey! Sneha cut it out,' Nandini tried to ward off the soft blows.

'Tere Mars ki to. This is all you could find!'

'Oww, my head!'

'She's big in the bust area? That's what you said, right?'

Nandini couldn't help her giggles. She tried to snatch the cushion from Sneha's hand but Sneha was too angry. 'Saali!'

'My laptop, it's brand new!' Nandini yelped trying to get away. She pinched Sneha on the arm.

'Oww!' Sneha tried to get Nandini who propelled herself as far away as she could. Sneha lunged and just realized that both she and Nandini where headed to the same destination—the floor.

Laughing and screaming, the BFFs collapsed on the floor. Chuckling, Nandini held her stomach and Sneha wiped tears of mirth from her eyes. 'Nandini, you will be the death of me one day.'

'Never!' Nandini got to her feet and helped Sneha up as her foot snagged in her dress.

'I'm going to check on my son!'

Sneha found Advey sleepily rubbing his eyes in Amla's arms. Sneha took him and he immediately thrust his face in her shoulders. Sneha gently rocked him back and forth, crooning endearments in his hair. He tucked his chubby arms around her neck and Sneha pulled him closer. 'Baba eat curd, fruits?' Amla asked, ruffling his hair.

'No!' Advey shouted, shrugging her hand off.

'Advey, we say no, thank you. What does my baby want to eat? Milk and a banana?'

Advey just shook his head vigorously.

'Okay, how about some chicken nuggets and milk?'

Advey again shook his head.

'Baba, smoothie?'

Advey did not say no or shake his head. Amla left the room to make him a smoothie. Sneha gently plopped Advey on the bed and rubbed his belly with her nose. Advey altered from a cranky child to a chuckling, wriggling and squirming boy. Sneha horsed around with Advey until Amla came back with a fruit smoothie and some cut up bananas.

A few minutes later, when Nikhil made his way to the restroom, he passed that particular guest room. On hearing the noise he stopped, curious.He popped his head inside and was amused to see Sneha dance animatedly to 'Itsy bitsy spider climbed up the window sill...' while Amla sat at the foot of the bed putting small bits of food into Advey's mouth. The child sat entranced, watching his mother make silly faces and big gestures with her hands and legs.

Advey saw him. 'Nik!' he called out, a bright smile lighting up his face.

'Hello, kiddo.' Nikhil walked over to the bed, not quite looking at the apparition in blue who stood quietly now.

Nikhil sat down on Advey's other side. Advey promptly shifted himself closer to Nikhil, who put a protective arm around him.

Advey then turned to his mother and ordered with a wide smile, 'Mama dance!'

Nikhil and Amla both burst out laughing at Sneha's expression. Amla excused herself. Sneha moved forward to feed Advey. Nikhil picked up the tray with the fruit and smoothie before she could. 'Nik will feed. Mama shall dance.'

Advey clapped his hands. 'Nik feed. Advey eat. Mama dance.'

'Genius, buddy!' Nikhil high-fived Advey and he goaded Sneha with a wickedly raised eyebrow.

19

Date with Dr Pradeep

Rolling her eyes, Sneha again started her song and dance routine, which was now considerably mellowed.

'Small bites!' she directed Nikhil.

Getting her approval on the size of the bite, Nikhil put it carefully in Advey's mouth. Sneha performed the 'itsy bitsy spider' with more vigour. A distracted child was easier to feed.

After ten minutes or so, by the time Sneha's throat was starting to hurt, Nikhil blurted out, 'I did it!' He held up the empty bowl to Sneha.

'Good job, Daddy!' The words accompanied by a broad smile slipped out before Sneha could stop them. She gave a small gasp, staring at him. Nikhil too seemed to freeze. 'I'm sorry, it just came out,' Sneha had to say, seeing his shocked face. He had lost some colour.

Nikhil put the bowl back on the tray. 'I'll be outside.' He got up from the bed.

'Nik!' Advey called out.

Sneha grabbed her son. 'He has to go. Nik has some work.'

Nikhil walked out without another word. Advey's disgruntled cries and Sneha's face in response to his reaction tugged at his insides. Nevertheless, Nikhil did not stop.

Just as Sneha was washing Advey's face, Amla came into the room. 'Nandini madam calling outside!'

'Is someone else there?' Sneha asked, wiping Advey's face.

'Barbie doll,' Amla said, taking Advey from her.

Sneha planted a quick kiss on her son's cheek. 'Play the alphabet game with him and then the blocks.' Ruffling Advey's hair, Sneha hurriedly left the room.

In the living room, she found Nandini sitting on the sofa, her face anxious, drawn. Aditya stood at the other end of the room, looking out of the arched window overlooking Mumbai. His shoulders were taut and he had his back to the others. Just near the door in the foyer, hovered Gayatri, her face pale, demeanour subdued. She was visibly nervous. Her dark eyes anxiously fixed themselves on Nikhil. Nikhil stood next to Gayatri, shifting glances between her and the other two. As she entered, Nikhil turned to Sneha, gazing at her. *What do I do?*

Make this short and quick.

Help me!

Last time!

Still looking at Sneha, Nikhil murmured a soft 'Thanks!' their recent angst pushed to the side.

Gayatri gave him a confused look, 'What are you thanking me for?'

Nikhil made a quick save, his eyes stern, 'For dragging all these people into a mess.' Gayatri stood, taken aback at his sharpness. For the last fifteen or so years that she had known Nikhil, he had never been rude to her—silent maybe, but never rude. She felt miserable; she had let even him down.

Nikhil and Gayatri saw Sneha walk forward. 'What is she doing here?' Gayatri whispered to Nikhil.

'Helping!' Nikhil snapped.

Sneha walked past Nandini and stopped next to Aditya who turned at her presence. His eyes were furious and she saw the muscles work in his cheek. 'How could Nandini agree to letting that woman enter our house? Did you know about this?'

Sneha laid a hand on Adi's forearm. 'Nandini too wants to put this behind her. Gayatri will keep hounding you both until she doesn't get to apologize. Today, next year or ten years after that, she will come back and bring up the issue again. Things went way out of hand last night. She needs to fess up and she owes you and Nandini an apology. And the sooner she does it, the better. You and Nandini,' Sneha emphasized Nandini's name, knowing that was the only word that always got through to Adi, 'need to close this chapter.'

Exhaling, Aditya rubbed his forehead. 'I don't want all this. All this is too bloody stupid.'

'Agreed!' Sneha nodded. 'Then let's get this over with. You and Nandini can enjoy the rest of the weekend. Please!' Sneha reasoned.

Aditya nodded. 'Fine!' He walked back and took a seat next to Nandini on the sofa, giving her a halting smile that came hand in hand with a frown.

'Please have a seat,' Aditya said to Nikhil and Gayatri, his voice curt.

Nikhil guided Gayatri to the opposite sofa. Sneha stood at the window watching Nikhil's protectiveness towards Gayatri, Aditya's toward Nandini. Sneha felt out of place standing by herself. 'Excuse me!' She walked past the four. She had done her part.

'Sneha!' Aditya called out just as Nikhil too was about to stop her.

'Stay, please!' Nandini said. Sneha perched on the edge of the chair next to Nandini and crossed her legs under her. Nikhil tried to keep his eyes from Sneha's fair, delicate calves.

Clearing her throat Gayatri began, 'I'm here to apologize for last night. I don't think words can even begin to tell you how sorry and ashamed I am for my behaviour. I was reckless and irresponsible and,' Gayatri took a deep breath, 'and completely stupid.'

Nandini glanced at her and Gayatri faltered, 'I was driven by my own selfish and wrong notions and caused such pain to someone I once cherished so dearly as a friend,' she said, as tears slithered down her cheeks, 'and much more.'

Sneha glanced at Nandini and caught her miserable expression.

Even Aditya seemed to have lost his ire, the darkness from his face was gone and in its place, she saw unease.

'Don't cry, Gayatri. It's okay. I'm fine,' Aditya spoke haltingly. 'We're fine too!' He glanced at Nandini. She smiled at him encouragingly.

Gayatri pulled herself together with some effort. Nikhil passed her a tissue, which she took gratefully. 'Thank you. You both are very kind.' She glanced at Aditya and Nandini.

'Can I ask what the plan was?' The question came from Sneha.

'The plan?' Gayatri asked blankly.

'Giving him four sleeping pills. There must have been a plan, right?'

'Four pills?' Gayatri appeared taken back. She swivelled her head to Aditya. 'You were given four pills? I was told on—' Gayatri clamped on the rest of the sentence.

Nikhil looked at Sneha. *What did I say?*

Sneha looked away.

'Bloody hell, Adi could have died!' Nandini burst out. 'Really, really stupid!'

'So what changed your perspective? Because the equation here,' Sneha pointed at Aditya and Nandini, 'is still the same. Adi doesn't want you.' Sneha did not mince her words.

Gayatri spoke solemnly, a sad smile sitting on her pretty face. 'Yesterday I finally understood what Nik has been saying to me all this while. It is not what I have or I don't that matters, Aditya only wants Nandini. Only Nandini! It is as if she is his last woman on earth.'

Hearing her words, Nandini inadvertently leaned closer to Aditya, who turned and pressed his lips in her hair.

Then Nandini stood up, walked over and sat next to Gayatri. Nikhil got up and stood next to them. Nandini took Gayatri's hand. 'I too have an apology to make. You have been hurt very badly because of us. It was the right thing to do because in the long run you and Adi wouldn't have...' Nandini changed her words, 'however, just because it was right, does not mean that it was easy or painless; not for us, not for you.'

Gayatri put up a hand to stall Nandini, 'You don't have to say all—'

'I do!'

'She does,' Sneha said and added dryly, 'Believe me, she does!'

Nandini quickly added, 'And yes Gayatri, you are welcome in this house as long as you choose your friends well.' Glancing at Nikhil, she hastily amended the sentence, 'your women friends well.' Nikhil bowed his head in deference to the compliment.

Aditya got to his feet. 'Nandini and I have absolutely no hard feelings for you and wish you the very best, Gayatri.'

Gayatri got to her feet. 'I am returning to Amsterdam tomorrow. And once again, I am truly sorry.' Aditya, Nandini and Nikhil walked with her to the door.

Nikhil turned to Aditya, 'I'll make a move too.'

Nandini pounced on him. 'No, please stay just for some more time. Please.'

Nikhil's eyes went past her to Sneha who sat in the chair, straight and proud, her face turned to gaze at the sunset visible through the French windows. 'I really have to go,' I really should go,' Nikhil murmured, entranced by the way the sunset illuminated Sneha's face with a muted, golden-orange glow. She seemed ethereal.

'Nikhil?' Nandini said.

'Yes?' Nikhil looked at her blankly.

'Dinner with us tonight?' Nandini asked.

'Hmm, ya sure...thanks,' Nikhil's words were rushed. Gayatri eyed him suspiciously. 'I'll walk Gayatri to her car.'

Nikhil and Gayatri went into the elevator. 'I'm glad you see things in a new light,' Nikhil said to Gayatri.

'I do!' Gayatri sighed.

'Talked to Mona?'

'No and I am going to keep it like that for some time. I

trusted her blindly. Four pills! That's scary!' Gayatri exclaimed. 'I just wished that the other nut job wasn't there today.'

'Nut job?'

'Sneha, Nandini's watchdo—'

'Gayatri! Show some respect,' Nikhil snapped at her. He suddenly found Gayatri a tad bit of a nuisance.

'Okay, sorry!' Gayatri said indifferently. The elevator stopped and they got off.

As they walked to her car, Nikhil relented. 'No, I'm sorry. It's just Sneha carries a lot on her plate.'

'You seem to know her well.'

Nikhil shrugged his shoulders. He nearly opened his mouth to justify himself but then thought better of it. 'So what time is your flight?'

'Four in the morning,' Gayatri replied.

'I'll drop you.' Gayatri opened her mouth to protest. 'I'm not asking you sis, I'm telling you.'

'Okay bro!' Gayatri impulsively launched herself into Nikhil's arms. 'I'm sorry, Nik. I didn't mean for it to get so bad.'

Nikhil held her for a few seconds and then broke away. 'The first time I saw you, you were all of eleven with two braids and a mouth full of braces.'

'Oh don't remind me!'

'Since the last fifteen years or so I have seen you get into innumerable scrapes, soups and situations and yet you emerge on top of everything because you eventually figure out the right thing to do. Just like you did today.' Gayatri looked up at him, her gaze loving. 'And as you are growing, the number of scrapes are decreasing so I think you are headed in the right direction.' Nikhil ruffled her hair.

'Heyy!' Gayatri whined in her familiar style. 'Anything but my hair. But thank you.' Gayatri got into her waiting car. Then she rolled her window down, 'Are you okay?'

'Yes! Why?' Nikhil replied.

'You are talking differently.' She gave Nikhil a closer look, 'There is something different about you.'

Nikhil took a step away. 'Have you been raiding the hotel's mini bar?'

Gayatri squinted at him. And then she snapped her fingers. 'You are explaining things! And being sarcastic, like witty sarcastic... and...and smiling, oh my God...your face muscles do work.'

Schooling his face to its usual impassiveness, Nikhil lifted his hand in a wave. 'Be ready by one in the morning. I'll meet you in the hotel lobby. Bye, bye Alice in Wonderland.'

'See? Another sarcastic but funny quip.' Nikhil turned and walked away from the car and Gayatri. 'Call me.'

'Will do!' Nikhil called out as he raised his hand over his head without looking back. Just outside the door to the apartment building, he stopped. Looking out at the lush landscaped gardens in front, he leaned against the exterior wall. He was wondering if there was any truth to what Gayatri had said, in which case it was time to bolt.

Nikhil only knew himself as a bitter, cold, brutal man who could bring no happiness to a child's life or to that of a woman who he thought was more beautiful and more complete than art painted by the gods. Nikhil shook his head wondering how and when he had fallen for Sneha. Was it when she came to him angry and damp or when she danced for her child or was ready to slay the dragon for her close friends or when she sashayed in that blue dress that only made her hazel eyes more alluring? Or was it just now as he had watched the setting sun cast a glow on her face? Bleakly, Nikhil closed his eyes. This would not do. No real damage had been done, no words spoken. He could walk away right now. He would.

Having made up his mind, Nikhil took the elevator to the penthouse. As the door opened, he walked inside and found everyone on the floor, including little Advey. 'Nik!' Advey called out, holding an alphabet book in his hand.

With a stiff smile, Nikhil walked towards them and sat on the floor next to Advey. He happened to glance at Sneha, who was looking at her son with such fierce determination that he was sure her thoughts were somewhere else.

'You think she'll be okay?' Nandini asked Nikhil.

Nikhil saw Sneha turn her face away, her curls covering her profile. 'She'll be fine,' Nikhil murmured not sure who he was referring to, Gayatri or Sneha. Why was Sneha not looking at him?

Sneha was recalling his expression when she had mindlessly called him 'Daddy'. Going by his expression one would think it was a blasphemous word. Sneha hated the hurt hammering in her heart. When Advey's biological father had washed his hands so easily off his child, why would any other man accept Advey like his own? And why would she be so stupid to even expect it? And Nikhil, he was nothing to her. Sneha fixed her eyes on the sky visible through the window resolutely. *I'm okay. No, better than okay, I am fantastic.* 'Nandi, can we have an early dinner? I have some work in the morning that I need to finish and then I have something at lunch.' Sneha's words were rushed.

Nikhil's ear pricked at Sneha's tone but he refrained from saying anything. Instead he concentrated on making a structure for Advey with Lego pieces.

'What lunch thing?' Nandini asked. Sneha just gave a smile which did not quite reach her eyes. 'What lunch thing?' Nandini persisted.

Sneha sighed; tact would never be Nandini's second name. Or third. Or gazillionth. 'Lunch with Dr Sai—Pradeep, I mean.'

Nandini eyes went wide. 'A date with Dr Pradeep?'

Nikhil's hand hesitated as he took another piece Advey offered him. He had to concentrate extremely hard to stack the smallest of the pieces on the largest one.

Sneha began, 'Well, it's not really.' Nandini gave her a glare. 'Okay fine, it's our third date.'

Nandini shot forward, 'Third? I mean, seriously, third?' She put her hands over Advey's ears. He began to laugh and squirm thinking it was a game. 'WTF, when did the second one happen?' She shot a quick glance at Nikhil and was satisfied to see a frown on his face. He too wanted to hear Sneha's answer.

'While you were getting super close to that warped shrink friend of yours.' Nandini pulled a face at Sneha's answer.

'Give me details—'

'Where is Aditya?' Nikhil interrupted, getting to his feet. Advey was immersed in passing his trucks through the bridge Nikhil had just made.

'I'm here. Great news!' Aditya came in, talking to Nikhil. 'Viraj is on board.'

'That's great!' Nikhil and Aditya shook hands.

'He is? Wow!' Nandini jumped up. 'We have to tell Badi Maa and Ajit Bhaiya.'

Aditya smiled. 'We will tell my mom and older brother but after we sign the papers.'

'And Nikhil is on board?' Nandini asked, peeking at Sneha who kept her eyes on her son.

'We are going fifty-fifty on this,' Nikhil replied politely.

'Oh wonderful, that means we'll be seeing more of you.' Nandini perked up.

'Not if Aditya still adheres to his rule of not bringing work home,' Sneha said icily, giving them a quick sharp smile.

'Champagne time! Let's celebrate. I'll get some.' Nandini made a quick exit and Aditya followed.

Nikhil turned and said to Sneha, his manner short, 'Do you have a problem?'

'With?' Sneha asked airily, her chin going up.

'I don't know, with everything it seems,' Nikhil snapped. *Why the hell am I fighting with her*, he wondered while he refused to back down.

'You are not everything.' *Megalomaniac*, Sneha scorned.

'So you have a problem with me?'

20

Hitch with such potential

Sneha opened her mouth and then shut it. Her eyes shot sparks. 'No I don't. I don't give a bamn!' Her lips clamped and brow furrowed, Sneha knew her argument may have steam but no logic. Hammit!

'Good!' Nikhil flashed a smug smile, the signature smile of the devil.

'Good! There is nothing good about you,' Sneha scorned. Using her foot, she pushed pieces of Lego closer to Advey.

'I'm not here to impress you.'

'You can't!' Sneha arched an eyebrow for effect.

'I don't want to.'

'You can't.'

'Fine, because I don't want to.' Nikhil growled, spending literally a minute over each word. His lips were pulled back, his look feral.

'Fine, because you can't,' Sneha retorted. She couldn't understand why she was experiencing an anger so fierce, it was sure to burst a few capillaries.

'Nikhil can't what?' Nandini burst in, followed by a staff member behind her.

'Nothing and everything!' Sneha muttered. Nikhil kept his silence. A tray holding a bottle of champagne and four flutes was placed on the centre table. Aditya joined them and picked up the bottle to open it.

'That's Bond's Champagne!' Nikhil remarked. His remark earned puzzled expressions from the others. Nikhil took the bottle from

Aditya and turned the label so the others could read it. 'Bollinger Champagne. That's what James Bond drinks,' he elaborated.

'You're a Bond fan?' Aditya's filmy bhoot, Nandini asked.

Nikhil's smile was rueful. 'Sorry, I am not. I just like to know my drinks.'

'Then you should open it.' Aditya raised an empty glass to the bottle Nikhil held. With a quick shake and few twists, Nikhil skilfully opened the bottle with a pop.

Advey was entranced by the froth spilling out. Clapping his hands, he called out, 'More! Nik more!'

Nikhil laughed. 'You are not starting that young kiddo.'

'Amla! Amla!' Abruptly, Sneha called out loudly.

Amla appeared, holding a tea cup in her hand. 'After you finish, please take Advey for a stroll in the garden downstairs.' Amla, surprised at Sneha's tone gave a rare, docile nod and went back inside.

Aditya handed Sneha a flute three-quarters full. 'I think you'll like this one.'

Sneha took the glass, flashing him a wide beaming smile. 'Thank you Adi. You are such a nice, sweet man.'

'Thanks.' Aditya was not used to such praise from Sneha.

Only Nandini heard Nikhil's soft snort. A little alarmed, Nandini watched Sneha finish her glass in two swallows. Aditya instantly refilled her glass. 'I told you, you would like it.'

Sneha giving him a quick smile took another big sip. Amla in the meantime brought out the stroller and strapped Advey in it.

Nandini asked one of the security guards to accompany them. Nikhil, over the rim of his glass, watched Sneha move on to her third glass of champagne. From the past, he knew her to be a one-drink-wonder; he wondered how much of that had changed. It hadn't. For several minutes, work-related conversation passed back and forth between Nikhil and Aditya.

'Hear! Hear!' suddenly Sneha called out. They all looked at her. Nikhil and Nandini immediately noticed her bright eyes and flushed cheeks, which had nothing to do with the temperature of the room.

'It seems today is a day of apologies.' Sneha carelessly waved her glass around at everyone. A few drops splashed out, falling on her dress. 'Oops!' she giggled at the growing stain. 'I owe you a dress kulta.' Again a giggle.

Sneha giggling was like watching a turtle move at 60mph. It was surreal. 'Are you okay, Sneha?' Aditya asked tentatively. Nandini was grinning and Nikhil had lowered his glass, watching Sneha, his gaze piercing.

'I'm fine! I'm so good that I can't even descriiibbbe it,' Sneha said. She gave a bright smile to Aditya and then Nandini. Then she glanced at Nikhil who was watching her with glinting eyes and a clamped mouth. Giggling, Sneha looked away.

'I shall not be left behhhind. I too have an apologggy to make.' Obviously, Sneha was having difficulty with words bigger than four letters.

'Who is the apology to?' Nandini asked, her eyes brimming with mischief.

Sneha pointed at Nikhil with her forefinger. More champagne splashed. 'Oops.' Again a giggle. 'To him! For outing him.'

Nandini eyes became wide as she looked at Nikhil, 'Oh my God, you are gay. No offence meant. It's great to be gay. I have several friends who are gay. I am all for...' Nikhil's hard stare caused Nandini to trail off.

'He's not, hitch!' Sneha put her head in her hands and seemed to be lost to her giggles for a few seconds. 'He's Devdas and his Paro is Kim didi,' Sneha giggled and then simultaneously finished the remaining liquid in her glass.

'Sneha!' Nikhil called out. 'I accept your apology, now forget it.'

'Not so quick.' Sneha wagged her finger at him.

'Kim didi, your first cousin in Europe? The one who came down for your—' Nandini bit her tongue

'My weddd-inng! Eggjactlyy.' Sneha winked at her.

'What was that about early dinner?' Aditya asked Nandini.

'Oh c'mon Adi, don't be such a buzz kill. I'm not finnisssed,' Sneha said, laughing.

Aditya got up. 'Sit!' Sneha's tone was like a verbal whiplash. Aditya sat down, his expression resigned. Apologetic, he glanced at Nikhil and was surprised at the manner in which he stared at Sneha. Aditya felt worried for Sneha.

'Nandi, you have been asking me how I know Nikhil. Welllll I know him because he was Kim di's college frieeend who came visitinnng her in the holidays. The time,' an unexpected giggle and a burp came out of Sneha. It seemed to surprise her. 'Oops, sorry. The time I wasss there tooooo,' Sneha's head wobbled on her neck, 'Nikkhill stood outtttt.' Again, that stumbling giggle and that word 'out'. 'Then he was this chubby boy witthh this big...' Sneha paused to put her glass down carefully. Finding a spot to place the stem was difficult for her so she rested the empty glass horizontal on the glass table.

'This big what?' Nandini said, then quickly pressed her lips shut as Aditya and Nikhil glared at her.

'Gooood questionnnnn! Bigg what?' Sneha blinked, her eyes confused. 'Whose big what?'

Nandini quickly, using her head and eyebrows, pointed at Nikhil.

'Oh yes! This bigggg,' Sneha pulled her arms apart as much as her shoulders would allow. 'Crussssh on Kimm Jong.'

'What crap!' Nikhil said, putting his glass down hard.

Aditya turned to Nikhil, 'Kim Jong, the Korean leader?'

'Ask the drunk,' Nikhil retorted coolly.

Nandini opened her mouth to defend Sneha who was giggling and winking her. 'I nursed a crush for the longest time on Rahul Gandhi,' she ended up saying instead.

'Sorrrrry not Kim Jong but Kim di! My Kim di,' Sneha said burping again. 'Excuse me.' Again, a giggle.

'Everyone has crushes. Big deal, Sneha.' Nandini kept the conversation going.

'Yaaa, of course kullltta, but how many write a diary full of horrendous poeemms,' Sneha paused to make a finger-in-the-mouth-to-barf gesture, 'and plannn to give it to the girl as a birthddday prasant.' Sneha intentionally mispronounced the last word.

'They were not horrendous poems,' Nikhil bit out. His cheeks were tight and colour darkened his face. What would he not give right now for that adorable drunk woman in front of him to simply pass out?

'How sweet!' Nandini gushed. Nikhil felt a muscle twitch in one cheek.

'How sttupiddd.' Sneha leaned forward besieged by a fresh bout of giggles. Nikhil picked up his glass and upturned it in his mouth. *How had things become so weird for him*, he wondered. Oh yes, when Aditya had refilled Sneha's glass the second and the third time. Casting a belligerent look at Aditya, Nikhil spoke up, 'To cut a long story short, yes I had a crush on Kim, yes she was hot and yes, I was fat.'

'Chubby!' Sneha corrected him, resting her chin in her right hand as she leered at him.

Nikhil forced himself to look away from the mischievous smile and sparkling hazel eyes. 'Sneha discovered the crush because of her habit of meddling.'

'Ouchh.'

Nikhil ignored Sneha's fake indignant expression. 'She opened a gift meant for her cousin.'

'Opened? It was in a plastic bag. An ordddinnary plastic bag,' Sneha yelled in her defence.

'Yes, with a rose stuck on the outside,' Nikhil snapped and then he felt like kicking himself.

'I picke-erd it up from the otherrr side,' Sneha's slurring became pronounced for she was trying to speak faster than her inebriated mind could keep up. ' DDid not see the rose you had taken from herrr room and stuck on with two yards of scotch tapee. TACKY!'

'It was an impromptu gesture,' Nikhil shook his head. He shifted uneasily in his chair. 'Anyhow with sheer consideration for my feelings Sneha, instead of leaving that bag on Kim's bed, took the diary out and read it. Then just as Kim's birthday cake was being cut and there were at least two hundred people in the room, including Kim and her parents, she pulled out the diary.'

'Sneha!' Nandini's tone was a soft rebuke.

'What?' Sneha turned her head to look at her. Her hand that braced her chin wobbled. Abruptly, she sat up straight. And then she recited a few lines.

'This life is a pain, without you,
Nearly like a drain, without you,
How will I go on, without you,
Without you is not an option,
It is only a prrremonition
Of an end without you.'

'Sneha!' Nikhil growled in his throat.

'Nikhil Keating's poem, firrrrst poem first page,' Sneha announced. 'I gave up readding poetry after that.'

Nandini clamped her lips and made a choking sound. Aditya did not know where to look; he stared into his glass, a smile playing on his lips.

'And then?' Nandini sobered up enough to ask Sneha.

'And then I was the laughing stock of that party. The diary got passed around, more poems were read and the evening was nightmarish, at least for me. Kim blasted Sneha. Sneha, showing some more stupidity, decided to walk out of the party. Went into the adjoining biker bar where she nearly got assaulted and had to be saved by some quick thinking.'

'Quick thinking by who?' Aditya asked.

'By the boy she had just dissed,' Sneha finished. She wasn't laughing any more. Her face was glum as she eyed the empty glass lying down on the table.

'Oh!' Nandini reacted with a single word.

'Why don't you check on the dinner?' Aditya suggested to Nandini.

'What happened then?' Ignoring Aditya, Nandini probed further.

'Sneha came to apologize to me next day. I called her an idiot and a meddling fool and closed the door on her face,' Nikhil replied.

'And then he went back to colleeege or wherever. Kim di did not speak with me for a year,' Sneha sniffed.

'I did not know that. We never talked about you,' Nikhil remarked. His expression was back to being aloof, his eyes no longer glinted, 'Get over it, Sneha. I have told you before, that was not the worst I've had.'

'Of course not. Your deevorce was that. We knows!' Sneha said, frowning mindlessly. Her head was beginning to hurt, which is why she was the only one who didn't hear Nikhil's harsh intake of breath.

Nikhil jerked to his feet. 'Apologies, but I have to leave,' he addressed Nandini.

'Please stay. I'm sorry on Sneha's behalf,' Nandini pleaded, getting to her feet. She had never wanted anyone to get hurt. 'I think she is sobering up. She is not slurring any more.'

'Some other time,' Nikhil replied with a tight smile.

'Aditya!' Nikhil and Aditya exchanged a quick handshake.

'Nikhil please...' Aditya shaking his head caused Nandini to trail off.

'I'll walk you out,' Aditya said. Nikhil walked out without as much a glance at Sneha who was now squinting and massaging her forehead.

Sneha glanced up a few seconds later. 'Where did he go?' she asked, glancing around the room.

'Sneh!' Sighing, Nandini sat down cross-legged next to the drunk. 'Guess what?'

'What!' Sneha asked with an indulgent smile, her eyes bright and cheeks flushed.

'You owe him another apology!' Nandini replied with an understanding smile.

'I do? Why?' Sneha tried to think and then snapped her fingers as she shouted and laughed at the same time, 'Because I'm such a hitch.'

'And with such potential,' Nandini announced wickedly.

The next day Sneha woke up in her bed with a head that felt like the stage of a rock concert and a mouth that tasted like its floor. 'Oh God!' Sneha moved her face restlessly on the pillow. Gosh, even her breath smelled like the behind of a truck's exhaust—nasty. Groggily she made it to the restroom, splashed water over her face and brushed her teeth for a full ten minutes. All she remembered of last night was Adi driving them home and Nandini helping Sneha into her bed.

As Sneha came out of the restroom, she saw Advey still sleeping. Gently she traced his cheeks and he moved his face away. Feeling somewhat normal, she came out of the room and glanced at the watch; it was still early—7.00 a.m.!

Making a cup of strong coffee, Sneha opened the front door and grabbed the rolled up newspaper. Taking the coffee and newspaper, Sneha went to the balcony. She didn't last long out there, just about thirty seconds, for every sound of the traffic felt like a sledgehammer to her temples.

After half an hour or so when Amla came out of the second bedroom she found Sneha asleep on the sofa, her head pushed uncomfortably in between some cushions, mouth open, soft snores coming from her. The open newspaper in utter disarray lay partly over her and partly on the floor nearby.

'Madam! Madam!' Amla shook her gently.

Sneha woke up with a start. Her eyes sprung open wide and alert.

'Aatha!' the maid uttered a startled sound.

'Huh? Why are you screaming?'

'Meter?' Amla muttered.

'What meter?' Sneha asked, irked, as she grabbed the papers on her stomach about to slip onto the floor.

'Bewardi!' Amla muttered to herself as she went into the kitchen. 'More coffee?'

'Please, and strong,' Sneha called back. Soon Advey, too, woke up and had her occupied. Around ten that morning Sneha made a call.

'Hi, Pradeep, Sneha here.'

She was greeted with much enthusiasm.

'Pra—Pradeep, I'm so sorry for the last minute change of plans but I can't make it to lunch today. Not feeling too well,' Sneha said and then she realized that it was the wrong thing to say to a doctor. For the next five minutes, with a suffering expression Sneha verbalized her symptoms.

Pradeep, like Amla, arrived at a similar conclusion. 'Someone was hitting the bottle hard last night. Celebrating?'

'Ya kind of, with Nandini and Aditya. Really sorry about this. I'm just not great company today,' Sneha replied honestly.

'No problems. Rain check?'

'Of course. I'll call you?' Sneha replied.

'You will call, Sneha?' Pradeep asked. Sneha hated the needy tone in his voice. It made her feel guilty.

'I will. Bye.' Sneha hung up. Why could she not reciprocate the doctor's niceness? A certain someone's face began taking shape in her head. Just as the green eyes came to life in her mind, Sneha panicked and switched on the TV and then switched it off almost immediately, realizing she would need a bigger distraction than the idiot box. Choosing work, she pulled out her laptop.

Post-lunch, Sneha got a call from Nandini who simply told her that she could have, she should have treated Nikhil better and before Sneha could respond, in typical Nandini style, she changed the topic and informed Sneha that she and Aditya were flying off for a mini vacation for seven days. Goa and Kanpur were their two destinations. 'Have fun kulta. I'm going to be stuck here knee-deep in work,' Sneha retorted grumpily.

'Listen, aren't your parents visiting Kanpur?' Nandini asked.

'Yup. They are staying at your place,' Sneha replied as she scrolled through her emails. She had several pending proofs and design reviews to look at.

'Sneh, why don't I take Advey and Amla with me and then he can spend time with the numerous grandparents there.'

'Numerous as in?' Sneha asked sharply. She was sure Nandini knew that her ex-husband's family, just like her ex-husband, had washed their hands off Advey.

Nandini read her mind. 'Sneh! I'm talking about your parents, my parents, Badi Maa,' she added, understandingly.

'Sorry!' Sneha conceded. She bit her lip. 'I'll miss him, Nandi.'

'I know! But think of Advey. He'll have company the whole day.'

'Damn! It's hard,' Sneha blurted.

'Think about it. We are leaving tomorrow morning.'

'How will you get the tickets for Advey and Amla so soon?' Sneha asked.

'I will, if the plane belongs to my husband.'

'Of course,' Sneha chuckled.

'Did you talk to N—'

'Bye, Nandini, I'll call you later.'

'Okay fine, I won't ask. How was your date with Pradeep?'

'Cancelled it. Because of the bloody hangover. And it wasn't like a date, date,' she said primly.

'So what was it, a meeting of similar minds?' Nandini snorted.

Sneha grunted.

'So sirjee.' Pause. 'Who would you rather date, date? Sadda Ni—'

'Nandini!' Sneha shrieked. 'MORON.'

'Nikhil, Nikhil, Nikhil,' Nandini recited breathlessly.

21

Dented armours and speed monkey

'What are you doing?' Sneha asked irritated.

'You were not letting me take his name so I took his name. Three times.' Sneha heard some voices in the background. She heard Nandini explain, 'Oh God Adi, will you calm down? I wasn't taking *Nikhil's*,' Sneha knew the emphasis on the name was for her benefit, so she blew a curl off her cheek, 'name for myself, it was for Sn—'

'I'm hanging up, bitch. Will call you in the evening.' Sneha hung up, a wry grin on her face. Nandini the town jester did that to her.

'Amla!' Sneha called out. Amla looked up from the TV she was watching.

'Want to go to Kanpur for a few days?' Sneha asked. 'Just you and Advey?'

'You no?'

'No, a lot of work. Mummy and Papa are there. You'll stay with Nandini's parents.'

'You miss baba.'

Sneha nodded glumly.

'I'll help you pack Advey's things.' Sneha snapped her laptop shut and went into her room where her son was practicing writing letters. 'I'm going to miss you,' she said, her eyes tearing up. Sneha, who had a rule of thumb about not crying, made an exception when it came to Advey. She cried the first time he got his immunizations, the first time he got an ear infection and the first time he walked. The emotional source code was different for the latter.

Next day close to 10.00 a.m., Sneha reached her office after dropping Advey and Amla off at the airport with Nandini and Aditya. Close to one-thirty, she got Nandini's text; they were home and Advey was super-duper excited to be with his grandparents. After that, Sneha threw herself into her work and tried to forget any wrong she might have done to whose-name-she-would-not-voice. Whose-name-she-would-not-voice too appeared to be festering a similiar desire for Sneha for she did not hear a peep or a tweet from him.

For the next seven days, Sneha's sunrise and sunset were only five minutes apart, or so it seemed. The life of a woman with impossible deadlines, an equally impossible addiction to caffeine and impossibly mesmerizing eyes that never quit haunting her. Stir those three together and what you get is just another long day at work.

The week passed, then a weekend and then life fast-forwarded to Tuesday. 'SEND!' Sneha screamed at the man in her room. Grinning, the young man in a graphic Tee and skinny jeans hit the enter button on his laptop.

He gave Sneha a toothy grin. 'Done, boss!'

'Now get out of my office and I don't want to see any of you for at least a day.' Sneha and he high-fived across the table.

'Good zzob, boss!' The young boy got to his feet. He might not look a day over sixteen with his thin frame and bony shoulders but he was one of the most brilliant graphic and design directors Sneha had come across.

'I'm sending an email to the team. I'm taking you all for lunch tomorrow to Goa Portuguesa at one o'clock.'

'Awesome. Are you leaving now?'

'Are you kidding me, Ozzy? I am going to organize my files and clean my computer,' Sneha winked at him. That was the code for surfing the net and essentially doing nothing.

Sneha's hope was short-lived. After Ozzy left, Sneha could only bask for a few minutes in the satisfaction of having executed the first phase of the print and TV ads that would run for the next quarter. A tap on the door roused her from her python-like pose on her chair.

'Yes?' It was Mr Baig. 'Hi, sir.'

'Gupta, just spoke to Ozzy. You're all are done with the first phase?'

'Yes we are. It has been a crazy few days,' Sneha said, trying not to stretch in front of him.

'Well, I'm glad you cleared that off your table.'

'Glad?' Sneha knew exactly what was coming next. 'Not exactly cleared; I do have a few very important action items that are going to keep me busy for at least some time.'

'Gupta, you are too quick for all that.' He leaned against her table. 'Listen, I have a friend who is starting a women's magazine and the whole operation is under the flagship of the Whisky Baron.'

'The Baron is funding that magazine. Their account must be big.' Sneha felt like kicking herself for that comment.

'I know. That's why I have set up a meeting with you and that friend of mine. Her name is Mallika Lall and she will meet you at her office in Powai at 3.30 p.m.'

'That is in the middle of nowhere. It'll take me over an hour just to get there,' Sneha protested.

'Then you should leave right away.'

'I don't have my car,' Sneha said. It was true; she had turned her car in today for servicing.

'Take the company car with the driver.'

'And I haven't prepared anything for that meeting.'

Mr Baig stood straighter. 'The meeting is an informal sit-down about her business. Just a very broad, open-ended discussion.'

Sneha was peeved. She had worked like a dog and she deserved a break. Mr Baig walked out and then popped his head back in, 'Don't be late.'

'Laala Custard!' Sneha fumed, as she gathered her stuff off the table. Five minutes later, a still-livid Sneha walked to the elevators. For a few minutes, she huffed and puffed in the car en-route to her appointment and then realized she could use the drive to call and talk to everyone in Kanpur. The next twenty minutes passed swiftly. Just as the car about to head for the JVLR road, it abruptly lurched and came to a complete stop.

Sneha quickly hung up, not too bothered. 'Perfect reason to be late for the appointment.' Getting out of the car, Sneha looked around. She saw a coffee shop.

'Excuse me, Shyam,' she addressed the driver of the car, 'I'll be in there. If the car gets fixed, call me okay?' She quickly texted Mr Baig, 'Car broke down. Looking for alternative conveyance. Thanks.'

'I will have to call a mechanic, madam,' he replied, scratching his head.

Sneha would have offered to take a look under the bonnet and probably diagnosed the fault, but not today. Especially after Mr Baig's tepid reply, 'Okay. See what can be done.' He texted her Mallika Lall's number.

'Take your time. If you want coffee, I'll order one for you too. Have coffee and then call the mechanic. Aaram se!'

'Okay madam. I'll lock the car and come.' The driver matched her wavelength.

Sliding her shades further up her nose, Sneha slung the laptop bag tighter on her shoulders and walked to the shop, a smile playing on her lips. She enjoyed the sun on her face and the wind ruffling her wispy plum blouse and knee-length black pencil skirt.

Of the many vehicles going past her, a motorbike passed Sneha. She glanced at it, her gaze offhand. Surprisingly, the biker slowed down, coming to a complete stop a few feet ahead of her and then turned, glancing at her.

Lecher! Sneha pressed her lips sternly as she was about to pass the biker in all black, including the helmet on his head.

As she went past him, she heard the biker start his vehicle. The bike casually kept pace at her side. Sneha shot an angry look at the biker. Dang, even his helmet's glass was tinted. Sneha felt threatened, especially with the spate of atrocious crimes against women on the upswing, even in Mumbai.

Sneha stopped and so did the biker, inches away from her. 'Listen, man!' Sneha began angrily and the biker just revved up the gears noisily, not increasing his speed but only the sound. 'Asshole,' Sneha, barely controlling her anger, took quick steps forward. The bike again started trolling at her side, maintaining its pace with her.

Sneha stopped. Keeping the element of surprise on her side, she leaned over and pushed the ignition off. The man did not stop her and the bike's engine ceased.

'Fine. Pervert. Let's talk,' Sneha challenged, pushing her shades over her forehead.

The driver, Shyam, came to a stop next to her. He was out of breath. He must have run to her defence. 'What happened madam?'

Sneha shot a condemning forefinger at the helmet, 'This creep—'

The biker with his gloved hand raised the tinted glass cover. 'Hi Sneha,' Nikhil spoke evenly, even though his eyes openly mocked her.

'You!' Slack-jawed, Sneha was startled. All she could do was make fish faces at an amused Nikhil. She ran her eyes over him. 'On...a motor bike? What happened to dark German cars?'

'Today I want speed over comfort!' Nikhil said, removing his helmet. Of course his hair was a mess but in a manner that added to his looks.

'Why?'

'Go-karts!' he said, placing the helmet on his leg.

'I saw you there in a car the last time.'

'True! But from today I'm unshackled,' Nikhil replied evenly.

'Umm...madam!' the driver called out tentatively.

Sneha glanced at him. 'Sorry! Why don't you go and order the coffee for yourself. Oh! Order some food too if you wish.' Sneha hunted inside her bag for her wallet. Nikhil was quicker than she was. He drew his wallet from the pocket of his jeans and handed over a very large denominator note even as Sneha protested. The driver thanked them and moved on.

Sneha turned to Nikhil. 'Unshackled?'

'Transaction's done, security is off, and I'm a free man.'

'What?'

'Whenever there is a big sale or purchase, the board of directors involved in the deal receive security for some time.' Nikhil's smile was brief.

Sneha looked at him, disgruntled by the happiness she was experiencing on accidentally bumping into him. 'You smile as though you don't want anyone to see it.' She coloured, wondering why she was getting personal here.

Nikhil shifted on the motorbike. 'No I don't.' He sounded defensive.

Sneha was tempted to argue but she did not. 'Okay, now that you have had your little laugh at my expense, I shall take your leave.' Sneha turned away and slipped her shades back on.

'Next time, you should play it a little safe. Stupidity can get you killed or worse,' Nikhil said, opening the straps of his helmet to put it back on.

Sneha stopped and faced him, tipping her chin up. 'As in?'

Nikhil straightened his helmet. 'What if it had been some idiot instead of me? Calling him out is not the smartest thing to do.'

'Why? Because I'm a woman?'

'And here by yourself,' Nikhil countered reasonably.

Sneha crossed her arms across her chest. 'The driver was there.'

'Even a sloth is quicker than him,' Nikhil retorted.

'I can look after myself,' she declared stoutly.

'Of course you can and a part of that also involves being

cautious. Going in guns blazing is great but at least make sure you have ammunition.'

Sneha opened her mouth to argue but Nikhil was on a roll, 'Until there are idiots in the society the smarter ones need to be smarter that's all.'

Sneha, who had been expecting a 'you-are-a-woman-you-are-weak' argument, was pleasantly surprised and conceded, albeit grumpily, 'I sometimes get carried away.'

'Sometimes?' was Nikhil's dry response. Sneha glared at him. 'How's the little fella?'

'Away,' Sneha replied. 'With his grandparents in Kanpur. He's coming back tomorrow. Anyway, I'll see you around.' Sneha sorely wanted to apologize for her drunken behaviour but she lost her nerve. If she could not do it in person she would shoot him an apology email today for sure, she decided.

Sneha had barely taken a few steps when Nikhil called out, 'Interested in playing hookey for the rest of the day?' Sneha half-turned towards him. Nikhil saw himself reflected in Sneha's shades. He wondered what the heck he was doing. Nevertheless, he couldn't bring himself to part with her just yet. Destiny only gave so many chances, right? 'You won't be disappointed.'

'What do you have in mind?'

Nikhil heard the doubt in her voice. He was just glad Sneha had not clubbed him. However, it was early and the day was far from over. 'Hop on,' he pointed to the back seat.

'In a skirt!' Sneha glanced at her clothes.

'Pull it up,' Nikhil replied, spontaneously lifting the helmet to put it on..

'You just want to see my thighs,' Sneha said and then froze. In her mind, she saw herself banging her head a few times on the road.

'Maybe!' Nikhil responded, sounding amused. The helmet hid his expression. 'Get on.'

'Let me inform the driver on his cell.' Sneha turned away,

agitated. She would have to be careful around the sunhaar, he had her feeling and speaking in a way she had never thought was possible.

Keeping that call quick, Sneha turned to Nikhil, who was waiting for her. He reached out, 'Let me hold your bag so you can sit better.'

Sneha handed him her laptop bag, feeling all thumbs and needles. What had she gotten herself into? Sneha, stepping closer to the bike, pulled up her skirt and sat down timidly behind Nikhil. She shifted a little back and forth trying to keep some distance between her and Nikhil.

'Spectacular!' Nikhil murmured, handing her the laptop bag.

'What's spectacular?' Sneha asked loping the bag around her.

'Your thighs!' Nikhil replied and he watched, satisfied, as the colour rose in her cheeks.

'I suck at this coquettish flirtatious hit so please just shut up and drive,' Sneha said, hating how shy she promptly felt.

Giving a crack of a laugh, Nikhil pulled down the glass on his helmet and the engine roared to life.

A few twists, turns and zip zap zooms later they arrived in front of familiar gates. 'Oh God, not here,' Sneha said, just as Nikhil brought the bike to a smooth stop.

'Scared?' Nikhil taunted, his mood light.

'Is that a word?' Sneha, feeling heady, matched his candour.

The gates opened. Nikhil drove in and stopped in front of the white structure. 'Seriously, what are we doing here?' Sneha asked, as she got ready to disembark.

'Something fun for a certain speed monkey,' Nikhil said, taking his helmet off as he balanced the bike with his legs.

'Junkie. Speed junkie,' Sneha muttered as she yanked and tugged at her skirt, which was hindering her movements and knotting at an indecent juncture between her legs.

'Should I help?' Nikhil asked, turning around.

'Noooo!' Sneha put her hands firmly on the spot between her and him on the seat.

'Hold on!' Nikhil tilted the bike to one side, making it easier for Sneha to slide off the back.

As Sneha tugged her clothes in order, Nikhil moved the bike to the side and got off, leaving his helmet on the seat. Sneha followed Nikhil into the carpeted hall. Sher Singh greeted her. His expression was comical as he saw Sneha and Nikhil together. Nikhil signed them in even as he and Sneha exchanged a knowing smile. 'Anybody else here?' he asked.

'Not yet, Mr Chandel. Your overalls are ready.' Sher Singh kept his eyes away from Sneha.

'Thanks. Can you arrange for an overall in her size, please?' Nikhil requested, motioning Sneha to come closer.

'A clean one! Thanks,' Sneha added, stepping closer.

Sher Singh went inside. Nikhil opened the glass doors that led to the racing area.

'I have never done this before,' Sneha said as she walked through the door.

'It will be fun.' Nikhil joined her.

Sneha took in the tracks. The smell of dust was strong.

Sher Singh returned with folded clothes. He handed an orange and white pair to Nikhil and a blue one to Sneha. 'Sir, no ladies come here,' he said hesitantly.

'I know it's only members. You can complain to the owner,' Nikhil replied as he handed his keys to him. Grinning, Sher Singh took the keys and moved away.

'Who's the owner?' Sneha asked, sniffing at the rough clothes in her hands. They smelled clean.

'You are with him,' Nikhil said as he put a hand on her lower back and guided her to the signs that boldly read 'Lockers and dressing room'. Sneha instantly went stiff at his touch. Surprised at her reaction, Nikhil dropped his hand and gave her a sideways glance.

'NICE! But why no women?' Sneha asked.

'No woman has come forth for a membership yet,' Nikhil replied.

'Tempting but it's probably beyond my pay grade,' Sneha said, wrinkling her nose.

'Not for you, it isn't. The owner's only condition is that you always bring him along,' Nikhil said, briefly flashing his pearlies at her.

Sneha controlled her smile as she gazed at him. *Why else would I come here otherwise?*

For speed, speed monkey!

'For the hundred time. It's JUNKIE!' She gave him a mock scowl.

Nikhil smiled with his eyes. 'In you go! I'll wait outside. Use locker number twenty. Put the overall over your clothes. Your skirt you might have to take off...' He trailed off, looking down at Sneha. An unbidden image of Sneha clad only in a plum blouse and black heels flooded his mind. His body temperature rose as Nikhil stared at her open face, parted lips and sparkling hazel eyes that with excitement shone enticingly. Nikhil commanded his fickle mind not to let him ponder over that image. However, it did worse or better. Nikhil imagined himself standing close to Sneha. His fingers had already undone a few buttons of her shirt and were trailing her pale, smooth skin. His lips were pressed over hers as Sneha arched her body into him, her arms wrapped possessively around his neck. They both were breathing hard, their breaths mingling as they moved restlessly against each other.

'Nikhil? Hello!' Sneha waving her hand in front of his face, snapping him out of his reverie.

'Sorry!' Nikhil's expression was distracted. 'Why don't you go inside? I'll wait here.'

'You okay?' Sneha realized she was talking to his back.

'Go in!' Nikhil spoke curtly. Confused, Sneha went inside. Nikhil stood glaring at the sky. Somewhere he had hoped that so many days away from Sneha would have fixed the chink in his armour. He should have known better! Why else would she keep butting into his mind all the time? Some people may label it 'missing someone' Nikhil had dubbed it as a 'short-term affliction.' Now he was wondering if he was mistaken about the 'short-term' part.

A few minutes later, Sneha self-consciously cleared her throat. Nikhil turned around, his face indifferent and composed and then he saw her. Sneha, even with considerably rolled-up sleeves and pants, appeared to be drowning in the suit. Positively adorable! Nikhil scowled at that thought. 'You'll have to tie your curls, your hair,' Nikhil said, hurrying past Sneha into the locker room. 'The helmets and gloves are on the racks near the tracks. Choose ones that fit you best.'

'Okay!' Sneha muttered, wandering off in the direction Nikhil had pointed. She wondered why his mood had taken a 180 degree turn. It was impossible to wrap one's head around his kind. Sneha tried on the helmet. She chose a white one with a tinted front. She picked the smallest of the gloves; they fit snugly on her hands. As Sneha grabbed her helmet with her gloved hands, Nikhil joined her.

'Found them?' he asked, loosening the Velcro collar around the neck.

'Yup!' Sneha held up her helmet with her gloved hands.

'Shall we?' Nikhil asked, quickly grabbing his gear.

Sneha followed him as they made their way up to the starting line where their carriages awaited. Sneha gleefully passed Nikhil to go to the meaner looking of the machines, painted a bright orange and white.

Nikhil opened his mouth to protest. 'Were you going to say that's mine?' Sneha teased, her eyes going up and down like a bouncing ball.

'No! You can have it. Just drive carefully. Go-karts tip over easily and the big ones like that,' he pointed at the one Sneha stood next to, 'can go up to 90 mph.'

Sneha felt an excitement she had not felt in a very long time, that she couldn't contain even if she wanted to. She clapped her hands. 'Let's get in then?'

Nikhil tried to stay indifferent to her little-girl buoyancy but failed miserably. Putting his helmet atop the smaller silver machine he would be driving, he began helping Sneha with the seat belt.

'That's the brake, the accelerator and those are gears. Five gears for different speeds,' Nikhil pointed at the appropriate places. Sneha nodded. 'What this?' touching the protruding lever next to the gears.

'That's what you call a "Hail Mary".'

'Huh? What does it do?'

'When you yank the lever out, it pulls in the lower rods of the carriage frame, increases the aerodynamics of the machine, giving the driver more speed but it also makes the kart extremely unsteady. So none of us use it. And once you pull out the Hail Mary it can only be pushed back once the ignition is turned off.'

Sneha nodded. Nikhil pointed at the red switch under the speedometer. 'That's the button for the ignition. Go slow, familiarize yourself and then after two practice laps, I'll race you for three laps.'

'You're on!' Sneha's finger pressed the ignition and her kart spluttered to life.

Nikhil quickly got into his kart and started the machine. 'Remember, no Hail Mary!' he said, tightening the strap of his helmet.

'Yes, Mom!' Sneha muttered.

'I heard that.' Nikhil slid the tinted visor on his helmet shut. Sneha's kart shot out under her and Nikhil gave her a head start so she had some room to practise. They finished one lap, their machines purring smoothly, displacing minimal dust. Nikhil tailed her.

Sneha loved the machine and the engine oil smell. Her hands held the wheel lightly as she adjusted and readjusted her legs to get a better grip of the pedals. She happened to look at the other kart, and at Nikhil who was using his two fingers to signal something to her. Sneha raised the visor of her helmet.

'What?'

'Do the second practice lap.' Nikhil raised his visor too.

'Nah, the race is on. The loser buys dinner.' Sneha shot her kart forward.

22

What had she revealed?

Nikhil followed her example. Sneha saw him in the tiny oval rearview mirror. He was close. He was coming up on her right. Sneha swerved her kart in his path. Nikhil fell back. Sneha assumed he would try to overtake her on the left. She swung her kart left. Wrong move. Nikhil gunned and overtook her from the right.

'Damn!' Sneha fiercely focused on the track and her driving. Adrenalin thundered down her veins. Sneha felt more alive than ever. Grinning, she sped up behind him. Roaring, the two go-karts hurled at a tremendous speed around the track. Just as they were about to take a bend in the second lap, Sneha used the opportunity she knew Nikhil would unknowingly present for he favoured the right while taking turns.

As they went into the curve, Nikhil was amazed to see Sneha hurtle past him. 'Bloody good, woman!' Nikhil chuckled, gripping his steering wheel tightly. They zoomed into the third and last lap. Sneha kept her wheel straight, giving little room for Nikhil to overtake her. 'Bamn!' Sneha saw the bend coming. If she didn't move to a side she would either crash into the adjoining tyres or at that angle her kart might tip. Keeping the accelerator still pressed she went into the curve holding her weight to the left of the vehicle while turning the kart right. She felt the kart shudder as it grazed the stacked tyres. She saw Nikhil immediately reduce his speed, just enough to let her win.

The karts passed the finishing line with the orange and white one leading. Sneha cut off the ignition and pulled her helmet off.

'That wasn't fair! You lost on purpose,' she called out loudly to Nikhil who had his helmet off.

Climbing off his kart, Nikhil sauntered over to her. 'How did it feel?'

'Awesome!' Sneha's smile reached her ears. 'But why did you let me win?'

Nikhil abruptly leaned down into her kart, bringing his face close to her. Sneha's eyes widened, surprised. 'I wanted to take you out for dinner.'

'Ohh!' Sneha made a strangled sound in her throat.

Nikhil did not bother to tame his wolfish grin as he straightened, satisfied at Sneha's reaction. She had not refused. 'More?'

'Of course.' To hide her confusion Sneha quickly put her helmet back on and closed the visor. Why did she feel tongue-tied? What did she expect him to do with her at dinner? The very thought sounded like a sensual dare. Sneha felt warm within the confines of the helmet.

'Hi Chandel!' A new voice broke in.

Sneha looked up but Nikhil's legs blocked her view of the person approaching. Sneha did not hear what Nikhil said under his breath but his stance was that of someone far from pleased.

Nikhil moved and Sneha saw a young man of average height and dusky complexion with a swarthy face coming towards them. There was certain swagger to his walk that added some bounce to his gelled locks.

He shook hands with Nikhil and said, 'Your friend kicked your butt.'

'Completely,' Nikhil replied, coolly extricating his hand. He turned to introduce him to Sneha but before he could even open his mouth, the newcomer extended his hand to her. 'Sharad. Call me Rad!'

Sneha choked on her laugh inside the helmet. She gave his hand a quick squeeze.

'Race with me. I'll show you how it's done. I beat Chandel

every week,' Rad declared to her. Then he turned to Nikhil. 'He and I are on next. I'm getting my kart readied.'

Nikhil and Sneha just then realized that Rad had mistaken Sneha for a man. Nikhil opened his mouth to clear the misunderstanding but Sneha's forceful shaking of her helmet stopped him.

'There she is!' Sharad pointed at the red and black kart the attendant drove to them. Sharad walked over to inspect his vehicle. Nikhil stepped closer to Sneha and squatted next to her. 'What are you doing?'

Sneha pulled up her visor a mere few inches. 'Please don't tell him. Let me race him. Please! Plleeeease,' Sneha pleaded earnestly.

'Sharad is a pompous peacock who doesn't play fair. You might get hurt,' Nikhil reasoned.

'I won't sue you. I promise.' Sneha tapped her knuckles against the steering wheel.

'Seriously, Sneha. I don't like this one bit,' Nikhil replied, his tone not the least indulgent.

'I promise I'll be very careful. I'll put my safety over my ego. I promise.' Sneha impulsively grasped Nikhil's hand closest to her.

Nikhil glanced down at their clasped gloved hands. Sneha instantly loosened her grip and pulled her fingers away. In response, Nikhil grabbed her hand, putting just enough pressure for it to be a gentle squeeze. 'Be careful. Remember: safety before ego.' Nikhil looked at her, a question in his eyes.

Sneha met Nikhil's deep green gaze even as she tugged her hand free. *Cross my heart and promise to die.*

'Dinner not death! Dinner.' Letting go of her hand, Nikhil stood up. He walked over to Sharad who was just putting an equally red—or 'rad'—helmet ready to slide into his kart. 'Be careful. I don't want anyone hurt,' Nikhil said to him, his tone stern.

Giving him a cheeky grin, Rad started his rad kart. Nikhil, purposely using one foot, bore his entire weight down one side of the kart. The vehicle quivered. 'I mean it. I don't want anyone hurt.'

Sharad gave Nikhil an irritated look. 'I heard you man. Now get off my kart. You'll break it.'

'It's metal.' Giving Sharad a sardonic look, Nikhil walked a few steps away. 'Three-lap race?'

'Bring it on.' Sharad for effect pressed down on his accelerator making a deafening sound. Sneha simply lifted her thumbs at Nikhil. To Sharad, she wanted to show a completely different finger.

Sneha started her kart and took her position at the start line, next to the rad man in the rad car. She saw Sharad inch the nose of his kart somewhat ahead of her. Grinning, Sneha glanced away and saw Nikhil standing at a gap between the tyres. He looked stern as he stared at Sharad. He raised his right hand, and counted one two and then made the 'go' sign. Sharad shot his kart onto the track, revving up his speed. Sneha fell behind him, her hands tight, body taut, and shoulders straight. All through the first lap, Sharad lead and Sneha tailed him. She could see she was making him edgy for he was glancing in the rearview mirror too often. She continued the tactic in the second lap. Sharad became complacent in the last curve of the second lap, giving her the opening she needed. Sneha, who had been driving at crazy speeds at a lower gear, moved to the last gear and floored the pedal. She smoothly overtook the other kart, her hands gripped the wheel tightly to keep her on course but the rear wheels went off the road. All she saw was a blur of red and the spew of dust washed over her as she went past him.

The two karts roared close to each other in the third lap. There were four curves to hit before the lap finished. Sneha managed to keep her lead in the first curve. As they raced to the second curve, Sneha's kart shuddered. She had to yank the wheel to the right and stabilize her body weight quickly to stop the kart from slipping from her grip. 'Bassbole!' she blurted out. Rad had just bumped her.

Sneha went into the second curve somewhat off her groove. Rad inched into the open space his underhanded manoeuvre had created. Sneha kept her eyes on the track and the wheels tight as both the karts hurtled together into the third curve. The fourth curve loomed at them. Sneha glanced at the kart zooming next to her. She saw Sharad turn the wheel; he was going to bump in her again. There was no way she could avoid crashing into the stacked tyres' boundaries.

Sneha got an idea. Crazy but maybe... She pressed hard on the accelerator. Her kart shuddered but moved a few inches past Sharad. Sharad panicked and tried bumping into her. In that split second, Sneha yanked the 'Hail Mary'. That move, in addition to the other kart's push forced her kart forward right through the fourth curve. Sneha sailed across the finishing lap with an undeniable lead.

The only snag was that now her kart was careening out of control. She saw Nikhil making some frantic gestures and shouting words at her from the side. Sneha understood, and threw her weight into the opposite direction of the tilting side and turned the wheel completely around. The kart did two circles and dust like a sandstorm rose, covering her and the kart. Sneha killed the ignition. She pushed the 'Hail Mary' back in. The boundaries rushed at her.

'Now!' Sneha heard Nikhil shout. She immediately pressed the ignition and floored the pedal. The kart's small engine roared and Sneha regained control of the kart. She yanked the wheel, the tyres straightened and the kart shot forward. Sneha hastily took her foot off the accelerator. The dust settled and Sneha missed Rad's ride by mere inches as she brought the kart to a smooth halt.

Letting go of the wheel, she put her head back and laughed out loud in the helmet. 'Oh my God!' She cried out. Nikhil reached her. He immediately unhooked her seat belt, his face concerned.

'You okay?' Sneha saw Nikhil mouth. Sneha's helmet bobbed furiously. A slow grin broke out on his lips. 'You were amazing,' he said. Nikhil helped Sneha stand up. Her legs ached, especially around the calves.

Sneha snapped her visor open. 'I know!' she hollered, excited. Sneha lunged forward and her arms circled Nikhil's neck, her adrenaline dominating her rationale. Nikhil did not move away, only lowered his shoulders to accommodate the embrace. Sneha came to her senses and pulled back. Her hands trailed his chest on their way back to her sides. Sneha gloved fingers tangled with Nikhil's bare ones. Unexpectedly, she wanted to rip off her gloves. Nikhil and Sneha started at each other for a few seconds, fingertips still touching. Awkward, Sneha was the first to glance away. She missed Nikhil's tender smile. His fingers reached under her chin to undo the helmet and touched her skin. Sneha felt familiar butterflies flutter in her stomach.

Sneha stepped out of the kart with a jerk. The helmet must be cutting off the blood circulation to her brain; why else would she swoon over Nikhil? She encountered a glowering Sharad. 'I think that was beginner's luck,' he scoffed to an older man who had joined him.

The man shook his head full of silver hair. 'Oh, give it up. You lost to him fair and square.'

'Who are you anyway?' Rad asked her patronizingly.

Sneha raised her finger, motioning for some time. She unstrapped her helmet and slid it off her head.

The older man gasped even as his wrinkled dark eyes twinkled with amusement.

Sharad threw his helmet and shouted, 'What the f—'

'Mind your mouth,' Nikhil cut him off, stopping next to Sneha.

'Did you know she was a girl?' Sharad asked Nikhil incredulously.

'It's kind of hard to miss, especially since I invited her here,' Nikhil replied even as he exchanged a handshake with the older man.

'Well then, the race wasn't fair,' Sharad retorted.

'Oh why? I had the advantage over you? Heck yeah,' Sneha stepped closer to Sharad and drawled. 'And you know what, doll? That advantage comes with skills and not sex.' Nikhil stayed mum and the older man appeared to be thoroughly enjoying himself. Then Sneha, casting another disparaging glance at Sharad, walked away, a fierce figure of 5 feet 4 inches.

Behind her, she heard Nikhil add, 'The next time you bump anyone on these tracks, your membership will be cancelled.'

Sneha stopped as Sharad yelled out, 'Do you know who my father is?' She turned to see Nikhil step closer to the blustering youngster. He towered over Sharad who stood his ground.

'I don't need to know your father. I know his boss and his boss, punk.' Nikhil sauntered over to Sneha, his face showing no expression but Sneha caught the anger in those green eyes. 'You okay?' Nikhil stopped next to her, taking her arm in reassurance.

'Y...ya, I'm fine.' Sneha cleared her throat awkwardly, shrugging her arm free. Nikhil dropped his hand. However, Sneha continued to feel his touch on her skin like a semi-permanent tattoo. 'I was just going to change.'

'Don't forget we have a dinner da—,' Nikhil chose another word, 'plan.' Stuffing his hands in the pockets, Nikhil stepped back. His demeanour cooled. 'I'll wait outside for you.' Nikhil walked ahead of Sneha and stopped just outside the door of the locker room. He asked the attendant loitering nearby, 'Please go and check that there is no one else inside.' Looking aloof, Nikhil busied himself on the phone even as Sneha stood quietly, waiting for the attendant to report to them.

Nikhil's eyes wandered to Sneha's face in silhouette. Her eyes flickered intermittently to him but she wouldn't meet his eyes. Sneha's obstinacy was frustrating and his fascination with her, perplexing. Nikhil disliked how she avoided or shirked his touch as if his fingers were on fire. If only he knew that for Sneha of late, his fingers did hold fire, the kind that started an answering spark, no, explosion in her.

'Locker room is empty, sir.'

Sneha passed Nikhil and went inside. A few minutes later, she came out smelling more like a woman than a dust mop. She found Nikhil where she had left him except he wasn't alone. Rad stood next to him. She stopped at some distance from them, hesitant. Rad was the first to notice her. Actually, Nikhil already knew Sneha had joined them but he behaved as though he did not; her floral perfume held a distinct sweet and light smell, which he had come to recognize.

Rad extended a hand to her. 'It was a good race,' he said grudgingly.

Sneha took his hand and returned the handshake. 'It was. Thanks.'

Rad turned around and stopped at Nikhil's side. 'Are we good?'

Nikhil turned to him and replied sombrely, 'We're good.'

'See you next week!' Sharad left them alone.

'I think I should head home,' Sneha said churlishly. To her disappointment, Nikhil did not argue.

'Let's go!' Nikhil reached out to guide her by her elbow. Then immediately Sneha saw Nikhil drop his hand as he briskly walked past her.

Oh, so I'm not good enough for him to touch? Sneha saw red. *Fine by me buster*, she thought as she marched up the steps, her head held high. Just as they walked outside, Sneha realized that her legs were aching and sitting astride a motorbike appeared an arduous task.

She caught the familiar dark German car next to the motorbike. 'Take the bike to the apartment. Thanks.' Nikhil handed the bike keys to the driver. He went on to open the door at the passengers' side and glanced in Sneha's direction. Sneha muttered a 'thanks' as she got in. She stretched her legs, trying not to draw much attention to her discomfort.

'Soak them in hot water,' Nikhil said, getting in from the driver's side. He had noticed Sneha's slow gait since she got off the kart and the manner in which she stretched her calves. 'Do you need some painkillers?'

Sneha straightened. 'No thanks. I have some at home.'

'We are not going home,' Nikhil replied, turning the car on.

'We're not?' Sneha replied, surprised.

'We're going out for dinner,' Nikhil said, putting the car in reverse.

'But it's...umm...early for dinner,' Sneha spoke haltingly, surprised by how pleased she was that their dinner da—plan was still on.

'So we'll have a drink,' Nikhil replied smoothly, putting the car in forward gear. 'Actually you are forbidden from drinking,' he added cheekily.

Tentatively, Sneha said, 'About that night. I wanted to apologize. I don't know what came over me. I'm really sorry!'

'Don't say it with such petulance. Sorry should be said with sincerity,' Nikhil goaded.

'I *was* being sincere.' Indignantly, Sneha turned in her seat to face Nikhil. His lips were sweetly pulled to a side as he teased her. Sneha lost her chain of thought. Without saying anything else, she sat back and stared right ahead. No man had bothered, irked and flustered her like he did.

'Are you okay?' Nikhil slowed the car and put the back of his hand against her cheek facing him.

Sneha stirred and jumped back in her seat away from his hand. 'I'm fine,' she blurted.

Unexpectedly, Nikhil hit the steering wheel with his hand. 'Stop doing that. I'm not going to rape you,' he bit out between pressed lips, his expression seriously aggravated.

Taken aback, Sneha stared at Nikhil's livid profile. 'What are you talking about? Rape? I never ever said or even thought...? Sneha's genuine horror turned into anger. 'How can you say such a stupid thing?' Nikhil now surprised, glanced at Sneha. Did she not realize it?

'Watch this.' Nikhil abruptly caught Sneha's hand placed at her side. Sneha flinched and immediately withdrew her hand.

'That. That's how you react every time I touch you, purposely or accidentally.'

Sneha stared at her hand and then at Nikhil, stumped. 'Oh! I do that every time?' she asked, her voice stoked with sudden self-realization.

'Every time,' Nikhil replied, emphasizing on 'every'.

'I'm sorry, I did not even realize I was doing that. I guess I'm not a touchy feely person,' Sneha said defensively

Nikhil snorted. 'Neither are a lot of us. But how you react is freakin' abnormal.'

Sneha could not contain herself, 'Well, if you had a spouse who forced himself on you, you too might react like that.' Horrified, she immediately clamped her hand over her mouth. What had she just revealed?

23

Either you are engaged or you're not

Nikhil's brief look at Sneha was filled with disbelief and anger. Sneha soon realized why the look was brief. Pressing his hand on the horn, Nikhil cut though the traffic and pulled over in a matter of seconds. He ripped his seat belt off himself and turned to her. 'What are you saying, Sneha?' he hissed.

Sneha was too overcome to talk. She shook her head miserably as sudden tears ran down her cheeks. Nikhil put a hand on her arm. Sneha raised wounded eyes to him. Her self-control was in tatters. 'On our wedding night. I was a virg...' She gulped and lowered her head, her shoulders shook. Oh God, she had held this macabre secret of her life so close to her heart and now it had just slipped out. Suppressed anguish shook her. Nikhil, swearing softly, undid Sneha's seat belt and gathered her to him. Sneha did not resist. She just lay limp against his chest as her misery poured intermittently from her eyes. Nikhil rested his chin on her head. He stroked her head muttering repeatedly, 'I will kill that bastard!'

After a few minutes, Sneha pulled back. Sniffing, she took the box of tissues Nikhil held out to her. He still held her close. 'I'm fine.' Nikhil, with obvious reluctance, let go. Wiping her eyes, Sneha sat back in her seat.

'You should have shot him.'

Giving Nikhil a sad, watery smile, Sneha stared ahead of her without really seeing anything. 'I ran away the next morning to my parents. Ankit came after me. He apologized profusely to me and my parents. He put the blame on me. Called me frigid and nervous.' Sneha snorted. 'Me and scared? But that night I probably was, for the first time.' Her breath came out broken. Sneha hung her head. 'My mom bought his lies and my dad…'

'And your dad?' Nikhil asked, his voice holding repressed rage.

'He pistol-whipped Ankit. One blow and Ankit was on the floor, face bleeding. My mother and sister stopped him before he killed Ankit.'

'I like your dad already,' Nikhil muttered between clamped lips.

'Ankit's parents were called. It was a big scene.' Sneha wiped her eyes again. 'My mom, his mom and his sister… everyone was of the view that we should give the marriage another chance.'

'Un-freaking-believable! And your dad?

'He was dead set against the idea.'

'Wise man.'

Sneha sombrely agreed, 'He is. Anyhow, I chose to give the marriage another chance but insisted that Ankit and I would live with my parents for a while. I felt safe there.'

'Arranged marriage?'

'Yes!' Sneha understood the look Nikhil gave her. 'I know, one would think I would never settle for something arranged. But honestly speaking, I never saw myself as the kind to fall in love. I never wore the rose-coloured glasses most girls my age wear.' Sneha became quiet.

'You should have ended the marriage right there and then,' Nikhil responded. The look in his eyes was angry yet empathizing. The kind that meant Sneha's anguish mattered to him…a lot. The kind that made Sneha want to tell him the whole story.

Sneha took a deep breath. 'I realized that within the four weeks we stayed with my folks, Ankit and I were chalk and cheese. But by then it was too late.'

Nikhil's gaze was questioning. Sneha flushed as she spoke haltingly, 'I was pregnant from the…wedding…night.'

'Oh!'

'Even though I'm pro-choice for others, I was dead set against hurting the life growing within me. Even my parents suggested that I move on. By then even my mom came to see what a futile effort our marriage was. But I was adamant; I would not kill my baby. I wanted my child to live.' Sneha eyes again filled up with tears, her vision blurred. She missed the tortured look that passed over Nikhil's face at her words.

Nikhil took Sneha's hand. Reflexively she flinched and then Sneha took a deep breath and relaxed her hand in his fingers. On their own accord her fingers tightened around his. Sneha did not have the courage to look into his eyes.

'And then?' Nikhil probed, holding on to her hand. It felt good in his.

'I went back to Ankit, but this time it was on my terms. Terms that included no crap of any kind. I hoped that our relationship would grow stronger with this baby. And the two years we stayed together, we did grow, but only more apart. In fact—' she broke off.

'In fact?' Nikhil asked, wanting her to go on.

Sneha glanced at him, her saucy eyes lacklustre for once, the tips of her eyelashes stuck together because of her tears. 'In fact, when I caught Ankit cheating on me with his ex-girlfriend from college, I was relieved. Relieved that I could free myself of a stifling relationship, I didn't ask for single thing in our divorce, just that I get primary custody of Advey. Ankit gave me sole custody.' Sneha twisted her lips in a sardonic grimace.

'He let you down again.'

Sneha gazed at him. *What was I thinking, right?*

Nikhil steadily met her gaze. *You weren't asking for much!*

'Thanks!' Sneha murmured.

'For what?' Nikhil asked, straightening.

'For what you just said…' Confused, Sneha squinted her eyes. Had he said that or had she…? 'Nothing!' She put the seat belt around her.

'I saw you!' Nikhil confessed.

'Huh?'

'That evening, nearly two years ago, at Gayatri and Aditya's supposed engagement party.' Nikhil's eyes were sombre, his lips wry.

'Back then! You were there? You saw me? Why didn't you come and meet me?' Sneha asked, perplexed. Then she remembered. Perhaps it was better Nikhil hadn't sought her out then—that night she and Ankit had had a big showdown. That night was the first time she had suspected that Ankit might be cheating on her.

'I don't know. By the time I thought I would look for you, I couldn't find you,' Nikhil said easily, hiding the fact that when he had found her, she had been in a heated argument with her husband in a corridor leading to the gardens. If he remembered correctly, it was something to do with some dubious texting her husband had been indulging in. It was time to change the topic. 'Where do you want to eat?' Nikhil asked.

'I really want to go home,' Sneha pleaded. 'I think I'm getting a headache. Crying doesn't suit me.' She confessed, rubbing her temples.

Nikhil started the car; as he was about to put the gear he paused and turned to Sneha, 'Regarding your ex, I think you should have shot him but regarding Advey you can be sure that you made the right decision. I—' Nikhil corrected himself, 'everyone can only applaud your guts. In the circumstances you just described it must have been extremely hard to do the right thing without family support.'

Sneha gulped. 'I guess I'm made of stronger stuff.' She had just announced that she rarely cried and here she was, getting ready to unleash a fresh set of waterworks. She swallowed a few times.

'You are!' Nikhil too put on his seat belt, his look perceptive.

Sneha sat back and said, her voice low, 'Everything bad, painful, simply disappeared the moment I first saw Advey and held him in my arms. Now even my family can't see beyond him.' Unconsciously, Sneha reached out to touch Nikhil's hand; however, she immediately realized what she was about to do. She stopped herself and her fingers bumped his knuckles. Sneha saw Nikhil purse his lips to hide a smile. Giving him a comical sheepish look, Sneha primly put her hands in her lap. She peeked at Nikhil under her lashes. He was staring at her. Sneha smoothed her hands over her skirt, her eyes grazed Nikhil's lower lip that came apart right under her gaze. She felt her breathing falter. Her nervous eyes clashed with his. Nikhil's gaze held something more than just amusement. Staring at him, Sneha silently howled in her head, *Oh God, I want to kiss him.*

Nikhil felt something tighten in his gut. The hooded look he gave Sneha held a promise. *And I'll kiss you back. Thoroughly!*

Nikhil's eyes became a darker shade of green as he stared at the woman beside him. The one with mussed hair, shiny cheeks, bewildered hazel eyes and a pink mouth that was sneakily pulling in deep, steadying breaths.

'We shoullld mo-ove,' Sneha stuttered. Her fraught nerves needed some alone-time or a call to her kulta. On second thoughts, forget about calling Nandini. Kulta would start planning her wedding.

'Of course. You said home?' Nikhil spoke slowly.

'Yes! Home…you remember where I live?'

'I do.' Nikhil started the car and merged with the traffic. Sneha chose to look out of the window, trying to straighten her jumbled mind. How could such uber personal shit come out of her mouth and to HIM? 'Nandini does not know about this,' she murmured.

'This stays between us,' Nikhil instantly allayed her fears, somewhat smug that Sneha had confided in him what she had not seen fit to share with her more-than-best-friend. Unknowingly, Sneha burst his bubble.

'Nandini is very innocent. She only sees the good in people and I wish her to stay like that,' Sneha added.

Nikhil merely grunted in response. Sneha, seeking some distraction, opened her laptop bag and scanned her phone for missed calls and messages. 'Excuse me!' she said to Nikhil and began reading them. What she saw had her utter a startled shout. 'No! Hammit.' She gently but repeatedly smacked her phone against her head.

Nikhil gave her a concerned look. 'What happened?'

'That damn driver took a picture of me with you on the bike and now half the office has it. Mrs Aiyyer just texted me the image. They fired the guy but what the hell?' Sneha appeared boggled.

'What will you do now?' Nikhil asked.

'I don't know' Sneha snapped. 'I will have to put out some fires,' she continued her rant. 'You know, that's why I avoid socializing or meeting people. Stupid unnecessary complications—' She paused when she saw Nikhil's expression. 'I'm sorry, I'm just frustrated.' Sneha crossing her arms fell back in her chair, her expression displeased. 'Now they'll think you are my loody fiancé.'

Nikhil almost struck the car in front of him. 'You are engaged?'

Sneha winced. Today was the day to reveal all the bloopers of her life. She bit her lip, her expression pleading. She hesitantly offered, 'Kind of yes, and kind of no.'

'Either you are engaged or you're not. What is kind of?' Nikhil asked, slowly and irritatingly emphasizing each word as he changed gears with unnecessary force. It was so hard to have a flat line of emotion around Sneha. She had him terribly happy, exceptionally furious, uncontrollably aroused, completely confused in no more than a span of a few minutes.

Sneha hurriedly explained, 'At work I just faked a fiancé story so that no one would hit on me.'

'What?' Nikhil's green gaze was as wide as it could be.

'Well, don't look at me like that. A divorced, unattached woman becomes target practice for all and sundry. I just go to office to work and not to bed my colleagues,' Sneha blubbered.

'You are that attractive.' Nikhil was surprised by his words but of course Sneha would misunderstand him. He saw her chin go up, and the nation was back to announcing its sovereignty.

'I didn't say that. Just that men can't resist playing darts with their dic—' Sneha flushed as she broke off. Nikhil's resounding laugh surprised her. She saw him leaning back in his chair laughing hard. He did have a beautiful laugh, the kind that was an even tone which fell smoothly on the ears rather than a mesh of emotional sounds at various decibels.

'Darts with their...!' Nikhil let loose another chuckle, a sound that went straight to Sneha's happy place. 'How do you come up with these expressions?' Nikhil shifted his bemused glance between Sneha and the traffic.

'I don't know!' Sneha replied, a grudging smile lighting her mouth.

Nikhil's quick glance lingered over her smile. 'How are you going to handle it?'

'I don't know!' Sneha's smile faltered.

'Kill the fiancé. Tell your CEO, DC Inc. is willing to let your firm make a presentation. I'll have my advertising head get in touch with you. And that is why you had this meeting with me.'

Sneha scoffed. 'Seeing how I was sitting with you, they'll never believe that this meeting was just work. And I'm not killing my fiancé, he's my knight in shining armour,' she added haughtily.

'Maybe it's time you get a new knight. Useless man can't even buy his girl a nice ring,' Nikhil teased.

'The girl brought it herself and sends herself flowers too,' Sneha added.

'Does he have a name?'

'Samar or Samarth, I think. I'm not sure.' Sneha liked Nikhil's answering hoot of laughter. 'Remember, this falls under the Nandini-must-not-know-category!'

Nikhil mimicked her earlier words, 'Because Nandini is very innocent. She only sees the good in people and I wish her to stay like that. In this case, you being the *people*, I presume,' he teased.

Sneha laughed and wiped the side of her eyes. 'On the contrary, kulta will alter a fictional fiancé in no time to a real one and have me marry him.'

Nikhil lost his humour. His expression darkened. 'Right!'

Sneha noticed Nikhil's mood change and something else too. 'Where are we going? This is not the way to my place.'

'You just said home! We are going to mine,' Nikhil smirked.
Sneha panicked. 'No, no! Please just drop me home.'

'Relax, Sneha. I'm not in the mood to play darts today, I
promise,' Nikhil's assuring words had the opposite reaction on
Sneha than he intended. Her eyes clouded with doubt. 'Look,
we both have to eat. My chef prepares extensive meals every
day and they go waste for I never reach the apartment in time
for dinner. So today, help me earn some brownie points with
him. Please!'

'Fine!' Sneha quickly acquiesced. 'FYI, I know when I'm being
played,' she added.

'You talk in riddles,' Nikhil replied, bemused as he pressed a
rectangular button on the steering wheel. The car filled with music.

Sneha sighed and rested her head back. Nikhil left her alone
with her thoughts just unexpectedly glad that Sneha had given
in to his demand of having dinner together. It was only altruistic
reasons that prompted him to spend some more time with her.
Sunhaar, in denial, drove to his house. And the luhaar all the
while cursed the high levels of contamination in the alloy that
her armour was made of.

Sneha and Nikhil drove into a sea-facing complex off Nariman
Point. The elevator ride was short and silent. They got off on
the sixth floor. Nikhil guided Sneha to an apartment on the left
side of the elevator. The carpet under their feet was thick and
burgundy in colour. Oval gilded mirrors and golden-plated artwork
dominated the walls of the corridor they were walking through.
Fresh flower arrangements were placed at regular intervals. Soft
music played in the corridor.

'What is this place?'

'Corporate housing.'

Nikhil pointed to a door on the right with the number eight
written in small metallic numbers. He swiped a key card and the
door quietly swung open.

'No retina scanning?' Sneha teased.

'Don't give them ideas,' Nikhil replied nodding at the ceiling where Sneha spied a tiny camera.

'Ughh!' Sneha hurriedly stepped in. 'Creepy! I actually prefer peelings walls, steps mottled with paan stain and the faint smell of urine in the air. How do you people live here?'

Nikhil stared at her slack-jawed. Then he recovered with a grin. 'Priceless!'

Sneha's answering smile was naughty as she pointedly peeped around. 'I know! For everything else there is MasterCard.'

Nikhil put his hand on her lower back and then realized he was touching her. Testing Sneha, Nikhil let his hand stay. Sneha at once stiffened and then forced herself to relax against his touch. She teasingly glanced at Nikhil over her shoulder. *You okay?*

Never been better!

Stop ogling.

24

I googled you!

'I'm not ogling,' Nikhil still kept his hand on her back.

Sneha was sheepish. 'Did I say that out loud...?' she trailed off, confused.

'No, I don't...' Nikhil's expression matched hers. 'Let's go inside.' They walked from the dimly lit foyer into the apartment.

'Oh my!' Sneha gaped at the two-level apartment done up completely in black, white and metallic colours.

'Welcome!'

'Very dramatic! Stark but beautiful.'

'It works well for me.'

'No fountains?' Sneha teased, settling into a recliner. She immediately sat up with a start, 'What the...?'

'Relax. That one has a sensor massage. Take the one next to it.'

'Actually I'm going to take this one. Where is the chef or the food?' she asked, easing her back against the massage chair.

'Italian or Indian?'

'Chinese!' Sneha said, smiling as she pressed her back into the chair. 'Hmmm!' The chair was doing wonderful things to her muscles. 'Oh this is better than sex.'

Sneha could have bitten her tongue off. Nikhil's wide grin only added to her mortification. 'Ignore that.' She closed her eyes tightly as she rested her head on the chair.

'Italian or Indian?' Nikhil repeated.

'Chin—fine, Indian.'

'Give me ten!' Nikhil walked away and went up the stairs that led to the kitchen fitted with modern, spotless, stainless steel appliances. 'There's a restroom there. The first door on the left, in case you want to freshen up.'

After a few minutes, Sneha got to her feet and followed his directions. Her body felt relaxed as it seemed to have lost a few knots. She splashed water on her face, brushed her hair and applied some watermelon gloss on her face. As Sneha was about to head out, she remembered.

'Dang!' Her impatient fingers ruffled the inside of her handbag until she found her perfume bottle. She quickly sprayed some on her wrists and behind her ears. As her finger went to open the buttons of her blouse to spray a hint of perfume in her cleavage, Sneha caught her face in the mirror. Eyes shining, cheeks that held colour and a mouth relaxed, face excited. She stared at her own reflection, shocked. Was she expecting something to happen? She shook her head to clear her thoughts. Sneha buttoned her blouse and put the bottle back in her bag without spraying any more. Even though she refused to acknowledge the perishing woman inside her shouting for a voice, she felt her pain, her acute pangs of solitary confinement.

'BS! I'm stronger than that!' Sneha muttered and with a defiant toss of her dark auburn curls, Sneha walked out. She found Nikhil removing white containers from the fridge and putting them in the microwave. He had changed into a pair of blue jeans that clung to his long muscular legs and a dark green T-shirt. His hair was brushed back as if, instead of a comb, he had run his fingers through it. He looked tall and freakin' mouth-watering. Sneha gulped going up the few stairs. 'Bhoot pisaach nikaat nahi aave, Mahavir jab naam sunabe,' she repeatedly muttered under her breath as she joined him in the kitchen.

'Have a seat!' Nikhil gestured at the four bar stools lined up against the brown-black granite counter top next to him. 'Or we can sit downstairs.'

'This is fine.' Sneha took the stool that stood at an angle furthest from him.

'You're okay?' Nikhil asked, glancing at Sneha even as he took out some black and white ceramic dinner plates from an adjoining cupboard.

'Perfect!' Sneha unknowingly, nervously licked the side of her lip as she lifted herself to sit on the stool. Nikhil stood mesmerized by the tiny, quick visual of her pink tongue wetting her full lower lip. Suddenly he felt as hot as the food sizzling inside the microwave. He could not take his eyes off the awkwardly tottering woman across from him.

'I hate bar stools. I'm always scared I'll fall off one,' Sneha gave a nervous laugh, carefully shifting on her perch.

'We can move downstairs.'

'No, it's fine. Seriously,' Sneha said as she stretched her hand out for a plate. Nikhil took out silverware from a drawer next to him and then he fished out napkins from another one.

'Thank you.' Sneha took the plate with the silverware and napkin. 'You seem to know your way around the kitchen.'

'I'm here most of the time by myself,' Nikhil replied as he opened the beeping microwave. 'What will you drink?'

'Anything non-alcoholic,' Sneha replied, her expression sheepish. 'I suck at cooking.'

'Kindred souls. I am only good at heating food in the microwave and making a mean omelette,' Nikhil shared seeking something inside the fridge. He pulled out a green bottle with silver foil wrapped around its neck.

'I'm not drinking champagne,' Sneha protested.

Nikhil held the label close to her, '100 per cent non-alcoholic, sparkling apple cider.'

'Okay! Thanks.' Sneha fidgeted with her silverware. 'Are we alone here?'

Nikhil who was delicately handling a hot container of appetizers, paused and glanced at her. His green eyes gleamed. 'Yes! What did you have in mind?' His gaze was searing.

Sneha's eyes widened, startled. An image of her and Nikhil making out on the granite counter-top flashed in her head. She experienced tightening and tingles in her lower belly. She flushed. 'Nothing! I was just wondering, that's all,' she glanced around the kitchen, awkward.

'There are staff quarters and a concierge on every floor. You need something?' Nikhil quickly placed the food in front of her. 'Please help yourself.' He opened the fridge door and poked his head inside the cool interiors to rid himself of the recurring image of him turning the barstool on which Sneha sat towards him and then lowering his head to grind his mouth against Sneha's surprised, soft mouth. Their mouths were locked with each others', the heat of her body ate at him through clumsily shed clothes. His fingers fisted in her hair, holding it in place as his mouth devoured her. Damn! His jeans felt tight in the wrong spot. Nikhil needed some instant cooling off and he had already used the shower in the bathroom. He did not understand this intimate oneness he felt with Sneha.

Keeping his movements efficient and brisk, Nikhil went on to place the food on the granite counter-top and Sneha gazed at the view through the large rectangular windows to the left of the apartment. The ocean was a looming dark mass of blackness behind the moving traffic lights of Marine Drive. It was as if life merely existed until that edge and then the world just fell away.

Silence, soaked only in the awareness of each other, stretched between Sneha and Nikhil. At this moment, a single look was all that it would take to kill the distance between their bodies. They were both suffering from extreme physical pain from not touching each other. Sneha's thoughts closely resembled Nikhil's as she stared out of the window. She imagined their intimately bound reflections in it. Her breathing became shallower, her body felt warm and lethargic and she felt something warm rush between her legs, something so painfully pleasuring that she crossed her legs with a sudden fierceness.

In her peripheral vision Sneha saw Nikhil take slow but sure steps towards her. She looked at him. Panic and something else filled her as she saw Nikhil's darkening eyes gaze sweep over her with raw hunger. Sneha had no will left to resist Nikhil; in fact, she craved him like a drowning man craving oxygen. She closed her eyes, powerless to do anything but await his touch with her heart thudding in anticipation.

She felt Nikhil stop next to her. His voice was a hoarse whisper in her ear, his words mirroring Sneha's feelings, 'I can't fight this any more. I don't want to. I'm done running, Sneha.' His guttural admission cut through whatever control Sneha had. Her head fell back inviting, welcoming his caress. Nikhil was close enough for Sneha's knee to brush his leg. 'Open your eyes!' Nikhil demanded, his voice hoarse, 'let me drown in them.'

Pulling in a deep breath, Sneha opened her eyes. Desire had turned her irises to a dark brown and the sultry invitation in them cleanly shredded all remnants of Nikhil's self-control. Holding her eyes captive with his, Nikhil's hand came up slowly.

Sneha gasped as Nikhil ran his fingers over the skin under her knees. 'Are the calves still hurting?' His voice was low and thick. His hooded deep green eyes left Sneha in no doubt that he was only and only thinking of her body. In response, Sneha brazenly dug the underside of her knee deeper into his hand, wanting to feel more of him on her. Nikhil did not disappoint her. His probing fingers very slowly, very intimately rose higher on Sneha's leg gently kneading her skin and drawing her closer to him at the same time.

Sneha could not breathe and then in sheer panic of the unknown and the moment, she blurted out, 'I googled you.' Nikhil's fingers that had now been replaced by his hand steadfastly stroking the soft skin at the inside of her thigh, stilled. Nikhil instantly withdrew his hand and for a second it stayed in the air, as he was unsure of where to put it. Sneha looked away and when she glanced back at Nikhil she saw the wary, hunted expression in his eyes. Sneha blinked, surprised. She had seen Nikhil exceptionally furious, uncontrollably aroused, completely cold, vaguely happy but this was a new one.

Nikhil took a few steps away from Sneha, going back to what he was familiar with. 'And what did you find?' His voice sounded as if it could freeze water.

'Stuff!' Sneha fumbled.

'C'mon Sneha, you can do better than that!' Nikhil's eyes were frigid pools of green.

Sneha fumbled, 'I'm sure it was mostly hearsay. Things about your divorce.'

'Tell me!' Nikhil's voice was like a crack of a whip.

Sneha's chin went up, bristling at his tone. She did not hold back. '90 per cent of the articles described you as a money-obsessed, greedy, opportunistic cad of a man who callously dumped his young wife in just over a year, leaving her traumatized and broke.'

Except for a muscle that twitched in his left cheek and the hard glint in his eyes, Nikhil stood still as a statue. Sneha watched him as seconds passed. After a few minutes, he coolly said, 'I'll warm the naan.' Nikhil turned away from Sneha and rummaged inside the freezer.

Sneha stared at him, her eyes narrowed. There was no denying Nikhil's anger and Sneha did not like the feeling of being ignored. 'Is it true?' she persisted.

She saw his shoulders heave and then Nikhil turned. His face bunched-up and feral, he snarled, 'None of your damn bloody business!' He flung the plastic bag on the counter-top between them. The packet with momentum continued sliding along the entire length of the slab and fell off, landing on the ground with a plop sound.

Sneha gazed at the fallen packet of frozen naan and then met Nikhil's angry eyes. Without a word and with whatever dignity she could muster, Sneha jumped off the bar stool and marched towards the main door. Her eyes shone brightly. Memories of fights from her past relationship dominated her mind. Fresh hurt pounded her head. Sneha was too mulish to accept that it was her heart being butchered here.

Nikhil watched Sneha go down the steps. How could she believe those things about him, especially now? His anger and ego pummelled his rationale, but not for long.

Just as Sneha angrily yanked her bag off the sofa, Nikhil called out. 'Wait!' Ignoring him, Sneha took hurried steps. She had barely touched the knob on the front door when Nikhil's grip pulled her away from the door.

Nikhil was surprised to see the dampness on her cheeks. For a second he could only gaze at her face. Deep contrition filled him. 'Sneha! I'm sorry.' His hand went up to wipe her tears, but Sneha smacked it away.

'You have no business yelling at me. I'm not your wife,' Sneha hollered as her face contorted, fighting more tears.

'And I'm not your ex-husband.' Nikhil stubbornly put his hand up again and wiped her tears gently. Holding her wrists he gently but firmly pulled Sneha closer, his expression sombre. 'I'm nothing like your ex-husband.'

Sneha glanced away. 'And neither am I all those adjectives you just used to describe me,' Nikhil added quietly.

'I was just telling you what I read,' Sneha mumbled, wiping her face against her upper arm as Nikhil still held her wrists.

Nikhil again reached out and wiped away all the remnants of her tears. 'Come back! I'm asking you, not telling you,' Nikhil let go of Sneha's hands. His action spoke louder than words. 'Maybe it's time I shared a few things with you,' Nikhil added quietly. His voice was proud but his face urged her to give him a chance.

'You don't have to. I don't mean to pry.' Sneha straightened her hair and flattened her palms against the side of her skirt.

In a heartbeat Nikhil replied, 'You are not prying and I want to. Please!'

Sneha turned around and walked back to the living room. She took a seat on the sofa. 'The food!' she said awkwardly.

Nikhil noticed she still wasn't meeting his eyes. 'It can wait. If you are not very hungry.'

'I'm not. I need some water though.' Sneha primly put her bag on her lap. She was ready for a quick exit if the need resurfaced.

'Sure!' Nikhil hurried back to the kitchen. He came back with two flutes filled with liquid that hissed and bubbled. He handed Sneha a glass. 'Apple cider. Let's go out there.' Nikhil walked and pulled the sheer white curtains on one end of the room. Sneha saw a terrace that opened out to the ocean. She gladly followed Nikhil out and the coolness of the night that held the sharp smell of sea salt soothed some of the turmoil bubbling in her.

'It is beautiful!' Sneha said, walking over to the cane chairs and sofa clustered at one end of the circular terrace. Dim lights shining all around them reminded her of the lights one saw from an airplane in the night. Sneha could see the outlines of various pots and plants. She could only imagine how beautiful this place must look on a rainy afternoon.

'Fountain!' Nikhil pointed sheepishly at the fountain on one end of the terrace that fell in steps over glistening and oblong pebbles lying in a marble basin.

Sneha's smile was weak as she sank into a cane chair. She kept her eyes fixed on the inky ocean. She heard Nikhil sit next to her. Sneha wanted to turn to him but she was unsure of how to begin the conversation. Nothing came to her head.

Nikhil did the honours. 'As a child—' Nikhil broke off. He tried again. 'In my marriage...no' He again broke off. He re-tried. 'My wife...no!' He again trailed off. Irritated, he sat back in the chair with a thump. He did not know how to begin the story even when he was so desperately eager to share it.

Sneha looked at him, her expression tender. 'As a child...?' she prompted gently, 'I want the whole story of you from you.'

Nikhil leaned forward and smiled a smile that truly reached his eyes. Then he started, 'I lost my father when I was seven and—'

'I'm so sorry!' Sneha could not help but say.

'Thanks. I still miss him. I wonder how my life would have turned out if he had been around. Anyway, my mom, who was a very sweet woman, found it hard to raise me by herself as she was not very emotionally or mentally tough…' He left the 'unlike you' unsaid but Sneha understood; she tried hard not to feel pleased at the unexpected compliment.

'Also I had a very greedy set of uncles on my dad's side that could not wait to get their paws on the companies my dad ran and they succeeded in doing just that. I had to grow up quickly for my mother and myself. My older uncle allowed my mother to start working with him, hoping she would know how to run the business but she wasn't cut out for that kind of work. Under my mother and my uncle, the family's jewellery business was about to go belly-up By the time I was thirteen, I had started going to office after school trying to fill in my dad's shoes and learn the ropes. That is when I bumped into Gayatri's dad who was an old friend of my late father. My father had helped him a couple of times and he repaid his debts to my dad in full and more. Gayatri's father took me under his wing, taught me how to manage the business and also helped us legally win our business back from my uncle.' Sneha, listening quietly, now understood why Nikhil felt the need to do all that he did for Gayatri. She had always felt that there was something rather brotherly about the way Nikhil behaved around her.

'All my growing up happened around adults. Somewhere I became a loner, keeping mostly to myself and work. The age where kids were getting their first car or first bike, I was negotiating my first million-dollar deal with people nearly thrice my age. When boys my age were partying night long, I was pulling an all-nighter in office conference rooms to avoid falling back on my college work.' Nikhil caught Sneha's sympathetic expression and couldn't help a soft smile, 'It wasn't that tragic.'

Sneha's smile was tender. 'I know when I'm being played.'

Nikhil's smile matched hers. 'As you in your immaturity killed all my chances with Kim—'

'I did not!' Sneha exclaimed.

Nikhil's look was very tongue-in-cheek. 'I continued living a few more years by myself with a slew of sporadic relationships. And then I met my ex-wife, Alisha Sarkar.' Nikhil broke off.

Sneha watched him as she saw a bevy of emotions skim his face; he was thinking of Alisha. She was surprised by the flash of jealousy within her. 'And?' she probed, shifting uncomfortably in her chair.

'And?' Nikhil recollected his thoughts and continued, 'Yes! Alisha was the darling of the Mumbai's page three society. Beautiful, educated, associated with numerous frivolous causes and the kind who partied hard and photographed beautifully.' Nikhil's face was bitter.

'When I met her for the first time I was immediately drawn to her.' Sneha took a hurried sip of her drink, hiding her face with her glass. Nikhil, with his gaze distant and fixed somewhere beyond the terrace's edge, continued, 'With all the maturity of a dolt, I fell for her...hard.' Sneha did not understand why she her mouth suddenly tasted of bile. 'Fulfilling her every wish and whim suddenly became the purpose of my existence.' Sneha again shifted her derrière in the chair and took a big swallow from her glass. She choked.

Nikhil snapped out of his trance and rubbed her back to ease her breathing. 'I'm fine!' Sneha said, her voice raspy. 'You were saying?'

Nikhil squinted, distracted. 'Where was I?'

'You were going to marry her,' Sneha suggested, wanting to skim over the tender boring details. Boring, right?

'I was?' Nikhil rubbed his chin thoughtfully. 'Anyway, to cut a long story short, I could not wait to marry her, which I did with all the pomp and show. I did all that even knowing that this was not what I wanted. I just wanted to please her. '

'Ya! Ya, I got that!' Sneha jumped, lest he start with the boring details again.

Nikhil gave her a puzzled look. Sneha gave him her sweetest smile to distract him. It worked, as he gazed at her longer then he needed to. Sneha pointedly cleared her throat. Nikhil shook his head as if to clear the fog inside. Sneha hid her smile. 'Sorry! Where was I?'

Sneha rolled her eyes at him. Nikhil said defensively, 'I'm not good at talking about myself.' Sneha gave Nikhil's hand a squeeze. She made sure her touch was brief even though both their fingers wanted to linger. 'It's okay! Carry on.'

'After marriage it took me only a few months to realize that parties, her looks and spending money was all that mattered to Alisha.'

'Being alone in a marriage is the worst kind of loneliness,' Sneha murmured, remembering her own unfortunate nuptials.

'It is. But I also realized that it was unfair of me to expect her to change. She had always been like this. She had never hidden these facets of her personality from me. Things were fine for nearly a year until the day of our first wedding anniversary. I came back early from a trip to surprise my wife and found her in our bed with another man and high on coke.'

'Oh my God!' Sneha whispered, shocked.

Nikhil stood up. 'I was devastated; I had to face not only the fact that my wife was cheating but she was also was a cokehead. Even though Alisha claimed she snorted cocaine socially, I did not buy it. I overlooked the cheating aspect and blamed the drugs for it. I had her enter a rehab programme and took an indefinite l eave of absence to be at her side.' Nikhil's pause this time was longer.

'And?'

Nikhil looked at her, his gaze blank. 'And?'

'And rehab, leave of absence...' Sneha prodded.

Nikhil shook his head. 'Yes of course. I'm sorry, in my head I was thinking about what happened next.' He sat back, his knees hovering close to Sneha's.

'And Alisha's stint in rehab did prove that she was a borderline addict with commitment issues. The man I had caught her with wasn't the first one she had cheated on me with.'

'I'm so sorry!' was the best Sneha could come up with. However, her pained voice did apt justice to what she felt for Nikhil at that minute.

Nikhil gave her a reassuring yet gloomy smile, 'Thanks. In all fairness, I decided to move on, divorce Alisha and cut my losses.'

Sneha heard the silent, 'but' and she said it, 'But?'

'But Alisha did not want the divorce. She wanted to stay married even if it was just for appearances. Our marriage would be in name only and open, leaving us both to pursue whatever else we wanted with whomever we pleased.'

Sneha could not help a reflexive, 'Ewww!'

Nikhil too grimaced. 'Exactly. Thus I refused point-blank and upped the share of money she would walk away with post the divorce. Alisha realized that my mind was made up and thus to spite me she hurt me where she knew it would hurt me the most.'

Sneha saw his face become pale, his green eyes throbbed with pain. Sneha could not help putting her hand on his knee. Nikhil did not seem to feel her touch. 'Being the only child growing up, I had always yearned for a sibling. After marriage I knew I would want several kids. Not a single corner of my house would be deprived of a child's laughter, no wall empty of a doodle…' Nikhil took a deep breath. Sneha's mouth twisted as she braced herself, knowing the worst was coming. 'Even though Alisha knew how much I wanted to be a father, in pure spite, she aborted a ten-week pregnancy…she aborted our child. She revealed the pregnancy only after she had had the abortion.' Nikhil's closed his eyes, immense sadness marring his chiselled face.

25

Lock your door!

Sneha gasped, shocked. 'She did not!'

Nikhil opened his eyes, rubbing a hand over his eyes and face. 'She did. Our baby. If she had just once, just once, told me about it I would have stayed with her, done all that a father, a husband is supposed to do. Even more. But to punish a child, finish a life. Kill your own child…forceps…the horror.' Nikhil covered his face with his hands. Sneha saw his shoulders quiver. Sneha was down at her knees next to him rubbing his back, murmuring incoherent soothing words. She felt her own tear glands open up. She laid her head on Nikhil's shoulder wanting to absorb all his pain. She heard him talk, his words muffled, 'After that I lost any sympathy I might have had for Alisha. I ran her to the ground.' Nikhil took a deep breath and looked up. He kept his face averted from Sneha.

'I exposed Alisha to her family and to her close circle of friends for the tramp and druggie that she was. There was indisputable evidence against her. Her family and closest of friends cut all their ties with her. I shattered the image Alisha held so precious. When I threw her out of my life, I took everything from her. She did not even have enough money to pay her legal fees. Broke, destitute and without any support, Alisha had no choice but to sign the divorce papers on my terms for a mere pittance of a settlement. After the divorce, Alisha used her media contacts to slander my name in the press. And then after a while, she completely disappeared. Not that I bothered to look for her.'

Sneha sat up. 'And you never tried to correct the press?'

Nikhil stood up with a jerk, nearly making Sneha fall. He walked up to the edge of the terrace. 'Who cared about what they wrote? My baby was gone! My marriage over! Who cared what they wrote and reported? I let my lawyers handle it and lost myself in my work. I went back to my old self,' Nikhil sounded bleak. 'I again became the cold, ruthless and unforgiving man I was. An ogre,' Nikhil added softly.

Sneha wanted to vehemently disagree, but she sensed Nikhil currently was more interested in venting his emotions than listening. She got up and walked to him. Leaning against the stone balustrade, she looked at him. Nikhil's face in profile was desolate and hard. 'Please don't get me wrong, but are you sure it was your baby? I mean, given Alisha's history…'

Nikhil's smile was grim. 'When Alisha got back from the rehab we lived together for a while.'

'Oh!' Sneha said woodenly. 'Are you in contact with her?'

Nikhil glared at Sneha but not really at her, just the question. 'I don't give a rat's ass where Alisha is or how she is.' He abruptly turned away and then stopped. 'I'm sorry, Sneha. I'm not good company tonight. I'll drop you home.'

Sneha felt hurt drench her. 'Sure!' The dim lighting gave her some good cover. *And FYI, you do give a rat's ass about her*, she thought. Guilt was stamped all over Nikhil's face.

As Sneha entered the living room, Nikhil let her pass so he could close the terrace door. Sneha reached the sofa and gathered her bag once again. Just then it hit Sneha, why this apartment and his office were so stark. Nikhil preferred starkness for it reflected his life; a reminder of all he had lost, a reminder never to trust again. The luhaar did something she had promised herself she would never do. She melted and for a man who wasn't born to her or she wasn't born off. Taking a deep breath, Sneha turned to face Nikhil who was moving past her to the foyer.

'Do you have a guest room?' asked Sneha, her chin raised.

Nikhil stopped short. 'I have two. Do you want to freshen up?'

Sneha slowly shook her head and then forced her mouth to say the words that were so hard to utter. 'I will spend the night in one of them...here.' Nikhil narrowed his eyes as he waited for Sneha to finish her halting monologue. 'In the guest room... me, alone. You in your room.' Sneha felt like a nincompoop for clarifying things but she was never the type to lead anything other than a dog or a meeting.

'You don't have to,' Nikhil's tone was sharp. He did not care much for pity.

'I'm not asking! Either you show me the room or I just walk into the first bedroom I find and lock myself in,' Sneha's tremulous eyes met Nikhil's rapier gaze. For a few minutes, they stood like that, staring at each other, sizing what really was on the plate, unable to look away. Then a nervous Sneha turned around and started taking slow steps toward the stairs that led to the kitchen and the bedrooms. With every step, she questioned her sanity.

Just as she reached the stairs, Nikhil called out, 'Second door on the right. The room next to mine. The bed in there is very comfortable.'

Sneha turned to him with forced nonchalance, acting as if such gestures were an everyday thing for her. 'I'm fixing a plate for myself? Are you hungry?'

'I'll have a drink before that. Not the apple cider kind. And I have some emails reply to,' Nikhil replied walking to her. 'You please carry on. Let me know if you need anything.'

'Thanks!' Sneha looked up and saw Nikhil's arrested expression as he stared at her.

Thank you!

Welcome. Sneha glanced at the TV in the living room. *I watch a lot of that before I hit the sack.*

'Knock yourself out!' Nikhil finally found something to smile about.

'Than—!' Sneha broke off, confused. Had she said anything about the TV?

Nikhil's face mirrored her expression. Had she actually spoken about the TV?

With a perplexed smile, Sneha climbed the stairs and walked to the kitchen area. She made a plate for herself and sat down on the barstool, trying hard not to remember what had happened between Nikhil and her the last time she'd been sitting on the same stool. Hastily, she took out her cell phone and browsed through her emails. Nikhil came to the kitchen and fixed himself a scotch on the rocks in a cut-glass tumbler. Giving Sneha a brief smile, he went inside his bedroom and returned with a laptop.

As Sneha spooned some food in her mouth, she saw Nikhil fix a plate for himself. Sneha couldn't help a pleased smile that she quickly hid. Keeping his plate down one barstool away from her, Nikhil sat down. Sneha and Nikhil sat next to each other eating food, sharing a funny SMS or an email with an ease akin to that of a couple. After dinner, they both cleared the kitchen and cleaned their dishes. A quick goodnight later Sneha escaped to the guest room. She made a quick call to Kanpur. Things were on track. Advey, along with Sethani, Aditya and Amla would leave tomorrow by the afternoon flight.

Sneha went into the restroom and scrubbed her face with a soap that smelled like aloe vera and lavender. As she came back into her room, her body screamed out for a shower with something as potent and strong as the toilet cleaner Hussain the TV actor advertises. Suddenly her clothes and body felt gritty. Sneha rummaged the bare closets hoping to find something to wear after her shower. 'Hit!' She shut the last of the empty drawers with feeling.

Sneha walked out of the room. The rest of the apartment stood quiet. Walking to Nikhil's room Sneha knocked hesitantly. She heard footsteps come to the door from the other side. Nikhil opened the door. His feet were bare and T-shirt no longer tucked in his jeans.

Sneha spoke with the speed of a freight train without brakes, 'I need something to wear, to sleep in. I can't sleep in these.' She pointed to her rumpled attire. Nikhil, standing at the door, quietly stared at her for a few seconds. Sneha nearly went back to her room. Something was passing between them back and forth, a frisson of awareness that was growing with every second. Sneha felt heat swarm her body. Nikhil saw her light eyes darken and his green pupils dilated in response.

'Sure!' Nikhil hurriedly walked back into his room before he behaved like a Neanderthal and dragged Sneha into his room and onto his bed. Just the thought caused his body to harden with painful intensity. He had never wanted a woman the way he desired Sneha. Even the damn pain of controlling himself gave him pleasure. He picked a clean, soft shirt from his wardrobe. He swallowed a few times as his overactive imagination immediately conjured the image of Sneha wearing only his shirt, revealing an indecent length of pale legs lying on a bed that was technically his. Nikhil muffled his soft groan within the depths of the wardrobe.

Sneha waiting uncertainly at the door, keeping her eyes away from the giant bed with a black and white duvet. Her colour was high and her breath uneven. She heard Nikhil come back. 'Here! This should work.' His tongue felt thick enough for him to choke on it. Nikhil stretched out his hand holding the shirt.

'Thanks!' Sneha quickly grabbed the shirt. Their fingers touched and something churned in her stomach in response. She fumbled and the shirt floated to the floor between them. Sneha refused to meet Nikhil's eyes; her body felt like an inferno that was pushing her towards the man with the beautiful green eyes with such intensity that she was having problems putting one foot in front of the other.

Nikhil bent down and picked up his shirt. The action brought him inadvertently closer to Sneha. He placed the shirt on her arm, making sure he did not touch her. But just as he was moving his arm away, he could not help himself and his hand trailed her soft skin. He heard Sneha's soft gasp but she did not move away; instead, she stayed close and raised her eyes to his face. Nikhil gently stroked the inside of her wrist. His body became harder, swelled, as he caught the answering desire in her awkward, tremulous gaze. Bending down, Nikhil lowered his mouth to her neck. Sneha felt his hot breath on her collarbone. His face nuzzled her skin, his head full of thick hair brushed her chin, giving birth to a longing within her. Sneha's fingers itched to pull him closer. She closed her eyes and nearly swooned onto him. Sneha was sure Nikhil would catch her before she fell. Her body tingled and every inch of her skin came alive and throbbed under Nikhil's touch.

Sneha blinked several times. Her lungs were constricting. 'Sneha?' Nikhil looked deep in her eyes, his voice guttural. It held a question, seeking her permission to cross the boundaries preventing them from becoming one.

Sneha was blank. What was happening to her? Nikhil saw desire and the bewilderment in her gaze. He sensed her uncertainty. With Herculean effort, Nikhil straightened away from her but not before he uttered a deep-throated warning in her delicate ear, 'Lock the bedroom door!'

Nikhil's lips purposely grazed Sneha's earlobe and the answering shiver that shook her petite frame made him burn. Nikhil could not help but dip his mouth to brazenly touch his eager tongue to the beat thumping above her collarbone. The sensation was like ice on Sneha's already sensitized skin. With a strangled groan, she turned and fled to her room.

On entering her room, Sneha turned around and locked the door. She went into the bathroom, stripped off all her clothes and took one of the longest showers of her life. Coming out, she rubbed the water off her but her thoughts were fixed on another thing far beyond the reach of any cloth or hand. She wore Nikhil's shirt and went back into the room. True to her word, Sneha picked up the remote and switched on the flat panel TV across from the bed. She twisted back and forth on the bed and then put some pillows under her head. Her hands were not their steadiest. Switching channels Sneha settled for the loudest of the reality TV shows.

Nikhil, in his room, raised his head from the Kindle in his hand. What did the *New York Times* compare to the flesh and blood woman in his shirt next door? Curious, he walked to the common wall between Sneha's room and his. He heard sounds. He put his ear closer to wall and his hand braced the wall at the height of his waist. Whatever Sneha was watching was definitely dramatic. Smiling, he leaned closer and his cheek touched the coolness of the wall.

On her side, Sneha glanced at the wall common to her and Nikhil's room. What was he doing? She slid out of the bed and shuffled over to the wall. She put her ear to the wall and put her hand on it as a brace at the height of her chest. Sneha thought she heard something. With an impish grin, Sneha leaned closer and put her cheek against the wall. Unknown to either of them, Nikhil and Sneha's hands were just a wall apart. And just for that brief moment, Sneha and Nikhil shared a picture-perfect moment. Nikhil felt some passing warmth from the wall and smiling ruefully at his romanticism, he walked away back to his bed and his Kindle. That very second, Sneha too came to her senses and went back to the bed and the remote.

26

Hope the shirt fit

The next morning, Sneha overslept and thus her ablutions happened at the speed of light, or so she wanted to believe. She stepped out of the room quietly but the apartment was silent. As she hot-footed to Nikhil's room, she walked into someone coming out it. The woman in green overalls and Sneha yelped simultaneously. The woman bobbed her head, 'Sorry! Madam, sorry.'

Sneha somehow recovered from her shock, 'No. It's fine. I should have been more careful. Anyway, is Nikhil here?' She pointed at the room.

'No, sir left. There is a note for you in the fridge. Sorry, on the fridge,' the house cleaner politely informed her.

'Thanks!' Sneha walked to the kitchen and grabbed the folded note stuck on the fridge under a magnet. She read the bold black scrawl across it. *'Had to leave early because of work. Call ext. 303 for the cook. Have the cook make you whatever you wish. Hope the shirt fit!'*

Cheeky dastard, Sneha thought, smiling and putting the note in her bag. The domestic help came to her. 'What shall you make, sorry, take…for breakfast?'

'Nothing, just a glass of any juice please,' Sneha replied. Sneha saw a thick blue and yellow book lying on the counter-top. It was a course book for English learning. The domestic quickly stepped up and grabbed the book.

'Sorry madam, it is mine. Please don't sell, sorry, tell. I should not have this at work,' she pleaded.

Sneha waved her hand. 'Don't worry. But what is this course?

Where are the classes and what are the charges?' Sneha grilled. Amla was about to get a welcome-back present.

A few minutes later Sneha made her way down to the lobby. She was all ready to flag down an auto or taxi from the road but as she stepped out of the building, Sneha caught sight of a familiar dark German car with a blue and white logo. Sneha's heart leapt briefly and then settled as she saw the uniformed driver step out of the car.

'Sir asked me to drop you.'

'Thanks!' Sneha sat in the back seat and rattled off directions to the garage where her car was being serviced. Sneha decided to take an impromptu day off. She called up Mrs Aiyyar and cited a migraine as a reason. Once home, Sneha got in her nesting mode, cleaning the place, sprucing it up for the welcome party tonight. She brought some balloons, cake and pizzas, everything Advey liked.

In the evening, when Advey and his entourage landed at the door, Sneha already had the door open. As she hugged her son, Sneha could not bring herself to let him go him for the next several minutes even though he squirmed to get away. Nikhil's pained face telling her about his unborn child swam in her eyes. Sneha planted soft kisses on Advey's forehead, chubby cheeks and his tiny soft hands, hands which on a usual day, she would give a closer look to make sure they were clean. A strange idea took root in her head. After dinner, as Amla whisked off Advey for a bath along with the multiple balloons he refused to be parted from, and as Aditya was on his cell, Sneha shifted closer to Nandini.

'Sethani, I need your help with something more up your alley.'

Nandini gave her a wicked smile, 'As in?'

'Butting into people's life is more you than me,' Sneha retorted.

'Are you asking for my help or insulting me?' Nandini said, displaying mock indignation.

'Help karegi ki nahi karegi, kulta?'

'Of course, babes. Tell me, whose life are we complicating?'

Sneha began awkwardly, 'There is one thing I need you to do—'

Nandini lost her smile and gave her closer look, 'Okay, what's going on with you? Are you blushing? Never seen you do that.' For effect, Nandini sported a horrified expression

Sneha went on the defensive. 'What are you talking about? I'm the same old cow you left behind.' Her words were rushed.

'Old cow with new udders.'

'Shuddup! New horns not udd—fine don't help.' Damn, the woman could read her better than her maker. Obviously in some cases familiarity does not breed contempt. Sneha immediately thought of Nikhil again. Sneha hustled to her feet. 'Do you want a drink?'

Nandini pulled her down, 'Okay ya. Tell.' Sneha fell down on the sofa with a thump. 'Going back to the original conversation, whose mind are we messing with?'

Sneha could not help the jibe, 'Missing psycho psychologist Mona darling?'

Nandini glared at her. 'Don't even talk about that chutiya!'

A laughing Sneha fell back onto the sofa.

'What?' Nandini said.

Sneha sobered with an effort. 'You know, when we started mispronouncing cuss words so Advey would not pick them up, you obviously did not get the memo of how it works.'

'Huh!'

'You wanted to say kutiya and you mispronounced it as chutiya which is a worse than the original. You are such a clown, Sethani.'

Nandini rolled her eyes, 'Ya, okay! For the millionth time, give me a name?'

Sneha pulled in a deep breath and said it.

Nandini scrunched her brow. 'I know the name but I can't put a face to it.'

'I know, that's why I need you to hire whoever the Sarins might have on their payroll.'

'And why are we doing this?' Nandini probed.

Sneha dropped another name. Nandini's mouth formed an 'O'.

As she was about to ask another question, Sneha put a hand on best friend's knee. 'Please don't ask me anything else! Please. I'll tell you later, I promise,' Sneha implored.

'Wohkay!' Nandini made a face but she dropped the subject.

Soon Nandini and Adi left after making plans to meet the coming weekend. A day later, Sneha received a call from Nandini. As Sneha put the phone to her ear, she heard Nandini humming CID's signature tune on the other end. Grinning Sneha said, 'Bolo Salunke!'

'Why do you get to be Pradyuman?' Nandini replied crossly.

'Because I'm the boss!' was Sneha's pat response.

'Pradyuman is bald!'

'So is Salunke and he wears a wig. That means he is bald and complex,' Sneha grinned.

'Pradyuman has scary eyes and dancing fingers,' Nandini argued.

Sneha sighed, 'And they both have my son and a million other kids and adults riveted to their TV sets every weekend. Can we move on?'

'You started it!'

'No, you did, by singing the tune.'

Sneha heard some silence on the other end. She knew Sethani was pouting. 'Are you pouting?' she teased.

'No!' Nandini lied. 'I have an address and a name for you.'

Sneha lost some of her cheer. 'Thank you in advance.'

'You get it only if you promise to hear me out regarding something I've been wanting to discuss with you. Saturday night over dinner.'

'Ménage à trios!' Sneha teased.

'Please! With Adi's frisky hands and mouth, its like I already have two of him in bed.'

'Ewwww! FYI, every friendship has boundaries woman.'

'No it doesn't. Haven't you heard that friendship knows no colour, caste, creed or *sex*?'

'That sex implies the *nar-maada* kind of difference moron,' Sneha laughed.

'It's open to interpretation!' Nandini gave a familiar giggle.

'Fine. The address please?' Sneha demanded.

'Are you agreeing to meet for dinner or no—'

'Ya! Ya, I'm agreeing.'

'Oh somebody is very eager for the address? Hmmm!' Nandini teased.

'I'm hanging up!'

Nandini, in a single breath blasted the address in her ear.

'You are sure?' Sneha asked.

'Positive! I have verified it in person.'

'Nandini, you didn't have to.' Sneha was touched.

'I had to! Even you agree all this stuff is more my *ishtyle*.'

'That I agree.'

'So what is the plan?' Nandini fished.

'I will tell you after the deed is done. Thank you very much.'

'Do you need someone to drive you there?'

'No!'

'Do you need someone to carry your bag?'

'No!'

'Do you need someone to open the door for you?' Nandini was persistent.

'NO!NO!NO!'

'Saali, chutiya!' Nandini grumbled whole-heartedly.

'Still mispronouncing, kulta?' Sneha gave the phone a long-suffering look.

Nandini laughed and said, 'Who's mispronouncing?'

Sneha growled into the cell.

A cackling Nandini hung up on her. Tucking her cell under her chin, Sneha grinned. Close to seven just as Sneha was about to head home, ignoring her life-long policy never to interfere in another person's beeswax, Sneha sent an email.

From: snehag@flagshipad.com
To: n.chandel@dnc.com
Can you take the afternoon off tomorrow?

The reply was quick.

From: n.chandel@dnc.com
To: snehag@flagshipad.com
About time! I'm good too, thanks. What's the plan?

Sneha smiled, even as she ran her hands over her plastic keyboard as if she were smoothing out a crease.

From: snehag@flagshipad.com
To: n.chandel@dnc.com
Surprise!

Yeah right, Sneha rued.

From: n.chandel@dnc.com
To: snehag@flagshipad.com
Who's picking who up?
From: snehag@flagshipad.com
To: n.chandel@dnc.com
I'll pick you up at around 2 p.m. post lunch.
From: n.chandel@dnc.com
To: snehag@flagshipad.com
Sounds good! C u.
From: snehag@flagshipad.com
To: n.chandel@dnc.com
Cool!

Why couldn't you have said that you were out of the country indefinitely? Sneha thought. Her hands felt clammy. Just as she was about to turn off the lights of her room, her cell pinged once again. She had a new email. She opened her inbox.

```
From:  n.chandel@dnc.com
To:  snehag@flagshipad.com
Looking  forward  to  it!  Did  the  shirt  fit?
```

Sneha felt her face flush. Smiling, she kept her reply simple.

```
From:  snehag@flagshipad.com
To:  n.chandel@dnc.com
```
☺

27

Surprise!

True to his word, Nikhil's marketing head, Boman Dinsukh, had called the very next day of the go-karting adventure and that afternoon, Sneha and Mrs Aiyyar had a long conference call with him. Sneha's CEO was happy with Sneha, which meant she could quote an appointment with Mr X of Xanadu and her bosses would not question it. Next day, citing an appointment with the marketing head of DC, Sneha left her office.

It was a hot afternoon as Sneha pulled into the parking lot of Nikhil's office. She texted him and did not have to wait for long. Nikhil came out of the building looking dapper in his metallic grey trousers and crisp white shirt over which a pale grey silk tie carelessly fluttered. Sneha was glad she too had made some effort while dressing up today. Her grey pencil skirt, teamed with a pale pink blouse with sheer sleeves was one of the finer pieces in her closet. On her freshly pedicured feet sat sliver wedges. Her make-up was impeccable and curls pinned flatteringly to a side.

Nikhil got in the seat and removed his shades to look at her, 'Hi and wow!' His smile was slow and did not disappear. He wanted Sneha to see his genuine pleasure at seeing her. She had not left his thoughts for a second since their last meeting.

'Hi and thanks!' Sneha too stared at him. She did not want to take her eyes off Nikhil and it wasn't like she was seeing him after ages. It had only been one very, very, very long day. 'What rubbish!' Sneha did not realize she had uttered that self-censuring thought aloud.

'What?' Nikhil quizzed. His smile turned wicked and his green eyes positively glowed. 'What were you thinking?'

Sneha swallowed. 'Nothing. Just…' She was not good at fibbing. 'Nothing.' She turned and started the car.

'Where are we going?' Nikhil asked as he put his seat belt on.

'Surprise!' Even to her ears, Sneha sounded deflated rather than buoyant.

Nikhil caught how Sneha rubbed the head of the gear as if she were ironing out a crease. 'Are you okay?'

'Awful! I mean awesome. Awesome!' Sneha flashed Nikhil a bright smile. Too bright.

'Are you kidnapping me?' Nikhil teased even as he wondered what had made Sneha so anxious.

'No. You are free to get off at any time.' Sneha secretly hoped Nikhil would take her up on that offer. No such luck; he only made it worse.

'I trust you! So did Advey have a good trip?' Nikhil steered the conversation to a topic that he knew would ease her. He was right, Sneha stopped trying to use hard things as acupuncture balls. The word 'hard' and 'Sneha' in the same sentence did not bode well for him. Nikhil shifted in his seat, cursing the minimal control a man had over the body parts south of his belt. This kind of thing had only happened when he was in his teens. But at that age it was okay to be obsessed with a female twenty-four seven. 'So where are we going?' He tried distracting himself.

'Santacruz!' Sneha flashed him a look.

'Okay. I'll ask no more on that subject,' Nikhil muttered. He then blurted out the first thing that popped into his head. 'Did the shirt fit?' He saw his own embarrassment reflected in Sneha's face. 'Scratch that! Was the bed comfortable? Scratch th—'

'The bed and shirt both were fine,' Sneha replied softly. The car felt too constricting.

Sitting beside her just then, it hit Nikhil. He was behaving crazy around Sneha because he was crazy for her. And there is only one way to deal with such a situation. 'Sneha, are you seeing anyone?' Nikhil asked quietly.

On seeing his earnest expression, Sneha panicked. 'Ughh! Ummm. Define seeing.'

Nikhil's beautiful eyes took on a teasing look. 'Really? I have to define that?'

'Are you seeing anyone?' Sneha asked, buying time.

'I was, up until a month ago and then we amicably ended it.'

'Oh. You miss her?' Sneha coloured. 'I mean…you don't have to answer that.'

'There is no comparison between you and anyone else… anyone else,' answered Nikhil, his voice low and guttural. 'You I miss like all of me is gone.'

Sneha felt happy enough to cry. 'I have a third date with Dr Pr—I mean Pradeep, this Sunday.' She sounded breathless.

'Oh!' Nikhil sounded crushed, and then he spoke lightly, 'That means I have only so many days.'

'Only so many days?' Sneha dared to peek at him.

'Only so many days to change your mind about it,' Nikhil replied smugly as he sat back against the car door looking at her. His smile was confident. As Sneha looked at him, she felt sad. By this evening, he might hate her.

'Oh!' Sneha said solemnly.

'Just "oh"? You sound morbid,' Nikhil was finding it impossible not to touch her. Currently, he had to satisfy himself by merely looking at her.

Sneha felt her heart leap to her eyes as she stared at Nikhil. 'Feel free to stop the car any time you wish,' Nikhil teased as his green gaze slithered warmly over Sneha's face to stop at her lips. His meaning was crystal clear.

Sneha came to her senses and quickly dragged her eyes back to the road. 'I don't know if it will work out between us.'

Nikhil scowled, 'Why?'

'Because my priority will be Advey and I don't do one night stands,' Sneha said glumly.

'*Our* priority will be Advey and I'm glad you don't do one night stands. Because one night with you just won't be enough,' Nikhil said, gently tucked a loose strand behind her ear and his hand caressed the side of her neck and then stroked her shoulder. Sneha shivered at his touch. Nikhil's fingers, like rough velvet, were lightly calloused and largely smooth. She closed her eyes as instant desire surged in her. She quickly opened her eyes. 'Please don't,' she implored, her voice thick.

'Why?' Nikhil demanded as his fingers climbed back to Sneha's neck. 'You focus on driving and I'll focus on you,' he said, his voice intimately low. To explain his argument more clearly, Nikhil's fingers stroking the skin below Sneha's ear roughly caressed her lobe. Sneha pulled her legs together ignoring the tingles that pulsated at her very core. She bit back her moan. Who knew getting your ears pulled could be so sexy? Nikhil saw the desire in Sneha's eyes in the brief look that she gave him. That was all that Nikhil needed, he could not stop. He had been enough of a knight last night, today he was the raider. Hurriedly unfastening his seat belt, Nikhil leaned over and kissed Sneha under her ear. His tongue touched and lapped up the taste and feel of her skin under his tongue. Sneha moved her head, baring more of her skin to his hot mouth.

'Nikhil. I'm driving,' she protested weakly.

'Then stop the damn car. Because…I can't stop,' Nikhil growled. His senses were drowning in the feel and smell of her. His hand rested on Sneha's thigh, stroking and squeezing the flesh under his fingers. Sneha moved restlessly against his hand. 'Stop the car so I can kiss you and touch you like this,' Nikhil groaned, his hand moving higher on her thigh.

'Ohh!' Sneha's self-control happily flew out of the window. She could not help but shudder and move urgently against his hand. 'Sweetheart!' Nikhil groaned in Sneha's ear and her body reacted impulsively by thrusting urgently and rubbing slowly against his palm.

'Please! Please! Stop!' Sneha cried out. She could not control her reactions any more. Shamelessly, her legs trapped his hand in between. Sneha felt such pleasure as she rubbed herself against his hand that she thought she would die. 'Don't stop!' Nikhil moaned against her skin. Nikhil's teeth were now gently biting and kissing her neck. His breathing was harsh. Glancing at the rearview mirror, Sneha turned the wheel and parked the car onto the side of the road. Nikhil impatiently moved to unfasten her seat belt. When Sneha grabbed his hands, Nikhil glanced at her. 'Please! No! Not like this,' she implored.

She saw the frantic desire in his eyes slowly mellow as he took in her nervous face. Squeezing her hands gently, Nikhil sat back. Sneha was drawing in gulps of air, looking dishevelled and Nikhil was breathing hard as colour sat high on his cheekbones. 'I did not mean to frighten you but as you can see, you have quite an effect on me,' Nikhil said even as his hand reached out to brush her hair off her temple. His fingers wanted to linger but he pulled them back with effort. 'Sorry! You do this to me.'

Sneha's responding smile was sheepish, 'Same pinch.' She looked away from his mesmerizing green eyes.

'To pinch me, you will have to touch me!' Nikhil gently reminded her. Sneha glanced at him, her mouth dry. Along with mischief, she saw the challenge in his veiled eyes.

Sneha felt her mouth go dry. Her hand lifted off her lap and Nikhil grabbed it. He turned her hand and planted an open-mouthed kiss on the soft skin of her wrist. Still holding her hand close to his mouth, Nikhil met Sneha's eyes over her wrist, his hypnotic eyes on her. *Be mine?*

Nikhil saw her breathing become raspy as heat bloomed in Sneha's cheeks. Gently and slowly Nikhil pulled Sneha closer and just as she leaned forward, he caught her mouth with his. Sneha's lips opened to gasp and Nikhil's hungry tongue found an entrance to her mouth past her soft lips. His fingers caught her face to deepen the kiss. Sneha with a soft sigh that Nikhil felt against his lips opened her mouth to him and inched closer. Nikhil groaned at her capitulation. He thrust his tongue hard into her mouth. His tongue tangled with hers, tasting her deeply. Sneha clutched his shoulders as explosive sensation after sensation rippled through her very core. Nikhil lovingly traced the shape of her sexy lips. His hand trailed to her blouse and impatiently opening it, slipped inside.

The sensation of Nikhil's fingers, tweaking, rubbing and tugging her sensitive nub was too much for Sneha to bear. She thought the pleasure would kill her. She had to feel more of his body. Moaning, she moved forward and her ribs slammed painfully into the gear. 'Ouch!' she yelped.

Nikhil moved just a little apart, still holding on to Sneha. He asked concerned, 'What happened?'

'My side!'Sneha pulled his hand out of her blouse. She needed some air. She hurriedly got out of the car and moved to stand behind her car. Her legs felt like rubber. It was only then she noticed the few bystanders who had stopped next to her car. She visibly cringed, wondering what they had seen. Sneha ran a hand through her hair. This was crazy. What was this? She hadn't experienced even one fourth of this urgency in her marriage. Nikhil made her want more. After this, maybe the life that she had so painstakingly built for her would not be enough. Would Advey really gain a complete family or would she just earn herself some real heartache for first time in her life? Sneha was HIT scared.

'What are you thinking?' Sneha looked up, startled at Nikhil's voice next to her. She had been so lost in her thoughts about him that she had not noticed when he had joined her.

'I'm so confused,' she said.

'I'm sorry. I did not mean to jump on you there back there,' Nikhil passed a hand through his hair. 'Things a got a little out of hand. I want you so much, it's driving me crazy.'

'It is?' Sneha asked, dazed.

Nikhil turned and stared deep in her bewildered eyes, 'Who would not? A beautiful woman who has so much to give.' He let a finger trail down her cheek.

'I have?' Sneha spoke as if in a trance.

'Stop parroting my words.' Nikhil fondly pinched her chin. 'You have and I'm a very greedy man, especially where you are concerned.' Nikhil leaned forward and Sneha did not pull back. His lips grazed the side of her lips. 'I want all of you Sneha, not just your heart and body...even your soul...everything about you. I want to spend my life with you ' Even though a smile played on his lips, Nikhil's beautiful eyes were deathly serious.

'Really?' Sneha murmured. She swallowed even though happiness like a fast-growing vine grew swiftly around her heart.

Nikhil tucked an errant curl behind her ear, 'We will go at the pace you want, I promise.'

Swallowing, Sneha tried to hide her dizzying happiness with a jibe, 'You are forgetting my Sunday date.'

Nikhil grinned, his smile boyish enough to charm the socks off her, amongst other things. Socks she wasn't wearing but the other things she was. 'I haven't changed your mind about that?'

Sneha gazed at him with such tenderness that her answer was clear, and yet she declared, 'Nooo!'

'Awesome! Then let's get back in there. Or better still, we could go back to my apartment.' Nikhil's hand wrapped itself around her fingers, tugging Sneha closer. His voice was a smooth suggestion in her ear.

'You just promised!' Sneha stepped away, flushing.

'Sorry!' Nikhil dropped his hand. The look he gave her was anything but apologetic.

Sneha threw her keys at him. Nikhil caught them, his look surprised. 'You're driving.'

'Aww come on, spoilsport. We are just beginning to have fun,' Nikhil teased, his face open and expression indulgent.

Sneha could only stare. Years fell away from his face. An image of Nikhil, Advey and her flashed in her head. Sneha blinked, startled. She wanted that picture to be true with a burning intensity that terrified her.

'Sneha, are you okay?' Nikhil asked concerned. He was about to come over to her side.

'Stay!' Sneha voiced, shaking her head.

Nikhil stopped and then gave her a knowing smile. 'Then just get in.'

Twenty minutes later, Sneha and Nikhil pulled in front of a three-storeyed, yellow and maroon building. Nikhil looked at it under the windshield. 'Here! My surprise is here?'

'Yes!' Sneha extricated her hand from his. Nikhil had insisted that he would only drive if they at least held hands. Feeling warm and fuzzy all over, Sneha had agreed. 'Let's go inside.'

Sneha gave him a soft smile and Nikhil was lost in it. Now he felt that even this ogre stood a second chance in this lifetime. Nikhil had to satisfy himself with blowing a kiss to Sneha as she snuck a shy glance over her shoulder at him.

Nikhil locked the car and waited for Sneha to lead the way. The board outside the building read, 'Sri Kamla Bai Women's Hospice'.

They climbed the few steps and entered a reception area with an old-fashioned desk and a wooden chair. 'Wait here!' Sneha told Nikhil as she walked into an office past the wooden swinging panels that passed for doors.

She introduced herself to the hospice warden who she had spoken to earlier. The warden, a middle-aged lady in a starched sari greeted her. 'She is waiting in the visitor's room. Is he with you?'

'Yes! He is. Can we see her now?' Sneha asked. Her earlier anxiety came back. Her hands felt like river beds.

'Sure!' The warden came around her desk and led Sneha back to the corridor where Nikhil waited. 'Hello!' The warden politely nodded at him.

'Hello!' Nikhil replied, giving Sneha a puzzled look.

The smile Sneha gave Nikhil was strained. She gestured for Nikhil to follow her. The three went up a flight of stairs and stopped outside a closed door with a sign on it, which read 'Visitor's Room'.

'Who are we meeting, Sneha?' Nikhil whispered in her ear. His voice was no longer soft or suggestive. It demanded an answer.

'You'll see!' Sneha tried to fake a laugh but her heart was thundering in her body and the blood was rushing in her ears. Now she was more scared than ever. When she had planned this, Nikhil had not confessed to his feelings nor had she acknowledged her own for him. Now the stakes were very high. They went inside the room.

Sneha heard Nikhil's harsh intake of breath from behind her just as she caught sight of the gaunt woman in a faded floral tunic with a weary thin face and unfashionably short hair. The woman lost any colour that she might have had in her pale, thin face as she saw them. Sneha glanced at Nikhil, who stood frozen as if he had seen a ghost. 'Alisha!' His voice was a harsh gasp.

28

ICU

Sneha ate up the buoyant 'surprise' she was planning to shout. The words 'May day', 'May day' seemed more appropriate. She stood awkwardly between them.

Nikhil walked past Sneha and held out his hands to the anorexic woman. 'What have you done to yourself?' His voice throbbed with emotion.

With a sob, the woman launched herself into Nikhil's arms. It seemed more like she fell down. Nikhil held the sobbing Alisha close. Sneha could not ignore the stab of jealousy that shot through her as she saw Nikhil hold Alisha as if she was something fragile, something precious. Just then, Nikhil turned his head half around. Sneha was startled to see his furious expression. The anger was directed at Sneha.

Just then, Alisha moved away from Nikhil's arms and looked at her.

'Who is she?' she asked coldly.

Sneha saw pure hatred for her in those eyes.

'No one. She works for me,' Nikhil voiced, his expression deadpan, his voice cold.

Sneha stared at Nikhil, stunned. She had just gone from being the 'the only one' to 'no one' in a span of less than an hour. These truly were the times when breaking news grew old in five minutes.

Alisha did not buy it. 'Liar!' She let out a blood-curdling scream and began hitting Nikhil with her fists and shrieking at an insane pitch. Sneha jumped forward to help Nikhil but Alisha swung her left hand and caught Sneha right across her face.

'Ouch!' Sneha faltered as she fell back. Nikhil caught Sneha's arm and pulled her back, saving her from crashing into the glass coffee table.

'Go now! Get some help,' Nikhil yelled as he stepped between Sneha and Alisha and took most of the blows and kicks Alisha was aiming at Sneha. A dishevelled Sneha wasted no time and somehow managed to stumble through the door and run down the stairs. 'Help! Help!' she called out loudly and a few women and two men who seemed to work there came to her. One of them was the warden. Sneha shouted hastily, 'Alisha has gone crazy. She is hitting Nikhil. Please help us.'

The men turned around and ran up the stairs and the warden followed. She called to another woman next to her, 'Smita, her medicine is in her room. Get it and come there.' Sneha too ran up the stairs. One of the men who had just gone into the visitor's room came out. He put a hand in front of Sneha. 'You cannot go inside. The man with Alisha says you have no business being here.'

Sneha stopped short. 'What? He said that? Are you sure?'

'Yes. I'm sure. Please leave the premises.' He said to another woman behind Sneha, 'See her out.' The woman grabbed her arm.

'Get off me.' Sneha shook her hand free. Feeling like something that had just crawled out from under a rock, Sneha turned around and walked down the stairs and out of the building. Sneha drove out and parked to the side. She then waited, keeping her rearview mirror fixed on the hospice gate. Too shocked to make any sense out of anything, she sat in her car, mute. Forty-five minutes later, Sneha saw a dark German car on the other side of the road. It made a U-turn and entered the hospice gates. Sneha sat up straighter. In minutes, Sneha saw the car drive past her.

After the car went past her, Sneha listlessly commenced her drive home. She did not bother with the tears that rolled down her cheeks as over and over her mind re-played the picture. As

Nikhil's car had driven past Sneha, she had caught a glimpse of Alisha resting on Nikhil's chest. Her smiling face was turned up to gaze at him, as he looked down at her, an indulgent smile creasing his features.

Sneha's drive back home was a blank. Her heart and head felt like they had split in two. Just as she pulled into her parking lot, Nandini called.

'Hi!' Sneha tried not to sound as low as she felt.

'And!' Nandini chirped.

'And what, Sethani?' Sneha asked wearily as she looked at the tubelight shining near where she had parked. Small insects in dozens fluttered around the light.

'What happened?' Nandini sobered, picking on her friend's misery.

Sneha exhaled. 'I don't know. It backfired!' Then she remembered the anger in Nikhil's eyes. 'Surprises are not really my freakin' forte.' Sneha felt humiliated to hear the catch in her voice.

'Oh my God! Are you crying?' Nandini sounded awed.

Sneha rubbed her eyes. 'No. I just wish I had never met that stupid man! It's all my fault.'

'What happened exactly?'

'The usual thing that happens with me. One wrong decision after another. I just flucking can't get it right. I don't even know why I try.' But Sneha knew exactly why she had tried.

'Sneh, don't say that.'

'No Nandi, it's true. I'm a fool. I let my guard down and look what happens?' Sneha closed her eyes and then promptly opened them for all she was HIS face, his ANGRY face.

'Just tell me what happened!' Nandini shouted.

Sneha in a tight voice told her all except for her and Nikhil's doings in the car. As Sneha ended her short and sour saga, all she heard was silence on the other end. 'Hello?'

'Ya, I'm here!'

'Then say something!' Sneha again heard some more silence. 'Nandini!' she said, grinding her teeth.

'I don't know what to say!' Nandini finally wailed at the other end.

'Well, that's honest.' Sneha was surprised.

'I can't help it, Sneh. I usually take your advice and now I don't know what to do. I'm such a moron!'

Sneha tiredly clucked her tongue. 'Don't be silly!'

'I am, Sneh! I suck at all this. Whatever I say will be so wrong. Even Aditya would laugh at me if he heard what I had to say.'

'Who cares what Aditya thinks of you? Don't doubt yourself, kulta,' Sneha rose to assure her friend. Her voice wasn't her strongest.

'You're nice, that's what you are. A piece of serious advice my friend, don't ask me what to do. Never, ever, NEVER!' Nandini added a sigh for full effect.

'Calm down, bimbette!' Sneha spoke soothingly. 'Tell me, what would you have me do?'

Nandini gave a self-mocking laugh.'I'm so not telling you. I'll totally muck it up! This is about you, not me,' Nandini insisted.

Sneha gritted her teeth. 'STOP IT. Just tell me, Nandi. I'm asking for your advice. There! I even said it.'

'No Sneh, you're too sweet. You don't have—'

'Don't be such a hitch! Just tell me already!'

Nandini sighed and then said softly. 'Go and meet Nikhil once!'

'What?' Sneha went completely quiet.

'See? I knew it. I knew it! It was such stupid, shitty advice. Listen, Sneh, don't even think about doing it. You just do what you think best, like you did today,' Nandini paused as she heard Sneha's sudden intake of breath. 'I mean you do what you think is correct. Because you know—'

'Will you come with me?' Sneha interrupted her quietly.

'What? You'll go? Are you serious?' Nandini sounded incredulous.

'Just to prove that you don't give stupid, shitty advice!' Sneha asserted.

'Umm I don't know. Ughh you think—'

'Yes or no, kulta?'

'Of course. Only if you are okay with it.'

'I'm okay with it!' Sneha's voice was firm. 'Is there any way of finding out where HE might be?'

'I can try!'

'Do that! Because I seriously doubt HE will answer my call,' Sneha confessed wearily. Even taking his name was hard.

'I'll try my best, babe. Listen, why don't I come over right now?'

'I'm fine, Nandi. We'll talk tomorrow. Seriously, I'm okay. I'll just spend some fun time with Advey and forget everything,' Sneha lied, forcing some cheer into her voice.

'Take care, Sneh. Okay?' Nandini sounded glum.

'Fine! Now go and make your man happy!' Sneha repeated Nandini's words. The latter used to say that often to Sneha while she was still married, not knowing the truth about Sneha's marriage.

'Jai Jawan! Jai Kisan!' Nandini hissed.

'Huh?'

'Nothing, got carried away. Sorry! Goodnight.'

Sneha could not help an exhausted smile, 'Jai Maharashtra! Goodnight.' She hung up and opened her car door.

Nandini, in her bedroom slumped back against the headboard. She had noticed something between Sneha and Nikhil but had been totally unaware that things had become so intense. If she had known! As Nandini went through her phone book searching for Nikhil's office number, she muttered ominously to her cell, 'Nikhil Chandel, I have talked Sneha into meeting you. That is your last chance to redeem yourself. If you hurt her again then in the future...always...*always* sleep with an eye open!'

The next day at around 2.00 p.m., Sneha got the call she was dreading and waiting eagerly for in equal measure.

Nandini wasted no time in greetings. 'I know where he is. I'm outside your office.'

'We are going now?'

'Yup! To a hospital.'

All the colour drained from Sneha's face. 'He's in the hospital?'

'Yes!' Nandini replied sombrely.

'Give me two minutes.' Sneha hung up, grabbed her cell and wallet rushed out.

In a few minutes, Sneha was sitting next to Nandini in her convertible. 'What happened?' she turned urgently to Nandini.

'Sorry babes! Don't know the details. Let's just go and find out.' Nandini gave Sneha's hand a comforting squeeze.

'Okay!' Sneha wore her seat belt. 'I'm sure the crazy hitch did something horrible to him.'

'He's in the ICU!' Nandini added quietly as she drove.

'Oh my God!' Sneha felt sick to her stomach. 'Just get me there quickly.'

29

Stupid shitty advice

Sneha and Nandini drove to the busy hospital near Kemps Corner. As Nandini drove into the parking lot, Sneha opened her seat belt, her hands shaking. Nandini put a hand on her knee. 'Hold on, babes.'

Nandini stopped the car in front of the hospital but Sneha was already out. 'I'll see you in there.' Sneha ran up the few stairs leading to the hospital. Nandini hurriedly parked the car and ran behind her. She found Sneha at the reception looking around wildly at the signs with floor numbers for various departments. She grabbed Sneha's hand, 'Come with me!'

Nandini walked to the receptionist and gave her her full name, the one acquired post-marriage. The receptionist promptly made two name-tags and sent off an attendant to guide them to the elevators. Sneha, Nandini and the hospital attendant got out on the fifth floor that had a signboard that read 'ICU'.

'Waiting area is on the left behind those doors,' the attendant guided them.

Sneha was about to head for the information desk in front of them when Nandini stopped her. 'You go to the waiting area. I'll get some more information.'

'Find out everything.' Sneha's voice was tortured.

'Of course. Go!' Nandini replied. She had never seen Sneha in such anguish.

Sneha walked into the waiting area. Her mind gnawed at all possibilities. All the scenarios in her head came up with morbid images of Nikhil an inch away from sure death. Entering the waiting room, Sneha glanced around and was shocked at whom she saw. Nikhil, very much on his feet, sporting an overnight stubble and harried appearance stared at her equally stumped. 'You!' he bit out angrily.

Sneha ran to him. She grabbed his hand, 'Oh my God! You are all right. I was so worried.' Sneha for once wasn't embarrassed either by her husky voice or the tears crowding her eyes. She was just crazily relieved. Nikhil was okay.

Nikhil immediately extricated his hand from her grip. 'Stop it! Stop behaving like this.' His voice and eyes were cold and harsh.

All Sneha could do was stare at him. She felt slashed by his coldness. She tried to compose herself as she pulled her not-so-steady hands back to herself. 'If you are okay then who is admitted here?' she asked, blinking rapidly to banish the humiliating tears from her eyes.

Nikhil put some distance between them. 'Alisha. She tried to kill herself last night. She slit her wrists. She has slipped into a coma.'

Gasping, Sneha covered her mouth. Nikhil glared at her. 'Why are you shocked? Isn't this what you wanted?' He walked towards Sneha, towering above her. His lips were clamped, his eyes two flaming points of accusation.

Sneha shook her head, distressed. 'I never wanted this to happen. I was only trying to help you—'

Nikhil fiercely grabbed Sneha's shoulders and pulled her close. There was nothing kind about his grip on her shoulders or his cruel hiss in her face. 'Who asked for your help? Who gave you the right to interfere? What do you know of me or Alisha to make that call? Tell me, who gave you that right?'

Sneha tried to rein in the hurt coursing over her, suffocating her, squeezing her heart. She somehow managed to say, 'I just wanted…you not to carry any guilt. I never thought it was your… your burden to bear. I just wanted you to be happy.'

Nikhil, wrapped in his fury, pulled Sneha even closer. His face appeared set in iron. 'Do I look happy to you? You forced a mentally unstable woman, barely coming out of chronic depression, to face her past in the most debilitating manner. I convinced her therapist to let her go home with me. She was on my watch, my responsibility. Do you know the meaning of the word responsible?' On her forehead Sneha felt Nikhil's rapid, angry breaths that accompanied his harshly spoken words. 'In the night when I was asleep, Alisha slipped into the bathroom and slit her wrists. If I had not woken up when I had...' Nikhil let Sneha go and ran a hand over his face and then pointed at her accusingly. 'All thanks to your bloody meddling ways.'

Sneha voiced the only thought that registered in her mind, 'You were both sleeping together?'

She saw Nikhil grind his teeth as he flung Sneha a look so vile that she took a step back. 'Get over yourself,' Nikhil raised his voice and then immediately lowered it. 'We were husband and wife once. That's much more than I can say for you...' He bit his words. Anger again dominated his features.

Sneha understood what Nikhil did not say. Something ugly and horribly painful gripped Sneha's heart, the pain excruciating. Sneha stared down for what she felt was an infinite moment at the floor. Nikhil, even through the haze of anger mixed with misery, noticed Sneha's hands smoothen her skirt at the sides. And then she looked back at him. Nikhil felt a tug at his heart as he saw the tears swimming in her hazel eyes. Grinding his teeth, he quashed any softness in him for her.

Sneha spoke haltingly, her voice thick with unshed tears, 'I'm truly very, very sorry for this. I will pray for her recovery and please let me know if I you need any help.'

Nikhil narrowed his eyes. 'I think you have done—'

Sneha raised her hand, stopping him, 'Then kindly fuck off. I hope you both live happily ever after.' Turning around, Sneha walked out, a proud, small figure. Sneha saw Nandini standing there, the door open in her hand. She wondered how much Nandi had heard.

'Don't even think of coming near Sneha! Rot in hell!' Nandini shot that and an angry glare at Nikhil and quickly followed Sneha who stood quietly in front of the elevators. Nandini took her hand. Sneha gripped it fiercely. They went down the elevators, past people, conversations, stretchers, desks, cars but no words were exchanged between them. Sneha felt as though she had zoned out of her own body and was watching herself from the outside as she saw herself go through a gamut of hurtful emotions; pain, betrayal and humiliation. She knew she was in shock.

As they sat in the car, Nandini turned to Sneha. Sneha probably for the first time in her life did not know how to hold back her tears. She threw herself into Nandini's arms and sobbed uncontrollably. Some time later, her copious tears dwindled to intermittent sniffs. Sneha looked up and saw the big stain of wetness on Nandini's cream blouse. 'Sorry I wet you,' she said, taking the Kleenex Nandini offered her.

'It's…okay!' Nandini sniffed.

'Nandini!' Sneha glanced at her. Her friend too was quietly crying. 'It's okay!' Sneha hurried to assure her.

'No, it's not!' Nandini hid her face on the wheel. Her back shook, she was sobbing inconsolably. 'I hate him.' Her words were muffled.

'Nandi, sweetie, it's okay. Please stop crying.' Sneha was bewildered, 'But why are you crying?'

Nandini stopped. 'Because you are! I can't see you like this. I've known you all my life and have never seen you break down like this.'

Sneha rubbed her back. 'Look at me.' Nandini shook her head. 'Sethani, look at me. I'm not crying any more. I just got a little carried away. Look up kulta.'

Finally, Nandini sat up wiping her eyes. 'Sorry!' She appeared embarrassed.

'Nutcase!' Sneha affectionately and gently punched her arm.

'I'll castrate him!'

'Then they both can lie next to each other in there!' Sneha met Nandini's eyes. Both friends gave each other weak smiles.

'Better still. We will forget this ever happened and just move on.' Sneha put up a brave front. 'I can do it, you know me.'

Nandini nodded and she started her car. 'Shall we go home?'

'My place!'

'Okay!' Nandini drove out of the hospital.

Sneha felt a mother of all headaches beginning behind her eyes. 'You were right!'

Nandini gave her a puzzled look. 'About?'

'You do give stupid, shitty advice!' Having got that off her chest, Sneha sat back and closed her eyes.

As Nandini pulled in front of Sneha's apartment, Sneha turned to her. 'I want to be alone, Nandi. I'm just not up to any anything right now, sorry.'

Nandini nodded understandingly and shut the car door she had opened. 'Okay! Come over for dinner tonight.'

'Not today!' Sneha replied weakly.

'But we are still on for tomorrow, Saturday! You promised you would hear the business proposition I have.'

Sneha got out. 'I'll call you!' She walked into her building, giving Nandini a small wave. She used the stairs, skipping the elevators. The moment Sneha was alone all the events of the day came crashing back to her head. She was probably one of those rare idiots who discovered how deeply in love they were post a break up. Sneha gazed out of the lattice window in the adjoining wall. Twenty-nine was somewhat late in life to fall in love for the first time. *How will I deal with this?* Sneha wondered, resting her head against the cold cement. Her brain could only suggest a single word, '*Work!*' Taking a few deep breaths, wiping her eyes and pinching her cheeks to get some colour in them, Sneha brushed her hair to cover most of her face and made her way to her apartment.

At that very minute Nandini was calling Aditya. 'Hi sexy!' Aditya's voice reverberated in the car for her cell's Bluetooth was hooked into the car's Bluetooth.

'Hi! Where are you?'

'At work!'

'Can I come to see you?'

'You have to ask, Nandini?'

'I'm coming.'

'I'm waiting.'

About to hang up, Nandini hesitated, 'Adi I really, really, really love you!'

Aditya paused as if he were trying to read her mood. Then he said, 'Me too!'

Nandini gave an equally long pause and then she said, 'You love you?'

'And you. Get your sweet ass here ASAP.'

Nandini hung up. In twenty minutes, Nandini reached the Sarin office. She made her way to the top floor where Aditya's office was. She no longer worked here and was currently on a sabbatical figuring out alternatives.

'Hi Simone!' Nandini waved at Aditya's secretary.

'Mrs Sarin! He's waiting for you.' Simone got to her feet.

'Please sit. I'll see myself in!' Nandini went inside.

Aditya, standing at the large windows at one side of his office, turned to her, a heart-warming smile on his handsome face. 'Hi babe!' Nandini quickly trotted to him and buried herself against his chest. Aditya held Nandini close and then realized something was amiss. Gently hooking his finger under her chin, he raised her face to him. 'You've been crying?' he asked, concerned.

Nandini again hid her face in Adi's chest. Feeling his heartbeats against her ear, she felt secure.

'Nandini tell me, what happened?' Aditya pulled back to look at her face.

'Nikhil is a jerk! Can't you cancel all his deals with you?' Nandini blurted out.

'I can! But what did he do?' Aditya looked puzzled.

Taking a deep breath, Nandini pulled away. 'He hurt Sneha!'

Aditya's face furrowed, his voice sounded deeper with concern, 'Sneha? What did he do to her?'

Nandini gave him a succinct version of what she knew and what she had seen. Aditya guided her to his chair. He sat down and pulled Nandini onto his lap. She tucked her face under his chin.

'Don't be so harsh on him,' Aditya said.

Nandini sat up. 'Harsh? How can you say that? After the way he treated Sneha?'

Aditya tucked her hair behind her ear. 'You remember a time when I was such a jerk to you?'

Nandini got up from his lap, protesting, 'You were different!'

Aditya leaned forward and rested his hands on the desk, 'You are being your sweet self. But I seriously think you should give this some time.'

'How much time?'

'As much time as they need. If Nikhil is even ten per cent of the person I think he is, he will come to his senses. And you know Sneha, she would not appreciate us meddling.'

Nandini gazed out of the windows. 'I saw her Adi, she was broken. I haven't ever seen like this. Not even during her divorce. It was horrible.'

Aditya got up and put his arms around Nandini, pulling her to him. Sighing, Nandini rested against him. 'Have you told her about your plans yet?'

'Tomorrow at dinner. But I don't want Nikhil coming to our house any more.'

'He won't! I'll try my hardest to make him feel guilty!'

'Yes, yes! Do that!'

Aditya turned Nandini around. 'Let's go for a movie.'

'Okay!' Nandini replied listlessly. 'Anything with a lot of action.'

'You want to watch porn?' Aditya asked, puzzled.

Nandini laughed in spite of herself. 'Tharaki! There are other kinds of action too. Bad guys being pummelled, car chases, things blowing up etc.'

Aditya gave her a sly smile. 'I would not know. For that is not the kind of action that usually comes to my mind when I'm with you.'

'Then why go to the movies?' Nandini replied throatily. She wanted Adi's love to drive the hurt from her mind and body.

Aditya came close to Nandini. Gently caressing her dark, voluminous hair away, he cupped her face and turned it towards him. 'I love you.' Both their eyes closed as his lips covered hers. Nandini melted against him and her arms possessively came around Adi's neck.

'Adi!' Nandini whispered as she threw her face back so Aditya could deepen their kiss.

'Hmm!' Aditya barely moved his lips as his tongue worshipped his wife's perfect mouth.

'Lock the door. And then take me hard on the floor.'

Aditya's eye widened. 'Seriously?'

Nandini nodded as she ran her tongue at the ends of his lips. She knew it aroused Adi terribly. 'That's the kind of loving my body is craving…as always…only from you.'

Nandini felt satisfied as she saw the desire flare in his eyes and the way Aditya's body went hard against her. Aditya swiftly moved and locked the door. By the time, he turned around. Nandini was stripping her clothes off her. Aditya was aroused beyond control. He was at her side in seconds, pulling her close as they went to their knees, kissing each other. Soon they were rolling on the floor, a hot tangle of naked, pulsating limbs.

As Aditya drove into her, Nandini's smile was that of deep contentment as she fused with the man she cherished more than life.

30

The old gang!

At that moment, Sneha, in her house, was busy putting up a front, a happy one. Finally, after Advey went to bed around nine in the night she decided to organize her closet, a chore she had avoided for over a year. Her iPod blasted music in her ears as she sorted out her clothes and other things. Finally done by one in the night, she took a quick shower and lay on her bed. Her mind, like a string tied to a yo-yo, kept bouncing back to a certain someone. Quietly, so as not to wake her son, Sneha snuck out of the bedroom.

Next morning when Amla woke up and went into the kitchen to make tea, she yelped a startled 'Madam!' Sneha astride a stool, her face and upper torso reclining on the slab, lay fast asleep, surrounded by containers and a few things from the pantry cupboards. Some of the drawers in the kitchen were pulled open. Silverware and other kitchen equipment lay scattered all around her. Amla gently shook her. Sneha got up with a start. She sat up, sharp and wary. Sneha's opening words to a spooked Amla were, 'Why am I sleeping in the kitchen?'

'You tell?' Amla replied, her eyes wide.

Sneha squinted at her, tapping into her memory cells. 'Oh yeah, I was organizing this place.'

Amla glanced around them pointedly and said sarcastically, 'Organizing?'

Sneha good-naturedly got up from the stool. Her body felt stiff and knotted. 'Is Advey awake?'

'Baba sleeping? You go in the bed!' Amla ordered her.

'I can help. Let me bru—'

'No madam you go!' Amla hastily said. Sneha did as she was bid. She climbed into the bed next to Advey. Just as she closed her eyes, her mind again did the yo-yo thing. Groaning, Sneha turned into her pillow and then with a single, quick movement she got up and went into the bathroom. Five minutes later, she was standing next to Amla. 'I'm helping!' she asserted.

Amla was shocked to see Sneha not only help but her usually quiet madam also chattered non-stop with her until Advey woke up.

An hour or so later on her drive to work, Sneha called up Nandini who was still asleep. After the cell buzzed five times, the cursing Nandini picked up. 'What?' she hollered angrily, casting a glance at Adi's side of the bed. It was empty. He must be having breakfast right now.

'Good morning Sethani!' Sneha chirped.

'Sneh?' Nandini sat up concerned. 'How are—'

'Want to join salsa classes with me?'

'Huh! What classes?' Nandini mumbled as she sank back into her pillow.

'Salsa classes, Sethani. Dancing n' all.'

'You've joined salsa dancing classes? Why?'

'Why not? It will be fun!' Sneha added enthusiastically.

'What are the timings?' Nandini asked doubtfully. Sneha told her. 'No ya, Sneh, I don't think they'll work for me. Sor—'

Sneha cut her off, not in the least offended, 'Don't be silly, you do your thing. I was just checking with you.'

Nandini began cautiously, 'Sneh, are you ok—'

'Gotta go, kulta and I'm fine. Going for work, for half a day. Go back to sleep. Bye.' Sneha hung up. She had reached her office. For the rest of the day, Sneha did not cease to work even for a minute and she even made it to the forty-minute dance classes in the afternoon. Close to 5.00 p.m. Sneha, Amla and Advey went over to Nandini's.

Sneha took a seat as Nandini and Aditya goofed around with Advey. 'So when are you having one of your own?'

Nandini glanced at her. 'Please, not before at least two years. Right?' She looked at Aditya.

He just shrugged his shoulders. 'I guess. Listen, I can look after this little fella if you girls want to discuss things.'

'What is this big secret plan you have going, Sethani?' Sneha asked. Her smiles still weren't reaching her eyes.

'You'll see! Adi, can we use your study?' Nandini got to her feet.

'Sure! Advey and I are going to play with something new.' Aditya picked up Advey and carefully placed him on his shoulders.

'What did you get him now?' Sneha asked, exasperated and touched at the same time.

'A remote-controlled plane and a Hummer,' Nandini chirped.

'You don't have to guys! You spoil him,' Sneha grumbled.

'Love to,' Aditya said, holding Advey in place with one hand as his other hand tickled Advey's feet. The toddler, chuckling and gurgling, squirmed on Adi's shoulders.

Just then, the doorbell rang. Advey instantly straightened. Looking at the door he called out, 'Nik! Nik!'

Sneh looked at Nandini with something akin to panic in her eyes. Nandini shot the same look to Aditya who in turn said, 'I haven't invited him.'

The grownups sighed in relief when the person ringing the doorbell turned out to be Aditya's driver who had come to drop off a parcel.

'No Nik!' Advey said disappointed.

'Let me call Amla. She can just hang around.' Sneha knew Amla was in the staff quarters on the floor below the penthouse. As she dialled Amla's number, to the present company Sneha casually mentioned, 'I got a new cell number today.'

'Why?' Nandini asked.

Sneha shrugged her shoulders as she put the cell to her ear. 'Just!' Sneha while talking to Amla, missed the look Nandini and

Aditya exchanged. They understood; if a certain someone did not have her number, Sneha would never wait for his call.

Soon Sneha and Nandini were huddled together in Aditya's study that was full of dark, mahogany and masculine furniture. Nandini opened her laptop and placed it between them. 'We, you and I, are starting our own advertising firm.'

'What?' Sneha's mouth fell open.

'I know it is all a little sudden.' Nandini smile was wry.

'You think?' Sneha mocked.

'You know Sneh, the core issue of Adi and my problems was that we have different ambitions. Advertising is what I want to do, the only career for me. I always wanted to have my own agency. And I want us, you and me, to do it together.' Sneha opened her mouth to speak but Nandini wasn't finished. 'We worked really well in the past and I know you are the only person I share that comfort level with. And I think I'm the only person you too can suffer,' Nandini paused as she waited for a reaction.

Sneha shook her head, bemused. 'I was not expecting this. Give me a minute.' She counted a few things on her fingers, 'Okay, kulta listen, you and I working on our business would be a dream come true. You're right, advertising is the only career I ever see myself in. But...and it's a big but...our finances are very different. Advey's school fees, house rent, everyday bills and what we eat literally comes from my paycheck. I have some savings but you know that is for a rainy day. And I do not want to piggyback on you.'

'Fair enough,' Nandini turned her laptop toward Sneha. 'I have made a business plan. Let's try this for four months. If we cannot sustain it, I have a built-in clause in the contract that you can leave with no obligations. We will take a loan from the bank and that financial burden will be mine to bear.' Sneha disapprovingly shook her head. Nandini raised her palm, 'And you won't be piggybacking on me. In fact, the risks are stacked up in your favour Sneh. Read it!' Nandini handed her a typed contract.

Sneha read the first few lines of the open document. 'You'll be working under your maiden name?' She was impressed.

'Of course. I don't want to take shortcuts or share credit,' Nandini winked at her. Torn, Sneha chewed her lips as her hands roved restlessly over her jeans.

Nandini pulled the laptop to her. 'Maybe this might help. Read these emails.' Nandini switched the screens and opened her email inbox. She handed the laptop back to Sneha.

Sneha read the brief emails. Her mouth turned to an 'O' of surprise. 'Tina is in?'

Nandini gave a smug smile, 'So are Roy, Riya, Vishal and Preeti.' The individuals Nandini had just named were a part of the fun team Sneha and Nandini had led in their earlier positions at Ace Advertising Agency in Kanpur.

'The old gang,' Sneha made a face. 'I'm so tempted.'

'Use your head. Study the plan. We'll have to hire more staff. People with more contacts and qualifications for the required departments.'

Pulling the laptop higher on her knees, Sneha perused the Excel spreadsheet. 'Give me some time. Where will our office be?'

'I have scouted a few places in Bandra East,' Nandini tried not to jump up and down as Sneha used 'our' instead of 'your'. 'Nothing big, but respectable and functional.'

'And all these people who will be moving here? They know the risks attached to a start-up?'

'I'm not painting a rosy picture to anyone. Not even to you.' Nandini linked her hands in front of her. 'Sneh, I'm very sure this is want I want to do. And Adi is not giving me the Sarin account nor am I asking for it. So we, I'm sorry, I will have to start from the scratch. Find leads and convert them into our clients.'

'Please, please give me some time,' Sneha requested. 'Can you email the business plan to me?'

'Sure!'

'Have you thought of a name?'

Nandini did not hesitate even for a second, 'Ace Advertising.'

'I hate you,' Sneha made a face. 'Let me work as a consultant.'

'Sneh, it'll be a conflict of interest. You'll get in trouble with your current employers.'

'I know. Okay, let me think about it. Give me a week.'

'Done!'

With mock seriousness, Sneha and Nandini shook hands. Sneha got to her feet. 'Okay then, let's go outside and see the new toys you have bought for Advey.'

Nandini too got up. For a second she hesitated and then came clean, 'I called.' There was no need to take names between them for they were on the same wavelength 110 per cent of the time.

Sneha paused. Briefly, her composure fell away from her face exposing the fragility and hurt beneath.

'Alisha's out of the coma. She'll recover fully.'

The mask fell back in place and with hard eyes Sneha murmured, 'Great. Here's to another happily ever after.' She could not keep the bitterness out of her voice. Turning sharply, Sneha walked out of the study. Just at the door, she met Nandini's eyes briefly. 'It will be okay, all right kulta? And this has nothing to do with anyone but I'm open to any and all blind dates you set me up for.'

Surprisingly, Nandini did not jump with joy but only nodded, her smile weak. The rest of the evening was spent sipping martinis, playing with a remote-controlled car and plane, and eating Peruvian food like empanadas and Arroz con pollo. Sneha, Advey and Amla ended up staying the night there and by the time they got home, it was Sunday evening.

After half an hour, when Amla came out of the room after having putting Advey to bed, she heard odd sounds coming from the kitchen. She went to the kitchen. Her eyes fell on the ladder propped up against the wall and the loft door standing wide open. 'Madam! Madam!' she called out.

Sneha, holding a torch, a dusting cloth hanging on her shoulder, face covered in soot and remnants of cobwebs in her hair, appeared at the tiny door. 'What? Advey's asleep?'

Amla nodded. 'What are you doing?' she asked, exasperated.

'Organizing! What else?' Sneha replied matter-of-factly and then disappeared inside the loft.

Amla smacked her head. 'Loosu!' she muttered, walking away to the living room to catch her favourite TV soap.

An hour later, Sneha covered from head to toe in dust, carefully made her way down the rickety wooden ladder. On her way into her bathroom as Sneha passed Amla watching TV in the living room, she stopped, 'These shows come every day? Even late at night?' Amla nodded dubiously. 'Awesome! Let's watch them together. I'll take a shower and be back!'

True to her word, Sneha came back fresh from a shower and joined Amla in front of the TV. Amla glanced at her madam who was behaving quite out of character. She was never the one to organize anything, not even her purse and here she was, tackling lofts and pantries. She never saw a single sitcom and here she was reading the TV guide in the newspaper and asking detailed questions on each of them as if she were researching a thesis paper.

'Madam, you okay?'

Just for a brief moment, the smile on Sneha's face faltered and then she quickly replied, 'I'm fine!' Amla watched her suspiciously. 'What's for dinner?'

When Amla went to bed, Sneha was still sitting in front of the TV. Stuffing some cotton in her ears, Amla fell asleep.

Next morning, sharp at eight, Sneha was at work. Close to 11 o' clock, her CEO, Mr Baig, stopped at her door. 'Hi! Any updates on the DC account?'

Sneha shot an angry look at his tie and then replied in a morose tone. 'None!'

'When are you meeting the MD next?'

'No clue!'

Mr Baig came inside her office. 'Why don't you meet him

this week to finalize a date for the presentation? Take him out for lunch or something?'

Sneha felt saying she was on an indefinite fast. However, she replied, her voice grim, 'He's in the hospital.'

'Better still!'

'Excuse me?'

Mr Baig hurriedly clarified, 'Go visit him. Take a fancy bouquet. That will add a personal touch.'

'It's not him; someone in his family is admitted there.' Sneha bit out the word 'family'.

'Then call him and ask if he needs anything. Anything we can do to help etc. That will definitely put us in his good books. Make the relationship personal.'

Sneha, tortured, closed her eyes. The nut in her room had no idea just how personal things were with the potential client. An image of her wantonly grinding herself against Nikhil's hand, flashed in her head. *Enough!* With feeling, Sneha banged the first thing she could find. It was her wireless mouse. Making a loud clunk it slid and rolled off the desk and made another muffled crack as it connected with the floor.

For a minute there was a complete silence in the room. 'In fifteen minutes see me in my office,' Mr Baig angrily exited Sneha's office.

31

Hitch, get to work!

Sneha made a call. Nandini answered in two rings. 'I'm in!'

Nandini tried not to scream in joy. 'Oh my God! Are you sure?'

'What the CEO is asking me to do, hell will freeze before I do it. So either I'll be fired or written up. Thus I need another job.'

Nandini gushed. 'It's not just a job, it's our dream! It's going to be—'

'Kulta, control!' Sneha rebuked.

'Sorry! Come over. I have the contract all ready.'

'Contract ready? You know my CEO or what?' Sneha asked suspiciously. She would not put anything past her loony friend.

'No, silly. Not your CEO; I know you.' Laughing, Nandini hung up.

Sneha quickly transferred important files from her PC onto her USB. She then typed a short email, sent it to the HR department and marked a copy to Mrs Aiyyar. That evening, Sneha stopped at Nandini's place and put some ink on her contract.

'Excited?' Nandini asked as Sneha handed her the signed copy.

'Nervous wreck,' Sneha shot back and then added. 'And excited and positive.'

'Positive is good.'

'Positive that I will need to change my house,' Sneha added casually.

'Why?'

'Just something closer to the office. We will be working crazy hours and I need to be close to the office, so I don't waste time in commuting.'

'New job, new house, new number? Sneh, who are you cutting yourself off from?' Nandini asked perceptively.

Sneha glanced away, 'From those who have done the same to me.' She hoped Nandini had not heard the tremor in her voice.

Nandini was quick to agree, 'Fair enough. So what do we tackle first?'

'Nandi, I know you mean well, but in future, can we let the sleeping dogs lie? Please?'

Nandini gave Sneha a quick look and then broke into a song, 'Who lets the dogs out? Who? Who?'

'Idiot.' Sneha sat down and then said, 'Hitch, get to work. We have a business to run!'

Nandini quickly came up and hugged Sneha and then she did as Sneha suggested. The two friends soon got busy making a list of action plans for the new business.

Nearly two months later, Sneha and Nandini, dressed in ethnic Indian clothes, stood outside an office door with a thick red ribbon tied in front of it. Nandini held a coconut and Sneha a pair of scissors. A subtle wooden plate with gold lettering proclaimed 'Ace Advertising Incorporation Friends and Co.' In front of the two friends stood a pandit, reciting holy mantras. Vibha Sarin (Aditya's mom), Shruti Sharma (Nandini's mom), and Sarla Gupta (Sneha's mom), stood flanking him.

Behind them stood Aditya, Mr Kaval Gupta (Sneha's dad), Nirbhay Sharma (Nandini's dad) and Seema Sarin (Aditya's sister-in-law) holding her daughter, Aadya Sarin.

'Did you call Ajit?' Seema asked Aditya about her husband in a hushed voice.

'What, and let him disturb you and me?' Aditya winked at her.

'Behave yourself. You have a niece now,' Seema grinned.

'Let me hold her?' Aditya took his niece and held her preciously close to his heart. 'She looks like me! Doesn't she?' he asked, gazing at the child fondly. Sneha and Nandini glanced at them over their shoulders.

'Two years, right? I'm telling you, if you can last two months without getting pregnant count yourself lucky,' Sneha teased.

Nandini rolled her eyes. 'I know. It's almost likes he craves to be a father. I have never seen a man like that before? Have you?'

Sneha face instantly became guarded. 'No!' she replied, firmly ignoring the face that came to mind. Starting a new business had Sneha running in ten directions simultaneously; Advey monopolized whatever little time remained. Sneha also regularly attended her taekwondo, salsa and French-for-beginners classes and yet, every second of her free time was spent thinking about HIM; visualizing his face like something precious, something lost.

Often when Sneha woke up in the middle of night, she would find her cheeks damp. Her heart always felt heavy, oppressed, but giving into her depression was not an option. Sneha would mask her misery as long as she needed to and hope that one day it would just disappear. Eventually everything died, right? Sneha hoped that she would some day forget Nikhil's face. Yet the thought that she might forget the face of someone who was causing her such torment hurt her more.

'Are you okay?' Nandini was staring at her.

Sneha blinked her eyes. 'Ya, I'm fine.'

Nandini gave her a closer look, 'You just looked so sad.'

For a fleeting second Sneha's eyes reflected her heartache and then she hastily glanced away, 'I'm fine kulta.'

The panditji gave a startled cough and the three older women in front of them turned to bestow righteous glares upon Sneha and Nandini.

'What? She said kulta!' Nandini impishly exclaimed. Then the pandit threw some rice and turmeric all over the door and blessed the place and his audience with some holy water.

'Nandini, it's time to cut the ribbon. Where's the guest of

honour?' Vibha asked as she put the vermilion powder first on Sneha's forehead and then on Nandini's.

Sneha's mother moved to the back of the crowd and called out, 'Amla, get baba.' Amla dutifully brought Advey who was dressed in a silk cream dhoti and red and golden kurta. He tripped over his dhoti and could not understand why everyone was oohing and aaghing over him. Sneha picked him and gave her son a big kiss. 'I love you kiddo.'

'I lub you too,' Advey replied, smiling at his mother.

Nandini grabbed him from her embrace, 'My turn.' Holding on to Advey, Nandini with the others advanced towards the door with the ribbon.

Sneha turned to Seema, 'Can Aadya join Advey?'

'Gladly,' Seema gestured at Aditya who, holding his niece, moved to the front of the group.

Aditya stood next to Nandini, 'Congrats, businesswoman.'

Nandini was feeling emotional, 'Couldn't have done it without you. Thank you.' She closed her eyes tight to hide the sheen of tears.

'Hey!' Aditya loped his free hand around Nandini pulling her close, 'Control, love.' Nandini sniffed and wiped her eyes on his kurta.

'Stop slobbering over our new business,' Sneha joined them, holding scissors. 'Make space, lovebirds.' Sneha pushed herself between them. She held the scissors near the ribbon. Nandini carefully placed Advey's hand over Sneha's fingers and Aditya did the same with Aadya's. And thus the ribbon was cut.

The pack led by the panditji came inside. Everyone seemed to like the pastel green and pale golden interiors Sneha and Nandini had chosen. Finally, after an hour or so everyone left the office except for Nandini, Sneha and Aditya.

'So when are the others joining you?' Aditya asked. He was walking around hooking printers and copiers to appropriate computers.

'Everyone starts tomorrow, ' Nandini replied.

'Great. Should I bring the champagne and beer sitting in the cooler of my car?'

'Excuse me, this not a watering hole for boozers. This is a place for work,' Nandini said with a straight face.

'And work is worship. Drinking is banned in a holy place,' added Sneha wickedly.

A grumbling Aditya had no choice but to make himself scarce.

'So what's next?' Nandini asked.

'I have a lunch meeting with the PR head of Magna Media tomorrow.'

'Cool. You have the presentation prepared?'

'Yup, finished it late last night.'

Nandini went into the conference room and came back seconds later. 'The lights are not working in there.'

'We'll have to tie up with some handyman services.' Sneha began to jot down points on the pad next to her.

'Already did. For all housekeeping services, Sarin Industries are helping us out,' Nandini winked.

'Nice, kulta.' Grinning, Sneha went ahead and checked all the switches. 'The TV for the conference room is coming tomorrow, right?

'Hmm!' Nandini nodded. 'Did you see page three yesterday?'

'Nope.' Sneha gave her puzzled look. 'Who had a wardrobe malfunction? Don't tell me it was you?' she teased.

'No, there was a picture of that Nikhil with his ex-wife. It was some black-tie charity event. They looked spiffy.'

'Ohh!' Sneha literally felt like someone had landed a kick to her head. She ducked and acted as if she was finding something on the floor.

Nandini gave her Sneha a closer look. 'You don't care, right? I did not mean to say anything that would make you ups—'

Sneha got up shaking her head, yet she kept her face averted, 'Don't be silly. I'm over...it.'

'Great,' Nandini stared at Sneha her expression sarcastic, which Sneha missed for she wasn't looking at her. 'How's Pradeep?'

'He's good. Advey, he and I went out for a movie last Sunday. Dr Pra—I mean Pradeep proposed,' Sneha said, casually moving around checking things. Suddenly Sneha felt a hard thump on her back. 'Ouch!' She turned around.

It was Nandini, looking far from pleased.

'I told you now!' Sneha put her hand up in protest. 'I haven't said yes.'

Nandini crossed her arms over her chest. 'Why?'

'Because I need time to think,' she tweaked Nandini's nose affectionately. 'Stop glaring at me. I'll get ulcers.'

'You should. Pradeep is right for you.' Nandini gave Sneha a coy look. Sneha made a rude gesture at her. 'When are you going to give him an answer?' Nandini persisted.

'I don't know. I have asked for some time. He's a good person,' Sneha said thoughtfully.

'Then why aren't you saying yes?'

'Chill, Sethani,' Sneha frowned at her.

'Someone—' Nandini smiled shamelessly, 'Sorry, I meant something, not someone. Something stopping you?'

'Mind your own business,' Sneha snapped, fully aware of what Nandini was up to.

'You are my business. Look at the sign,' Nandini pointed at the door. 'Friends and Co.' Her grin reached her ears.

Sneha glared at her. 'I have some actual work to do unlike you. What are your plans tonight?'

Nandini groaned silently. Trying to make Sneha miss Nikhil, Nandini was overdoing coupley things with Aditya. It was taking a toll on her alone-time or her time to generally vegetate in front of the TV. 'We are probably going out with the family. You know you are invited by default?'

'Thanks but no thanks, sweets. I'll spend some time with Mom and Dad. They are leaving tomorrow morning,' Sneha smiled.

'Sneh, what did you think of that guy who joined us for dinner last Saturday? Guess he was no good huh?' Nandini asked sweetly.

That had been Nandini's below-the-belt attack on Sneha. She had hunted long and hard to find some other single Nikhil. Finally, short of adopting a grown-up man and renaming him, Nandini had finally found the caterer who worked in Sarin Industries, Nikhil Bhomick.

The poor man would not stop stammering in Aditya's presence who, dismayed, eventually had to leave the house for some night golf with one of his buddies. However, all that work was worth it just to see Sneha's expression when Nandini had told her her date's first name only. And then Sneha's expression when the door had opened and Nikhil Bhomick had walked in. Nandini was surprised Sneha had let her live.

Sneha took a deep breath and answered, 'That Bhomick chap was definitely a big no. Getting Advey to drop his lisp is hard enough. Please, no stammering men for me.' Of course, Sneha would never acknowledge the real reason she had been peeved with Nandini that entire night and the following few days. Sneha was surprised by her self-control; Sethani was still alive.

Nandini's cell phone buzzed. 'I have gotta take this one.' She moved to her new office. The call did not last long. Nandini sat on her chair and gazed at her new room. 'I love it,' she said to herself and then a frown settled between her eyes. Sneha and Nikhil's situation was bothering her big time. Not once did Sneha mention Nikhil's name but Nandini had often caught her staring into space, looking dismal.

Nandini also knew that Nikhil and Aditya had met a few times but not once had Nikhil even breathed Sneha's name. In fact Aditya had told her that the meetings were quite brisk and to the point. Neither of the men had wanted to linger more than they had to. 'I have to get them to meet. But how?' Nandini scratched her right temple.

If only Nandini knew what would unfold at Sneha's lunch tomorrow she would have promptly called Aditya and asked him to come back with the chilled champagne.

32

Do you know French?

Next morning, Sneha drove through the crowded streets of south Mumbai to get to Vile Parle's popular Maharastrian restaurant famous for its seafood dishes. She had already made the appointment and had left early enough to reach fifteen minutes before the appointment. The restaurant was like a revolving door, people just kept coming in and going out. Sneha had requested a table at the back. She chose to take a chair facing the door.

Sneha took out the bound and laminated company profile and placed it on the table in front of her. She smoothed some genuine creases in the orange and white tablecloth and then sat back in her chair. Even though she gazed at people around her, in her head she was going over how to lead the conversation to what she wanted to discuss with the client. A sudden awareness crept up her nape. Sneha turned her head slightly to the right and then froze.

Sneha was looking directly at Nikhil Chandel sitting two tables away from her and he was staring right back at her. Sneha couldn't blink, blood rushed to her ears, her heart raced and colour appeared on her cheeks and paled almost instantly. She was back to being pulled in, drowning in his veiled green gaze. Sneha didn't know how long she and Nikhil stared at each other but finally when she could bring herself to break the eye contact, she felt compelled to draw deep stumbling breaths to gain some composure.

Nikhil kept his eyes on Sneha even when she looked away. Just looking at her made him feel like a very important organ in his body had just kick-started after a really long time. Sneha looked so beautiful, so entrancing, so much, much more than what he had imagined her to be every day, every night. Nikhil was about to get up when saw a man stop at her table. Nikhil's face darkened as he sat back down. Who was she talking to? They way they shook hands made it seem like they were meeting for the first time. Why was Sneha shaking hands with him? Was this a date? Nikhil angrily watched them as his hands drummed the table impatiently.

'I remember her,' remarked Mrs Ali, Nikhil's secretary, who had just returned from the restroom.

'Please sit.' Nikhil was terse.

Nikhil saw Sneha place a hand at the base of her neck. He thought he saw a slight tremor in her hand. *Good*, he thought smugly. *What if it is not because of me?* The sudden thought caused him to frown some more.

Nikhil met Mrs Ali's questioning gaze. 'Sorry. Give me a minute.' Picking up his cell phone Nikhil typed and sent a quick text to Sneha's number. 'Hi!'

He waited for Sneha to respond. She did not even glance at him or her phone. Nikhil lost some more patience. He re-sent the message. Just then, Nikhil saw Sneha's cell make some noise for she glanced at it. Nikhil watched, waiting. To his surprise, he saw her pick up the phone and start talking to the person on the other end. Just then, his cell buzzed. He had received a message from Sneha's number. It said, 'Do I know you?'

'What? Of course you know me.' Nikhil, highly irritated, voiced to his phone. With quick fingers, Nikhil typed, 'Of course you know me. It's Nikhil.'

Mrs Ali hid her amusement as she saw her usually aloof boss display the sudden churlishness of a child. Nikhil's phone again buzzed. 'Nikhil who?' he read off his cell. A muscle began to twitch in his cheek. Grabbing his phone, Nikhil got up. 'That's it.' With a few determined steps, he was at Sneha's table. 'Hi Sneha. Nikhil.' He put his hand out as if to shake her hand. 'You know me?'

Sneha shot Nikhil an angry glance, stoked with all the hurt and horror of what she had suffered because of him. She mulishly did not shake Nikhil's hand. Nikhil, in response, just crossed his arms over his chest, his stance challenging. He wasn't going anywhere. Finally Sneha spoke, her face a rigid mask, 'Yes Nikhil, I know you very well.' Her lips curled and the words came out as a sneer.

'Then why did you text this to me?' Nikhil thrust his cell close to her face.

Sneha glanced at the man across from her. The look he was giving them was questioning. 'That is not my number. I have a new number,' she replied, without glancing at him. She cast the PR head of Magna Media an apologetic smile.

'You changed your number?' Nikhil's icily spoken question came from somewhere above her head.

Sneha skirted it with a withering look directed at Nikhil, 'I'm in the middle of a meeting here so if you will excuse us…' She kept her smile polite but stiff.

The PR head leaned forward to speak but Nikhil did not give him a chance, 'Well, I could be your client too. Is this how Flagship treats their prospective clients, especially the big ones?' Nikhil felt quite like an ass for throwing his weight around but if that is what it took to get a reaction from Sneha then he was willing to do that too.

Sneha maliciously enjoyed bursting Nikhil's bubble, again, 'I would not know. I'm no longer with Flagship.' Priggishly, she eyed Nikhil's slack jaw.

Too late, Sneha saw the PR head extend his hand to Nikhil, 'Hi Mr Chandel. It's Martin Rodericks. We played golf together at Bombay Presidency Golf Club last month. You were playing with my boss, Rishi Sanghvi.'

'Oh yes, of course. Small world! How are you, Martin?' Nikhil, distracted, gave Martin Rodericks a quick smile and he shook his hand. Nikhil brought his gaze back to Sneha.

Sneha gave Nikhil the evil eye. *You have no clue who he is.*

Nikhil smirked. *Well, he doesn't know that.*

Just as Sneha opened her mouth to speak, Nikhil beat her to it, 'Mind if I join you for a bit?'

Nikhil did not wait for either of them to answer and simply took the chair across from Sneha. He turned to Martin. 'So how's Rishi?'

'Mr Sanghvi is good.'

'Great.' Nikhil then turned to Sneha, his expression cold and his eyes seething. Sneha was surprised he wasn't frothing at the mouth, Nikhil appeared just that livid. 'So you are no longer with Flagship?'

'Yes, in fact they have just started their own advertising agency. Ace Advertising.' Martin handed over the company profile Sneha had placed in front him.

Nikhil sat back. 'You and Nandini?'

'Yes!' Sneha replied aloofly even as she winged a genuine smile at Martin. 'Shall we order?' She pointedly asked only Martin hoping the man across would take a hint and spare her more of this torture. In her mind, Sneha had always envisaged herself to be cool as a cucumber if she ever met Nikhil but here she was getting hopping mad and angry like those colourful birds from the iPhone game.

Nikhil, with a composed face and precise movements, placed a call to his secretary seated two tables away, 'Mrs Ali, kindly cancel the appointment I have day after with Flagship Advertising.' Sneha gave him a surprised look. After not wanting to see her, Nikhil had set up an appointment with a company where he knew her to be working. Why? Nikhil, meeting Sneha's sceptical look with a bland one of his continued, 'There is a new advertising agency in the reckoning. Ace Advertising.' Martin gave Sneha a sly thumbs-up. Sneha responded with a feeble smile to Martin and glanced at Nikhil. Nikhil reached out and took Sneha's business card lying next to the company profile. Sneha tried to grab her card but he kept it out of her reach. Short of getting into a tug of war before her would-be-could-be client, Sneha had no choice but to let Nikhil keep her business card. 'Here's the website and the number of one of the partners.' Nikhil prattled off Sneha's number from the card he held.

Nikhil ended the call and then turned to Martin, 'Gotta run. Say hi to Rishi.' Nikhil was on his feet, already shaking the other man's hand. He then turned to Sneha, 'I'll keep this card. I'm sure you have another for him. Bye!' Sneha clamped her lips and stretched them, giving Nikhil a grotesque smile.

Nikhil and Mrs Ali walked out of the restaurant. Sneha got to her feet. 'Excuse me just for a minute,' she said to Martin and trotted out behind Nikhil and his secretary. 'Hold on!' she called out loudly after them. Nikhil and Mrs Ali turned at her voice. 'Just him,' Sneha clarified, pointing her finger at Nikhil.

Nikhil nodded at Mrs Ali. She walked away from them. Sliding his hands in his trouser pockets Nikhil watched as Sneha came closer to him. Both of them regarded each other like opponents inside a ring. However, their gloves soon came off. Sneha was the first to fire, 'You have some nerve marching—'

'And you Sneha, you've changed your number, your job and you didn't think it was important to inform me? You've probably moved to a new house too?' he finished sarcastically.

Sneha could not hide the sudden flash of unexpected guilt.

'Nice!' Nikhil gave her an incredulous look. He rocked on the balls of his feet. 'Very nice.'

Sneha crossed her hands over her chest. 'Some nerve you have. Why the hell should I tell you anything about myself? The last time we met you very clearly threw me out of your life. So don't you dare put this on me! And have you tried to get in touch with me in the past months?' Sneha waved an accusing a finger in Nikhil's face, 'No! But I'm expected to keep you informed about my life. Who the hell do you think you are?'

Nikhil thought it better not to remind Sneha that he had just revealed that he had set up an appointment with her former advertising agency. His only reason behind it had been to meet her in a neutral surrounding. 'Not even a friend?' Nikhil muttered darkly.

'Friend? You are no friend of mine. I can cut you off too and I have done it. You are nothing to me and let's keep it that way.' Sneha was about to storm off when Nikhil caught her arm and stalled her.

'It seems you have forgotten a time when you could not wait to get close to me. At my apartment,' Nikhil saw the colour rise in Sneha's cheeks even as she met his eyes without flinching, 'And the car, remember the car,' he goaded angrily. He wanted her to remember those moment, dammit!

Sneha hauled her hand free, 'Classic, really classic. In this lifetime, everyone is allowed a few mistakes. Consider yourself one of mine.' Sneha strove for some composure. Nikhil had cruelly thrown some of her sweetest memories in her face, the ones which hurt her most.

Nikhil lost some of his anger. 'Sneha.'

Sneha continued with tremulous eyes and a mutinous face, 'And if your company were the last company on this planet then I would rather go out of business then have anything to do with you. So stay away from Ace Advertising.'

Nikhil's expression hardened. His green eyes glinted sardonically. 'If this is how you work, you might as well close the agency right now.' Tauntingly, he waved her business card between them.

Sneha looked at the business card and then at him. 'Do you know French?'

Nikhil seemed taken back with her question. 'Yes.'

'Well then you don't need a translator for this. Va te faire foutre.' Sneha stormed off in the direction of the restaurant. She had barely taken a few steps when Nikhil called out.

'Classic Sneha, really classic,' Nikhil had understood the colourful expletives. His French was good.

Even though she kept walking, Sneha turned around and called out, 'Glad you think so.' Her smile was insulting. Just then, a loud horn sounded in front of her. Nikhil had seen the car but Sneha hadn't. He pulled her away from the vehicle practising a Grand Prix run in the busy parking lot. Sneha fell and bumped into him. Before her body could react to the fleeting touch of Nikhil's body, Sneha pulled away but it wasn't fast enough. Her body remembered his and it tingled and hummed for more. Gazing into her eyes, Nikhil's eyes became abruptly hooded, colour rushed into Sneha's face as Nikhil's fingers purposely and slowly trailed down her shoulder, the entire length of her arm, her hand and finally brushing the tips of Sneha's fingers before they withdrew completely from her.

Sneha felt breathless and warm as her body betrayed her. Sneha hated the gleam of victory she saw in Nikhil's eyes. 'Do give my regards to the wife!' Sneha threw at him and then turned away. With Nikhil still looking after her, Sneha hot-footed it back to the restaurant, her composure intact on the outside but her insides feeling shredded like grated cheese.

33

I'm no friend to her!

After that unfortunate meeting, in the following days, Sneha's mood spiralled down faster than a fire-fighter going down the pole. She was only animated and lively around Advey but apart from that, she became a shadow of herself. She was talking less, hardly eating, or smiling and working longer hours. No one around her dared to ask what was wrong but everyone saw it. Tina and Preeti had confided in Nandini that they thought Sneha was doing drugs. Vishal warned Nandini to watch her back because Sneha was going to ditch the company. Roy told Nandini Sneha was having a rather long time of the month and Riya, the ever- romantic Riya, was the only one to hit the nail on its head. She told Nandini, 'Mark my words, Sneha is miserable in love.'

Nandini heartily agreed with Riya but she was yet to find a solution to Sneha's problem. She was scared that Sneha would soon completely break down. Chewing her thumb, Nandini covertly watched Sneha in the room across from her. Sneha was talking on the phone and simultaneously typing something on her computer. Just then, Nandini's cell buzzed. Languidly, Nandini picked it up and saw the number: it flashed as restricted. Pressing the talk button, Nandini put it to her ear.

'Nandini. It's Nik—'

Shocked, Nandini hurriedly ended the call and glanced at Sneha, who was focused on what she was doing. Nandini's cell rang again. The name again came up as restricted. Grimacing,

Nandini pressed the talk button and put it to her ear, 'Nandini, it's me Nikhil C—' Nandini again hung up on him.

'Who's calling, Sethani?' Sneha called out distractedly from the other room.

'Adi. Seems like a bad connection,' Nandini hastily got to her feet and went to close the door.

'If you close the door, won't the reception get worse? Go out,' Sneha said, not looking up from her computer.

'Good idea.' Just as Nandini grabbed her cell, it rang again. The word 'restricted' flashed repeatedly on her screen. Nandini quickened her pace and when she reached the corridor leading out of her office, she once again pressed the talk button and put it to her ear.

'Is this Nandini? Has she changed her number too? Whose number do I have?' Nikhil sounded bugged.

'It's Nandini!' Nandini heard the startled sound on Nikhil's end and then she promptly hung up again. 'Squirm, dude, squirm,' she said to her cell.

It immediately rang again. Nandini let it ring a few times. Finally, she answered it. 'Please just hear me out? Hello. Hello?' Nikhil had mellowed down.

'Why?' Nandini did not hear a response from Nikhil. 'Are you there?'

After few seconds of silence, Nikhil asked suspiciously, 'Are you again going to hang up on me?'

'I should!' Nandini replied nastily.

'I got your number from Aditya after some verbal arm twisting and begging. Please help me out here. I have to talk to Sneha. I have really, pardon my language, screwed up things.' *Only if he heard the language Sneha and I use*, Nandini thought, without interrupting. 'And I have to meet her. I just have to.' Nikhil sounded quite out of his mind.

'You want to meet her? That's rich! And why? Haven't you done enough damage already?' Nandini argued.

'Nandini, I mean no offence but the why is really and truly Sneha's and my business but I do need your help in meeting her. Alone and somewhere private. Please? I'm begging here.'

'Tall order,' Nandini retorted, 'And frankly, I don't trust you.'

'I don't blame you. This mess is completely of my making. I misunderstood her intentions and...' Nikhil trailed off and he repeated his earlier request, 'Just one meeting. Somewhere private and alone. Please.'

Nandini chewed her thumbnail. 'I don't know. She won't listen to you. You know that right?'

'But if you get her there?' Nikhil said hopefully.

Nandini shook her head. 'She won't listen to you. If you were the last man on earth she would jump off the planet,' said Nandini with a wise smile, not realizing how eerily similar she sounded to her BFF.

After that, Nikhil stopped arguing with her. 'How should I get her to listen to me?'

Nandini prattled off an idea to him.

'It sounds crazy,' Nikhil breathed softly.

'How has wonderfully sane worked out for you so far?' Nandini scoffed.

Nikhil swallowed, 'And where should I execute this?'

'At the party next weekend at your farmhouse in Karjat! Where you and Aditya are introducing Viraj and his idea to the others. That's perfect!'

'There will be at least three hundred people there,' Nikhil reminded her. 'I wanted a private meeting.'

Nandini rolled her eyes. 'Ya and I want Antilla. Look that is the best I can do. Sneha has agreed to come to that party and we will be there overnight so you'll get two days and ample opportunities to talk to her.'

'Sneha knows what the party is for?' Nikhil asked surprised.

'Yesss,' Nandini answered without hesitation.

'She already knows that Aditya and I are collaborating on this so the chances are pretty high of me being there. She still agreed to come for that party and stay overnight?'

'Ohh!' Nandini saw his point. 'You think she is going to cancel on me last minute, don't you?'

'What do you think?'

'I think you are right. I missed this one,' Nandini agreed and then added confidently. 'You know what? Actually, never mind. You shall have Sneha at your doorstep that day. I promise.'

'If you get Sneha there, I'll be obliged to you...obliged to you...' Nikhil seemed to be overwhelmed with gratitude, 'forever.'

'Nikhil?' Nandini's voice softened.

'Yes?'

'If you, pardon my language, screw this up and hurt Sneha again I'll hurt you worse. Get it?' Nandini threatened dulcetly.

Nandini heard the smile in his voice. 'Got it.' And then he added soberly, 'You know what, Sneha was right. I'm no friend to her. Thank you. Bye.' Nikhil hung up, leaving Nandini wondering what his cryptic words meant.

34

Traitor

After talking to Nikhil, Nandini stomped inside the office and banged loudly on Sneha's open door. Sneha looked up. 'Quit breaking my new door. What's up, kulta?'

Nandini walked in with long quick strides. 'Your Nikhil Chandel is a jackass.'

Sneha raised a warning hand.

Nandini was unstoppable. 'No Sneha, you listen. Now poor Adi, apart from getting the demo ready for display has to work on that damn party. If Nikhil had some work, he should have planned better. Two days before the party, he's off to Europe for a fortnight for a so-called critical situation. C'mon yaar, we all work, but who works like that?'

'Well maybe there is a crisis.'

Nandini gave Sneha a beleaguered look. 'How would you know? He told you?'

Sneha opened her mouth and then shut it. Then opened it again. 'You're right. He's a jackass. Now what is Adi going to do?'

'No clue. Until the thing gets over, he'll probably come home just to crash. It sucks. Nikhil sucks,' Nandini glared at her.

Sneha quickly offered, 'Anything I can do?'

Nandini pretended to mellow down, 'Can you help us with the initial meet and greet? Maybe you can supervise the caterers.'

Sneha's eyes widened. 'Me? There? At the party?'

'Ya, you, at the party. You were coming right?' Nandini asked in all innocence.

Sneha's expression said it all. Nandini narrowed her eyes. Nikhil was right, Sneha wasn't planning on coming.

'I'll be there,' Sneha's reluctance was obvious. Then she said with more enthusiasm, 'Make a list with Adi of things you need me to take care of.'

'Thanks, we won't try to burden you too much. BTW I have already ordered our dresses for the party.'

Sneha shot her an ominous look, 'Cancel it. I'm wearing my own clothes, thank you so much.'

'Please ya, Sneh, don't be a spoilsport. Please no.'

'No thank you.' Sneha grimaced. 'You'll probably dress me like a "Sheila Ki Jawani" type.'

Nandini put a hand on her Adam's apple. 'I promise I won't. Please ya, Sneh!'

'Fine, but I'm paying for my dress so please get me something I can afford.'

'Wohkay.'

'Now Ma Poupeé, can we get back to work? Actually, I'll take care of things here. Go and be with Adi,' Sneha suggested picking up her cell phone.

'French and all, very impressive. What did you call me just now? It had better mean something nice. It sounded much like poop.' Sneha wrinkled her nose and tossed a paper clip at Nandini who dodged it. 'Will Advey be able to stay without you for two days?'

'Mom is coming back. And Sethani, don't mind but I'll leave early the day after the party. I'm taking a driver with us for that reason. Please.'

'Of course,' Nandini agreed, wondering who would be driving Sneha back the next morning. 'Is Pradeep coming?'

'Are we allowed dates?' Sneha asked nonchalantly.

'Date? Have you said yes to him?' Nandini hid her nervousness.

Sneha gave her a sheepish look. 'I haven't.'

Nandini tapped her chin with her fingers, 'If you haven't said yes for so long so it must mean no. Logical, right?'

Sneha gave her a dry look, 'Good you don't stay in Agra.'

'Hain. Why?' Nandini's mouth twisted, puzzled.

'If you lived in Agra, you would be admitted every morning and discharged every evening. Mad woman with your crazy logic,' Sneha grimaced.

Giggling, Nandini went out. Sneha alone in her room tried to not to feel anxious about the upcoming event. She had planned to call Nandini and cancel at the last minute. Now the situation had changed. However little she may want to attend anything to do with Nikhil, if Adi and Nandini needed her then she would be there, no questions asked. 'He won't be there. What is the harm now?' Sneha muttered to her whizzing heartbeat and the pulse throbbing in her neck. They ignored her and continued to race at their pace.

A day before the party, close to late afternoon, Sneha knocked on Nandini's office door.

'Come in,' Nandini called out.

Sneha walked in and took a seat across from her. Nandini noticed Sneha's expression. 'Why the long face Sneh?'

'I said no.'

'To Pradeep?'

Sneha nodded glumly. 'Feeling bad because you said no or because *you* said no?' Nandini asked quietly.

Sneha glared at Nandini, 'What does that mean?'

'As in are you feeling bad for him or for yourself?' Nandini elaborated.

'For him and a little for myself.'

'Why for yourself? You liked him?'

Sneha shook her head and then confessed, her voice low, 'I feel scared sometimes Sethani. I don't want to be alone all my life.'

Nandini's face was sympathetic. 'You've never said something like this before.'

'I've never felt like this before,' Sneha mulled, her chin resting on her hand.

'How did Pradeep take it?'

'Like a perfect gentleman. That's what makes it worse. I wish he had said something nasty,' Sneha rubbed her forehead.

'I can do that for him,' Nandini's smile was cheeky. 'We are leaving tomorrow at 2 o'clock. You want to go from here or shall I pick you up from home?'

'From home. The driver will simply follow us in my car,' Sneha suggested, feeling new butterflies in her stomach at the mention of the party. She stopped. 'Umm listen, Sethani, has he left?'

'Who?' Nandini chose not to understand.

'Umm…ugh!'

'Adi? No, he is leaving for the venue tomorrow morning. Early.'

'Not Adi. No.' Sneha shook her head. 'Umm—'

'Viraj? He's going with Adi.'

Sneha felt like chucking something at Nandini. 'Umm not Viraj…umm…'

'Nikhil?' Nandini asked innocently.

Sneha acted as if she had just remembered his name. 'Yes him. Yes.'

'Yup he's gone. Left last night. Traitor.' Nandini made a face.

Faking some sympathy, Sneha retreated to her office. The familiar oppressiveness hung around her like a low fog. It was becoming harder and harder to keep up pretences.

35

Man, I feel like a woman

Next day, close to 2 o'clock, Sneha left with Nandini for Karjat. Sneha had said multiple goodbyes to Advey and checked innumerable times with her Mom and Amla that they had everything they would need for Advey and themselves. Sneha and Nandini were travelling in Aditya's Maybach and a make-up artist and hair stylist were following behind in Sneha's car with her driver.

Nandini gave directions to Adi's driver for a hotel in Karjat.

'Why the hotel and not the farmhouse?' Sneha asked, puzzled.

'The owner is a little picky and he has a few guests of his own. We are only using his grounds and the living area of the farmhouse, not the bedrooms etc.'

'It's not yours? Whose is it?' Sneha asked.

'Some business associate of Adi's. I don't know him.' Nandini then diverted the conversation to topics related to their advertising agency. Finally, after doing a few weeks of pro bono work they appeared to be close to getting a big account, Magna Media.

After they checked into a hotel, Nandini let loose the stylist and make-up artist on Sneha.

'Why don't you get ready first? Who cares how I look?' Sneha wailed.

'Don't be like that, Sneh. I have to go to the farmhouse to check on a few things. And your dress is in the black dress bag I have asked to be taken to your room. There is a pouch in it with the accessories. And the shoes are kept under the dress bag.'

'Let me come with you. I'll get ready later. It takes me five minutes anyway,' Sneha protested.

'Oh c'mon, Sneh. How often do you get pampered like this? Soak in the bathtub. Order some wine. Relax. I'll be back in an hour and we have to leave by 8.00 p.m. so we can reach before 9.00, well ahead of the time of presentation. Okay?' Nandini squeezed Sneha's arm and walked to the door.

'I don't know but thanks!' Sneha called out. Nandini waved and walked out. Sneha sent for coffee and ran a bath for herself in the tub large enough to fit four. Forty-five minutes later, Sneha stepped out of the tub, wrinkled like a prune and very sleepy. She decided to take a nap. A gentle hand shaking her shoulder woke her up. 'Sneh, get the suck up.' It was Nandini.

Sneha sat up sharply, eyes wide open and alert. Nandini jumped. 'You are such a freak.'

Sneha blinked her eyes. 'What?'

'Who gets up like that?' Nandini made a face. 'You overslept, it's close to 6.30,' Nandini informed her. 'I'm getting ready first as I have showered. I have ordered some coffee and sandwiches for you. Have them and get your ass in that robe.'

'Stop bossing me, kulta,' Sneha said, stretching her arms over her shoulders. 'Oh, that felt good.'

However, Sneha did as Nandini bid. As she gobbled the food, she observed with amusement as Nandini had some foul-smelling paste applied to her face and as her hair coiled around large rollers. Sneha could find excuses only for so long and fifteen minutes later, she too was sitting with smelly paste slapped on her face and her hair wound in rollers large enough to flatten roads.

After having their hair and make-up done, Nandini and Sneha disappeared into their rooms to change. In less than a minute Nandini heard a loud rap on the connecting door between Sneha and her room.

'What?' Nandini yelled out as she took her sandals out of their case.

'I'm not wearing this,' Sneha called back.

Nandini grinned. *So she had seen the gown*, she thought. 'Yes you are.'

'I'm not going to the party,' Sneha called back.

'Then I'm staying here too,' Nandini said placing the sandals near her bed. Next, she picked up her dress bag.

After a few seconds, Nandini heard Sneha mutter with feeling, 'I hate you.'

'No you don't and you are welcome,' Nandini giggled as she unzipped the bag and took her gown out. Minutes later, as Nandini stepped out of her room all dolled-up, she heard the door of the adjoining room open. Nandini saw Sneha. 'Holy cow. Look at you!' Nandini crowed, delighted.

'I feel so exposed,' were Sneha's opening words as she stepped out of the room. 'Do you have a stole or a few safety pins?'

'What is the point of wearing a backless gown with a thigh-length slit? And I don't have either. You look stunning,' Nandini announced.

'This evening you shall only find me against a wall and not moving,' Sneha threatened. 'And you look bootiful as always.' Mispronouncing a word, Sneha gave a thumbs-up to Nandini's burgundy colour, chiffon off-shoulder gown with a beaded neckline, empire column skirt and a short train. With her dark hair in loose curls around her face and impeccable make-up, Sneha knew Aditya would be the source of envy for anyone who had eyes.

Walking alongside Sneha, Nandini only wished Sneha would see herself as others would see her tonight. Sneha's strapless gown was black with hints of red. The stiff black and red embroidered flower bodice began a few inches below her shoulders and ended just under her chest. Her back till her waist was bare. A thin red belt accentuated her tiny waist and voluptuous chest. The black taffeta full skirt was A-line with a small chapel train and a long thigh-length slit that showed Sneha's legs tantalizingly. The black gown was lined with red cloth. As Sneha walked, she flashed quite a bit of red and her legs. Her hair was tamed and softly curled, brushing against her shoulders and falling below in a silken wave. Her earrings were simple white drops, her neck was bare and she wore a thin diamond spidery bracelet on her left wrist. Her make-up was subtle in muted shades of red and bronze to bring out the hazel in her eyes. 'I feel so over-dressed and yet so naked,' Sneha muttered and mumbled several times.

Nandini stopped short. 'Once in a life every woman should look like this. You look beautiful. Enjoy it,' she said simply.

'I don't know. But thank you. I feel different.' Sneha took Nandini by her forearm. 'Shall we?' Both of them, holding small black clutches, took the elevator. Nandini and Sneha chose to ignore the way the people in their way stopped to gaze at them. Both the girls did have the tiniest of smiles, enjoying the attention. In their heads, Shania Twain hammered away on her guitar, 'Man I feel like a woman.'

The drive to the farmhouse was a mere ten minutes but just getting from the gates to the entrance doors of the party, took them well over fifteen. 'This place is huge,' Sneha murmured, eyeing the tents set up on sprawling green lawns. To the left of the tents stood a two-storeyed Victorian mansion with many glass windows that were all lit up. 'Wow!' Sneha eyed the house and attendees. Seeing the fancy gown and black ties milling around at the entrance, Sneha was secretly glad that even though no one knew her here, she had not come under-dressed.

The car stopped in front of the large doors where everyone seemed to be going in. Sneha carefully got off and joined Nandini who was giving some last minute instructions to the driver. Nandini turned and gave Sneha a quick smile. 'Ready?'

'Ready.' Sneha knew she sounded breathless but that is how she felt. The venue was overwhelming. Sneha quietly walked behind Nandini as they carefully went up the seven broad marble steps; Sneha was counting. Just as they reached the top step, the group of people in front of them moved to the side. Sneha waved at

Aditya who stood there, dazzling in a black and white tux. And then she glanced to his left. Sneha turned to stone. Standing right in front of her a few feet away was Nikhil in a dark tux. The light from above made his hair gleam and threw most of his face in shadows except his gleaming green eyes that came alive with some secret inner thoughts. Sneha caught her breath at how striking he looked. Nikhil too only had eyes for her. His expression was tender and awed as he studied Sneha from the hemline of her gown to the curls around her face but it wasn't one of surprise. He was expecting her.

36

Hammit

Shocked, Sneha turned to Nandini whose face held an apologetic look. 'How could you?' Sneha whispered furiously to her.

'Sorry!' Nandini hastily stepped to the side to join Aditya. Nikhil came forward towards her. Sneha sprung into action as she whisked past Nikhil and tried to disappear in the crowded foyer. Nikhil wasn't slow. He intercepted her move and stepped to his right, blocking Sneha's way, 'Sneha, please listen to me.'

Sneha put a hand to her unexpectedly flushed cheek. 'Please, not here,' her voice came out strangled. The magic of the night, Nikhil's presence and the treachery of her own head and heart were overwhelming her rationale.

Nikhil grasped Sneha's elbow, his manner familiar and voice urgent, 'Then where? I have to talk to you.'

'Please, not here,' repeated Sneha, stepped a little to the back where Aditya and Nandini stood watching Nikhil and her. Nikhil did not let go of Sneha's arm and backed in with her. Thus, in a line, they all stood at the door as the welcoming party. Whoever came in, Aditya greeted them followed by Nandini. Inadvertently, Sneha ended up showing similar courtesy to those who talked to Nikhil. Sneha could see the open curiosity in their eyes as Nikhil only introduced her by her first name.

Sneha stiffened as she felt Nikhil slide a possessive arm around her waist. Sneha felt his touch on her bare back. She closed her eyes as treacherous hot feelings unfurled in her. Nikhil's hand too kept roving over and over on her skin as if his fingers had an amorous mind of their own. Lowering his head, Nikhil whispered in her ear, 'Angry?' He had the gall to tease her even though his eyes held some tension.

Beyond that, buster! Sneha came to her senses and shot Nikhil a fuming glance. Just then, Sneha spied someone she knew. Stepping forward, Sneha greeted him like a long lost friend, 'Hi Rad. Long time.' Before the poor man could react and Nikhil could go past the two men standing near him, Sneha grabbed the puzzled Rad and holding on to his arm, she moved into the crowd thronging the foyer.

'I'm sorry I seem to have forgotten where we met?' Sharad spoke, his smile extremely pleased.

Sneha dropped her sweet smile. 'Dude, I'm the girl who creamed you at go-karting.'

'Ohh, Sneha, right?' Sharad had no trouble recollecting her name. 'You look stunning.'

'Thanks. Can you take me to the restroom?'

Sharad seemed taken back. Sneha, holding his arm, kept up as brisk a pace as the crowd permitted, 'You want me to take you the restroom?'

'Just drop me till there,' Sneha said even as she turned to glance behind her. 'Hit!' Nikhil was determinedly coming behind them. The only thing that worked to Sneha's advantage was that no one knew her here but everyone knew Nikhil. Thus, he was interrupted often and Rad and she weren't.

Sneha tried to find Nandini but she still seemed to be at the door. Sharad seemed to have come here before because he led Sneha straight to the restroom that had been labelled 'W' for women. Sadly, there were quite a few Ws already in line ahead of her. Sneha let go of Sharad's elbow but he caught hers.

'Listen, we did not really get a chance to talk that day. Here's my card. Keep it. Call me.'

Because of his recent forced kindness, Sneha gave him a quick smile and took the business card. 'Thanks. Excuse me,' she hurried past the women. 'Sorry, emergency! Emergency!' Sneha did not wait for a reaction as she just pushed open the black door and went inside. Sneha realized what she had done only after she had done it. She had just walked into a restroom without knocking. Luckily, this was only a powder room, which was occupied by a few Ws. A door behind them seemed to be the actual restroom. Sneha snuck to her side and took her cell out of her clutch purse. She called Nandini several times but Nandini did not answer. After hearing repeated rings, Sneha cursing in Hindi, English and French thrust her cell back in her purse. She felt cornered.

Obviously, Sneha wasn't cornered enough. A woman came out from behind the closed door. Her eyes met Sneha. Sneha sucked her breath in, and prayed Alisha would not recognize her. 'Dang!' Alisha came straight at her.

'Hi! Sneha, right?' Alisha asked quietly. A serene smile rested on her face. Alisha had changed much since the last time Sneha had seen her. She had put on some weight that suited her and her hair was styled in a chic way. Tonight she was looking every inch the sparkling socialite she had been in her expensive gown, crystal jewellery and shiny stilettos.

'Hi. How are you?' Sneha mumbled, fidgeting.

'Thank you and sorry.'

Surprised, Sneha voiced, 'For what?'

'Thank you for getting me and Nikhil back together and sorry for acting the way I did at our first meeting. It was quite abominable. I had gone off my medications.'

Sneha felt a knot the size of a football field form in her abdomen. All she heard was, 'Together?'

Alisha nodded, 'You know my shrink kept telling me I was not ready to meet my family yet but you made it happen. And the way Nikhil has looked after me. All the bad of the past has been wiped clean. It's like a fresh start for us. And all thanks to you.'

'Sneha? Hi! Alisha?' Sneha closed her eyes in disbelief. This could not be happening. Mona darling too was here. 'I haven't seen you in a while. How are you?'

Sneha opened her eyes and realized Mona was talking to Alisha.

'I am well. It's good to see you too.' Alisha then glanced at Sneha and Mona, 'You know each other?'

'We met briefly,' Sneha offered when Mona's only answer was a barracuda smile.

'You know, Alisha, Sneha and Nikhil are very close. Like best friends or more,' Mona spoke suggestively.

Alisha gave a polished smile. 'I know. Sneha is so kind. But I'm back now. I can look after my husband.'

Sneha did not know how her mouth opened and uttered, 'Ex-husband.' Alisha narrowed her eyes at her. Mona did quite the opposite. Her eyes became wide as if she had found a pot of gold.

'Oh c'mon Sneha. You are barking up the wrong tree. You don't know them from before. Nikhil and Alisha were inseparable. That kind of a bond does not break,' Mona spewed her venom.

Sneha really did not how to refute the claim so she didn't. It slammed into her like a punch to her face.

'Thanks Mona.' Alisha then gave Sneha another one of those serene smiles. 'What she,' Alisha cocked her head at Mona, 'is saying is true. I'm sorry, neither I nor Nik want to hurt you,' Alisha seemed to search her thoughts, 'you were simply in the way.'

Sneha's mouth worked but no sound came out. She felt her head would explode any second. Her stomach was heaving. She felt powerless to distinguish between the truth and fiction as her gaze swung between a serenely smiling Alisha and Mona's piranha-like expression.

Just then, another voice joined the circus. 'Hi Alisha.'

Sneha gave a small groan and closed her eyes. Her torture was about to worsen. She wasn't sure if her frayed nerves were up to it.

Mona flashed an uncomfortable smile as she greeted the newcomer, 'Hi Guy. Didn't know you were back in town.'

Gayatri smoothly glided to their side, looking pretty and haughty in a silver gown that fit her like a second skin. Her hair was pulled back and knotted in a sleek ponytail resting at her nape. Her make-up was stark, silver with hints of lavender. 'That's because I did not call. Oops,' Gayatri replied, her smile cold. 'Nik and my dad insisted that I come down for the demo so here I am. I flew in last night,' Gayatri's eyes were hard as they rested on Mona.

Sneha used the diversion to leave. 'Excuse me.'

'Oh, don't go just yet. I really wanted to talk to you,' Alisha butted in.

Gayatri stepped aside, making way for Sneha. 'Don't you have to pack? Nik said you are leaving tomorrow!' Sneha saw the fuming look Alisha gave Gayatri. Unaffected, Gayatri glanced at Sneha, 'The girl looks like she needs some air.'

Sneha bristled at the 'girl' part but she allowed Gayatri to take her hand and lead her outside the powder room. 'What was all that about?' Gayatri asked Sneha as they came out. Her tone wasn't friendly. 'Don't believe a word either of them says. One is clinically insane and the other just hasn't been diagnosed yet.'

Sneha was barely paying any attention to Gayatri as she glanced around. She saw no Nikhil and she breathed easy. 'I need to get out of here. Are you familiar with this place?'

Gayatri gave her a disbelieving look. 'Yes of course. This is Nikhil's farmhouse.'

Sneha's mouth fell open but she quickly recovered, 'Perfect.' Nandini's end would be painful. 'Can you show me the way out?'

'Who are you avoiding?'

'Your brother?' Sneha said under her breath.

Gayatri snapped her fingers with the metallic nail paint. 'Oh, so you are the one Nik's been looking all over the place for. Why?'

'I don't know. Do you know the way out?' Sneha repeated.

'Way out? Not right now. Wait for ten minutes or so, they will gather everyone in the tent for the demo. I can tell you where to hide till then,' Gayatri offered.

'Why are you helping me?' Sneha asked suspiciously.

Gayatri rolled her tongue in one of her cheeks and gave a nippy smile, 'Because Nik is looking for you. And I don't like you.'

'Ouch!' Sneha recovered quickly. 'Honest enough. Where do I hide?'

Gayatri raised a toned arm where a few thin, silver bangles sparkled and pointed to the corridor which led to the restroom. 'Go right from there. After that, take the second door on the right that leads out to the back lawns near the tennis court. Just before you reach the tennis court, there is a small gazebo. You can sit behind the gazebo; there are some stone benches there.'

'Thanks.' Sneha was off like a bullet from a gun. Holding up her gown, she blindly ran past people lounging around in the dim mood lights. She did not stop until she was outside and the gazebo loomed close. Walking on her toes as her heels sank in the grass, Sneha leaned against the gazebo structure, wondering what had she gotten herself into.

Just then, the bushes across from her moved. Her startled cry died as she recognized the man's outline. She simply hid her face in her hands. 'Hammit.'

37

Take the damn picture

Pulling in a deep breath, Sneha pushed herself away from the structure determinedly. She started the toe-more-heel-less walk again, retracing her steps back to the house.

'Sneha, please,' Nikhil stepped in her way. The light was on her face and she could not see Nikhil's expression but his voice was urgent.

'Excuse me.' Sneha tried walking around him. Nikhil held her arm and Sneha tried shaking it off. Alisha's words rang fresh in her ears. 'I swear to God I'll scream and then I'm not responsible for who hears me or what happens next,' Sneha threatened.

Nikhil saw Sneha's dogged expression. 'So you will not listen to me?'

'No,' Sneha barked. For a second, Nikhil looked away into the darkness.

He let go of Sneha's hand, 'Fine. I won't say a word. Just humour me for the last time. It will take less than a minute. Please.'

'NO!'

'Please! Less than a minute! No words!'

Sneha exhaled. 'What?' she asked sullenly.

'Hold on.' Nikhil went back in the bushes. Sneha's eyes widened as she saw Nikhil pull out a chair from behind the bushes. He easily carried the chair up the few stairs inside the gazebo and placed it smack down in the middle. Then he came down to Sneha who was eyeing him, irritated and sceptical. 'Can you please take a seat, just long enough for me to take a picture of you? Please.'

'Are you mad? No,' foxed, Sneha protested.

'If you do this for me, I promise I will never chase you or stalk you or try to get you to work with me. One small thing and I'm out of your life forever.' Nikhil added challengingly, 'If you want it.'

Defiantly, Sneha thumbed her chin at Nikhil, 'Absolutely! If this is what it takes.' Sneha quickly clambered up the stairs. 'Don't expect me to smile.'

'Hold on. Sit under the light.' Nikhil hurriedly followed her.

Making a face, Sneha sat down with a thump and crossed her arms over her chests, her look baleful, 'Take the damn picture.'

'Sure.' Nikhil standing close to her reached inside his right pocket. Sneha looked away disdainfully. Big mistake! In a flash Nikhil straddled her and before Sneha could yelp, she felt the first line of a thin and smooth nylon string go around her shoulders.

'Oh my God. Stop it, right now. I order you!' Sneha shrieked.

Nikhil had already wound the rope in three lines across her and the chair. He quickly knotted it behind her back, even though Sneha kept cursing and shaking the chair, Nikhil quickly tied her legs to the chair. Finally satisfied, Nikhil stood up to admire his work—a well trussed-up Sneha. 'There! You are going nowhere now.'

Sneha used all her force to break the binds, shake them loose, but to no avail. She doubled up, shook the chair, cursed loudly and tried to grab the ropes by her teeth but except moving the chair and herself a few inches here and there with some loud thumps, Sneha stayed tied to the bloody chair. 'Are you freaking insane? Untie me right now,' she hissed at Nikhil who stood a few feet away, eyeing her. His grin was broad.

'No!' Nikhil replied and smugly perched on the protruding concrete ledge that went all around inside the gazebo, serving as a seat. 'Not until you hear me out, please,' he softened his voice.

'Never!' Sneha exclaimed with feeling. She again heaved against the binds. Sneha realized—and Nikhil knew—that the knots were secure. 'Ugghhh!' Frustrated Sneha used her legs as a lever and tried to push against the binds. Sneha felt the chair totter on two legs.

'Careful!' Lunging forward, Nikhil grabbed Sneha's legs tied to the feet of the chair. Just as Sneha and the chair were about to fall sideways, Nikhil pulled all the legs of the chair and her back to safety.

A few strands of Sneha's hair bounced on her cheeks. Nikhil's hand came to brush them aside. Sneha turned her face away. Then she turned and snarled at him, 'I can smell Nandini in this foolish scheme like a fish in macher jhol. Where is she? Is she too hiding behind the bushes?' Sneha locked her angry eyes on the bushes. 'Nandini, come out right now. Untie me and I just might let you live,' Sneha hollered.

'Macher what?' Nikhil moved back and once again, took his seat. 'Nandini is inside the house. She must have locked the doors leading here by now,' Nikhil informed her.

'And Gayatri? She too is part of this hare-brained scheme?'

'I told you before, Gayatri and I consider each other family. Guy will help me whether she agrees with me or not.'

Sneha glared at him. 'What are *you* doing? Your wife just thanked me for bringing you and her back together and here you are…' Sneha trailed off. 'What are you doing?'

'I knew it was a mistake to let Alisha come here. Anyhow, my ex-wife among all her wonderful qualities is a compulsive liar and no more my burden to bear.' Nikhil purposely used the phrase Sneha had used in the hospital.

Sneha too remembered. She shot Nikhil a fuming look.

'Early morning, tomorrow, Alisha is flying to her brother in the USA and as a part of a binding agreement that I signed with her last week, she no longer has any rights over me or anything that I own. Also as a part of the agreement, her lawyer may contact my attorney in emergencies only. Any attempt on her part or those associated with her to get in touch with me or my future family will rescind the earlier agreement thereby ending the annual sum she is to receive from me for the next ten years.' Nikhil saw Sneha's hand move in familiar manner over some creases of her gown. He could not help a tender smile. She was anxious just like him. It took some effort not untie the ropes and haul Sneha in his arms, hold her close to his heart never to let go and crush her mouth to...Nikhil got up with a start. It was hard to think straight when he was alone with Sneha. Sneha, from under her lashes, followed Nikhil's rapid movements.

Sneha still looked vexed. 'Sneha, I'm deeply sorry for the way I behaved with you at the hospital. I'm so sorry. I wasn't angry at you, not because I thought you had caused Alisha to go over the bend but really...because you hurt us.'

'Excuse me!' Sneha could not help the startled words. 'Hurt us? What are you talking about?'

Nikhil lowered himself on his haunches, bringing his face at the level of her eyes. The green eyes stared deep into hazel ones. 'Us, Sneha! You and me. That day in the apartment when you had stayed back, I knew something amazing was beginning between us. And in the car it hit me that I was crazy about you. I wanted you for life. After an age of waiting, something good, something truly meaningful seemed to be happening to me.' Sneha felt her lungs constrict.

Nikhil eyes shone with sincerity and sadness. 'In the car, I knew I wanted to marry you...take Advey as my son, have twenty more kids with you. In a few minutes, I had mapped out my whole life with you and I could not wait to begin it. I thought my heart would stop or crack or something with all that happiness when we made out in the car.' Sneha looked away, blushing. Nikhil gave an awkward smile, 'Because of the act of course, but primarily because you seemed to have similar feelings for me. I was just so happy, so, so...' Nikhil trailed off, his face held an animated, arrested expression even though he could not find words to quantify his love and hope.

Nikhil did not need to, Sneha understood. Because that day she too had shared that spot under the sun with Nikhil. Sneha felt a tennis-sized lump in her throat. Nikhil continued, 'And then I came face-to-face with Alisha and all the bitterness of the past, the painful memories, the betrayal, the lies, the feeling of having failed slammed into me. And you had brought her back into my life so, wrongly, I blamed you. In that moment I hated you because I was so much in love with you.' Sneha clamped her lips, wanting to cry relentlessly. She had this all wrong.

Nikhil cupped Sneha's cheek and his thumb lovingly stroked her soft skin. Sneha was humbled to see his eyes glisten. Her eyes shone overtly brightly too. Nikhil wasn't done. 'You were the reason I was looking forward to the future yet you brought my painful and sordid past right back in front of me. And I felt betrayed all over again,' Nikhil broke off turning his face away. She saw the way his Adam's apple bobbed and his mouth twisted tortuously.

Sneha immediately hastened to comfort him. Only then would her misery ebb. Her body strained against the binds. Her voice shook with the intensity of her feelings, 'Nikhil, I'm really sorry. I never meant to hurt you. I was just trying to—'

Nikhil turned around and put a finger on her lips. 'You have nothing to apologize for. You were right. In life there are some things you can't run away from, some loose ends have to be tied, only then can you truly get over them and walk towards a new beginning.' With feeling, Nikhil pushed himself closer to Sneha, 'Then life, or the one you desperately and endlessly love, just might consider you good enough to give you a second chance.' His eyes were wet. 'Will it?'

Sneha simply gazed at Nikhil and then she whispered, choking on her words, 'Come here.' Tears dripped down her chin. Nikhil leaned forward. Sneha rested her face against his. That is the comfort their souls needed; skin against skin, her tears mingling with his. Sneha felt similar to the earth washed by rain. Finally, she shifted her face, her nose bumped against his upper lip. 'Sorry!' she murmured.

'That's fine.' Nikhil too opened his eyes, giving her an

uncertain smile. Both their faces held tremulous and faltering smiles. Now what?

'Can you untie me?' Sneha asked.

'One last thing and then I will,' Nikhil spoke as he gently wiped each and every one of Sneha's tears with his fingers. It sounded more like a request.

Sneha nodded.

'I'm sorry for cutting you off from me the way I did. That day at the restaurant, I realized how deeply I must have hurt you.'

Why then? Sneha's face was puzzled as she peeked at him.

'When I found out that you had changed your numbers, your job, even your house, I just felt cut to the deep. I could not bear the thought of being a stranger to my love's life. I'm really sorry, Sneha. Please say you'll forgive me,' Nikhil begged, his manner urgent. He still lovingly cupped Sneha's face.

'But why did you cut me off? Did you not miss me?' Sneha asked, her eyes still held remnants of her past pain.

Nikhil winced at the hurt he saw swimming in Sneha's hazel eyes. 'Because I'm an ass. Even when I was in hospital with Alisha there was not a single doubt about how strongly I felt about you. Only you were on my mind and in my heart. And no, unlike the idea I gave you, I haven't even touched Alisha in a manner a man touches his woman. Like this.' For emphasis, Nikhil brushed his lips lightly over Sneha's mouth and then he trailed tiny, open-mouthed kisses across her jaw and then down her neck. Sneha arched under Nikhil's lightly tasting tongue, her breath came out unevenly and she bit back her moan as Nikhil's mouth dipped into her cleavage.

'Stop!' Sneha raggedly called out. Nikhil raised his face, his breathing as harsh as Sneha's, his eyes shining with unfulfilled desire. 'Finish what you were saying first,' Sneha spoke feeling hot and heavy. With an effort, she tore her gaze from Nikhil's mouth.

Nikhil blinked, trying to recall the conversation. It was so easy and so deliciously arousing to get side-tracked around Sneha. 'Yes! What was I saying? Hospital...yes. Once Alisha got released from the hospital her immediate treatment was my first concern. Getting her on her feet was imperative and so was making her family accept her. I flew to the USA with her, convinced her family to meet her, brokered peace between them. With my financial aid, her family has agreed to keep Alisha with them and continue her treatment there.'

Just as Nikhil began to dip his head familiarly, Sneha fondly forbade him, 'Stop right there, mister!' Pausing, Nikhil gave her a rakish grin, the one that Sneha felt straight in her heart. 'Finish what you were saying.'

Sighing, Nikhil obliged. 'I did all this to close Alisha's chapter once and for all. Clear my conscience. Also, Alisha repeatedly questioned me about you and to keep you away from any of her insane maliciousness, I decided to stay away from you until Alisha was out of my hair. All that while not even for a second did I doubt my feelings for you or forget your place in my life, Sneha. I did all that so I could begin my life with you and Advey with a clean slate. My murky past is out of our lives...for good.' Nikhil lovingly cupped Sneha's face. His eyes dazzled with his need to convey the honesty of his feelings and actions. 'Please forgive me!'

'I forgive you,' Sneha did not hesitate a second in whispering back. Too much time had been wasted already.

Nikhil leaned back surprised, 'You do? Just that...that...simply?'

'Just that...that...simply.' Sneha sniffed, her smile questioning, 'You don't want me to?'

Nikhil's smile was self-deprecating. 'I was looking forward to convincing you.' Nikhil's thumb stroking the soft skin of her cheek left her in no doubt about how he would be convincing her.

'Stop!' Sneha gave an awkward laugh.

Nikhil sobered. 'It takes getting used to being with someone so sweet.'

Sneha coloured at the way Nikhil looked at her and touched her. The feeling that they both were truly alone suddenly made her nervous,'Can you please untie me?'

38

A small ring, three children, two dogs...forever!

'Of course,' Nikhil got to his feet and went behind Sneha to untie her binds. By the time she was free, Sneha was flustered and breathless, for Nikhil had left not one bit of her body untouched by his trailing hands as he slowly untied and removed the ropes from her body. The act of untying her had become a hot and heavy act of seduction for both of them. Nikhil's face had been in Sneha's hair all the while as he breathed her in. Sneha mouth was dry and her body warm as Nikhil pulled her up. His green eyes were full of desire and love and a soft smile played on his lips as if all he wanted was her. 'I'm never going to let you go!' he promised softly.

Sneha more than willingly went towards Nikhil. Her lips parted and face fell back even before Nikhil lowered his face and closed his mouth around Sneha's parted lips. As their mouths took hold of each other, Nikhil's arms came around Sneha and pulled her to him. Their deep kiss was a sweet promise of the complete love they felt for each other. And then Sneha and Nikhil's soul-searing attraction to each other took over. Nikhil's tongue tangled with Sneha's. Their bodies strained to get closer as Nikhil's hungry mouth worked over Sneha's eagerly parted lips, tasting her as intimately, as deeply as it was humanly possible.

The gown offered so much of Sneha's soft skin for him to touch, taste and tease. Nikhil kneaded her hot skin roughly with his fingers, stroked it with his tongue and mouth over and over again until Sneha's fingers were digging into his shoulders, running repeatedly through his hair, pulling him closer. Sneha's soft, urgent moans could be only satisfied by repeatedly bringing Nikhil's mouth over hers, so she could savour him as deeply as he was savouring her.

Finally, Nikhil roughly broke his mouth from Sneha. 'Please can we go to my room? I need you Sneha, I need you to be mine. I can't wait any more.' His hands left her breasts to cup her face. His green eyes burned as he looked into hers.

'Yes!' Sneha breathed throatily as her fingers languidly traced his lips. She rubbed herself wantonly against him. Nikhil's sucked in his breath. Heady from the effect she had on him, Sneha increased the pressure of her lower body against Nikhil, moving her hips in a circular motion. In complete surrender to the crazy desire he felt only and only for the woman in his arms, Nikhil closed his eyes and let his hands hold every inch of Sneha to his eager and painfully hard body. As Nikhil's hands shifted, stroked and kneaded intimately, Sneha bit her lower lip to still another deep, pleasure-laden moan. Her skin tingled all over and her heart was racing, craving the pleasure Nikhil's hand and mouth promised. 'Let's go!' she breathed urgently.

Giving Sneha a tight, quick hug and then a brief kiss, which she tried to turn into a lingering one, Nikhil pulled away. His gaze was full of love; his green eyes pulsing with his need for her. 'You are beautiful.' He ran his fingers over Sneha's cheeks and the side of her face. Holding her face, he planted a reverent kiss on her forehead. And then Nikhil pulled away to stare deep in Sneha's eyes. *I love you!*

Sneha felt her heart constrict and tears pricked her eyes. She did not hide her raw feelings for him. *I love you more!*

Sneha saw the flare of possessiveness in Nikhil's eyes; he brought her even closer to him. 'Say it,' his voice was thick, pressing.

Sneha quickly hid her face against his jacket lapel. When she looked up seconds later, she had to tease him even though her heart happily thundered. 'What?'

Nikhil looking down at her face, laughed quietly even though the ardent look in his eyes made Sneha shiver with pleasure. 'There are other ways I can have you say it. Shall we?' He pointed at the direction of the house.

'Not right now.' Sneha rested her head back on his chest and snuggled there, revelling in his racing heartbeats. Sighing contentedly, Nikhil wrapped his arms around her and thrust his face in her hair, holding her as close to him as he could.

'You missed the demo!' Sneha reminded him, her face tucked into Nikhil's muscular chest as his strong arms held her securely and tightly.

Sneha felt Nikhil's laugh against her cheek, 'Who cares for a demo? I just cut the deal of a lifetime.'

Smiling, Sneha snuggled even closer in Nikhil's embrace; two souls lost to the world as they had found each other.

'Forever?' Nikhil whispered into Sneha's soft hair.

Sneha nodded and then replied thickly, 'You, me, three children, two dogs, a small ring and…forever!' Nikhil chuckled softly and sank his head in Sneha's nape. Sneha fit perfectly against him. His woman, his life! And now he even had an adorable son. Looking up, Nikhil sent a brief thank you to the skies and destiny. He could not have done this alone.

Epilogue

Five weeks later, give or take

Sneha and Nikhil clapped as they stood at the periphery of the dance floor. 'Your mom is quite a dancer,' Sneha said, watching her mother-in-law dance and gyrate enthusiastically on the floor.

'I know. Look at Nandini.' Nikhil was actually laughing openly as his mom and Nandini danced together to 'Sarkaye lo khatiya jaara lage'.

Nandini had begged to be Govinda much to Adi's embarrassment. Soon enough the bride and groom, Sneha and Nikhil, were pulled onto the dance floor. 'We already did the salsa number,' Sneha protested as Nandini pulled her on the dance floor.

'Saaali angrez do desi now,' Nandini hollered back and kept pulling Sneha, who, in turn was holding on to Nikhil. Aditya, holding Advey, Vibha, Shruti, Namit, Meghna, Nandini, Sneha's parents and a few others surrounded them as the turbaned crew beating the dhol played live for them. Nikhil enthusiastically danced with Sneha and then took Advey from Aditya as Sneha and Nandini took over the floor, everyone else forgotten. Advey did not like the noise and turning, snuck his short hands around Nikhil's neck.

'No more dance, Dad!' he crowed in Nikhil's ear. Nikhil tried to act casual whenever Advey addressed him as 'Dad' but he could not help the tug his insides experienced and the overwhelming sense of protectiveness he felt for the little boy in his arms. His son!

No one in the family, including Sneha and Nikhil had tried to force Advey to call him 'Dad'. One afternoon when Nikhil and

Sneha had taken him cycling, Advey had done it on his own. Just as his little feet and his sharp mind had figured out how to work the pedals to move the bike forward, he had excitedly called out to Nikhil, 'Dad, see, see!' Sneha and Nikhil, standing close, had frozen in their places and then Nikhil had abruptly walked to Advey, swallowing the lump in his throat.

Advey, giving him a closer look, stopped just as his tiny legs were again about to hit the pedals, 'Something in your eye, Dad?'

Nikhil ruffled Advey's soft curls, giving him a watery smile. He still did not trust his voice.

And then Sneha had addressed Advey over Nikhil's shoulder, 'Yup, he has something in his eye, just like me!' Nikhil clearly heard the thickness in her voice. Walking back to Sneha, Nikhil had pulled her close against him as he dropped a kiss on the top of her head. Sneha in answer had wrapped her arms around Nikhil as she hid her wet eyes in his chest.

Advey had watched them for a few seconds and then with a disgusted and loud, 'Eeeww!' and a shrug, he had gone back to focusing on the pedals. At his reaction, Nikhil had smothered his laugh in Sneha's hair and she in his chest.

Coming back to the present, Nikhil tried not to puff his chest or make his embrace around Advey too tight. 'Okay kiddo, let's go.' Holding Advey protectively, stood Nikhil at some distance from the dance floor as he talked to some guests at his wedding. His eyes kept wandering to the woman on the floor wearing a beautiful, ethnic red and golden, traditional ensemble. His wife! And his son. Nikhil shifted Advey a bit more comfortably in his arms.

Fifteen minutes later, a heavily breathing and sweating Sneha excused herself with some effort from Nandini and the rest of the family and wound her way to where Nikhil stood holding Advey and talking to someone she did not know. The wedding photographer instantly followed her. 'Please, not for some time,' Sneha begged, dabbing her face with a tissue. He left her alone.

'Hi!' she greeted Nikhil. The couple standing with Nikhil

congratulated her and the four stood there making small talk. As they moved away, a smiling Nikhil turned his shoulder to her.

'Has he fallen asleep?' Nikhil asked.

Sneha gave him an amazed smile. 'He has! Good job Dad!' she winked at him.

Nikhil came around her other side so he could embrace Sneha with his other arm, which he did promptly. 'Thank you.'

Sneha fully turned into him. Content, her face rested against Nikhil's chest and her hand rested on Advey's leg as she said, 'You don't have to thank me for anything. I never thought I could ever be so happy.' Unknown to them, the photographer clicked one of the most honest and beautiful pictures of that night.

Nikhil placed a kiss on Sneha's head. 'So what happened to a small wedding?' he teased, running his eyes over the wedding that he knew boasted of more than two thousand people.

Sneha looked up and gazed at him, her eyes shining with mischief, 'This is what happens when you hand your entire contact list to the wedding planner.'

'I was marrying her best friend, how could I say no?' Nikhil replied smiling down at the face of his beautiful bride. The photographer got another stunning candid shot. 'But with all the work at the agency, how did she manage all this?'

'She had help.' Sneha winked at him. Nikhil's eyes widened. 'So even though you initially wanted a small wedding, you planned it this big?'

'Oh what the hell, my husband was picking up the tab,' Sneha smiled, looking at him from under her lashes.

'He is and very, very happily. Lucky man,' Nikhil moved Sneha a little closer against him. Sneha knew what he was up to.

'Are you mad? Behave.'

'Just stand close to me. Like really close.' Nikhil gave Sneha a longing look.

Grinning, Sneha moved away even though she stayed in

Nikhil's arms. 'Serves you right! Who asked you to become all righteous and wait until our wedding night?'

Nikhil grimaced. 'I could kick myself. That night when we came back into the party, I was in a very generous mood. What can I say, I wanted to impress you?'

Sneha cast him an incredulous look. 'Do I look impressed?'

'No, just horny!' Nikhil chuckled and Sneha joined in. 'Don't laugh like that!' Nikhil bit out, his voice hoarse.

'Nikhil,' Sneha glanced away, embarrassed.

'I can't help it if you have such a sexy laugh.' Nikhil was about to turn Sneha fully into him, when he saw who approached them. Nandini.

'Hello, tharaki newly weds. Hanging in there?' she teased them.

Nikhil shook his head and addressed Sneha, 'You told her?'

'Noo!' Sneha replied, grinning.

'Let me lay my son down before I make an ass of myself. Where's that snotty nanny of his?' Nikhil walked away, winking at his wife and her friend.

'Snotty nanny? Amla?' Nandini asked.

Sneha grinned. 'Amla and Nikhil are always arguing over Advey. Amla told me to my face and that I was marrying the wrong guy; she was like, "Pradeep was at a least a doctor."'

'She did not!' Nandini gave a hoot of laughter. 'And Nikhil knows?'

'He has been wanting to fire her ass from day one. His grouse is that, because of her, Advey watches too much TV and pouts like a twenty-year-old woman.' Sneha could not control her mirth. Nandini heartily joined in.

Just then, a woman and a man's raised voices drew Sneha and Nandini's attention.

'What do you mean animals urinate to mark their spot? And how dare you ask me how I know if this is my spot? What kind of marking do you think I'd leave?'

Viraj, pushing his glasses back, spoke firmly, 'You were saying that this chair is yours? I see no name on it so all I wanted to know was, how you can be so sure. Did you leave any marks on it? And about the animals, I was just telling you how certain animals mark their spot due to their heightened sense of smell. I never meant to say you urinated on the chair.'

'You are mad. SHUT UP! People are looking at us. Take the damn chair and make a house for yourself. DISGUSTING!' Waving a fist at poor Viraj who watched her bewildered, Gayatri stomped off in the opposite direction. Listening to her curses, Sneha knew Gayatri spoke French, among other languages.

Grinning, Sneha and Nandini gazed at each other. 'Oh my God!' Sneha covered her mouth to subdue her laugh.

Nandini squeezed Sneha's arm. She whispered, delighted, 'Look at him. Look at Viraj. He is smiling. He was purposely baiting her.'

Viraj caught the two friends staring at him. Becoming self-conscious, he hurriedly walked away from the chairs.

'Yay! I'm so excited.' Nandini nearly clapped her hands gleefully.

Sneha gave her a puzzled look, 'Why are you excited, kulta?'

Sneha and Nandini did not notice Aditya who was approaching them from the front or Nikhil who was walking to them from the side.

'I saw the sparks between them,' Nandini replied, her grin reaching her ears.

Aditya smacked his forehead, turned around and walked right back to the dance floor.

'I'll help you,' Sneha promised Nandini, her smile evil.

Nandini was surprised. 'You'll help me with Gayatri. Why?'

'Because she doesn't like me,' Sneha winked at Nandini and the friends collapsed in titters. Nikhil bit off an expletive and hastily retraced his steps. Nikhil and Aditya knew that together, Sneha and Nandini were unstoppable.

That night was not really the night Sneha and Nikhil could finish off what they had started in her car. The wedding noise had left Advey cranky and restless. Around 6.00 a.m. the next day, Amla knocked at Nikhil and now Sneha's bedroom door in Nikhil's ritzy apartment. The door swung open in her hand. Peeping in, she saw Nikhil still in his wedding suit sleeping on the bed. Sneha in her wedding attire and jewellery slept, her head resting on her husband's shoulder. Her arm was wound around Advey's leg, who, in his Spiderman nightsuit slept peacefully on his Dad's chest. Amla retreated quietly, emotional that now her baba's family was complete. She made a quick call.

Sneha felt a gentle shake on her shoulder. She sat up, alert and straight, her eyes open wide. She spooked a few people. She glanced around frantically. This was a strange nightmare. 'What are you, my mom, your mom and your mother-in-law doing in my bedroom?' Sneha whispered to Nandini who had woken her.

'Get up, Sneha,' her mother called out.

'You did not even change your clothes, you must have been exhausted,' clucked Vibha Sarin, gazing at Sneha.

'You and Nikhil were sleeping so peacefully!' Shruti Sharma added.

'Mom!' Nandini shushed her as Sneha gaped at them.

'Where are Nikhil and Advey?' Sneha asked, red to the roots of her hair.

'In the living room with Adi. Nikhil woke up with Advey.' Nandini said.

'What are you all doing here?' asked a puzzled Sneha, repeating her earlier question.

Nandini replied, 'We are taking Advey. He is spending the day with us.'

'Why?' Sneha asked perplexed.

The three older women simultaneously cleared their throats pointedly and Nandini winked at Sneha to drive the point home. Embarrasment had rendered Sneha speechless.

'We are even taking Amla,' Nandini whispered as they all were about to exit Sneha's room. Sneha slithered off the bed with some effort, hindered by her wedding attire and chunky jewellery. As she was about to walk outside, she heard Nikhil's voice requesting Amla to make sure she kept everything Advey might need. Next, Sneha heard Nikhil request Adi, Nandini and Sneha's mom individually to call Sneha and him if Advey got cranky or needed something. Smiling broadly, Sneha walked back to the bedroom and then into the bathroom.

A few minutes later when Sneha stepped out of the room, she found Nikhil sitting on the bed. With an incredibly sexy smile, he rose to his feet, 'Hello, wife.'

'Hello.' Sneha felt herself grow warm as desire for her husband coursed through her. Nikhil, in two steps, was upon her. He picked Sneha up and nuzzled his face in her throat. Sneha sighed and tightened her arms around his neck. Nikhil lay her down gently on the bed and quickly joined her on it.

Sneha and Nikhil then went on to finish what they had started in her car, on the brown and black granite counter-top in the kitchen, on the floor of the living room and finally, when it became dark, near the fountain on the terrace.

Sneha could only smile in the darkness as her husband rested his sweaty forehead against her equally damp and bare shoulder. 'You are an amazing woman. I love you, Sneha,' Nikhil whispered ardently into her skin, planting soft kisses there.

Sneha joyously wrapped her arms around Nikhil's bare back and fighting happy tears, she whispered right back, 'I love you most, husband!'

Acknowledgments

Thank yous to a few very important others:

My late father—my loving memories of him and his encouraging words continue to guide me to this day.

To my husband Sumit for his continued support and love. To my in-laws, Mr and Mrs Mehrish, and the rest of the family.

To my Snehas or Nandinis, Richa Vaidya, Nidhi Agarwal and Seema Chowdhury—this book would not be half of what it is without your opinions, advice and encouragement.

A heartfelt thank you to Kausalya Saptharishi for her immense and invaluable contribution as my editor and partner in arms. Thank you to Prerna Vohra and Maithili Doshi for their insightful help with the manuscript and the book cover.

A very big thank you to the entire team of Rupa Publishers especially Mr Kapish Mehra for his guidance and belief in my work. If he weren't my publisher, I might not be an author.

My deep gratitude to all my readers who show such immense love to me and my work. You all enrich this journey and empower the writer in me. Thank you.